ABSTRACT/CONCRETE

KIRSTY NEARY

A Wild Wolf Publication

Published by Wild Wolf Publishing in 2011

Copyright © 2011 Kirsty Neary

All rights reserved. No part of this book may be reproduced, stored in a retrieval system or transmitted in any form or by any means without the prior written permission of the publishers, except by a reviewer who may quote brief passages in a review to be printed by a newspaper, magazine or journal.

First print

All Characters appearing in this work are fictitious. Any resemblance to real persons, living, dead or undead, is purely coincidental.

ISBN: 978-1-907954-13-9

www.wildwolfpublishing.com

You *cannot* train yourself to successfully and sustainedly unsee and unhear.

China Mieville, *The City and The City*

The really important kind of freedom involves attention, and awareness, and discipline, and effort, and being able truly to care about other people and to sacrifice for them. The alternative is unconsciousness, the default setting, the 'rat race' - the constant gnawing sense of having had and lost some infinite thing.

David Foster Wallace
1962-2008

To my family:
Stranger than fiction, the lot of you,
yet the concrete to my abstract.

In loving memory to **Granny Anne and Granda Fitz**
Thank you for making and keeping me curious.

PART ONE

REVISION

March 13th 2024

There used to be so many places to go when you don't want to be seen. When he was around, we'd been pretty creative. The list of options is now in constant and rapid decline, thanks to whichever new restriction the Management send thundering down. They're hoping we'll be so poor and sick and pissed off we won't notice what they're up to.

They'd have us believe that it's all our own fault.

Once, I could live off the map. Fall right on in: sheer density of shadow and insanity of light shows allowed the city to follow up on its promises of anonymity. Not anymore. Couldn't stop it, no matter how far I pushed the boundaries of information, of permission. I read the paper. I watched the news. I trailed after protest marches and signed petitions, all the while knowing it was fruitless. You take what you're given, around here. I sat back and watched it rot, peel, burn. Give over to the blank drapes of the eye's irrepressible trickery.

It should be spring. The calendar says so. It makes no difference: dark in the morning, navy to greyish murk to shifty white as the day rumbles to its nexus. It's fine by me; I don't miss morning's pale slant across the bedroom wall, across the clock face, watching it watch me willing myself out of bed. Nice to be free from the implicit criticisms of yet more misspent time.

See, I'm trying to look for the gold, the silver, but fixating on the good of a situation usually involves a *something* to begin with. Last week I lost another of the odd jobs I'd been hoping to hold down. Just waitressing, nothing special, but it had been nice to have some human contact once in a while. Something to take the edge off that morning hurt – pawing the chill by my side in the bed again, forgetting. Still. Silver, gold, tin, stone, heat, light could be out there somewhere, maybe hiding, like the smartest of us.

I'm luckier than most. I live in a box tacked to the top of a tenement building. A bedroom twice the size of a single bed; a toilet-shower-cubicle; kitchenette with just room enough for a kettle and sink. No lounge, of course, just a chair and table by the bed. I'm not presumed to be partaking of much dedicated leisure time. No entertaining. But it's all I need, now. Lucky, lucky me.

There are a few things I have to do before I leave my flat. Processes. They're not written down anywhere, no checklist or instructions or pamphlets, which disconcerts me to the point of being glad I live alone – no one to see the arrangements I've made with myself.

I start with the phone. It's an ancient model – stuck in mere Audio – but still armed with features I'm afraid of. It sits, waiting, on a small steel-bracket telephone table. This has a neat little drawer, in which I've locked headphones, sensors, infra-red trackers, caller-ID satellite navigation system, polygraph, scrivener template, translator and light-years of wiring. I don't need a print-out, don't need geography, don't need to know my caller's height, weight and body temperature, whether their moon is in Scorpio. I don't care whether or not they may be lying to me. A voice would be enough.

Which leaves me with the answering machine: haemorrhaging wires, perched next to the phone like a plughole spider. I press play, squeezing my eyes shut against the sound of my own voice. There hasn't been a message since I moved in here – or left the hospital, whichever marker I'm geared toward by relative degrees of self-pity – but that doesn't keep me from the machine, jabbing *DELETE* over and over again just to make damn sure there's nothing lurking on the tape. I know all about these digital recorders. They mess with your head, don't follow instructions, as capricious as the weather used to be.

Then I record a fresh message. Every morning. Just in case something should change. I used make jokes, quote cult fiction, a shard of the zeitgeist to make myself sound more interesting. I don't bother anymore. I'm running out of words, things I've heard or read and folded away for rainy days that never come. I don't want to waste them all on recordings only I will ever hear. Post-post modernism –fear of being swallowed up in your own self-references.

I can't face the television yet.

I put a coat over my pyjamas. I'm going downstairs to the almost-garden out back. I don't trust a glance from the window anymore. Tiny two-foot square, quadruple-glazed, so many pearly reflections built up between the separate panes that I can see the room behind reflected in its own image many times over. I could use a coffee, but I have to keep out of the kitchen until I've taken care of everything else. However pared back my breakfast options have become (one cereal, one freeze-dried loaf) there are always migraine minutiae to account for – deep bowl or soup plate, cup or mug, powdered milk or sterilised, wash up now or later. Debates can rage for hours before I'm even approaching a decision, thus rendering my morning useless. Besides, the longer I leave it, there's more time for evidence to be cleared, should anything have happened outside.

Sometimes I'll run into my neighbours on the stairs. I've shaken hands with these people, seen names on their mail-slots, and yet I can't hold onto anything to remember about them. I've no idea how old they are, what they do for a living, whether they have children or pets. Might as well be a fresh tenant in each flat every time I pass, for all the noteworthy characteristics I'm able to retain.

The passage from the lobby to the garden could have been one of my hidden places. Still smells like it should, of solitary pottering in darkness. Of oil, wood shavings, rusting tools; of candle wax and battery fluid leaking from emergency torches. Each time I open the back door, I can't help but hope for a surprise. It's inbuilt, I guess. Those who remember Advent calendars, cuckoo clocks, game shows. Fifteen billion open windows into fifteen billion inboxes on the one small screen haven't done away entirely with the pleasure of the *wait* for something real. Something we can reach right into and grab what's ours.

I'm better, now, at coping with the same slew of grey-green. The lawn's an exercise in taxidermy. Grass shoots long dead still push up from the ground, neither growing nor sinking for want of meteorological momentum. Handfuls grabbed pass through fingers like cobwebs, drifting straight to the ground in an absence of wind. A pine-plank back gate provides an illusion of access: the Management have been kind enough to keep the bars and chains hidden on the other side. A thick pipe runs from the roof to the bin shelter, stopping at each flat's rubbish hatch along the way. I don't use it myself. I produce so little waste: besides, taking it out manually is something of a novelty. Breaks up the day.

Checks to make. I take the perimeter, tight-roping across a concrete divide. The sky hangs white and waiting, hoarding all of its light bar a grudging LCD blur. Looking up at the building behind me, I don't need to see past the light bleached on the window panes to know there's a drawn pair of curtains in each one.

I've never met anyone down here. There's nothing to see. Nothing to feel. Which makes it all the more satisfying, in a quiet, private sort of way. It's reassuring to be properly conscious of the holes in my head where my logic should be. I was out of it for a bit when I got out of the hospital. Numerous versions of reality colliding in the sky overhead. Constantly in that state of mind in which you *know* something isn't right, you can't put your finger on *what* exactly. Trying to walk in a straight line with one leg shorter than the other.

At first I thought I was checking the lawn for crop circles. Seriously. Embarrassing, yeah, but in that cloud around my head, anything seemed possible. Soon realized that any extra-terrestrial life forms would take one look at the place, at the mess we'd made, get the hell out of here before we passed on our diseases, our bastard ideologies. I can halfway blame Caleb for this slice of delusion – it's his voice I hear. Those nights we spent pressed up to the window, unfurling strings of numbers to try to explain the vastness of space, the incomprehensible ratio of what we knew to what we never would.

Now I'm just checking for *anything*. Something different. Something that might imply a shifting of time since I last checked, something to shake the freeze-frame held over the city. I'm not after flowers or birds or a fresh blade of grass. I'll settle for a weed or a lump of animal spoor or a scrap of product packaging I haven't seen before. I'll settle for the movement of a crumpled wrapper from one end of the garden to the other. I'll settle for a ghost, a stain, an echo of movement, a sliver of weather.

I'm on the third bar of the oblong when I see it. A gouge in the turf three feet from the border. I have to break my own rules and step onto the lawn for a closer look, first leaning back to look up at the windows above for any flutter of curtain. Closer. There's more than one. Three, four, five, six leading from the corner of the bin shelter across the lawn to the back door. Footprints. Okay. Another deep breath. I take the notebook from my pocket and make a quick sketch, standing very, very still for fear of interfering. For fear, I guess, of shifting into another of my pet realities, in which all such random factors disappear, smoothed under a fresh pool of tar. Things have gotten pretty drastic to get me this excited by a set of footprints. I lose time. The sky doesn't help, just sits there adrift in its own shiftless light.

I'm stood there for a minute, for an hour. Just staring. I know it wasn't me. They're far too large. It wasn't me. It takes a bit of time to work this out. Sometimes I'll be in the middle of something, in the middle of nothing, and find myself losing track of where and who I am, what I'm doing, where I'm going. It's easily done, as these blank days pile up with no real marking of junctions between sleeping and waking. But it wasn't me. This is good. This is news. This is movement.

This alters my routine. Every day a newspaper appears in my mail slot. I don't know why – I never order one. There's a spine-rattling of static as I lift it, shifting my gaze about the stairwell as I fold it into my coat.

I count out every step on my way back upstairs. There's no reason for doing so save the calming effect of knowing it's the same number each time. I keep a record in the back of the notebook. I keep a record of a lot of things. Steps on the staircase. Tiles between the bathroom door and the sink. Spoonfuls in the average jar of coffee. Incidences of persons passing in the street outside. Incidences of voices in the staircase. It pays to keep an eye on things. I've already had to start over, reshape reactions and routines post-discharge. I can't let anything slip.

Now I have to deal with the television. I didn't buy the damn thing, it came with the flat, and I'm too scared to move it. It's got a standard-issue dissemination device built into the top, for the recording and storage of programmes of interest. I have never touched a button save the power-on switch, yet every single morning I'm met with the red-eye alerts beating from the box. I learned the hard way not to ignore it – gone unchecked, the drivers in the machine swell to a roar of components, whipping up sufficient frenzy to set the whole room abuzz. It gets so loud and static-furred my eyes begin to hurt, nose and throat choked with a Laundromat lint of unspent electricity. Then the klaxons begin, a sound loud enough to have a colour and smell, a taste of crab apples in the back of the mouth, so heavy I half-expect the flat to topple from the building. So yeah, it's best not to have to deal with a backlog.

I switch it on and jab at the remote control. Manufacturers have long since disabled the fast-forward, skip and mute functions – you can play, pause and rewind, but everything must be seen right through one way or another. I don't understand the logic or order behind the programmes stored. I used to try to enjoy it, especially in the weeks following my discharge, in the interests of catching up on what had been happening. Pointless– every broadcast comes from a local network, all the news is regional, all the sights and scenes are in-studio craftworks, and none of the names or faces or places or subjects concern anything outside of the city.

Every broadcast begins with a shot of a Management suit, sat in a club-chair in front of a roaring fire. Something from the Scottish tourist board on the wall behind – a Saltire or Lion Rampant, a set of antlers, a claymore, a pewter thistle. For a while they'd a clutch of china figurines from that song about the city's patron saint – bell, fish, bird, tree – but they canned that after anti-iconography complaints from Secular Enforcement. The suited figure in the chair begins with a pleasantry and ends with a warning – *Welcome to today's Conurbation network broadcast. We, the Management, hope you will find our schedule informative, efficient and productive.* Another recap of edicts and rules. Then a window opens up in the corner of the screen, in which appears the faces of those suspected of anti-policy activities. *We would ask you to pay attention to the contact details at the bottom of your screen, should you have any information regarding infringement of policy.*

The broadcasts I've seen are a laugh-riot. The TV shows us how to make the most of the taut spaces in our homes, how to make a five-course meal using only three packets of freeze-dried goods, aerobics routines made for five-feet square living spaces. Then it's the news, and it's more of the same –success stories and dire warnings. Shots of shiny new boxes for people to live in. Miniature gardens with cellophane glass. Management heads scissoring lengths of tape from new stretches of intra-city Tube. Footage shot in streets still open for walking. Uniforms clapping cuffs around crocodiles of people with smudges for eyes, clothes torn and blackened, images branded *CRIMINAL, INSURGENT, TRAITOR, PORNOGRAPHER, ACTIVIST, DRUG DEALER, VIOLENT OFFENDER, RISK.* Then back to the club chair and the final remark. Just in case we've lost track since fifteen minutes ago. Call this number. Contact this address. Report, inform, keep yourself and your city safe, clean, neat, efficient.

And always a slogan. The current favourite's been around for a while. All over posters, broadcasts, broadsheets and pamphlets:

THIS IS ALL FOR YOUR OWN GOOD.

There's no room for argument with that. It's hard not to just take it in. Switch on and switch off. There's a gulf in me once occupied by original, *organic* thought. Rubbed up against Caleb's, sounded off and argued about, laughed and cried over, pressed close between us to block interference. It's hard not to buy into what I'm looking at, when there's no-one urging a look further in. I give up. Switch on the box and let it play on. I shut myself in the kitchen until it's all over. I don't want to know. Can't make up my mind.

Humming to drown the sound of the set, I spread out the newspaper. The usual shit on the front page, the editorials – riots quelled, dissenters uprooted, new Tube lines up and running. Weather mild, thirty per cent chance of rain. Calls to mind your manners and your own business. Whole pages devoted to mug shots of folks caught in the act of protest. A slender article at the bottom of page sixteen calls for increased vigilance around about the outlying casinos, in the

10

wake of several reported disappearances. Vigilance, though, nothing more. No need to panic.

The Opinions section. More of the same - extolling efficiency, deploring disorder and calling for the punishment of the outspoken. Then froth: diary entries and diatribes, from housewives and leather-upholstered execs and rehabilitated rough-housers, folks who simply *can't* believe how much time they used to *waste* on such useless pursuits as drinking and fighting, having sex and going to parties, as the Arts, as debate, as anything remotely unplanned. I can pity them or loathe them if I want to, but it's not as though I'm doing any better. It's not as though I can remember what all of that fun really felt like.

Broadcast continues in the next room. The techno-bagpipe theme to the Management bracketing slots comes up every fifteen minutes. By the sixth time I've heard it, it's safe to leave the kitchen. The last pages are all just adverts. There are no competitive sports anymore, not with that legacy of disorder and violent crime. So, no anomalies in the newspaper. I'm not sure whether to be disappointed or relieved.

I don't take much time getting properly dressed. You don't want to be attracting attention, and it's best to be practical. Jeans, leather boots, denim jacket, it's all about blending in, the blue of the denim long since faded to the same non-colour as the sky.

I square up before I leave; needless, really, but there's no sense letting standards slip. Then out onto the stairwell, trying to avoid making too much noise; every misspent footstep rattles the floor tiles, the remaining panes in the windows, and the neighbours are paranoid enough as it is. I can't handle heads peering over door-chains, inquiring as to my business, all in a whisper on the off-chance someone else is watching. I'm always disproportionately satisfied on these occasions I make it all the way to the street without being seen; another small mastery. They all add up, so he said.

I'm the only one left out of everyone I know who stayed behind – or had to – after the Management took over. That's when the flat started to clot, stink, choke. Those four walls and roof did for *sleep*, when it came, but I miss my hiding places. Having people to call, places to crash. Means of quelling the rise of his name in my throat. I'd spent months, trying to choke it off, his memory, hide from it in those few remaining safe apartments. Now the others are all gone, too. God knows where. I certainly don't want to.

Today, one more thought-tamping field trip. All other options throttled, I make it my business to find more interesting things to get

11

on with in that widening gyre between waking and sleeping. I was bored already with the smouldering ruins of the buildings.

These buildings formed your maps and pathways. Do you remember that summer between leases? You'd both go for walks wearing too many layers, the occasional surprise splash of heat inching between the buildings, wiping cool shadow from half-hidden grins. You two, the two of you, the link between skin and thought and breath, was all still a secret plumped and glossed with novelty.

You didn't mind, you figured on all things in good time. You had it all worked out: he'd scamper his way through exams whilst you battered away at your thesis, both of you saving every last penny afforded by those odd jobs you just couldn't keep. Practicalities: a basis for dreams pleated from hanks of light and streams of wine, coils of smoke and wisps of good intention. Back then you both thought body heat was all you'd need to keep you warm. Still full of that scholarly arrogance, truly believing in life after graduation. Convinced, even in all-black gear and switched to your night vision ,that you were really doing nothing wrong. That everything would come together, that, with enough time and effort, a slice of one of those beautiful buildings would be yours for the taking. Space for just the two of you, untainted. Nobody would care where you'd come from, who you'd been.

Now he's gone, you're going to have to work harder than that. Look deeper. It's all still here.

The Management couldn't, I thought, touch the garden. I'd walked past so often without seeing it, figuring it as an attraction shoehorned in for the benefit of those tourists we used to have. Plants are plants; they don't *do* anything, don't dance or sing songs or take off their clothes on stage for money. I can deal with that, now. Everyone's a tourist, an alien, these days.

The garden once grew so lush and rich with plants I'd only otherwise see in dreams. Meaty leaves of electric green and acid yellow; plants with teeth and claws and limbs and hearts like red-eye in cheap photos. Plants whose growth and breath I could hear, roaring, white noise spread thick over the clamour from the streets. I'd duck in and wander between rows, watching the disembodied heads of other explorers floating over the foliage. I'd mingle with the marble nymphs and angels, rare long-term residents: nestled back in recesses, squatting on plinths, chasing cigarette trails of steam as it rose to the moon from the flowerbeds.

I used to come here with him when we'd needed to be sight unseen, unheard. For a taste of words wrapped round clean air.
Climate change. That was it. Global warming. Pollution. A bunch of stuff I didn't know enough about to have much of an opinion.

It's had its way in here. Such random factors should have worked the other way around; slaked the plants in enough bad chemistry to really give them eyes and hands and voices. Tearing themselves up by the roots, wandering down the streets, clamouring for clean water. Now they're just husks, a dirty grey-green spread of rot, kicking up such a sick-sweet stink I have to breathe through the sleeve of my jacket, wobbling over the cracked slabs of the pathways. Those concrete angels stare up into whiteboard skies, hands clasped in prayer, waiting for it all to be over. Graffiti tags mark the flanks of deer and rears of nymphs. Kids have pierced bared nipples with ring pulls from drinks cans.

There is a stillness here my head can't hold in. I'd never thought there was such a gulf between peace and death. Grey light shears every surface to the matte of a still photograph; movement works to a delay, flickers there then gone in peripheral vision. Once, they kept plants so delicate they'd only bloom three minutes out of a whole year. Care was taken to provide the right conditions: moon phase, moisture, serenity. Now, the glass cases have been shattered. The padlocks lie smashed to pieces. Now, nothing grows but a sense of resign; acceptance of time grudging its forward momentum, a passage of hope into gaseous clot. I light a cigarette. It seems the thing to do. An old woman with a plastic bag over her head turns to glare, then halts, looks up at where once was the glass dome. She shivers, shrugs, moves on. I don't enjoy it anyway. A cigarette smoked from a teenage bedroom window. All statement, no taste.

I follow on. I'm done here. I need a little something else if I'm to sand a few edges of conscious space. Turning back, just the once, the garden and glasshouses are as grey-green spray-paint over photographs faded with time.

Your focus is sharper in here than it is on the present. You've just mislaid the bones of those fairytales. You can feel his breath on your neck more keenly than the nip of the wind through the patchy green. His hands, still warm, pressing through the touch of dead branches. Stone yourself on news and facts, relentless information, but you're still haunted.

They wouldn't like this, you know. Holding onto anything from before. And in such colour and texture, too. Misusing nostalgia. You could share this, if you weren't so mired in self-pity. Call everyone you meet to an awakening of their own. There'd be quite the uprising. Demands made. Put things back the way they were. The Management won't have that. They'll kill you first. Keep it clean, sterile. Keep to the facts. Lips and fingers locked in step. Behave yourself: or at least look it.

This is the season of the *ish*. Never too hot or too cold, never properly rains and certainly never snows. Weather words a blur: warmish, coldish, kind of damp, a touch of frost. Used to piss me off, being unable to get a grip on where I was and when. Not so much, now. The Management take care of orientation.

I remember the last time it snowed. Really snowed. Thick clots slathered pavements for days on end. Weak thaws simply glazed the slough yet to melt, turned every walking surface into glacial plates. People were afraid to leave the house. Walking without falling over was impossible: the brave and stupid wound up enacting their own slapstick skits, smacking heads, knees, elbows of the ground with sick eggshell cracks. I had to go to work, though. Didn't want to give my boss an excuse to let me go. I was a hundred yards from the platform when I saw my train into town. Instinct took over and I started to run. I landed in my own cartoon, legs and feet wheeling, unable to get a grip, running without getting anywhere. I was black and blue for days. The Management might have borne that in mind. You can't run if you can't trust your own feet. In the season of the *ish,* I'm still unbeaten.

There's further encouragement at the top of the road. The traffic snarls like electric tape around the assault course of lights at the junction. Two legs reign supreme. I didn't think it'd have to get this bad to make of a pedestrian one happy traveller. Traction-less wheels spin in potholes; taxed bumpers clatter to tarmac; drivers lean from windows to smash steering locks and wrenches into the windshields of over-takers. The lines don't so much crawl as seep. Cars tend to make it past the lights in pieces, sometimes with a car-jack hanging, carbon-monoxide blue, to the undercarriage. Drivers hiss and spit as I weave through; the trick is not to look, not to taunt, at least not till I'm on the other side. I've lost blood, that way; pulling faces, rude words, obscene gestures. Very childish.

Safely across, there's still a gauntlet to run past the Management presence clotting the top of the street. If it's a slow day, they're the type to stop and search just for the sake of running through comfortable motions. I hand over my ID without being asked, looking for shapes in the smoke in the air as they match me to my photograph. Nonchalance pisses them off.

'Take your time,' I say to the hands clamping my shoulders. 'I don't have anywhere to be.'

'Stand up straight. Legs spread, arms out.'

I don't recognize any of them anymore. Time was, I'd spot a friendly face floating somewhere atop the black and blue. Guys who'd walked the same beat I had along this street. Back when *knew* people, in that backwoods American television kind of way. When we'd names instead of badges, instead of faces dodgy or otherwise. The officers keep it brief, despite my offer of a session. I honestly wouldn't mind. It's a touch, a time-kill. It's contact.

'She's clean,' he says to the rest. 'What's your business today?' he asks me.

'Cigarettes. Groceries. Coffee with a friend.'

'You sure about that?'

'Yes.'

'Right. Move on.'

'Yes, officer.'

There's a way to walk on. Purposeful without being hurried. Move too quickly and you look like you're up to something. Saunter and they take it as a mockery. Cigarettes, groceries, coffee – all, none, some could be true or untrue. It doesn't matter, so long as I'm clean and quiet on my way back home. Just something to say to project an illusion of purpose.

This street was once a twinkling rope of drinking establishments. The place to be, for loose-change students and moneyed execs alike. Not so much anymore. The posters pasted over the windows are kind of off-putting. Red letters against black prohibit happy hours and cheap drinks; warning of spot-checks, late openings and early closures. High-definition photographs of casualties tumbling from ambulance doors: broken, bloodied, stippled with shards of glass. Statistics in speech bubbles reel around the bodies: death and rape and brain damage and criminal records. A cartoon liver weeps green tears, bemoaning its maltreatment.

All self-inflicted, all our own fault, all our excesses and freedoms hollowing us out in cross-section, in spite of numberless warnings. We've been hearing it all since we were in high school. Yet all those initiatives, adverts, health visits, seminars, price hikes, measure shrinkage, curtailed hours, increased police presence and tightening of licensing laws had come to nothing, at least not at first: the people of the city continued to drink and drug and fight and fuck and stir up all kinds of merry hell. Governments don't like to be caught looking ineffectual: they needed a more hands-on deterrent. Hence the beatings, the kidnaps, paralysis and coma, sometimes suicide, the occasional death in the course of resisting arrest …the results of which were perfect photo opportunities for the posters outside.

All self inflicted. All our own fault.

Sure. However brutal their methods, you couldn't argue with the results: slowly but surely the city's drinking population fell to a to a low ebb, neon skies given over to a smouldering rug of gloomy streetlamp orange, nightlife whittled down to hushed gatherings behind

15

heavy curtains, killing the lights at the glimpse of blue light. Anyone with any sense was too terrified to step over a pub threshold after dark. I am one of them. Maybe if he'd still been around, we'd have had fun kicking up a fuss, heading on in anyway. These days I've too many harsh lessons under my belt to go looking for trouble.

He'd have started, you'd have carried on, you'd both have finished on your backs, rolling about and howling with laughter. You wouldn't have felt the beating; even if you had, you'd have loved it. Bruises for him to kiss, wounds for him to lick, markers on your bodies uniting you both in fight you barely understand. Not just you, either; he'd have called down the whole lot, people willing to jump into the fray in defence of a tenuous freedom, or even just for the fun of the fight.

Those remaining became caverns, dark dens of ill repute tense with the wait, all clientele poised to scuttle under tables like cockroaches at the first jackbooted footstep. Outside a place I used to frequent myself, a dim den nested in police tape, an old regular sits on an orange crate, smoking a rolled-up cigarette. He looks like shit, but then, we all do. We've more to worry about than peeling threads from crusty old overcoats.

'Hey Davie.'

He turns to look at me through eyes battered purple, cupping his shoulders round his torso, resting an arm in a sling on a trembling knee.

'Wha …?' he mutters, bringing his free hand up to steady his chin.

'Davie. What's happening?'

He's looking right through me. I'm simply not here. Better that way, I guess. Don't ask, don't tell. He shifts his gaze back to the pub door, long since boarded up. Might as well be open, the way Davie stares. Worships. No real difference between drunken and dazed, insanity or bafflement, accident or assault. He's just another of the lost, shuffling backward into a past slowly erasing its own trail.

'Take care of yourself, Davie.'

I'm no longer sure what that means.

I carry on down the street without looking back. I don't want to see officers swarming round. Davie's unnoticed just *sitting* there, sure, but now there's been a ghost of an interaction, they'll be honing in to see if he's any plans as regards those shuttered doors. Pubs are the new supermarkets. Aesthetic vacuums. If you really, really have to, just get in, get it done, pay up, get gone. No looking or talking. No social circles. And absolutely no fun.

I've made up my mind what I'm doing with my afternoon. The last preserve of the damned. None of the fires have yet reached the city's constellation of casinos: the only public leisure premises the Management have kept running.

Caleb would know it and call it for what it is – another control measure. Keep us all in one place. Since curfew means passing the guard boxes, which means you'd better be sober, there's nothing propelling a mad rush for last orders. Plus, on the few occasions I paid a visit *before* the changes, I couldn't help but notice the calm. You just don't pick a fight in a casino.

People hunch over their tables or games of choice, fixed on nothing beyond the numbers; shoulders hunched against intruders, drinks sipped slowly, with care. Bouncers and back rooms poised over the threat of any altercation. Prowling the floor, stewards, security guards, packed tight into their uniforms like sleeping bags stuffed with pure muscle. A far-off look in the eye, peeling the middle distance, needling the vanishing point, ears and nostrils twitching for trouble. Stock-still and speechless, yet you respected, you understood, as you would an electric fence or a scattering of landmines.

Traffic clamours all the way to the edge of town. Motorists seem to take the increased Management presence as a challenge: they hang from the windows, screaming threats and obscenities, still believing in the protection of their metal boxes. I've seen what happens. Agents move in formation, eyes dead ahead, arms at perfect right angles. They surround the offending car, one at each corner and bumper, and just *look* for a minute or two. They wait for the driver to simmer down. He will, always. Then panic, try to roll up the windows. Then it starts: a truncheon to each side of the car, sometimes the windshield. They'll drag him from the car. They won't beat him right there on the pavement: they'll cuff him and take him to the nearest Facility. The empty car will sit there for days – other vehicles simply smashing it out of the way, driving over the top – or until a vulture takes his pick of the saleable parts. I used to make such a fuss out of not being able to afford to drive. These days, I owe more than ever to two working feet.

He'd be pretty upset if he saw you just walking past, head to the pavement. Where are the actions to support your running commentary?

You thought you knew everything, back then. You thought you could get a grip on the world and its workings simply by reading the editorials in the liberal newspapers. He's surprised you, hasn't he? He's gone and done something, or tried, at least. Wherever he's ended up, alive or dead or sick or mad, he's made a move.

You fell far short of expectations when the time came for you to be brave. Do you even remember what he told you? Things that didn't to those dreams you drizzled away in pipe smoke? Concentrate as hard as you like on how stupid he'd

17

been to put up a fight, but there's no denying he's proved himself worthy of those ideals you both spouted. He's on his knees on piss-streaked concrete with his mouth strapped shut, giving nothing away, still holding on. And you are on your way to the casino to work on forgetting. Very disappointing.

I used to hate it here. Lights and noise, glitz and bleep. Not agreeable on rough mornings. Living inside an epileptic fit. When I still had a job, I'd sometimes end up here after work – the only place with a last-orders loophole. I'd deride this den of pathetic fallacy, all garish costumes, faux-Egyptian interiors, lacing every word and glance with a contempt I thought fitting for premises thriving on falsehood and scams. I still think it abhorrent: bad taste swollen to epic proportions, spilling down the walls in streaks of neon and cherry cellophane. But now, that's what I'm here for. Colour, shape, movement unchecked. Fakery, true, but there's only so much of the grey I can take before I get to thinking I've gone blind. A bit like Christmas, back when we still *did* it. The way glitter and pine, cinnamon and clove, crunch of snow and wrapping paper underfoot was still a little bit magical, long after busting the Santa Claus myth.

Everything in here is a lie I can't help but swallow, starving, willing. The gloss I used to mock, bleeps and squeals that had once had my head in my hands, false promises of riches beyond wildest dreams: I'm so tired of seeing right through everything. There's got to be a safe house, a place to wallow in illusions just a while.

I've never been one for gambling. Few are, anymore, it's too easy to get carried away. We're just here for a break from the outside. I make for the bar, squinting through shards of light blazing from the mirrors and chrome fixtures round the gantry, spirit bottles casting jewelled blooms on champagne-coloured carpets. I don't recognize any of the staff: I don't expect to, any more. They're carefully circulated: never the same premises for more than a few nights at a time. It minimizes the risk of relationships established between staff and customers.

'Good afternoon.' Blonde girl, black shirt. 'What can I do for you?'

Her voice rehearsed, controlled, every syllable purged of inflection, of possible double-meaning. They don't get it, not yet – they've won. We're too tired, too bored, to carry secret messages.

'A coffee, please.'

'Cappucino? Latte? Espresso? Something fancy? Or just black?'

'Uh, cappuccino, please.'

'Certainly. Anything else?'

It's fun to watch her making it. They still do it the proper way in here, one of the few places yet to switch to buttons and sachets. I savour the gurgle, grind, patterns of steam on the side of the machine. The roll of foam over the top of the cup a tumbling pack of white horses. I even get chocolate sprinkles. Sugar-free, but you can't have everything.

'Cheers.' I pay up, still squinting for something, anything other than service with a smile.

'Enjoy your coffee!'

I'm here so often now I have a favourite seat; a booth tucked into the curve of the rotunda, prime position for seeing without being seen. By people, anyway. No use hiding from the cameras strapped to the inner rims of the lighting braces, the CCTV playback on screens behind the bars and booths. Still, these don't make the skin crawl quite so much as a gathering of stewards and staff, peering shameless every time they wander past on invisible pretexts.

I'm looking for Murray. A familiar face. He hated the casino, too, but it'd be just like him to come here to hide out. We go way back – well, as far as a stoner's living memory will take you. Met at a handful of parties. Did a bit of dealing, back and forth. We'd help each other out, no charge, when one of us was falling short. People did that, back then. Favours, I mean. Nothing in stone, no payback or deadline, just a helping hand out of a tight spot. I haven't seen him around for weeks, which begs the question – where do you go to hide when you're already underground?

I mark further depopulation. Those clients remaining become imbued with significance, have more to be read into; gathering meaning like household objects in an avant-garde movie. I know them all so well by now, even only by sight, the odd knowing nod, it's almost a pleasure to construct a little family, like those crowds of regulars from before.

Today, the older woman in the black spangled dress has been crying again. She hunches over a round table in the centre of the room, picking through gambling chips. A steward moves in for a peek; just on the off-chance she's spelling something out in yellow plastic disks. *SOS. Send Help.* That kind of thing. We've only ever spoken briefly; I know she's far more likely to be trying to remember how to spell *GOD*. Tragic set of circumstances as far as I'm aware – rich husband banged up in one of the facilities. Tried to set up a few games of poker outside of the perimeter. On the outside. They couldn't be having that. She's in here playing both sides of each game, waiting for him to come back. Peeling the fringing from the hem of her dress, slowly unravelling time.

The guy in the far corner is here on his own; no partner or family as far as I could gather from snippets of conversation. He

20

speaks in epigrams, spoken mainly to his barrel of a chest. He wears a zoot suit – a mythical get-up I'd seen only in costume stores. A fine piece of attire it is, too; powder-blue with navy lapels and tie. He's trying very hard not to look too bothered that they took away his wide-brimmed hat. He understands. Wouldn't want to interfere with their surveillance.

He expends every last gram of energy into making believe it's just like before; maybe the power's in the suit, since he's always got a smile on his face and a kind word for the likes of me. He wanders between booths and tables, wheels and slots, tongue thrust into lower lip as though sampling a mouthful of fine wine. Running chips through his fingers, clacking them about his pockets. Must just like the feeling of all that potential energy in his hands. We don't get a lot of that anymore; no concessions, no exceptions, no surprises.

And no Murray. Time sucks itself dry, shrivels, dusts the roulette tables, the cup and saucer between my hands. I can't muster the energy to sketch him a probable set of circumstances – he's here or he's gone, I'm scoring or failing, I'm drinking my coffee and killing more time. Christ, it's depressing in here anyway, that's reason enough to stay away. I'm here for reasons that would not stand up under interrogation, trying to forget something I don't remember being told.

So what the fuck do I do now? I've long finished my coffee – which, I must say, almost convinced me – and taken a look around. There's something awkward about sitting here without a plan. It's like being a student again, too poor to afford much of anything, sat trying to make the one cup last and knowing there's nowhere to go when I'm done. Looking like I'd been stood up. Looking friendless, jobless, useless. It's not supposed to be like this, when you grow up and move on and know a little about the way the world works.

So no scoring, nobody to talk to, no real reason for sitting there taking up space, dirtying dishes. Poor you, indeed. You have no idea what you think you're really missing.

Feeling sorry for yourself, you're allowing the past to mist over into tear-blurred sepia frames. Just pick yourself up and get out. Go home. Things are only going to get worse. He'd tell you if he could. There are mechanisms in place. Just because you're out of reach of traffic clatter and handcuff burr doesn't make it all go away. The woman in the dress peels herself of what's left of her mind. Zoot-suit creaks through blood bruises, broken ribs. The bar staff are so pumped with medication they have to be folded into bed at night. That's the price of this loophole at land's end. This illusion of freedom. You're on camera right now. You're a weave in the pattern. Are you sitting comfortably? You should be – that funny taste in your mouth is not accidental. They'll allow a cup of real coffee, sure, but with added extras.

Your arrogance matches only your complacency, brocaded with a sick hit of self-pity. He'd be so disappointed. He fought for you, and this is the sum of your hours. You've let him become just a ringing in your ear, a buzz of winged insects.

He's asking for you, you know. Getting into a lot of trouble. He's got it all wrong, backward — the harder he works to get through to you, the tighter they pull the strings.

Finish up your sad little cup and go home. Go home and don't think about what you're not doing. About what you could have done.

I'm making my way to the exit with my under-surveillance stroll. Outside, the car park lies bare of vehicles, even of dry leaves. I have my hands pressed to my temples, staring past my feet into surface water. Reflections and adjacent headaches creeping up again. The cameras topping the posts are almost idle, turning over in a half-sleep.

Watched or otherwise, I am not ready to go home yet.

Around the curved wall of the rotunda, a couple of benches remain from when this once was a manicured garden. I take a seat, just a minute, just to calm down, take advantage of the quiet. Fuzz creeps round the edge of my vision. Stupid to think they'd leave the coffee alone. My own fault, small delusions of sanctuary. Still, comfort to be had in the press of cold steel against the back of my legs; I'm still here, just. I used to drift, sat out here before – look out into the city lights, picking out places I knew from shades and shapes of neon. Before, cars had streamed along, stitching the city together in bands of coloured light. Now they drag like wax blobs trundling from candles, suspended, waiting, pushing, waiting, writhing, waiting, straining, waiting. Before, I'd have conversations to play back in my head, things I couldn't wait to tell him, ideas I was eager to share. Now my mind dribbles on like rain on tin, nothing going on but the reminder to keep breathing. I'm rubbing hands together to keep hold of slackening sensation when a voice cuts through the rustling of dry palms.

'You shouldn't be here,' she whispers, not unfriendly.

A woman I last saw behind the bar inside. I know her, we've spoken before. I just can't remember what about. She's attractive in a grungy sort of way. Blonde hair striped through with a splay of dark roots, makeup pressed into the ridges around her eyes in ghosts of blue and peacock green, a keen smile twitching at the edges. Can't be any more than thirty-odds, but you never can tell. We're all looking a little scattered, these days.

'I'm not doing anything.'

'That's not the point,' she says, shifting round to take a seat on the bench. 'You've come here to get away from something, right?'

'Not really … well, kind of. I like it here. At least you can't *see* them.'

I'm not so stupid as to believe this is a safe house. It's just that there's a sliver of comfort to be had from not being able to *watch* them watching.

'You're not hiding from them, though, are you?'

'I'm not hiding from anything.'

'Yes, you are. You're hiding from Caleb.'

A sharp pain in the gut. I haven't heard that name out loud since I left the hospital. She has no right, whoever she is, to come out with such statements.

'What the fuck are you talking about?'

I immediately regret cursing. If she knows something, I'll want to remain on the right side of wrath.

'Your Caleb. He's still about, you know.' She scratches her left nostril with a raw fingertip.

'What? Where?' Not the most useful line of questioning. There is no *where*, anymore – it's all one plane, under greater or lesser surveillance.

'Shhhht. Keep your voice down.'

'Makes no difference, they're listening anyway.'

'Sorry. Habit,' she says, leaning back into the bench, lighting a cigarette. She's watching coils of smoke rising up to meet the orange chaos of the sky. As though we're just a couple of friends having a chat. Drawing too deeply on the filter, drinking instead of smoking, she buckles, splutters, clutches the bench for leverage.

'Hey! You ok?'

'Yeah! Yeah …' she offers a wet smile, picking grains of tobacco from lips dissolving in cracks and flakes of dried skin.

'Look … look … do you know something I should know?'

I've given in. I don't know how to play games. No wonder I always skipped out on the casino tables. She almost smiles; tentative mouth corners peeking up into unknown territory.

'Nobody really *knows* anything,' she says. 'Like, the word doesn't really mean anything anymore. You can *know* something without understanding it … or remembering it.'

'Please. You were talking about …'

'Caleb? That's what you're after, isn't it?'

'I haven't heard from him for months.'

The orange foam arcing over the twilight sheets her eyes in glass. She shifts back on the bench, attending to her posture, crossing and uncrossing her ankles. Silence. I've said the wrong thing.

'You make it sound like he's been off on holiday or moved house or something and just … forgotten to call you.'

'He might as well have.'

Only curiosity keeps back an outburst, from walking away.

'What? What are you talking about? You mean you–'

'Look, I don't know who you are or what you want from me.'

Gangster-speak springs to the lips in the absence of any other kind of sense. 'The thing with … with Caleb, right, that's our business. He left. No word. Maybe you two are best of friends, these days, I have no idea, but I don't want to talk it over with a perfect stranger, if that's quite alright with you.'

She laughs. It's not pleasant.

'You really don't remember, do you?'

'Remember what?'

'Where he's gone. And why. And with whom.'

I'm pressing my hands to my temples again. She's stopped laughing. There's a rushing in my ears, blood or wind or cars crashing miles and miles away.

You'll be getting and giving grief over how much you have failed to remember. Yes, it doesn't look so good, not good at all, but where's the credit for recalling all that you do? You've a puzzle box of treasures spread the length and breadth of your insides; head memory, heart memory, recollections of the skin and eyes and teeth and tongue. You've an inner language, whole encyclopaedia of words he'd spoken; acres of cartography outlining where he'd been. And you. This was not always a show for one.

Your favourite isn't the where and what of how you met, although it's worthy of note. Favourites come later, when the tension slackens and you're able to make of it as you wish and will. Not so much pressure – see, back then you'd still head-space to devote to unpicking gestures, analyzing phone messages, squinting at the spaces between lines of an email, unsure of where you stood. It's just a shame your enthusiasm for secret messages has so waned without him around.

Back then, there were actual whereabouts. Places had names instead of numbers; people used them whether or not they were difficult to spell or took up too much disk-space. You were still a student. You still are, technically, by the way, although they tend to give up looking for you after six months or so. You're lucky you worked instead of taking that loan, otherwise you'd be in more trouble than you are already.

You were on your way to the library (or so you told yourself – you were often on your way there, it seemed, never quite making it past the door before you'd hung a left and slipped into the student union. For the warmth, the cheap food, the coffee, yesterday's news-papers. Sure). It was raining, proper raining, over Glasgow; the kind of rain you haven't seen for years, walloping the roofs so hard and fast it turned silence inside out, wrapping the senses in this fuzz of white noise spun about you in a half-meter circle. The buildings propped up on stems of silver streaming from the gutters. The turrets swathed in a cloud of shrapnel as one by one the roof tiles gave themselves over. Thick drops you could hold in the palm of your hand like a pearl or a prized soap bubble. Remember? Rain these days is just a smear, a sticky breath addling the air. You were soaked through, having failed once more to spend your pay-check on any kind of sensible outerwear. Student uniform of torn jeans, concert T-shirt, camouflage-print jacket rattling with badges, shoes so ravaged you could see your mismatched socks underneath. Between two fingers, lengthways, a half-smoked joint it was too wet to re-ignite. You were halfway up the hill, passing a few of the cheaper flats – tenement floors meant for one property split and plaster-boarded into two, popular with students unable to afford the modern slicks of glass and chrome poised at the hub of the nicer parts of town.

You felt it before you heard it, sound dampened by the rain – a thought which still jerks your stomach if you think on it too long. A rumbling underfoot, like the underground train swooping past, needing a bit of a repair job. You'd stared at your feet, trying to remember where you were headed and why. Then it happened. A great white oblong on its side, careering down the inside stairwell, past the open door, over the front steps, scattering shards of broken paving slab on either side before coming to a rest three feet from your right ankle; then catching on an unseen gutter, righting itself to its six-feet thunder, dithering back and forth as though pondering whether you were worth the crushing. You were too surprised at first to do anything but stare at the refrigerator, still rattling and shuffling, trying to find its feet; an image crossed your mind of a black stick figure cowering under a hypotenuse of a great black triangle, the business end of a vending machine making to flatten any customer stupid enough to shake it for money or product gratis. Then it was funny; you couldn't think of any manner of death more ridiculous than being crushed to death by a rogue piece of kitchen equipment. You sat down by the machine; right there on the pavement, amid floods of rain still tearing up the gutters, too shocked to do anything else. Your first taste of the nicer manifestations of hysteria; when was the last time you laughed out loud in public? Laughed like you meant it?

Then one voice, then another. Two skinny figures skiing down the inner staircase, thundering over the front steps and down the pavement. You couldn't make either out, at first, the rain blurring the sodium around the streetlamps to a pinkish fuzz. Sherbet pink. Valentine pink. You'd be seeing it again, many night walks across campus. You read too much into it, even then.

A proffered hand.

'Uh … are you okay?' said the first figure; the second darting around both you and the refrigerator, checking for damage. You stopped laughing, took the hand. You didn't drop it once you were on your feet. A nice hand, a shock of heat in the damp chill, pleasantly rough in the way of – you knew by then, through experience both positive and negative – artists and musicians. The face attached to the hand laughed, not unkindly, when you noticed and pulled back.

'Yeah … yeah … I'm fine, just … erm, is this yours?' you said, patting the refrigerator, a mad grin marching across your teeth and tongue.

'Kind of got away from us a bit, there,' said the second figure, who by now is laughing as hard as you had been. You decided, quite calmly and without too much concern for etiquette or shyness, that you liked these men – boys, really – and their flying machine. The laughter is addictive. You remember that, right? The way laughter used to swell a room, rippling the shoulders of everyone present one by one by one like a stick drawn over a xylophone? It was nice. You liked it.

The three of you stood in the rain around the monolith for what seemed like eons, or no time at all, the rain pouring down your throat and into your eyes and jacket collar as you held your stomach, the small of your back, forgetting where you were or where you were going or the fact that you could be justifiably irate or shaken by the whole ludicrous near-death experience. Finally the boy with the warm

27

hand levelled off, turned his head as well as his gaze to where you were stood half-drowned. He'd been watching you the whole time – maybe you didn't know that.

'Look, ah – sorry, what's your name?' he asked.

'Lucy. Hi.'

'I'm Cal, this is Fred. We're, ah, really sorry about the … the thing. Would you like to come up for a cup of tea or a drink or something? Get dried off a bit?'

'That'd be nice.'

You couldn't have done anything else. That's how these things start. The story of the refrigerator went straight into your pocketbook of precious recollections you'd want to tell your kids and grandkids or at the very least pore over, clutch to your chest, cold nights you're tempted to fear that you've never really lived.

You'd no need to feel ill at ease. It was the laughter that had done it. Something about laughter, in all its release, leaves people too sore round the ribs for pretence. Enjoy it, the memory of awkwardness peeled back. The guys were as unsure as yourself. Strange; they could throw a refrigerator down a flight of stairs in plain sight, yet got all tongue-tied and fidgety with a girl in their flat.

Six flights around a spiral staircase brought you to the third floor, soggy denim and hi-tops squeaking all the way. Fred charged on ahead at Caleb's urging; you'd heard mutterings of check and state and you bit back a grin of pleasure that they were keen to make a good impression.

You stepped into a marijuana haze. You'd been around it once or twice before, but never with such clout, even with the front door open. A wicker mat spread over a three-legged dining table confirmed your suspicions – you were in the company of some serious stoners. Hand-moulded clay pipes and many flavours of tobacco; steel tweezers and antennae laid out like a surgeon's tray. A six-skinner lies half-smoked in an ashtray enamelled with a Warhol Monroe. You'd never seen so many half-empty glasses. It was a room culled from mythic annals of student lifestyles, the stuff of warnings and encouragements you'd never imagined to be so close to the truth. Pizza boxes teeter on the arm of a battered sofa upholstered in questionable stains. The posters on the walls were of the kind you'd always wanted in your own bedroom at home. So many books, CDs, DVDs and records in the room that, were you to sit down immediately and charge through them twenty-four hours per day, you'd still be reading, watching and listening halfway through the next century. Stringed instruments propped up against the far wall – standard electric and acoustic guitars, some you'd only ever seen in museums. Amplifiers, cables, and pedals sprawling from corners. You'd smiled and wished you'd kept up your high school lessons.

'Eh … ah, sit down …?' said Fred. The other boy snickered, began knocking various items of debris from the couch to the floor.

'Sorry,' he said, 'We're … ah, moving flats. The place is a bit of a state.'

28

'Hey, don't worry,' you replied, trying to be cool, to say the right thing, 'You should see mine, it's a shambles.'

Lying. You didn't want to think on why your flat was in such order – a dearth of opportunities for parties or visitors; an unwillingness as yet to fill the place with books or films or music in case you got caught by the Management. Besides, you didn't know what you liked, yet. You took a seat, gingerly. Troubled etiquette; you weren't sure you should make yourself too comfortable. The guy named Caleb slumped down into the depths of the next sofa, sighing.

'Fred ... Freddy ...' he called. Fred appeared in the kitchen door, a lidless kettle in one hand, a teabag box, empty, in the other.

'Yeah?'

'You making tea? Or are you rolling?'

'I dunno, mate. Having a bit of trouble finding the rest of the kettle. Kitchen's all over the place with wires and dust and crap. Besides which, we've no milk, now, have we?'

'Ah ...' said Caleb, leaning forward, slapping his knees. 'Seem to have got you up here on the back of some false advertising, Lucy – as you'll no doubt have noticed, we're sort of lacking a fridge. And stuff to keep in it.'

'No worries,' you said. 'I'm not much of a tea-drinker anyway, it's just good to get out of the rain.'

'Shit!' yelped Caleb, 'Jeez, sorry! You're sat there all ... wait a minute. Freddy – fuck the tea, just get rolling, eh?'

'Ayuh.'

Caleb leapt from the sofa and sloped off down the hall. You heard doors slamming and the wrenching of drawers, bone-thumps and curses. Fred bent over the table, didn't say a word; the process required all his powers of concentration. You didn't mind; you were too busy looking over everything, every glance throwing back a fresh turn on a kaleidoscope. The boy Fred didn't fascinate quite so much as Caleb. Handsome, yes, but his image failed to flip the same switch. You'd barely had a decent look at Caleb, yet there was something fascinating in the languor of his stride. Shambling as it was, carelessness suited him. He was certain the air through which he moved would accommodate any fumbles or staggers.

He shuffled back brandishing a faded handful of denim and cotton.

'Eh ... I don't know if you're funny about clothes and that, but if you want to dry off, you can wear these for a bit. Could put your stuff over the radiator ... you know, just so's you're not going back out there still soaking ... or you could stay, whatever, we've plenty of space.'

He'd actually looked a little awkward, hands locked across the back of his neck, peering up at you from under a nest of petrol-coloured hair. You'd had to be brave. You were so very, very keen to do the right thing, so desperate to be liked. In the corner, Fred lit the half-smoked joint to help him through the rolling of the next one. *The fresh smoke made your mind up. You'd never get another chance like this, to find out your limits and your preferences.*

'Thanks. I wouldn't mind a chance to dry off, if that's okay.'

'No bother. Bathroom's down that way.'

You'd taken your time. Pressed your face into the fabric, inhaling grass and aftershave phantoms. You'd had to bunch up a handful of denim at the back to get the jeans to stay on, tying up the excess with a hair elastic like a tail. Two tokes of the joint and this was a point of much hilarity.

You took your seat. Caleb perched on the arm of your couch, picking at a guitar. You were still too shy to look at him directly, but conversation soon came more easily, with the addition of music and marijuana haze. Everything pulsed with green light. You took in and stored every word he said, packed them in tissue, pressed them close to your chest.

You're allowed to picture him, you know. However you try to frame yourself as being above and beyond aesthetic concerns, you've enough of the words and smarts down pat to linger over the form as much as the content. Slowly, now. Pan down as you would a painting in a gallery; the way you used to do when there was no-one else around, to hurry you up or make you feel awkward or try to dictate what you were supposed to see.

Start at the top. Hair so black it's almost blue. You'd thought it a bottle job, and were pleasantly surprised to discover otherwise. Pale translucence of skin; he didn't get out much during the day. You're never sure whether the green light in his eyes came from the haze surrounding everything else; it was uncanny, almost unholy, spilling out and over the lips of the lids like drips of liquid glass. Bone structure women would pay hard cash for. Dips and hollows purpling eyes and scoring the cheeks. Remnants, you'd learn, of many nights like this, of assignments called up from the depths of sense at the last minute.

Move on. Go deeper. How did he feel? You liked the hard-packed crunch of his back and hips, knees and wrists and elbows, sure; even better the slight slackness of the belly, point to point with your own. Perfection in imperfection, you know. Or maybe you've forgotten what it is to be moved by that which can't be quantified. Just remember how it felt to be held, pressed up close and tight to another's skin, heat, scent. That came much later. Caleb was either a perfect gentleman or far too stoned for any process of seduction.

You'd liked that they'd asked you questions. They seemed to appreciate your taste for the obscure and old-fashioned – books and music your parents had had before the latest run of trips to the junk depots. They were students, too. English and French with Politics and Sociology. Subjects far beyond your fragile grasp of text and framing, but no matter. Caleb never, ever made you feel stupid. Every time you spoke, his responses always interacted with your statements. You'd never been in a dialogue, before, a proper interplay of fact and idea.

'Caleb, man ... I'm a wee bit ... argh ...' said Fred, eventually.

30

'Long day, Freddy-boy. All sorts of weightlifting and aerobics ... you shuffling off?'

'Aye. Got to ... probably ... something tomorrow ...'

'Cool. See you then.'

'Was nice to meet you, Lucy,' said Fred, pausing at the door, remembering to mind his manners. 'Sorry again about the fridge.'

'No ... no, it's okay ... thanks for letting me stick around.'

'Anytime.'

With Fred gone, questions of sleeping arrangements could no longer be ignored. You couldn't believe how much time had slipped from your grasp without your notice. You got up and made your way over to the radiators, very slowly, stoned and reluctant to leave. Your gear was dry. You'd no excuse.

'Lucy ...!' Caleb drawled. 'You're not leaving now, are you?'

'It's really, really late,' you said, 'I'm beyond dried off ... beside, need to give you your gear back.'

'Sit down,' he said, grin spread across the entire lower half of his skull. 'It's still pissing it down, and it's way too dark to be walking home. Seriously, just crash. No funny business, I promise.'

And there hadn't been. You weren't sure why you were so disappointed.

Eventually it crosses your mind to ask about what had brought you up here in the first place.

'Caleb?'

'Yeah?'

'What were you and Fred doing with that fridge?'

Caleb started up that infectious chuckle, characteristic of career stoners and their foibles.

'I told you we were moving flats, yeah?'

'Yeah ...?'

'Well ... it's kind of a last-ditch bird-flip to the, uh, powers that be. They're kicking us out since we can't keep up with the rent hikes or the bills anymore – fucking fuel crisis or something, they're saying, but I know for a fact they're planning to chop these flats in half, twice as many bodies means twice as much rent for the bigwigs. I know it's daft, but ...we figured we'd make the place as unappealing as possible. Steal or trash the appliances and furniture. Put a few holes in the walls. Disappear into the night.'

'Won't they catch up to you? Your next place?'

'Nah, we're moving into a squat a mate of mine's been keeping. Just for a while.'

'But, like, what's the point? Trashing the furniture, I mean?'

He'd looked puzzled and guilty in equal measure. You didn't know this at the time, but you were the first person to call him on the futility of his anarchies. The first one to point out he'd achieve nothing by destroying that which meant

31

nothing anyway to the people with money. The first to have him question the outcome desired from the statements he was trying to make. The first to be that legendary promontory from which arrows of intent are launched.

'I honestly don't know, Lucy,' he said, his voice clearing the haze, eyes becoming more defined, like pressure points on screens of liquid crystal. 'Kind of childish, I guess. We figured, if we couldn't keep the place and everything in it, nobody else would. Just wanted to make it difficult for the bastards. They can't just push us out and expect us to go quietly. We've been chucking bits and pieces out the top window for days, now. We've quite the collection, out back.'

And he did. You looked out over the accumulated ruins of everything on the landlord's inventory. Your shoulders pressed up close in the window frame. He hung his head.

'It's ... ah, it's pathetic, eh? No point. Changes nothing. I don't know what we thought we were up to — seemed a good idea at the time, you know? Sticking it to the man, or something. Only thing keeping us from tearing out the cooker was, we were scared we'd gas ourselves in our sleep.'

'So who's the man?'

'You know that. It all comes down from the Management, doesn't it? Can't turn around without some dire warning, clamping down on your right to ... fuck, I don't know anymore. All I do know is, things are getting worse. Another fucking crisis, another initiative, another ...'

He broke off, laughed a little. At himself, you were sure. He'd a ways to go yet before he'd learned enough, been around a few more groups and protests, picked up enough underground publications to know what he was fighting for. Later.

Hang on to the early stuff. From back when it was enough to just be: angry or excited or desperate for truth. The freshness made it all seem possible. A nameless enemy to have you clutching one another that much tighter, hanging on to what you knew. That night in the window was the first time you'd struggled to make out the stars, just beginning to disappear. You'd never really bothered, before, happy enough to know they were there.

There you were, first time ever up close to a guy who threw white goods down tenement steps in protest. A boy still honing his tantrums. Back then, you still believed in the poetry, the purity, of just being angry enough. Naive enough back then to believe that this was the only formative experience had by anyone, ever. To believe in bright lights and magic words. The proximity and posture all set up for a kiss. You'd never had a man's undiluted attention. You didn't want to spoil it by asking why.

'Are you still in there?' she asks, rapping knuckles on the bench. Steel static burr thrums skin. I can hear her. Sure. Doesn't mean I want to.

'Pay attention. Not going to look too good if I have to get physical, eh?'

'Look, just talk. Tell me. About Caleb.'

His name hurts my throat. Broken glass in the soft vowels.

'You know he's alive, right?'

I can't help it; I laugh, head shot back, mouth slack as a pin-jabbed balloon. I know things are pretty bad, but folks' status as being living or dead isn't some a quantity as changeable as the weather used to be.

'Look, maybe we didn't end well, maybe we weren't as grown-up as we should have been, but I'm pretty sure I'd know if he were *dead.*'

'You sure about that?'

'Well, he still has some of my stuff, for a start, and he owes me money from the rent on the last place.'

He hated that. The use of sarcasm in tense situations to deflect unease.

'Christ, you really don't remember.'

'You've said that, already. And I was there, you know. I think I have all the information I need. What makes you think you can tell me anything I haven't played out a million times already?'

I'm getting angry again. I'm giving too much away. Soft spots.

She tilts her head like an animal squaring up to a hostile environment. A shrug of pause. Another fumble in her cigarette packet. She's picking up pace, I notice; discarding them half-smoked, lighting another as the last still smoulders, as though the lighting were the addiction itself. She coughs, offers a half-cocked smile. Accustomed to sweetening bad news.

'You're forgetting something. Well, forgetting lots of things, really, but for starters – I'm a *bartender.* For now, anyway. I *know* things about people just by paying attention – what people drink, the way they walk into a room … whether they look around, or into the bottom of the glass … and I know all about *you.*'

'What … the *hell?*'

'I remember you from before. The way you clung to the edges of the room with this far-off look on your face, as though you were just *waiting* for something. Missing someone. Like you had your

33

happiness on pause, just hanging on until you could get out of *here* and back to what you knew. Back to your Caleb.'

Pressure of thumbs against closed lids shocks up a rush of colour and shape far more appealing than anything else I'd care to look at. I say nothing. She can talk on, if she likes. A fun . I've seen it before – folks these days enjoy constructing vast epics of experience and influence, keen to keep hold of what their lives once meant.

'Not for months, now, though,' she continues, getting right on into it, the warm burr of a radio play. 'Didn't see you around for ages … thought they'd got hold of you, too. . Used to run into you on my smoke breaks – you'd sit right there, where you're sitting now, with at least half a packet's worth of cigarette ends at your feet. You'd talk about your Caleb - never said *boyfriend* or *lover* or *partner* or anything like that, but I got the idea. You'd speak of him like the pros inside spoke of the great big win – a hope to hold onto. I'd tell you stories from on the job – daft stuff, customers and pranks and all that, but you *got* it. How important it was to keep in constant touch with the *why* of any given day. To know where you were, and why. To know what was important, however much the Management worked to take it all away.'

She breaks off. A long sigh, and I know without taking my hands from my eyes that she's leaning back, taking in the view of the city spread out before us like a model railway. She shifts closer, her breath against the side of my neck. I don't move away. I want to know.

'Then you're back, all of a sudden. Wandering about the place on your own, staring up at ceiling like you were trying *not to look* like you were looking for something. The way folks do when they've been stood up. Or hoping to be *picked* up. Not you, though. You couldn't figure out what you were missing. What was lost.'

'Look. I can't … I can't–'

'You can. Just listen. I don't know what you think happened, but you've got it all wrong. I've *seen* him, he's *talking* about you, and he's got no idea what's going on, whether you're alright …'This is crazy. I do remember her face, her voice, but I can't place her in context. Flashes and shards, zoetrope blurs. I've lost bits and pieces before. Very uncomfortable, like my head's a box of confetti upturned, fragments of thought drifting off without my permission. They warned me about that, after my accident. That some stuff would be a bit mixed up. It's been a while since I've consciously misplaced anything, though – I guess it's easy to lose track of how much you've forgotten when you've no-one around to remind you.

'Where … where did you see him?' I ask, finally taking my hands from my eyes. It's now as dark as it's ever going to be. Ice-cream swirls of pink and green slake the city in a haze; car headlights no less condensed, pressed taut, but shorter. Maybe a few drivers really have made it all the way home. She sit with hands folded in her lap, the cigarette, forgotten, burning ever closer to the back of her hand. as the ash crumbles and drifts over her lap, until she flinches from the heat, flapping the butt from her hand, expression unchanging.

'Where?' I repeat.

'Where we all end up. When we don't do what we're told.'

'Please. Tell me.'

'I can't. Not here. You talk, now. You tell me what you think really happened. With you and Caleb, I mean. Just so I know where we both are. Then we'd better get a move on – it's getting late, we don't want to be caught out.'

This is private stuff. Sort of. Relationship crises too banal to relate to anyone but the most tolerant of friends, family, parents. Those I don't really have any more.

'Come on,' she says, chuckling a little. 'There's nothing you can't share with your friendly neighbourhood bartender.'

'Okay ...' If we're going to be on more intimate terms, there's an etiquette. Embarrassing, but I have to ask. 'Uh ... really sorry, but ... what's your *name?*'

She doesn't look the least bit surprised that I have to check.

'That's a puzzler, sometimes. Full name ... ex-Agent Number Forty-Four, Sector Nineteen. But, these days, just Bethany. Between friends.'

Friends. Another language I've forgotten. It sounds far better than a return to clock-tick, air-con, traffic noise. I'm sure I'll pick it up.

You've been slumped. Sinking. Clutching only to the hope that the more you're able to forget, the better off you'll be. When you do allow a mote to float to the surface, recall tends toward the negative, the prosaic, or worse, the cerebral.

You can't blame the medication.

You can't blame the cracks in your skull.

You can't blame solitude or routine. You're not working hard enough.

Bethany's trying to return what's lost: ownership of your thoughts. This won't work till you're willing to take a closer look. And face it, you're not exactly reeling with distractions, crack-backed around a calendar heaving with better things to do. If you see Caleb again, you'll want to start over, skip the digging-down through all the rot. You won't want him to know just how much effort you've put into forgetting. Think. Pick a nice one, there are more to choose from than you'd have yourself believe.

Here's something to make you smile. One of the first projects you'd got up to in the tower blocks. He'd amassed a team of volunteers; guys with whom he'd shared flats or classes; worked alongside in one of his many bar jobs; or just got talking to when stoned outside a gig. Back then, you both had so many friends. He wouldn't tell you what he had in mind. He wasn't sure yet, himself, but you knew whatever happened would be spectacular.

You shambled about barefoot in your underwear, raking the wardrobe for something that said covert ops, midnight prowlers, secret mission. Still playing a kid's game. He lay on the bed, just watching, talking, drowning in coils of marijuana smoke. Laughed as you wrapped your hand in sticky tape to brush lint from a pair of black jeans.

'Just go naked, Lucy. You can distract the robots whilst the rest of us slip in through the prison laundry.'

'Uh-uh, don't you go objectifying,' you said, a joke between the two of you – political correctness having taken on whole new levels in your Identities seminars on campus. His phone rang as you wrestled on the bed. Freddy. Jake. Colin. One by one they pulled out. He was furious, but he understood – matching the walk to the talk meant climbing higher stakes than ever before.

He took your hands and said, in his best pre-Millennial film star accent, 'Hey kid, looks like it's just you and me.'

The look on your face caught him by surprise. You didn't know just how frightened you were till you saw yourself reflected in his gaze. Dropping your hands, he said, 'Look. This was a stupid idea. Just you wait here. I'll take care of it myself.'

You knew you couldn't turn down the chance to see what he did. You set your jaw.

36

'Caleb. I'll never know what to be afraid of if I don't get to see for myself. And … and I trust you. To take care of me.'

He didn't say a thing, just kissed your closed lids and led you over to the window. To show you what you were both seeking to protect.

It had been snowing. The last proper winter. No stars in the sky, but no clouds, either. The chill peeled the smog from the city like a milk-skin. A bal three-quarter moon looked on, a great glass eye strung between the distant tower blocks. It turned the snow bright blue, bounced sheets of glare from the flawless spread to the window pane. It was his turn to speak, but you had to say something.

'Maybe this is one of those little things that are supposed to make us glad. Little things to fight for. Like you said.'

He didn't laugh. This was enough.

He led you once more to the wardrobe. Things were getting serious: his spliff forgotten in the ashtray. Soundless, he lifted a black shirt and jacket of his own and dressed you up. Lip caught at mouth-corner, an artist, a patient father. Your eyes locked together, the fraction of a second when you disappeared behind the fabric felt like too much of a strain, too much like a goodbye. You two, the two of you, felt like you were spilling the light of church flames. Every motion a statement footprint over historic dust. Something filled the room for which you didn't have a name.

And even when you were both clothed and ready to go, shutting drawers and pulling blinds and checking locks three, four times over, neither of you tore it down with your characteristic sarcasm. You let it lie. You cherished. Maybe even then you knew there would come a time when such things would be precious, a globe of memory, fully-formed, petrol rainbows swirling the surface.

Then the fun began. He still didn't know what he was doing – he just brought his usual bag of party tricks. The target was a security firm on the other side of the city. They'd been laying folks off to make room for Management experts keen to supervise the manufacture of devices. Device – a word that came up far too often, applied to so many objects that their reputation buried their true purpose. Consumers and technicians were so awed by the numbers, prices, capacities, and qualities that nobody paid much attention to what they could be used for. The target was developing a seventh generation of undetectable, indestructible surveillance equipment. The Management had purchased developments in the hopes of installing them in every home in the city. Complete visibility. No midnight REM or picked nose or pawed-at creature in the depths of sleep would go unrecorded. Dispensing with each and every original employee meant no independent civilian would know enough to disable the equipment. No civilian would ever think to check every last inch of their home for such invasion of privacy. You didn't ask Caleb how he knew this – he had a way with people. They told him things. He had a gift for betraying no reaction at the time to any slice of scandal – he merely nodded, murmured, poured the storyteller another drink and stored away the information for future use.

37

You did have to ask what was so horrifying about the manoeuvre. You should have known better than to speak without thinking it through.

'I'm not keen on being watched in the bathroom, sure, but if we're not getting up to anything … isn't it something we could all just get used to? I mean, drug dealers and terrorists and paedophiles and murderers get up to their bad shit in their own living rooms. Maybe a little privacy's a small sacrifice for improving the odds of catching them.'

He didn't say a thing at first. He pulled the car over to the side of the road. You sat watching neon mimic sundown. His jaw clicked as he chewed over a response. Finally, 'But that's just how it starts. Has already started. We've been watched, recorded, monitored for years, now. And are we any better off? Wasn't so bad in the Nineties, like – you'd only really notice if you were doing something out of the ordinary, like taking a flight or being fingerprinted in a police station. But since the Millennium, it's just gone crazy. Everything, I mean. I'm not sure what happened first – whether people started pushing the limits of just how fucking insane their criminal – no, fundamentally inhuman acts could get, or whether overreaction on the part of the authorities pushed their limits even higher. It's an interesting premise, don't you think? That maybe some psychotics like a challenge … that maybe they wouldn't have gone to so much bother if the Management hadn't kept trying to make it more difficult.'

You shook your head, lit a spare spliff kept behind the shade on the passenger side.

'You're digressing again. Sum it up, Caleb, for the love of God. I get it, in principle, yeah, but just what so you think you're trying to prevent? They'll have back-ups, they won't …'

He took the joint right from your hands and smiled.

'You've still so much to learn.'

He went on. You listened, trying not to cry. He said your naiveté would be cute only up to a point – a point at which you'd have to decide whether you'd the courage to stand up for yourself. The right to be who and what you were. To exist. To move across the surface of the planet without interference, neither hurting nor being hurt. To remain fascinated by depths of thought and limits of experience. To never, ever believe in one hard-copy, indisputable answer, in one unbending truth. 'Keep it simple – there always have been, and always will be, plenty psychopaths and criminals and deadbeats on hand to keep the Management busy, however many measures they put in place. These just prompt great leaps of imagination, an irony I'm sure they won't appreciate. Look … how old were you when you started smoking?'

'Fourteen, fifteen. I'm not sure.'

'So what was the appeal, at first?'

You felt like a child reading a simple sentence from a chalkboard.

'Because I knew I was doing something I shouldn't.'

'Bingo.'

Caleb winked and handed back the spliff.

'Lucy, you'll start to get it once you've stopped over-analysing. Once you get it into your head that a stripping of permissions and privileges won't happen all at once. The teeniest niggle of something being not quite right ... time to look around and take note of what's happening.'

You made promises. Said you'd keep yourself informed, on the alert, that you'd fear complacency and laziness. Learn to use your voice as a weapon, whether spoken or written, gestured or detailed. He pointed to the rattling spectrum of spray-paints in the backseat of the car. Said they'd never change the world taken purely as they were, a clutch of chemicals and plastics — but that the act itself of doing something other than what was prescribed, permitted, held a shy power of its own. Even better if there were some artistry involved.

'Your idea, Lucy. That day with the fridge ...you got me thinking about ... meaningless destruction. We're not doing that anymore. There should be a context.'

If half the battle was the catching of the eye, the sight had a far better chance of fixing itself to a consciousness if there were a quirk, flair, something undeniably other. The city wasted further every day — a fire or a bomb, a toppling or sabotage, would blend right in. No-one would care.

'Get your beret on, Lucy. How do you think we should spruce the place up?'

'I've a fair few ideas. I'm going to need a screwdriver, a pair of pliers, probably a chisel.'

Caleb flipped out a kit as dextrous as his grin.

I doubt Bethany could have been much of an agent. If part of the job description is to appear and disappear without a trace, the slow-piling anthill of smouldering cigarette ends is kind of a dead giveaway. I give her my version of events, wondering if there isn't a trick handkerchief to flourish to make the whole thing sound less *teenage*. Embarrassed, we're both avoiding eye contact. Feigning coughing fits, shoulders hunched, watching the smoke sketch alien cursive up into the gathering dark. I'm not breaking the silence; I've said enough. And she *did* ask. I didn't promise a page-turner.

I wasn't prepared for the sound of so much of my own voice. Weak, cracked, fumbling for words, like an old man set in plaster in the bars my grandfathers used to hide from tomorrow.

'So … eh, that's it?' says Bethany. 'You had a tiff? Rent, job, money, future?'

'Well, yeah, but … I mean, when you can't agree on simple things like—'

'—when you can't agree, you have a difference of opinion. That's all. And from what I know of you two, that's the type of thing that'd have lit a fire under *both* your arses. You don't strike me as the kind of couple who'd have been happy with tea and Hob-Nobs and Radio Four till bed before midnight. You'd have thrived on conflict. And you're telling me you jacked it all in because you couldn't stop fighting about whose turn it was to take the bins out? Come off it.'

A less exhausted version of myself is thinking *cheeky bitch*, thinking *shut up*, thinking *you don't know a damn thing about me*. But she does, it's clear. The more she speaks of fire and conflict, the more I'm picturing – not just picturing, but hearing, *feeling, tasting* – things I've been trying not to think about. I don't know why I would've taken such an about-turn in what I was and wasn't willing to put up with. Forgetting the way he made the small stuff disappear.

'So you have a more reliable sequence of events?' I say. 'Something you've picked up in your presumably long and successful career in relationship counselling?'

'Touchy, touchy. He was right, you *are* one for the sarcasm. Lowest form of wit, don't you know? That drove him crazy. Told me … told me it was like you were never quite sure whether your words counted for anything. You thought you'd be shot down for voicing an opinion. So you mouthed off, cracked jokes, self-deprecated …to give yourself an out. He wished you'd stand up for yourself. You'd potential to be so *powerful,* he said – you just hadn't made your mind up, yet, which way you were going to go.'

I'm supposed to get angry, here, listening to her talking about him as though they'd been best of friends. Something's stuck in the mechanism. Every hot word clots in my mouth, fails to launch. Bethany, shakes a drizzle of tobacco dust onto her lap, scowls and throws the pack over her shoulder. Mute, I hand over a fresh one. We're silent for a stretch, eyes fixed dead ahead. We're smoking the smoke of a mortified couple after an unsuccessful tryst.

'Bethany ...' I say, finally, the silence beginning to strip the skin, 'Why are you here? Why are you even *interested?* And why are you telling me things I already know? Sarcasm? Guilty as charged, but what does it matter? It's finished with ...'

'That's the thing, though, Lucy. You *don't* already know. I saw your face when I told you what I'd heard. You've not only forgotten what you had between you – you've forgotten who you *were*. The old Lucy ... she'd have squared me up, fought it out. You're just *taking* it.'

'Stop talking about *me!* You haven't come all the way out here to sit and listen to my sad wee sob story, to give me a personality assessment, for no reason other than to ... Christ knows why you'd do that. There's something else going on.'

Looseness rolls from her sockets. She takes her time over this particular cigarette end; stubbing the concrete, grinding with her boot heel, before turning to look me right in the eye, shoulders stiff and straight enough to hang wallpaper by. The beetle-shells of her eyelids are cracking further with every cigarette, scattering chips of green and purple on her cheeks. The brutal cut of her brows, twitch in her jaw, care taken with every movement in her finger – it does kind of add credence to this Agent stuff. Looks plenty capable of swimming silent through the black of any alley or tunnel in the city, clattering those neat ankles against jaw lines, unsheathing invisible weapons, washing down cyanide capsules with luxury vodka.

But I don't have to like her. *Bethany*. What a stupid name for an agent.

'I'll tell you.'

'You keep *saying* that, and then you turn it around and start asking *me* more stupid questions!'

'I had to know, Lucy. Had to know how much has ... gone. How much is *still there*. We have a lot of work to do, but ... you're going to have to make a decision. You might not want to know. There are mitigating circumstances.'

41

'Jesus Christ, will you *please* stop speaking in *code?* All this *I know, you know, they know we know* stuff means *fuck all* to me, I don't have *anything* to tell you other than what I already have!'

She falls silent again. I know I'm running headlong into farce, but sometimes you've got to fall back on cliché in the absence of any other options.

'What do you want from me?'

She laughs. Credit where it's due, she recognizes the absurd.

'Nothing, Lucy. Except that you listen. And that you trust me.'

'Why should I?'

'Caleb did. I tried to help him, I *did*, but ... I didn't take ... enough care. Things ... got out of hand. This time I have to get it right.'

'I don't *need* this.'

'Oh, Lucy,' she says, rolling her head back over the bench. 'You need this more than you've ever needed anything. You just don't know it yet.'

That's enough. Whatever slow-burning soother they've put in the coffee has well and truly worn off. I am not about to be teased and poked and prodded for reactions. I get to my feet – stiff peeling from the slats of the bench, the affronted jerk upright I'm going for not quite coming off– and lean right into her face. She doesn't budge. She must be used to it.

'Look, you've five seconds to tell me exactly what's going on. I can't believe I've sat here telling you all this *stuff* about myself – fuck, even *I* don't know where it came from – and you've the nerve to think you can sit there making out like you *know* me–'

'–We covered this, Lucy. I *do*. Know you. And you didn't tell me anything you didn't have to. You *needed* to talk. I listened. You've lost nothing. Well, nothing *tonight*, anyway.'

I can't keep doing this; readying myself to walk away, only to be jerked back with a breath of a clue, a shadow of a doubt. I turn toward that loathsome trudge. Back to my flat. Back to white noise.

'Lucy.'

I remain taut, watching traffic ribbons braid the low brow of the cityscape. I can't go back with *nothing*. I can carry on fooling myself that I'm a master of my own portion of this slow-stripped universe, but that can't excise the fear of empty spaces, dead time, blank walls. I'd never have imagined getting past childhood, adolescence, university, first job and flat and relationship, only to be so bound and drawn by another human voice. Spend your life trying to *find* yourself, *make* yourself, declaring independence and all that sloganeering bullshit, and in the end all that remains is *other people*. They make you who you are. She could be performing a character assassination, tearing up my family tree by the roots, scorching every inch of skin with abuse, and I'd still far rather listen to her than go back to my hovel. I turn back. I always do.

'Uh-huh?'

'I will. I'll tell you everything you need to know, but … it's … will you take me seriously if I say this could be dangerous? For both of us?'

I laugh, filling a gap, palm-flashing a pause while I make room in my head for the question. Danger. Such a fluid concept. Used to be pretty simple – the possibility that an action taken will result in accident or injury. Danger used to have colour, shape, sound – road signs, sirens, numbers you could call. Means nothing, now. I'm living proof that bad things will rock up out of nowhere whether or not you'd been paying attention, whether or not you'd been reading your tea-leaves and guidebooks. And that's thinking solely in terms of biology, the body's limits and soft spots. There's still a million danger signals twitching switches in your heart and mind. Plunges cerebellum-deep, ripe to cast you right out of yourself, drive reasonable human beings over edges they can't see until it's too late. Which is why I'm not going back to face down the dead gaze of a blank wall. No more taunts hissing through empty rooms. If she's saying *danger*, I'm saying, *yes please*.

'Go for it, then,' I say. 'I've a high threshold for … all sorts of things.'

'It's like this,' she says, rising from the bench with far more poise than I'd managed. 'All this *knowing* of things – I'm not the only one who's keen to see what you've got up there.' She taps her forehead with a ravaged fingertip. 'If you walk away right now, it's finished. You're fine. But if I tell you what I need *you* to know, what I think you *might* know if you think back long and hard enough, well … there's no telling what might happen. No *knowing* who will be wanting more than a word with you, or when. You're going to have to ask yourself – *Can I leave things as they are?* Or …do you take the apple? Heh-heh …' She cocks a thumb over her shoulder, at the blaze of neon fox-fire in the building behind, '… do you roll the dice? Take what's coming?'

We stand, silhouettes in the whipped orange haze. Sliced moonlight through cloud tinges upper edges of lips and brows an arcade blue. Something has to change.

'I'll take it. Just tell me what I have to do.'

'We can't do this here,' she says, squinting up. CCTV has us butterfly-pinned. 'Nowhere near classy enough for a de-briefing.'

She chuckles; again, we might as well be colleagues, friends, casual acquaintances sharing a gossip and a smoke. Which reminds me.

'True ... and if we've more talking to do, we're going to need more cigarettes.'

'We could go back inside ...' she says, sucking her teeth, winking at me, 'Or ...?'

'There's ... I mean I ... if they're watching, it's going to look a bit odd if I've been out for a smoke all this time, then coming back in with an old staff member ...isn't it?'

'You're getting it! Of *course* we're not going back in there! But you're learning ... for everything they'll tell you you're paranoid about for no good reason, there's a million things you'd step right into if you weren't *just* paranoid enough.'

'Yeah, well ... I've been in trouble a couple of times,' I say, 'Nothing serious. Being in the wrong place at the wrong time. Giving lip to the Management guards. I'd rather not push it.'

'Let's go to your place, then,' she says. 'They'll see us going in and coming out, fair enough, but if you're still living in that shoebox of an attic flat, your place won't have been fitted with surveillance kit, yet.'

'Huh? I didn't think they—'

I remember something. About in-house surveillance. Something Caleb wanted me to help him try to stop. Another mission I told him would accomplish nothing.

'They do. Slowly but surely. Right now, it's just the houses and larger apartments, places with more than a couple of voices and movements to keep track of. Your place is fine, for now.'

'Ha. Never thought much of it. Fuck, the city's in serious trouble if *that's* one of the mod-cons, one of the selling points. *Not yet fitted with surveillance kit. Shit and shower at your ease.*'

'Trouble ... funny, it used to *mean* something, didn't it?' says Bethany, fingers tracing the line of a ghost cigarette from her lips, down the length of her arms. 'Thought for a long time I was helping. You know – see trouble, fix trouble, hand troublemakers over to those higher up. It was only when the men in charge kept ... *shifting* the definitions, when getting into trouble just got easier and easier ... wasn't long before something *I* did or said or thought was *trouble* needing dealt with. But that's another story.'

She slings an arm over my shoulder, grinning madly, raising a brow toward the cameras.

'*Let's go,*' she says, through gritted teeth. '*Smile, you're on You've Been Framed ...*'

I've been wandering up and down these test tubes in a daze, too fixated on trying to lock down a vanishing point to bother making sense of the dimensions. Bethany shifts back and forth across the tunnels, tilting her back into to each curved arc every ten feet, managing to do so without looking like she's up to anything at all. Taking the view. Power-ambling. Up close, though, her eyes are everywhere, reeling about in her head like laser-pointed pin-balls. She needn't worry, it's empty up here, like always, and getting past the guard was merely a case of flashing a smile and insisting that we were on our way home to our respective dwellings. Tunnel guards are like the night-club bouncers and taxi-drivers of before – suspicious as hell when you're on your way *in,* on a course toward high-jinks, but nice as pie when you're on your way back to where you should be, tucked up in bed with tea and a book. The tunnels are genius, in that respect – there's nothing between here and the guard stops at the top of the road, nothing we could possibly be getting up to between flashes of badge and declarations of intent.

Halfway along, Bethany stops short. We're in the midsection, at which point the steel and glass give over to thick lengths of fibreglass tubing, utterly opaque. Pretty little scallops on the ceiling and silver paisley fishes streaking a half-drop across the surface add interest, with head tilted at the right angle; the kind of thing interiors manufacturers used to etch into worktop linoluem. It's the dark that gets me, though. When you're facing onto the blocked patch, before your next step sets the motion-sensor lights flickering, it's the oddest sensation, a tugging at the limits of the visual spectrum. Nothing else, outside or in, day or night, is as black and thick and depthless as this section of suspended animation. The murky halogens and furry neons can't penetrate here; there's no seam, no graduation, no hint that there's an end and a light to come out into.

'Do you know what this is for?' asks Bethany, darting a fingertip in and out of the darkness, flirting with the lights.

'I dunno ... reinforcement, or something? Aesthetics, maybe? Just to pretty the place up a bit?'

She's kind enough to spare me a scathing brow. I'm really trundling out the quips this evening, I notice. Nearer the moronic than ironic end of the comedy scale, I'll grant, but at least I'm not just staring at my hands and feet. Bethany beckons me over, pulls us both into the fibreglass womb. Even with the lights on, the effect is just as startling – behind the smooth black panels could be anything at all, land or sea or sky, over-ground or in the damned centre of the earth. She leans right into it, palms flat, eyes closed, listening for breath or heartbeat.

'This part of the tunnel ...' she says, 'Is barely a quarter-mile long. Barely worth noticing or mentioning. Might as well be a *feature*, like you say. A bit of roadside sculpture. And yet, that's the ... that's the fucking *genius* of the Management, Lucy. People are ... *reverent*. You'll notice, by the way, there's not a single tag, not a drop of paint, not a scratch. Folk who wander through have no idea what it's for, or why it's necessary, yet they know enough not to *touch* it. Doesn't that strike you as a wee bit odd?'

'I guess so.'

Time was, in Glasgow, nothing sat still without a branding of some sort. Vandalism, sure, but I'd taken part in a few tagging matches myself, and I know it went deeper than that. Those scratches, blobs, fluorescent rainbows were a railing against a spoon-fed aesthetic. Sick of looking at endless industrial planes of beige, mushroom, cat-shit green. Colours so dull they went by *numbers*.

'It's a feature, all right,' she spits. 'A development on an original idea. Trompe l'oeil. You'll maybe remember those godawful statues and sculptures and shit they used to string along the motorway?'

'Yeah. Sheesh, I was just a *kid* the last time I —'

'—perfectly reasonable, if not quite innocent. They'd spend a fucking fortune commissioning these eyesores to distract attention away from the shit that was even *worse* ... decrepit satellite towns, rotting fields, miles and miles of road-works always *in progress*, never finished ... roundabouts and retail parks chomping up the green belt ... if we'd been paying attention, we'd have got it right away. Every time we spotted a *feature*, we'd ooh and aah and barely notice everything else falling to pieces around about.'

'Hey, I get it. Roadside artworks *bad*, opium for the road-raged ...'

'Sorry ...' she says, snapping upright, shutters pinging from her eyes. 'I just ... I'm never *out* out with anyone. Sometimes I have to talk, just to remind myself what I've seen. You should try it.'

'Have done. Don't change the subject. What's the deal with the tunnel?'

'Trompe l'oeil. It's what they *don't* want you to see. What do you think's down there?'

'I dunno. We'll be ... what, right above the city centre? Near the shopping centres and train stations?'

46

'The eye of the storm, so to speak,' she says, curling a lip. 'You ever take the subway?'

I had, ages ago. Glasgow's clockwork orange, a city-wide underground rail network carving up the perimeter, linking compass points.

'I used to live in London, ages ago. You seen the underground map for down there?'

'Aye.'

If the subway systems were rings around a body's ten fingers and toes, linked up along spinal columns and nerve endings, Glasgow's own would be dainty pinky finger to London's whole-body complications. We were always a bit too big for our boots.

'I used to met folk who lived from station to station. Like, they'd pretty much walk out the door, onto the subway, out at the next station and straight into work or the shops or the pub or wherever they were going. The spaces between stations ...just didn't exist. London was just a series of nodes. If they'd wanted to, the folks in charge could have gotten away with a hell of a lot in that dead space, since nobody was paying attention anyway.'

'So Glasgow's just a ... what?'

'Same idea. Smaller series of nodes. These tunnels, checkpoints, home and workplace. You can get away with seeing nothing but the hundred yards or so between your front door and the nearest guard box.'

'But that's not true! There's the park! The whole of the main drag! I walked it on my way here!'

'Ah, but that's it – they're very *selective* about what you can and can't, should and shouldn't see. Tunnelling the park would be going too far, at least for now. There's nothing there anymore anyway, just more cameras and officers than the command centres know what to do with. Keeps you sweet, though, doesn't it? Remnants of that *dear green place.*'

'Not so green anymore,' I murmur, recalling this morning's lament.

'Nope. They'll let it rot until it's a *favour*, getting rid of it. And as for the street ... that drag's under constant surveillance – it has to be, unless they finally close the road. You get to see the sheer volume of police and official *presence*. You get to see what happens when folks don't do what they're told.'

Davie. Like Davie. Closed off, beaten down, staring into the door of a pub as though it were a family photograph, members deceased. As for the garden, I can see it now: vitriol splashing the

47

letters pages in the over-ground newspapers, then the columns, editorials, then the front pages. *Tear it down. It's an eyesore. Get rid, redevelop, potential site for far more lucrative and functional enterprises.* They're already more than halfway there with the rainforests, the deserts, the tundra, the mountain ranges – nature doesn't have the nerve, anymore, to get in the way of progress.

'So …?' I say, waiting, again, for a point to be reached.

'So … down there. You're right, it's a vast chunk of the city. You used to work somewhere down there, if I remember correctly …?'

'Glory days. Bartending.'

'You lost your job when the place shut down, yeah?'

'Yeah.'

'They told you and your colleagues that they couldn't afford the rent. That they had to sell the site on to a council body.'

'Yeah.'

'Your place, and a hundred, a thousand others. And They took it over. That's what's down there. One of *my* old workplaces, my time coming a little after yours, mind. Facilities. And they don't want any old passers-by leaning into the tunnel windows for a peek.'

'Facilities …?'

'You're not stupid, Lucy. You know how it is. People going missing for a while, or for good. If they *do* come back, they're looking and sounding a touch …*tried.* Spaced. Not quite there anymore. They've loosened up on the beatings, these days – people *do* still talk, even just a little – but it's the same idea. You disappear, so completely that even the *hiding places* are hidden.'

Bethany leans back into the tunnel walls, exhaling, weary, sliding down the surface to sit cross-legged on the floor. Following suit, I'm sat there nodding my head like some fucking neon-tubing Elvis strapped to the walls of the casino. I used to know far more about all this stuff; I'd have it drilled in, branding a fury, inciting a violence I no longer seem to have the energy for.

'So … what now?'

'I don't know. In fact, I do. Tempting fate. You ever wondered why you never meet anybody in the tunnels? Coming up behind you, or going the other way?'

'No,' I say, again, mortified. Caleb used to have a thing about degrees of questioning one's environment. *There's a difference between looking and seeing, he said. And then, between seeing and understanding. Opt out of any element of the process, and you may as well be shrink-wrapped, treading gelatine, every step and every thought just another to add to a pile of shapeless moments. That's you quit, that's you* stopped, *for all intents and purposes, and that's you* fucked.

Enough, though. I'm trying, aren't I? I'm here listening, I'm looking *and* seeing, even if I do need Bethany for the *understanding* part.

'They time you. Like, when I worked the tunnels … back in the early days, when They'd still to close down many of the streets, when folks needed *encouragement* to come up here. If a party approached while there were others still up here, we'd to …delay them, a little.'

'But that makes no sense,' I say, '*We're* up here, talking. They're not about to stop us.'

'Subtlety, again, Lucy. We were together already, two mates out for a stroll. We're already ID'd and computed as entering as a pair. Would look pretty scary if they'd split us up, no? We're not supposed to be *aware* that it's one party at a time. But what happens if you …I don't know, bump into somebody you haven't seen for ages? You'd stop to have a chat, wouldn't you? Even if you were talking about the fucking *weather,* that's enough to spark off prior associations, similar conversations. The nostalgia disease. Makes people edgy, makes them ask questions.'

Nostalgia disease. I haven't heard it put quite like that before. It's kind of fitting, though; starts off with a niggle, a xylophone patter across the tines of the ribcage. Unexplained aches and pains, a perpetual headache, the prevailing sense that something's not quite right, like one small section of your mind's at a half-drop from the rest. And we ignore it, hoping it'll go away. Find something constructive – or destructive – to patch it up, push it down. Questions imply the existence of answers, and when you're sick, you know you won't like what you hear.

'Bethany … what are you trying to say? That we're all so stupid we'll just *forget* everything and everyone we know? It can't work like that … you're talking mind-control shit, and that stuff just doesn't happen anymore. There's always a thought, an idea, a voice … they can't–'

'–haha, what – they can't hold us down? That we'll *fight the power?* God, you're still so naive, Lucy. They don't have to *do* a damn thing to our *minds* … at least, not to … we'll talk about that later. No – we do it to ourselves. Once you're used to one small change of circumstances, you're easier to talk into another, and another, and another. Too much fucking *effort* to say anything, to do anything. Nobody wonders or cares what's going on – not because it's not interesting or exciting or frightening, but because it's too much fucking *hassle* trying to crane your neck to see around the edges.'

'So what *do* we do about any of it?'

'We get it anywhere we can. Talk. Information. Contact. Me and you, we're going to your place. I'm going to tell you what you've been missing. And you're going to get ready for a reckoning.'

She strikes out, footsteps on fibreglass like juggling balls in a washing machine. I scuffle behind, fresh thought-patterns keen to scratch over patches I'd rather not have bared.

I'm paying attention. I can't help it. Coming down the ramp toward the check-point, I'm scouting for trouble. Both guards stand in profile at either side like Egyptian etchings, inner arms tensed at sharp right angles. They're becoming living carvings of the same fibreglass they use to line the tunnels. Losing a little more of who they were with each stop-and-search, eyes furred as pewter in dire need of polishing, lips straight and functional as parentheses. The one on the left is the same guy from this morning, but any recognition stems from my ID card, not my face. Otherwise Bethany might have worried about being remembered from her prior incarnation. When they're only checking from the neck down, charting attire, and scanning for questionable lumps, a bright dash on the eyelids is a disguise as good as any.

'What's been your business tonight?'

'Coffee, catch-up, casino,' says Bethany, syllables factory-belt autonomous. The guard purses his lips. Could be trying to remember how to smile, to remember what comes next in the exchange. His partner catches up.

'Positive outcome?' he asks, the words a ticking beat across a snare drum.

'Yes,' I say, 'Lovely night.'

All four of us nod in time, allowing a moment of pause to settle the farce.

'That is ... *that's* ... what we want to hear,' says the first, straining to batter discrete words into casual conjunctions. Keeps things friendly.

'Well ... ah ...' says Bethany, 'We should really get going, shouldn't we, Lucy? It's getting late ...'

The guards lock eyes over the tops our heads, frowning. I'm convinced I'm carrying something I shouldn't. Information has an atomic weight all of its own, both greater and smaller than the walls of the skull can hold, plates of bone and wraps of skin a semi-permeable membrane prepped for involuntary osmosis.

'Hold on, please, ladies. Checks.'

I'm stepping forward, raising my arms and spreading my legs without thinking. Bethany does the same. I've gone from feeling

50

violated to being obscenely grateful for the touch, my skin rising up to meet their hands as though keen to confirm its presence. Bethany has her eyes screwed shut. Must be doubly unpleasant to be on the other side of a procedure in which you'd once had the power.

'All clear,' says the second guard, disappointed. I shift closer to Bethany. I can almost hear the fury whirring from her every pore. She's solid, defiant, spine and shoulders an upturned anchor refusing to budge.

'Thank you for your co-operation,' says the first guard, rubbing his lips with thumb and forefinger. Coaxing out the pleasantries.

'No problem,' says Bethany. Zero inflection: neither sarcasm nor sincerity detectable.

'What are your plans from here?' asks the first.

'Home,' I say. 'Straight home.'

'On your way, then.'

'Straight home,' repeats the second.

Amazing what you notice when you're paying attention. Sanded edges, shrivelled discourse. Half-sentiments. Conclusions long foregone. No need tell us not to talk to strangers. Not anymore.

PART TWO

MACHINATIONS

He doesn't come quietly at all, despite that spare frame. A mess of violence strung into his reeling limbs, kicking, punching, possibly snapping his jaws. Anarchists such as him were always so stupidly proud of their powers of rhetoric over kinetics: this one clearly hadn't been prepared for situations in which the former would be of no use.

It begins politely enough: a knock at the door, answered before the pounding had to get too heavy. All sat neatly on a pair of ruptured couches. Three Agents and the Manager; the latter designated as such by the absence of a standard issue helmet. No other noteworthy characteristics: all wore the regulation sharp-cut beige fatigues; all shaved too close to detect a hair colour; all wore lips and eyes slung loose into a uniform lack of expression.

The girl isn't home. The boy purports not to know where she might be. This is just fine – she is an accessory, at most, just a voice in a clamour. She'd come in useful later on, perhaps, as an instrument of coercion, but for now, they want only the anarchist.

'So, sir … where would you like to begin?'

Coaching ensures such words as *sir* emerge as the insult intended: a sneer kept in the throat without ever reaching the lips. Just a formality. Once on the premises, behind closed doors, negotiations are just for fun. The anarchist had nothing to say that would keep him out of the trouble he's already in. Denials mean portable polygraphs – some old-world technologies were unnecessary in light of Agents' body-language drills, but Agents liked gadgets. They provided an amusing interlude, before things became rather more arduous.

Caleb shrugs. Prompting may not be necessary *at all*. Defiance thrums through the expression, the posture. The Agents look forward to smoothing the excesses of each.

'I have a problem. With the way things are going.'

Eight eyebrows strain to stay in place, instinct angling them toward invisible hairlines.

'Go on,' says the Manager.

'Things are getting out of control. We're not animals, you know. We weren't doing anything wrong, and yet we're stopped and searched and arrested for just going about our business. My girlfriend's about to lose her job, since you've taken it upon yourself to close down the pubs. Friends of mine are disappearing, turning up black and blue, if at all. We're all afraid to go out, afraid for our families, afraid for … well, you know. You can't just *do* this.'

'Gossip, hearsay, exaggeration. If anything, a few minor casualties. Mild inconveniences. I'm sure you'll agree that there's been a notable improvement in terms of anti-social behaviour. Which brings us to your activities, sir. They have been a cause for concern for some time, now.'

Caleb gets angry. He knows he should keep his cool, but they are right *there*, on *his* couch. The real deal, no longer avatars, rumours. The Management.

'I just don't see why grown men and women should have to abide by a curfew, let ourselves to be searched, watched, arrested for no reason at all. We were doing nothing wrong. At least not till you *pushed* and *pushed* and …'

'Nothing wrong …' repeats the Agent on the left. 'The Candidate seems very keen on this particular turn of phrase. Hmmm?'

'Yes … yes … the Candidate seems to think it up to himself to decide. No mention of the importance of rules and regulations.'

No-one need mention the schemes and plans and protests. The petty anarchies. He needn't fool himself – he knows they know.

The Agent on the left tilts his head toward the door. Footsteps on the stairs; careless footsteps, too, no regard for the echoes and chatters of sole against tile. Someone who's not learned, yet, the advantages of discretion. Memories of what it meant to smile twitch the corners of the Agents' lips. They like this part. Caleb freezes, teeth chewing air.

'Look, let me–'

'Too late for that, Sir,' says the Manager. 'You have refused to co-operate.'

'But you haven't asked me–'

'It's the girl. Best keep them apart.'

The Agents rise from the couch, each a half-beat behind the other, drilled in motion. The Manager and one Agent make for the hallway, pulling the lounge door closed with the neatest slam Caleb had ever heard. The remaining two Agents circle the chair in which Caleb sits. One removes his hat and glasses, sneering at the yellowed foam spilling from the cushions upon which he sets them. The other grabs Caleb's forearms from behind, wrenches them stiffly up and out into a taut crucifix. Caleb does not cry out as the fist slams into his gut. He's heard too many rumours that turned out to be true; heard that in this case, submission was the best defence. A friend had recently lost an arm, another currently nursing a pair of shattered kneecaps, putting up a fight. Further regulation blows bring Caleb to his knees. The Agents snap the cuffs around his wrists, fix straps across his mouth, slip a polyester sack over his head. Wipe-clean, standard issue.

In the hallway, the Manager holds a hand over the latch, keeping the girl from opening the front door. She curses, rattles the handle. He smiles, turning to whisper to his inferior.

'You have prepared the other premises?'

'Yes.'

'Band C? Bare necessities?'

'Yes.'

'We'll bring her in. Just for a bit. Fond farewells.'

The girl was no fun. They can tell by the rouged glaze around her eyes that she's been ingesting substances. Reports indicate all such employees are on their worst behaviour, pushing the very limits of regulations before the premises were closed down for good. Drinking after hours, exchanging baggies and tablets. Even smoking *inside*. The Manager had been unfazed. Let them exhaust themselves one last time. They were only clocking up convictions.

'What the fuck are you doing in my flat?' she drawls. Her body language is textbook hostile.

'Come inside,' says the Manager. 'We would like to speak with you.'

'Where's Caleb? What have you done with him?'

'He is in a great deal of trouble, we're afraid,' says the lower-rank Agent. 'Would you please step inside?'

'I'm not being invited into my own damn flat! Do you even have a warrant?'

The Agents can't keep back a chuckle at this. Warrants. How quaint. Those haven't been in use for a long time, now – a stroke of genius on the part of the Manager. Cut out a great deal of paperwork. Allowed no time for excuses, evidence disposal or vanishing acts.

'Come with us.'

They take her into the bedroom alongside the lounge, arms locked tightly round her shoulders. They place her in a chair by the dressing table and stand before her, arms folded.

'What the bloody hell is going on?' she demands. She makes quite a production of pulling her jacket round her torso, crossing her legs tightly together. The Agent glances at the Manager, a question in his eyes only rigorous training can detect. The Manager nods, pats the Agent's elbow.

'Stick to the torso, for now.'

That hurt, just in case you're wondering. It's not like the movies, where a grimace and a tautening of muscle will see you through. You can't just bite down hard and hope it will all go away. This is what it feels like. Fire wrapped in ice exploding at the core of every nerve cell. It's electric blue, neon green, tadpole shapes knotting, unfurling, running wild over your retina. They asked you questions you hadn't the breath to answer.

Then they started on your legs. Remember those nights at work, running trays and plates from table to table in the half-light? Sometimes you'd bash the cross-bar of a bar stool. The kind of pain that makes you wish for a sea-deep pillow into which you can scream. Twenty times over. More. All the while you could hear the riot in the next room. Every gasp, howl, crack, lash, splutter, wail poured between the cracks in the plaster. Caleb fought hard, writhing even as they had him pinned, chewing carpet.

You gave up pretty quick, though. You didn't know, or didn't care enough, for what he was fighting for. It wasn't about the drink, the noise, the laughter, the smokes. He was fighting for something so often dragged out in defence of something worthless that it has become a thread in a cross-stitched epigram.

Freedom. Doesn't sound so flash or powerful as it once did. It's a word on a tea towel. Independence. That's another one.

These once meant the right to the movements of your own body, the words from your lips, the privilege of taking responsibility for your own actions. These days, a watchword in a campaign speech. A pivotal argument in a political manifesto. A word sprayed out all over actions otherwise inexcusable. All these slippery terms sliding into and over one another, rendering the result meaningless — your excuse for taking a back seat on the whole thing, preferring to keep your mouth shut on issues of which you weren't sure.

If you'd been paying attention, he would have talked you through. You're not stupid — you just liked to pick and choose what you wanted to hear, keen to steer clear of anything that meant trouble. That's why he's gone and you're still here.

That's why you're still killing time, kidding yourself, skulking around perimeters. Those hidden places, niches and alcoves you both once so loved — you can't find them out because you're still hiding too much from yourself.

    And you're not listening. You're tuning out the inside. Look deeper, think wider, otherwise you're unlikely to come across much they haven't meant you to find all along.

The Candidate on the cot looks carved from marble. Shadows in the blanket stretched over her frame winnow like faces behind frosted glass. Plastic tubing in the back of her hand. A complex nest of wiring surrounds the head. Steel wire straps chunky metal discs to either temple.

And headphones jammed into ears. Under the blanket, taped circles clamp pads and conducting gel to her chest. Wires unfurl from the discs, headphones and chest-pads, stream across her neck and torso into metal boxes equipped with dark-green screens, heavily studded with buttons and switches. Agents in the control room pipe gentle strains of cello music into her ears, the rhythm dictating the slow beat of her heart.

The Manager stands before a sheet of soundproof glass splitting the puce-coloured cell from a room full of audio equipment. He is unsure of himself in the Stories department. Three agents sit behind steel desks covered in buttons, levers, plugs, wires and switches. At the top of each revolves a reel of sleek black tape. Fluorescence flooding through each of the soft spoke-triangles scatters the room. A flickering zoetrope. A grand mal.

These particular Agents make the Manager uncomfortable. Specialized recruits, employed solely for such services as these. Never called upon to prove their mettle in the field, yet they *were* necessary, in the light of recent developments. The Manager loathes bending to statistics researched and published by civilians, but the numbers didn't lie. Notice was being paid to rates of disappearance and inexplicable injury. On top of which, Facility was becoming overcrowded.

The Stories department is firmly based in disciplines formerly known as The Arts. Agents likely to be found bent over desks, writing or sketching, or in one of these rooms, strapped into audio equipment of the kind last seen in the late Nineties.

Barren classrooms at the lip of the corridor are dedicated to Premises and Scenarios. In the former, architects, designers and artists hunch over drafting tables, sketching and painting plans for new homes. These are intended for interned Candidates awaiting release. More elaborate projects require scale models. When the Manager is feeling unpleasant, nothing improves his mood like flattening the finished models with his heaviest pair of regulation footwear. In Scenarios, scriptwriters recruited from the Management-facilitated television network type and file narratives loosely based on the

Candidates' life. These are accurate up to the point of detention, before said circumstances require the crafting of safe, if elaborate, rewrites.

In the very heart of the Facility, isolated and soundproofed under thirty feet of concrete and topsoil, are the rooms dedicated to selection and re-enactment. Candidates are suspended in a suggestive stage of consciousness apt for hypnosis, at which point experts extract any pertinent information necessary for the next stage. This takes place in the next room: painted black from floor to ceiling and muffled in thick carpeting. Here, specially recruited Agents – those who had once wasted so much valuable time on the theatrical arts – put their talents to far better use. Taking Candidates' information and vocal patterns, they record Audio Scenarios: flawless mimicries of those which could plausibly have taken place in the Candidate's reality.

The Manager overlooks one of the final stages. Transmission and Rewiring: not much of a visual experience, but the room afforded the Manager the least confusion. He can track the exercise from beginning to end, if he so wishes. From behind the glass, he can watch the Candidate writhe with every flick of switch or touch of button as new lives are implanted; memories and preferences rewired; gentler replacements for any overly stimulating details smoothed over blanks and gaps. The tapes were often unpleasant. Candidates must be taken through traumatic events and disagreeable details in order to build up a necessary aversion to looking too deeply into the past. The Manager knows well that there is nothing so dangerous as nostalgia.

The Manager peers over the shoulders of the audio-tech agents immersed in the task. He can't fathom the satisfaction they seem to take from random, unchecked words and images. A positive recipe for revolt, he thinks. Threads of insurgency unfurling from one creative mind to another; no strict formula or protocol save a requirement for orders to be approved. *This* is why he finds himself in the cavernous basement of the Facility when he could be out in the field, over-ground, in the thick of the city under his control.

'Sir,' says the middle agent, removing from his headphones, 'We're ready to go when you are.'

The Manager glares at his inferior. He'd neglected to salute. It takes a moment or two for it to dawn on the Agent, eyes glazed and ears furred from hours spent in the murky isolation booth. He snaps to it, hoping the dim light will sheathe the hint of insolence playing about the corners of his mouth.

'The girl is ready?' asks the Manager.

'Sir, yes, Sir. She has been under for approximately one hour; wave patterns indicate she is approaching REM, primed for rewiring. Permission to begin transmission.'

'Permission granted,' snaps the Manager, trying to avoid looking too closely at the chaos of equipment surrounding the officers in this room, and the girl on the other side. Every liquid crystal screen beats with information he has no hope of understanding. The girl, though; the Candidate: those were always worth a look, just to remind himself what he held in his hands. A sliver of the overall aim for the city. Calm, subdued, controlled. A few minor casualties along the way were a small price to pay. The girl was in good hands; they were *fixing* her, *rehabilitating* her, releasing her back into a landscape over which his influence spread further by the day.

Everything was coming together. Everything was slotting into place.

EXCERPT FROM TRANSCRIPT OF REWIRING:
    CANDIDATE No. 42
    VOICES FROM SPECIAL AGENTS NUMBERS 117
AND 189 - ARTS DIVISION: PERFORMANCE

Programme notes: several edits over live transmission through Manager #15 - slight imperfections passed without Candidate's notice.
    [RECORDING]
    'You don't understand. That's not what I wanted.'
    'You clearly do - you've got the agreement and the keys right there, don't you? You didn't have to go behind my back - we could have talked about this.'
    'That's what I'm trying to say! Talk! I'm listening!'
    'Just ...tell me what you want. Or what you don't. We can fix this - you don't have to leave.'
    'It's the same story every time, Caleb. You're always out doing ....whatever the hell it is you do, losing jobs and getting drunk and causing trouble, and expecting *me* to pick up the slack!'
    'Hey! It's not my fault you're not interested in coming out for a bit of a

laugh, is it? You'd have a much better time
of it if you cut loose a little, had some
fun.'
    'I do, you know that! I'm just a little
better at remembering when I've a shift, and
knowing what I have to do with my money
before I spend it on getting wasted. We're
six weeks behind with this place, you know!'
    'It's not about that, though, is it,
Lucy? You're always saying there's more to
this stuff than money. And if you were that
bothered about it, by the way, you wouldn't
be smoking half the [BLEEP] contraband
[BLEEP] you do, would you?'
    'Oh, for fuck's sake, Caleb. Maybe I
just need a little space, eh? I've got to
grow up, start taking myself seriously, for a
change. Doesn't mean we have to stop, but-'
    'So you
[TAPE SNARLS, SLOWS]
need a little space
[TAPING RESUMES WITHOUT INTERFERENCE]
do you?'
    'Yes.
    'Fine. Fine, fu
[TAPE SNARLS]
get lost
[TAPING RESUMES]
then?'
    'Maybe I will! I have my own place now
anyway, I don't need you!'
    'Fine!'
    'Fine! Have a nice life!'
    [SOUND OF DOOR SLAMMING (TWICE FOR
EMPHASIS) KEYTS RATTLING, FOOTSTEPS ON
STAIRCASE]

    [RECORDING STOPS]

    [SEGUE TO CELLO MUSIC]

Agent 12A claps a hand to his forehead. Agent F63 trusts the
flood of light from the other room in the lens of his large spectacles to
mask his rolling eyes. 12A cocks his head toward the door, listening
out for the approach of heavy footsteps. The Manager had seemed

60

keen to allow the specialists to get on with it, but there's still a chance he'll come back for another look at the girl. Silence outside.

'That was a fucking … shambles,' says 12A. Agent H5 crouches under the switchboard on the pretext of fixing something. A rhythmic thud shakes the table as he slowly, deliberately thumps his forehead against a table leg.

'Hmmm,' says F63, trying very hard to remain still. 'It's just a Candidate. Not to worry.'

'Oh, come on. That was horrendous. I'd never have bought *that*.'

'Uh … well, it'd certainly have sounded a lot smoother, had our Manager refrained from interrupting the recording … messy, indeed.'

'Yeah, but even at that – where'd Scenario get that dialogue? Sitcom re-reruns? Morning chat shows? Jesus, people haven't talked about needing *space* since the bloody Millennium.'

'We're looking for a scenario, Agent, not a psychiatric history. It's enough to give the Candidate *something* – she'll fill in the gaps herself, things she and her companion *would* have said.'

'Still, it's … ach, clumsy. Once is enough, right? We don't have to put her – us, I mean – through all that again?'

'Once should do it. Certain key words and phrases will play out over the course of her stay here, whilst she's under ether. Plus the Manager will be conducting interviews, making sure to ask and answer all the right questions.'

'Hmmmm …'

12A still has his doubts; not so much as to whether the Candidate will take on board the suggestions, but of something deeper, something he can't quite name.

The rewiring process always calls up this nausea, a damp flutter in his torso; that same dread characterising dreams in which the dreamer is prevented from reaching a goal that's somehow very important to get to.

It's not guilt – it can't be, it's gone too far for that. He'd always had such faith – before, before everything had so changed – that the power of the arts was beyond mere application or dosage. That it couldn't be quantified. That people couldn't be so easily fooled. Part of the process, he knows – he must keep his distance. Artistic and aesthetic concerns must be put aside. Treat the Candidates as such – let them figure it out on their own back Outside, in their meticulously constructed apartments, jobs, if so they chose. They had a job to do, in here, as F63 never ceases to remind him. Fixing, mending, smoothing over, creating a nice blank canvas over which the Candidate's new manners of living could be played out without injury.

None of that brainwashing nonsense that were rumoured to have gone on backstage over the war years of the previous century – there was no need for that. Candidates were free to think and move and do as they pleased, within reason. They had names and identities all of their very own; it was just up to them to figure out what that *meant*. There was nothing implanted telling them what to do or where to go or anything *crazy* like that. In here, they were merely given a few suggestions, moved gently through and away from a few uncomfortable memories.

Despite knowing that all exertions were for a good cause, a small unquiet part of 12A craved a failure. That some day would come a Candidate who could not be so easily placated. One who'd make demands, ask questions, reject those lives so meticulously arranged. One who'd question the past.

Nothing, so far. 12A was coming to realize how much hinged on the Candidates' thirst for Stories. The headaches involved in resurrecting something cracked and furred seemed far too complicated, too painful – especially when a fully functioning narrative was ready and waiting. A brand new existence without sharp edges or dread smells, migraine lights or seasick colours. Vulnerable persons seek the path of least resistance, and the accepted truth becomes merely the version with the least effort required. A little push in the right direction; that's all this was. Rehabilitation, F63 calls it.

12A has another unnamed feeling attached to watching and aiding the constructs, easing the Candidates along into their seamless version. It's probably fear, but it shall be pressed aside. There's simply no room for such random factors.

'What do we do with the girl now?' he asks F63. 'Just wait till they come by to collect her?'

'She'll be under for a while,' says F63, any attempts to read his expression still deflected by his rimless glasses. 'An unfortunate side-effect of the rewire, I'm afraid – woken too quickly, Candidates suffer terrible migraines as the brain works to take on board the suggestions. A couple of days under should do the trick.'

A low groan issues from under the switchboard. H5 is still under there. He's stopped banging, and instead presses his hands to his eyes, his fingers tangled in lengths of wire. His lower jaw twitches with effort – biting back pain or holding tightly to silence, 12A's not sure. F63 pretends not to see him; if he's seen him at all.

'So what ... we just leave her here, then?' asks 12A. F63 shrugs, indulges an almost imperceptible twitch of lip.

'She's perfectly alright. Our Manager will send someone by to take her back to her room.'

'Oh. Okay. What do we do now?'

'Shut down the equipment we've finished with. File the duplicates. Then to the studios to take levels for the next recording.'

Slowly, as though from a deep sleep, Special Agent H5 emerges from under the desk, stretching his arms up high, tapping fingertips across the purpling of his forehead.

'Ah, you've joined us,' says F63, no inflection in his tone betraying sarcasm or censure.

'Hmmm. Yeah. Next assignment, then. Go on.'

'Start collecting the cables, H5.'

He does so without a sound, every manoeuvre about the room choreographed to keep the other side of the pane from his line of sight.

12A stares at the floor as he rolls coils of wire, flips switches, stretches a tension from his shoulders. If H5's display was all the Audio department had by way of protest, there was the question of trouble: this meant either a little too much, or none at all. 12A can't decide which is worse.

The Candidate wakes from a sleep the colour and shape of a drunken collapse. Crimson addles the eyes in splashes and spots. Wet warmth swaddles the skull. Pressure on the abdomen. Later, sight slid from the fuzz, efforts will be required to dull the memory of the bruised fruit of her flesh. Chemicals to tear up flowers of pain splashing her skin.

Her left hand streams with tubing attached to a metal stand, hung with bladders of clear liquid. The room is grey and blank and windowless, as all such rooms should be. A door without handles or visible hinges seeps with magnolia light. Shuffling in the outside corridor intimates rubber soles on damp concrete. A drip, drip, drip of dank water rattles the bones of rusted plumbing. As she rouses, each instinct to jump or flinch is drowned in an opium haze, pinning her back to the stiff cot. Slowly, very slowly, her eyes force a crack. She is cold, and in no small amount of pain.

The Agents hadn't been as strict with themselves as the Manager generally recommended. There had been a small issue with possible internal bleeding, necessitating this short-term stay in the Facility. Her new Premises were ready and waiting, though, it was merely a case of tying up loose ends before sending her back out Outside. She has been checked, screened, stitched and approved by the in-house medics. She will be just fine; there was simply the matter of making sure she has a feasible sequence of events around which to structure any unlikely complaints.

The door swings open without a knock. In walks a man who, at first glance, has shifting monochrome squares for a face. The Candidate struggles to sit up, grasping the frame of the cot. She cries out as the muscular contractions required for the manoeuvre pull piano strings across her stomach and thighs. The nozzle in the back of her hand stings; she slaps, scrabbles, to no avail; rolls of bandage and tape fix it too firmly into her network of chalk-blue veins.

'That sounds painful.' A voice like paper bags crushed between heavy hands.

Some ghost of a learned response prompts her to ask, *where am I, what's going on?* – as they all do, sooner or later. As yet, she is too scared to open her mouth. The bones of her skull feel taffeta-light, her teeth rattling loose in her jaw. She presses both hands to her temples, trying to hold it together.

The Manager sits down on the end of the cot. The squares resolve into a face no more informative; skin the dull sheen of natural yoghurt, hair of no particular colour, cropped close to skull of a kind just *made* for battering at doors in the middle of the night. Lips and eyelashes the same shade as the skin, as though the whole head had been dipped in pale wax and left to set.

'How do you feel?'

'Hungggh?'

'That's the analgesic. You've been getting a strong dose on the hour, every hour for a few days now. It affects muscular control to a certain degree, particularly around the mouth and eyes. Take your time.'

'What's ... what's going on?' The Candidate manages a slack sentence. She sounds strange, even to herself, as though speaking from the bottom of a well. The Manager permits himself a small smirk; there's no real need to check whether or how much she remembers. Certain officers may have taken it a bit too far, but the results speak for themselves. There are benefits to unpick from certain ineptitudes. Only one of the myriad elegancies with which he credits this new system of government.

'You've had a bit of an accident. Don't worry, you'll be perfectly alright – a bit sore for a while, that's all. We've taken good care of you.'

'Accident? What ...'

The Manager is having some difficulty curbing his amusement. He never tires of the initial daze; the stirring-around in fragments of thought; the resultant speech a blur of childish nonsense. Neither will he ever quite understand that automatic clamour for a Story – that desperation for a context, a cause and consequence for everything. Rumours of a lack of imagination are clearly unfounded.

'You were crossing the road at a tricky junction. The car didn't see you in time, I'm afraid; slowed, yes, but not enough to avoid a rather nasty thump. You're very lucky – some bruising, a touch of concussion, that's all. No breakages, no major bleeding. You were certainly in a hurry – looked terribly upset, according to the driver. Were you running from somebody, or something? Had you been ... having an argument?'

Of course not. She doesn't remember a thing, but it helps to frame suspicions, pre-empt the fictions right from the off. The truth is *always* stranger. Candidates are far more inclined to believe neatly folded falsehoods.

'I, uh, I don't remember ...'

Between the walls of the Candidate's skull, a face and a name drift as flurries of snow. A man formerly known as Caleb. He is of

65

some importance to the Candidate, and thus the Manager. She can't quite bring this Caleb into any strict definition, but feels his lack as one feels the cold in a bared patch of skin recently pressed to another.

There will be time for details later. At present, a concrete location is of paramount importance. The Manager removes a roll of official papers and a set of keys from his inside pocket; as the Candidate processes the information given so far. This story will no doubt have to be repeated several times before she has taken everything on board, committed it to a new age of memory.

'These were found in your purse. You were moving flats, am I right?'

'I, uh … I, uh …'

'Shhh, calm down. You won't be going anywhere for a while, yet – we have to make sure you're ship-shape, right as rain. Well, these are your keys, your contract. At least you'll know where you're going once you're ready to leave.'

The Candidate grabs the back of her neck and groans. Too much information for her skull to hold. The story requires enacting, to be played out in her head with herself in the lead role. All the while, fractured shards of the image of the man known as Caleb scratching at the inside like a dream dragged on after a waking.

'Okay … but … *this* is a hospital?'

The Manager makes a mental note to have a word with a few Agents about the decor. It's passable, yes; not too much of a problem when the Candidates are still dazed and malleable. Still, no sense in cutting corners simply because few who pass through the doors find their way back Outside.

'Yes. Yes. It's a new hospital in Sector Twelve – not quite finished off yet, but the nearest available bed after your accident. The doctors and surgeons are the best in the country for impact injuries such as yours – again, you're very lucky.'

'Oh … okay …'

'You must be very tired.'

'Mmmm-hmmm.'

'You'll be due another dosage, for that bruising of yours. I'll call a nurse, shall I? Then you can take a rest. After that, everything will feel much better.'

'Hmm.'

The Manager presses a button on a device in his inside pocket. Clearing his throat, he says, 'A nurse to room sixty-four, please. Sixty-four. Our latest admission. Please.'

Another waxen figure enters the room. She wears a navy trouser suit and sensible court shoes, looking far less like a nurse than a school-board administrator. The Manager rises, nods a greeting she doesn't return. The woman is not at all pleased about having to assume the role of Medic; she already plans to sketch out a damning report as regards this confusion of roles.

'Would you kindly give this young lady her dose of pain relief, please, Nurse? And – perhaps a few …extra pillows and blankets? Let's make this room a little friendlier, eh?'

'Why certainly, *Doctor*,' she sneers. The Candidate on the bed is beyond processing sarcasm, beyond registering errors of costume or set design. Still, it paid to be careful. The Manager glares, a silent promise they'd be having words later.

The woman who is not a nurse slips a syringe into the tubing running from the Candidate's hand. She pats the top of the Candidate's head, gently pressing her back onto the pillow. The Candidate smiles, popping a seam in her lip. The Manager stands by the door, waves a hand.

'You get some rest, now. I'll be back to see you soon.'

He places the papers and keys back inside his jacket. For now, it's enough that she's seen them; pieces of information planted, to be dredged up and resolved once she's ready to absorb fresh streams of logic.

The Candidate slips back under streams of velvet dark, sinks once more below scarlet blooms and flares. Back under, where there are no rules, no need for which to break them. Back under, where she'll find Caleb fully-formed in all his contours; colours, shapes, textures and words unbound.

Two Agents line up in the corridor for inspection. More than one body constituting a *line*, the Manager marches slowly back and forth in front, lips pursed in approval. Agent H5 from the Stories Department wears a gentle variation on the Medics uniforms: neat black shoes and trousers, crisp white shirt, his laminated swipe cards and Medical ID swinging between the lapels of a casual denim jacket. D16 from Re-enactments is in civilian garb of the type favoured by off-duty teachers and priests: crisp jeans, polo shirt, a rumpled waterproof jacket and deck shoes.

'Splendid,' says the Manager. 'And you're sure of your roles?'

'Yes Sir,' says H5. 'Dr William Brogan, Hospital Consultant.'

'Yes Sir,' says D16. 'Harry Weiss, Rehabilitation Officer and Care Worker.'

'Marvellous ... marvellous ... and you've both met with the Candidate before?'

'Yes Sir,' says H5. 'Established therapeutic relationship as of Wednesday last week.'

The Manager turns to the screened window in the door of the Candidate's room. He has been in to see her many times himself: tugging at the edges of fresh memory, making certain the Stories were adhering. She's certainly in far better shape: on her feet for much of the day, pacing the limits of the room. Losing interest very quickly in the Approved Archive reading materials the Manager had saw fit to provide.

She has been asking many questions, too, for which the Manager had to be on hand. Rarely did he take such specific interest in any one of his Candidates or Interns, but Number Forty-Two *had* something that was definitely worth watching. He knows it has no little to do with the fact of her prior acquaintance with Intern Number Nineteen. It is fascinating to see the process at work, tracking the efficacy. A splendid job all round: he gets rather a thrill from watching and listening to the results of this crafted division, cast down between consciousnesses once so tightly entwined. There was nothing, he knew, of which he and all the other officers in the Facility were not capable. Not with the right resources at hand, amassing a variety of disciplines in careful cooperation. All were on their way to a neater, cleaner, brighter, tighter future.

'You know where you're going?' asks the Manager.

'Yes Sir,' says D16. 'Fresh apartment in Sector Eight.' He scowls, resisting the urge to shove his hands in his pockets and slouch, sulking.

The Manager nods. There had been a minor dispute as to the Candidate's new premises. Certain of the agents in the Stories department are of the opinion that the place is far too blank and Spartan for the Candidate's apparent aesthetic sensibilities. They'd read far too much into the unlawful arrangements of books, records, posters, draperies and glitter-crusted knick-knacks found in the Candidate's previous residence. The Manager had had none of it. Not only is it crucial to keep the Candidate's environment as stripped of tastes, preferences and prior associations as the rooms in which her new thought-patterns had been generated; it also hints at the possibility of Agents growing *attached* to the Candidate concerned. There are to be no special concessions, no privileges, and *no decorations*. Why, that would be just the beginning: pander to their original preferences as pertained to an apartment, and it wouldn't be long before they'd be after an unlawful lifestyle and paraphernalia to match. Then there would be trouble. Pinpricks of memories from before, inching through the drop-cloths the Manager and his Departments worked so hard to craft. It would bring about the chaos against which he was constantly at war.

'Excellent,' says the Manager. 'I have spoken with the Candidate myself. She is, of course, a little anxious about leaving the Facility. I've explained that it's perfectly natural after a period of inpatient treatment, particularly following head trauma. She has been instructed to look to you two for guidance, should there be any … *gaps*, as regards such matters as administration and conduct. You have the necessary papers?'

'Yes Sir,' says H5, holding up a plastic wallet. 'Discharge papers, rental agreement, Care Plan. The latter gives details of out-patient treatment situated in the civilian Medical Centre in Sector Nine – D16 and myself are to be called to the surgery immediately, should the Candidate wish a follow-up, or experience any difficulties.'

'Good work, H5,' says the Manager. He turns to D16.

'And you have prepared a Welcome Pack?'

'Rations for a fortnight stocked in the kitchen unit. Rent paid up for a quarter; situation to be supervised in case of financial difficulties. Prior savings transferred to new bank account and augmented with sufficient funds for the next three months, perhaps four. Candidate will be *just fine*, for the time being.'

'In that case – shall we proceed?'

'Yes Sir,' says D16.

'I'm certain you can take care of this yourself,' says the Manager, 'However, I *am* keen to supervise the final In-Facility procedures. I don't mind telling you that I'm really rather proud of this one. Excellent work from all teams involved, wouldn't you agree?'

'Yes Sir,' both agents speak in time.

The Candidate's reaction speed has finally begun to level out. Following the laconic post-transmission haze, she had become something of a nervous wreck: starting, shrieking, jumping from the bed at the least movement or sound. Earlier, she'd taken to hiding in the trench between the cot and the wall. Then, when feeling more adventurous, to prowling on all fours around the perimeter of the room. Pressing her palms to the walls, as though checking for reality's seams. D16 and H5 had been instrumental in bringing the Candidate back into herself, calming her down. Reassuring her that all she saw, heard, felt and thought were completely normal, to be expected, and that she would, in time, be right as rain. Today, she barely flinches at the hissing of the door. She sits on the edge of the bed, idly flicking through dated magazines before arranging them in stacks on the bedside table. The Manager steps back behind the frame, refraining from entering the room. This part of the process was extremely delicate; the fewer faces the Candidate had to deal with over the next few days, the better for her rehabilitation.

'Good afternoon, Lucy,' says D16. 'How are you feeling? You must be excited!'

The Candidate shrugs. Her shoulders continue to shake even after the gesture has run its course. She twists and untwists her fingers, taps her toes, nibbles her lower lip.

'Yeah. No. What?' Her lessons are yet to settle: still uncertain as to which is the correct response. Her eyes are perfect circles, taking in the Agents stood before her.

'Shhh ... it's okay,' says H5, as the Candidate stand ups, sits down, then stands again. 'Calm down, Lucy. You're alright.'

'Sorry ... sorry ... I just ... uh ...'

'Don't be sorry, Lucy – this is a big day for you! Going home!'

The Agents take seats on either side of the Candidate, H5 removing the plastic wallet, D16 handing him a pen. The Candidate smears a hand across her face, throat, stomach, before placing palms on either knee to quell the shaking.

'Home ...' she murmurs, staring up at the ceiling. Her gaze shifts to the mesh screen on the door. Outside, the Manager does not move from his watch. He needn't worry. The Candidate's system still writhes with sundry medications, enough to keep her calm until she's been settled into her new apartment.

'Home!' chirps D16, catching H5's eye across the top of the Candidate's head. Such non-sequiturs form the coda in many of the scripted scenarios run through in Re-enactments. Neither can quite believe the palliative power of a single word, an incremental inflection. Part of the job satisfaction for many of the Agents – such results, from so little effort.

'We're heading off very shortly,' says H5, 'We just have to get some of this paperwork out of the way.'

'No … problem …' says the Candidate. 'But … where's the man?'

'What *man*?' says D16, knowing perfectly well of whom she speaks.

'The man with the … clipboard … he comes … to talk to me … very nice …'

'Ah, you're talking about the Director! You're a lucky girl, Lucy, getting visits from the man in charge of *everything* here in the Fa – in the Hospital! He's a *very* nice man, but I'm afraid he's also a very *busy* one. He'd have been here if he could, I'm sure, but–'

'That's okay,' says the Candidate. 'I just … wanted …'

'To say thank you?' asks D16. 'We'll pass that on, of course.'

'… no … wanted to check … I can't … remember … he knows … things …'

'Shhh …'

In perfect synchronicity, H5 and D16 wrap an arm each around the Candidate's shoulder. Stiff, as drilled: close enough for comfort without breaking non-threatening contact regulations.

'You're still a touch confused,' says H5, 'Just wait until we get you home and settled. Everything will be just fine. You trust *us*, don't you?'

'Uh-huh …?' says the Candidate. There is really no reason not to. There are no other options. This Consultant and Care Worker had been spending a great deal of time with her, after all, telling her Stories, asking occasional questions, gauging her responses to the prospect of returning home. As for the other man – she's not quite sure why she's so keen to see him before leaving. Everything had been so hazy and unsure. Whenever he entered the room, there appeared a concrete answer to every question, a set question to every answer.

'Good … good … we're here for one reason, and one reason only, aren't we, William?' says D16. H5 is not as quick as he should be

71

on the uptake, too much of a delay between the unfamiliar name and his response.

'Yes! Yes, that's right! As your consultant and key worker, myself and Harry are interested only in making sure you are as fit, healthy, happy and settled as you possibly could be.'

The Candidate's eyebrows quaver, an uprising of phantom irony buckling her stomach. She'll do, say, sign anything to have this over with. She will be pleased enough just to never again see these four soggy walls. She is waking up, now at the mere prospect of *motion*, of extending muscles of calf and thigh along corridors and pathways, one step unfurling into the next without a wall necessitating another about-turn.

'Okay ... well, what do I ... need to do?' she asks, squirming slightly under the Agent's arms.

'Just cast your eye over this form,' says D16, handing it over, making crosses in the appropriate places, 'And if it's to your satisfaction, sign here ... and here ... and here.'

'What does this stuff ... actually mean ...?' asks the Candidate.

'It's just a form, Lucy. Red tape. Nothing too important.'

The Candidate signs. The words mean very little, with the exception of the phrase at the top. *PATIENT DISCHARGE.*

RECORD OF PATIENT DISCHARGE
FAX TO OUTPATIENT FACILTY: *Sector Eight Medical Centre*

Discharging Consultant:	Dr William Brogan
Care Worker:	Harry Weiss
Tel:	09837 733710

Date of Admission:	September 17th 2020
Ward:	14 – Cranial Trauma, Acute
Date of Discharge:	March 9th 2021

Patient Name:	Lucy Chalmers
Date of Birth:	22.4.1997

Hospital Number:	862549-YZ
Address:	Flat 4/1, 23 Park Drive, Glasgow Sector Nine

Dear Doctor XXXX, Sector Eight Medical Centre

This is to confirm that your patient *Lucy Chalmers* has been discharged from *Glasgow South Neurology Hospital* on 9.3.2021. Please see enclosed discharge letter.

In the meantime please note the following key facts:

CFT-11 Diagnosis: Head Trauma, Acute. Function temporarily impaired: no sign of permanent damage. Expect slight confusion due to short-term memory loss. Full recovery expected in time with outpatient monitoring.

Risk Assessment: Amber. Requires intermittent monitoring esp as regards memory loss/possible delusions.

Discharge was:	Planned.
Mental Health Act Status:	N/A
Discharge Medication:	
Fluoxetine 40mg	4 weeks
Sodium Valproate 300mg	4 weeks
Chlordiazepoxide 80mg	Indefinitely
Discharge Plan:	Outpatient
	Monitoring
	Surveillance
	Rehabilitation

Patient Signature: Consultant Signature:

My whole head feels like the business end of an electric toothbrush. Constant blurriness about all edges; every object a magazine cut-out pasted onto an LCD backdrop. I'm not paying as much attention as I should to the route we're taking: in the car, I just stare down at my hands and feet, flexing digits, tensing muscles. All the way down the stairs and out through the blank concrete wasteland of the car park, I watch toe, heel, toe, heel touching the ground, barely lifting my head to look around in case I fell over.

I am not thinking about Caleb. I do not have space between headaches.

Harry, the smaller one, is behaving so strangely. Every word and gesture borrowed from an actor in one of those American soap operas from the Seventies; his hands forever tugging at his lips, feeling around for where his moustache should be. Jumping ahead, pulling open doors, throwing his hands out like a magician flicking a handkerchief. When we got to the car he has a kind of *panic attack* over where we all should sit. William is in the driver's seat already. Harry jitters along the length of the Volkswagen, trying to unpick the shotgun etiquette for a recently-discharged head injury. Rather proud of myself, I suggest both of us sit in the back. That's what they call logic, I believe.

Three flights of steps up to this place I'm supposed to be living from now on. I've no idea what made me choose such a hole in the wall, but William's quick to inform me – with lashings of tact – that I'm not currently in the most flexible of financial situations. I can deal. I just want to be settled and left alone.

'Here we are,' says William, handing me the key. 'You should be the one to open the door, don't you think?'

'Cheers.' The door's about as substantial as a paper lantern, and doesn't so much *click* as *tear* open under my palm. I might as well have hung a beaded curtain, for all the security I'll have in here. 'Oh … well …'

It's horrible. I do remember living in some hellish slums as a student, but this is something else. It's not that it's actually *unclean*. It's not staggering under dry rot or damp. It's perfectly functional, which is kind of the problem. It's like someone's stuck a roof and a door in a refrigerator drawer: utterly soulless, blank and bereft of any color or texture.

A square-yard hallway leads into one of those *slash* rooms. A bed made up in shiny, shiny white sheets – the squeaky kind that catch your every hangnail – is pushed up against the far wall. Over the pillow, a foot-square window, its wire-mesh screen tastefully concealed behind a beige scroll blind. A small round table of pebble-dash linoleum and pair of grey plastic waiting-room chairs accounts for the other half of the room. Along one wall, a stack of shelves empty save for a plastic daisy peeking over the edge of a polystyrene coffee cup. Grey square carpet tiles on the floor, the kind I know will buzz with static with every footstep. Three smallish cardboard boxes against the wall on the other side, LUCY CHALMERS inked in felt-pen between strips of brown tape. I have no idea what's in there – I figure I'd remember if I'd anything worth holding onto. I'm already flirting with the idea of making some grand gesture, flinging the whole lot out of the window, unopened. But that's too much like something Caleb would do. And we didn't end well. I'm done with his stupid, pointless anarchies.

'Well?' says Harry, throwing an arm over the room. 'How does it feel to be home?'

'It's a bit ... well ... I thought I'd have *done* something with the place.'

'You just got here,' says William, 'There's time yet to make the place your own.'

'Is that ... all my stuff?' I ask. I'm not convinced that's the shape and weight of all my worldly possessions.

'Why, yes!' says William. 'Don't you rem ... uh, you probably don't. You said something, in one of our sessions, about a fresh start? After you, ah, parted company with your, ah, previous housemate, you set about getting rid of many of your things. Gave most of it away.'

'Something about ... not wanting to be reminded, constantly, of certain ... things.'

That *does* sound like something I'd do. Never mind; I'll just have to stock up on new stuff. Maybe clothes, if I really have to. Another thing I *know* I know how to do for myself. Okay. No sense in panicking. I am going to make this work. I have to concentrate. Take my time. Ask for help. Keep calm, like they told me.

'Ach, better that way. You should have seen my last place,' I say, hoping I sound more upbeat than I feel, 'You couldn't move for the mess. Me and the guy I lived with ... we had serious issues over what to keep and what to throw away. No sense of proportion.'

We move on. Another door leads into a crawlspace of a kitchenette. Miniature fridge, hotplate, kettle, sink, a microwave oven and toaster. No washer or dryer. No panini machine or smoothie maker. I like it. Fewer complications within the flat mean more reasons to venture out for whatever I'm after. Harry swings cupboard doors open on a supply of canned, freeze-dried, chemi-sealed and just-add-water foodstuffs. I'm trying not to laugh; it's a nice thought, but it'll take a certain level of desperation before I'm driven to this particular array.

It's the same deal with the bathroom. Never before has the term *water closet* so rung with meaning. Toilet, sink, shower cubicle. Small shelves stacked with boxes of single-serving sachets of shampoo and shower gel. A cabinet with plastic mirror, inside of which I find a rank of familiar square brown pill bottles. Stuff to keep my head pieced together. I'm supposed to keep taking it till they tell me otherwise.

I'm very calm and polite once I'm back in the lounge. I know the Management have been revolutionising all kinds of things, but still – all this efficiency is more than a little creepy. I've never known doctors to take such an interest in their patients that they'll go to all the trouble of filling their homes with care packages. I'm not ungrateful, it's just … it should have been different.

If things hadn't gone so wrong with Caleb, he'd have been the one to bring me back from the hospital. To our place. His hand in mine. There'd have been no need to flinch the touch of my own flesh as though it were a school uniform I didn't want to be wearing. No need, perhaps, to have ever been in this situation at all. But I suppose it keeps things interesting. If he should ever show up, ever come looking for me, *I'll* have a story, to make up for all those times I sat wide-eyed and slack-jawed, utterly convinced he was … I don't know, a Messiah or a lunatic, depending on whether we'd been in each other's good books.

'It doesn't look up to much,' says William, 'But it's all in good working order. There's a laundry room on the ground floor. And I'm sure you'll have fun kitting this place out with anything else you might want or need.'

'I'll be just fine,' I say. 'Thanks.'

I just want to be left alone. If I've any chance of many any kind of imprint on this place at all, me and the blank cubic feet are going to have to get to know each other.

'You know you still have a care plan to follow up on, don't you, Lucy?' asks William.

'I guess so … I thought all I had to do was call the number in the wallet-thing if I start feeling … weird again.'

'Yes, of course, but you *are* going to have to attend outpatient sessions at the Medical Centre – routine tests, repeat prescriptions, checking in with how you're feeling. Is that alright with you?'

'But I feel fine! Honestly! I'm feeling better all the time, now that I'm back at my own place!'

'Lucy ...' murmurs Harry, shaking his head. 'You've had a very, very serious injury. You've made a remarkable recovery, that's true, but the last thing we need is to get too complacent. I mean, you miss one day, just one day, of your medication, and God only knows what might happen ...'

'I'll take it,' I say, keen to be polite, yet unable to keep sharp edges forming on syllables. They *are* taking good care of me; I just wish they weren't quite so efficient. 'I'll come to the appointments. How long do I have to keep going? I mean, no offence, but I just want everything to go back to normal.'

'Normal!' says William, far too loud, practically *cheering*, 'Everything *is* back to normal! Will be! As normal as you could possibly desire!'

There is *definitely* something funny going on. I'd be able to see it more clearly, figure it out a little better, if my head didn't fizz quite so much. All thoughts sort of *bitty, strained,* as though my brain were being sifted like flour.

Normal. Caleb loathed the word, the very concept. He couldn't bear the taste, sight, sound, smell of conventions or givens. Seemed to spend every waking hour chasing after ways and means of bucking anodyne shackles. Quite the riot. True, it was a *kick,* shoring up and tearing down limits and presuppositions of my own, but ... God, it was exhausting. There's a tremendous amount of energy involved in trying to force your thoughts out of the proverbial box.

'I suppose so,' I say, 'Got it all sorted ... flat, keys, address, bank account, care plan, medication, appointments, stocked kitchen and bathroom ...'

I don't think I've ever been more organized in my life. Probably shouldn't accord too much significance to the fact that *organized* can be both an adjective *and* a verb. Still, I've been living in the city for long enough now to know when I've to take what I'm given. So I don't like the flat. I don't like my headache. I don't like being strung to appointments at the Medical Centre. I don't like having no idea of what's in those pills. So what. It's a hell of an improvement on that wretched hospital room. I can deal. I can manage. I just have to concentrate.

Intern Number Nineteen is attempting refusal of his sedative. They had these little fits, sometimes: this was not to be permitted. Sent out all kinds of errant messages. Questioned efficacy. The Manager thinks it, on a personal level, an insult.

The Intern crouches in a gully between cot and wall, head buried in arms folded on his knees, glancing toward the door every handful of breaths. There's barely sufficient space in here to turn over in bed without touching the damp concrete at either side, yet he's gone to all the trouble of making himself a den. Curious. Perhaps Agents in the Neurochemistry Sector would have an insight into why there remained such an instinct for the Interns to burrow, to protest, to fold themselves up in delusions of autonomy.

'Stand up. Step over the mattress. We can't be having this.'

The Intern raises his head, hands scrabbling at his scalp's re-growth. This has more of a *smell* than a colour; clotted with grease, seasoned with smoke, braided with ether's low rumble of spice. Bruised slicks of mahogany and mauve gather round the eyes, drinking the light from the depths of the iris. The bones of the cheekbone, temple, jaw-line hold up the frame for what could have been an inoffensive face; spaces between sagging and hollowed, pinched between thumb and giant forefinger, left to set still in need of refining. The top corners of his beige cotton Issue shirt fold over themselves to reveal his neck and clavicle; further deep pools of darkness, collarbones so pronounced that it's difficult, sometimes, for Agents to keep from reaching in, using them as handles.

'Stand up, Nineteen. I do not wish to have to summon reinforcements.'

The Intern sneers. Perfect set of teeth: slightly viscous on the surface for want of a brushing, but still pushing forth the illusion of thrice-daily servings of calcium; caps and settings fixed in the Cranio-Facial Block before the Intern had destroyed his last chance at Release. Back when even the lower-ranking officers really believed in the powers of rehabilitation. That the Facilities were merely stop-overs en route to a cleaner, more functional future. The Manager does not like that glare, that sneer, one bit. He's not used to such activity about the musculature of the face– Interns are supposed to be blanks and gaps, drawn for information until empty, pliant, calm.

'I said *stand up*, Nineteen. Make this easier for us both.'

The Intern growls – *growls*, the Manager can't believe it, shifts his hand to the button on the device in his pocket – before slowly gathering his feet up under his torso, sliding himself up the wall to an upright position as though drawn up gently on strings. Such insolence.

'Do not interfere with the layout again. Should it displease you in any way, we will remove the furniture entirely. Come here.'

Nineteen does not fumble and roll over the mattress: he steps up one foot at a time, as though mounting an escalator, over the surface and onto the floor without a wobble. Expression inscrutable; simply taking in the view. The Intern's chest is barely a foot from the Manager's, yet he stands easily with arms loose-folded. Waiting for a bus, queuing in a supermarket. And still not a word.

'Shift it back to where it was.'

The Intern does so without stooping, without dropping his eyes from whatever moves across the ceiling of his mind. He stands blank, still, unnervingly upright in what remains of the centre of the floor.

'Good. Now, remember. It gets very cold, in here. You won't enjoy sleeping on the bare floor.'

Nothing. Neither argument nor concurrence. The Manager remembers why he's here.

'It has been reported that you have been refusing your dosage.'

The Intern shrugs.

'What do you have to say about that?'

'I'll take it if you want. Makes no difference anyway.'

Brief silence as the Manager starts at the sound of the Intern's voice. They should be – they *were* – cowed, level, rusted, no inflection. This one rings out clear against the concrete. With ten words, the Intern invokes all the power of speech with which he'd made so much of his original trouble. This was not to be permitted. For the sake of morale. For the sake of peace and pliancy in the Facility. The Manager backs up to the door, listening out for footsteps, uncertain as to whether the Intern was really speaking at volume, or whether the clarity-shock has heightened his own response.

'Sit down, Nineteen,' says the Manager, biting a neat edge around each of his own syllables, enjoying the taste of the ranks in his mouth. Perspective. The Intern does so, again, with effortless precision, pressing his limbs into origami folds.

'Now. Why have you been refusing to take what is given?'

'I told you. It makes no difference. Nothing is hidden. You can't keep me from tasting it all, however much I'd like to spit it back …'

'Nonsense! I won't tolerate this … this *drivel*. If you are no longer responding to the treatments, we'll have to find another way to keep you on your best behaviour.'

'Not my drivel. *Manager.* You should see what it's like on the *outside*.'

The Manager draws up to his full height, suit buttons chinking under the pressure of his breath. Illogical: Nineteen has not seen the Outside for months. The Manager himself knew the score – each Outside patrol turned up further proof of efficacy. Sacrifices made for the good of order and public decency were a small price to pay; soon the ratio of casualties to calm would slide in favour of the latter. Soon, ingrates, scum, random factors like the Intern would be mere paperwork.

'You have no idea what you are talking about. Since your Internship, there have been so many developments. So many wonderful happenings. Peace, order, precision, stability of which you and your *kind* could never have dreamed.'

'Enjoying it, then?' says the Intern. 'So …what are you doing down *here*? Underground, out of sight? You, or any of us?'

'Necessary period of adjustment, Nineteen. Had you been more *amenable to change,* less *vocal,* you'd be up there right now, reaping the benefits of the smooth-running system your kind had been so desperate to overturn. And … who do you think you are talking to? Yours is not to ask questions. *I* want to know what your intentions are with regard to co-operating with your *own* programme.'

The Intern laughs. The Manager's fingers fly up to his ears; sonic departments of the brain unsure as to what to do with the sound.

'I think I've been pretty well-behaved, so far,' says the Intern. 'Although you really had me for the first few months or so …I could have been wandering the Gobi Desert or orbiting Saturn, for all I knew.'

'Well behaved? That is debatable. You realize you have *still* failed to furnish us with any worthwhile information.'

'I told you before, I don't know a damn thing.'

'We want names. Locations. Plans. Our success depends on rigorous maintenance, detailed scrutiny, identification and swift dispatch of insurgency. People like yourself. Unable to see the bigger picture. You *people* don't seem to understand – this would all be so much simpler, easier, less painful if we all *worked together*.'

'And by that, you mean *we people* working toward what *you* want. That's not co-operation. That's slavery.'

'Enough! I will *not* be debating the finer points with *Interns*! Either you co-operate, or we're going to have to find a suitable replacement for your sedative!'

'Sedative, eh? Tricky, tricky. You should have known, Manager, how quickly *we people* grow accustomed to having our minds altered ... And that's before we've even *started* on non-toxic opiates, Manager. All those free and easy pleasures ... talking, laughing, joking, *reading* ...'

'I said that's enough!' barks the Manager, blank planes of his face quivering, a geological battle for control.

'And *I'm* needing a sedative ...?' whispers the Intern, smirking.

'Intern. Number. Nineteen,' says the Manager, each syllable a gale-torn granite block, 'You appear unable to fully understand the gravity of your situation. You have no *control* here, don't you understand? Your *humour*, your *rhetoric*, your – ha ha – *debate* – they're of no use, not anymore. Where are your teammates now? Who's listening to your protests?'

'I'm not protesting,' says the Intern. 'I'm stating a case. You want information. I have none. You want me to do what I'm told. I have neither space nor resources to do anything other than what I'm doing right now. Sitting here. Listening to you. Taking your drugs and waiting for ... waiting.'

'Waiting for what? Nothing can happen until you tell us what we need to know.'

'And if I did? Know something, I mean? If I told you? I'm not about to be fitted out with a brand new apartment, a job, a clean record. Not like some of the others.'

'I wouldn't say that, young man. We have an excellent rehabilitation programme up and running, as I'm sure you're aware. For the right candidate, we can ... well ... again, it all begins with co-operation.'

The Intern's sneer slips. Rehabilitation. Images colliding. A girl, a name, the shared heat of a sun-struck bedroom. A beating. Screams. Bruises. For every memory stolen from her, the Intern's replay of the same sequence of events grows shape, texture, colour so sticky and vivid he must squint to keep from going blind. He knows things. He's not sure how much, can't tabulate the degrees of estimation at either end of a spectrum of horrors, but he knows she's still out there. He listens. Those in command say least when they're trying to make themselves heard. The Manager knows, too. They've been keeping an eye on her. Waiting to see if she could be as useful to them as she is important to the Intern.

'So what? I give you a few names?'

'We want,' says the Manager, pacing, chest thrust out to force the Intern up to the wall, 'To know every detail of everything you got up to, prior to your apprehension. We understand you had quite the career, but as yet, we're unable to align your activities with any one particular faction.'

'Oh, for fuck's sake,' laughs the Intern, 'All this time, all this effort, and you *still* don't get it.'

'Explain! For your own good, Number Nineteen! Tell us what you know!'

The Intern, smiling, shakes his head.

'You're thinking factions. Groups. Organized efforts. Yeah?'

'Reports would indicate a certain attention to detail, yes.'

'Here's the secret. There *are* none. *Were* none. There is no *we*, there's only a *They*. You guys. The rest ... whoever you've got in the rest of these rooms, whoever you're keeping an eye on Outside ... it's all very, very personal. Very, very specific. Nothing burns down, no rules are broken, for the sake of the good of a group. It's all the work of single minds pushed to personal limits. I'm not saying every act's the work of an individual – that's what friends are for, yeah – but it starts with a single flipped switch. One man says to himself, *this is shit. Let's go.* Whoever else is up for joining in ... that's a matter of luck. What you're fighting, what you're trying to control ... if you're looking for a *movement*, you're mistaken. Movements can be crushed. What you *can't* control is the instinct, the impulse, of a single entity. You can try – you're *trying* – but until you've got *everyone* locked up in their own little hole, you've no hope. Dissent is fragmentary, Manager. It starts with a thought, an idea ...and those always begin in isolation.'

'Nonsense,' says the Manager, finally. 'The *anarchies*, the *destructions*, these can't be the work of single people! If all of *you people* got it into your heads to do the ... the *things* you do, why, the result would be ...'

'... chaos?' smirks the Intern, shifting further along the wall. 'Isn't that what you're up against, Manager? Or have I missed something?'

The Manager loses his temper. It's part of the job, he knows; stuck down here in these cramped rooms, with these cracked psyches. Swallowing hard, he strikes the Intern across the jaw. The Intern, tissue-light and wasted from months of barely edible rations, soars clear over the bed to smack his skull against the concrete. Still conscious, he laughs, cradling his head in his hands.

'Nice. See what you're dealing with? Imagine having to do that

82

to every skull, every time it lit up with an idea. Fun at first, yeah, but I'll bet you'd get hellish bored after a while. You lot need visible results ... and you can't count what you can't see ...'

'Your own fault, Nineteen. I'm afraid we can't come to any kind of arrangement, if you continue to fly in the face of order. Telling such *lies*.'

The Intern struggles upright, swiping the heel of his hand across the bloody web draping his mouth and chin. He holds a hand up with a burlesque flourish, requesting a pause, as he roots around in his mouth with the other, withdrawing a loose cap from a premolar. He places the tooth on the bed as though waiting for it to turn into a penny, then raises his brows, a chuckle still rocking his shoulders.

'I think I've given you plenty to be getting on with,' he says, his voice still a shock of clarity even around masses of bruising and fluid. 'If you'd been listening, you'll have a far better idea of what you're trying to deal with.'

'You have given us *nothing*!'

'There you have it. That's what you're after.'

'You have just pushed yourself even further back from release,' says the Manager.

'I wasn't holding my breath.'

'You're not thinking, then, of your dear one? Such a shame ... She has no idea where you are ... what you're doing ... how easily this could all be resolved ... perhaps we should bring her in ...'

The Intern blanches, a pallor startling against the black blots of blood clotting his mouth.

'You don't ... you can't ... you *STAY AWAY FROM HER!* You—'

'Again, that depends on cooperation. Give it some thought.'

The Manager jerks open the door, snaps it shut neatly behind him. He watches through the porthole as the Intern reels about the surface of the cot, palms flat to the wall, stretching up to the ceiling, face contorting through a spectrum of unlikely expressions. The Manager straightens the seams of his suit. He frowns, rubbing at brown smears on his cuff. Still capable of making such a mess, these Interns, even under the tightest of controls.

'Any progress?' comes a cool, dark voice from the other side of the corridor. The woman who is not a nurse steps out into the halogen pool, arms folded, lips pursed.

'Indeterminate. Nineteen certainly *talks* a great deal, but the *content* ... No information of any use, as far as I can tell.'

'Perhaps ...' says the woman, pale peaks rising at the jagged edges of her smile, 'Perhaps it's time for a visit. From an old friend.'

'Funny, we were just talking about ...'

'Candidate Number Forty-Two?'

'Candidate Number Forty-Two.'

PART THREE

NONFICTION

14th March 2024

I am not ready to hear this.

I've been making it, so far. Might not have been a bundle of laughs, but at least I've been *present*. Most folk *do* just trundle by, no need to be seeking out revelations and epiphanies, too busy or bored or frightened or clueless to tugging at thread hanging from reality's seams. Existence is no physical entity, after all; you can't map it or track it or throw posts about the borders as the scientists do continental plates. It just *is* – questions and comments are for the philosophers, folks equipped to deal with concepts whose very circumference would take the top off my head.

So now I'm finding out my own little existence can be managed, held between paperclips and sheets of copy carbon. Not just mine, either. Turns out there are many lives in need of a tinker's touch. Mine is only one of many half-dead pocket watches, springs replaced, levers polished, cranked back up to full and quasi-functional pelt. As a stopped clock tells the truth twice daily, I have my own pair of truths – where mine ended, and theirs began.

Bethany's not impressed with the flat; nor is she surprised.

'Standard issue,' she says. I nearly choked when she made straight for the bathroom, wrenching lids from bottles, clattering pills down the sink.

'Pills you've been taken as recommended, eh?'

'Well, aye, the doctor–'

'–is not a doctor, Lucy. But we'll get to that.'

I'm not ready for this, either. Less shocked to discover I've been pouring numbness down my throat than to realize I've known, somewhere, full well what I've been doing all along. I just didn't want to look too closely at the label. I didn't *want* to know that there's more to it than a levelling of neurons, that I could have tried a little harder to find out. And I'm certainly not ready for the panic at the sight of them tumbling down the drain. That I'd be ready to keep knocking them back, no matter what else they were doing to me.

Then shows me what she's made of. Drawing the curtains, she peels off her jacket and lays it out on the bed. She runs a blade around the seams of her jacket lining, pulling back to reveal a handful of those *gadgets* I've been looking for all along.

'Lucy. One more time. Are you sure you want to go through with this?'

'Yes.'

'Which first? Audio or the visual?'

'Errr ... visual, I guess.'

She flips open a device about the size and depth of two Nineties-era credit cards.

'Sit down, Lucy.'

She clamps a free hand on my shoulder, points the device at the wall. Presses a button.

She needn't have bothered holding me down. I'm not budging an inch, looking at *that*.

This is what skin looks like when the owner has gone AWOL for a while. Injuries properly computed only with a hit of the objective. The body in the frame lies on a blank bed, naked, shown only from the clavicle to the kneecaps.

This is not *me*.

Not yet.

That can't be *anybody*.

Behind the bruising, skin the colour and texture of milk on the turn. Bethany is quick to point out a pattern: violet clam-shells side by side on the lower abdomen, around about the region of the kidneys. Half-ovals of a putrid green demarcating the lower edges of the ribcage. Comet tails trailing from collar bone to underarms. Bra straps. Breasts oddly untouched, rising up in pale protest, bluish shrivels of nipples indicating a chill. Bethany balls her hands up, presses them against me, point-to-point with the marks in the photograph.

'Cars don't have fists,' she says. 'Cars aren't so precise. The body in the picture has borne the brunt of a systematic and choreographed kind of impact injury.'

Words blur to a phonic soup as she continues. Tells me that the body in the picture is *me*, on the other side of a confrontation I don't remember entering into. Logic throws up a palliative distance.

Suggests it's not unusual not to know what you look like when you're unconscious. Like your own voice on an answer-phone message, there are degrees of remove. I don't notice I'm hyperventilating until I start seeing little blue spots.

'Calm down, Lucy. Breathe. I know this isn't easy, just take your time.'

It's the absence of hue I can't get over. These are high-quality colour prints, yet, other than the bruising, there's no spectrum-swaying shade deeper than a petrol rainbow, a soap-bubble reflection. Closed eyes pushed back into the shadow-shrouded skull. A Halloween pumpkin. Face dented inward around the jaw-line where I'd lost teeth, swollen about the cheekbones, contoured only in various shades of grey. A spider-web of ink-black blood splits the skull from hairline to mouth-corner.

'I've had enough, Bethany.'

'Just one more. Then I'll talk.'

The last slide's a little easier. One frame, four photographs. An old-fashioned chalet window looking into an anatomy lesson. A head. A pair of legs. Two torso shots, one from the navel up, one from the bust-line down. I know I shouldn't, but have to ask, squinting at the yellow thumb-prints denting the tops of the thighs.

'Have I been … you know?'

Bethany glares.

'The next time I hear you inching around the truth, you'll be getting another smack. Rape is the word you're going for. Harsh, isn't it?'

Not a nice word, tightening crotches and buckling knees together across the globe. She has a point. Hiding behind socially acceptable dinner-party terminology only works to throw further gauzes over the act.

'Anyone who's been under the heave and thump of bodies taking ownership of bodies knows better than to dance between the terms.'

'I just want to *know*.'

I'm near tears, so fucking frustrated. She doesn't think I'm trying hard enough. But I'm *working* on it. Trying to peel back the anaesthetic. She softens.

'I don't think so, Lucy. The fun's in the *struggle*, and you'd been doing none of that. They can't chase you if you're not running; they can't take from you what you're not conscious of protecting. That's another hidden message. When you awoke to hear all about how lucky you were, you didn't know the half of it.'

I want to know where she got those photographs, why she's been carrying them around. I have to push and push at silence before she finally breaks it open.

'I did some awful things. When I'd been one of the moving parts in the Facility.'

'Uh-huh? Go on.'

'The worst thing of all was doing nothing. This is why I need you to pay attention. To move parts of your brain you haven't worked or touched or even known you had, for too long now. Too long. I know now how easily a mind and body can come to accept the unacceptable.'

I am now to understand that the photographs show a fraction of limits that should never be pushed. That to do nothing from here on would be to deny that I've lived to tell.

A seasonal hissing at the back of my head. I'm waiting for a mention of Caleb. He has to fit into this some way or another, if, as she said, we didn't part on quite such acrimonious terms. She clocked my expression, all right; more of that bartender's sixth sense, unless she's bullshitting about even *that*.

She taps gently on my forehead with a fingertip. 'We'll have to combine knowledge to form just the right kind of picture of who he is, who he was. But he's in there.'

This is not reassuring. But it's time for the second half. She switches off the projector. I don't feel any better. Then she stares down into her hands, cracking knuckles, weaving finger-webs.

I wait. I wait. I wait.

'Look, what do you want me to hear?'

I'm staring at the lining of that jacket, expecting another device. So naive, she'd called me. I'll show her.

I am not ready to hear a reply in my very own voice.

A rustle, a click, in the back of her throat. Then it's *me*, talking to Caleb, a long time ago, on the other side of something too large to ignore. Horrible things were said. I'd been hanging *on* to that, throwing my current circumstances over the bars and chords of this conversation like dust sheets over precious paintings – acknowledging the importance by obscuring them from sight.

God, I sound so pathetic, trundling out accusations, yammering on about the Small Stuff that Caleb had always been so adept at brushing aside. I'm still looking for something, anything, in her hands or in her pockets, a streamlined button-box of black magic in which my voice is trapped. There's nothing but throat, lungs, mouthful of articulators of the woman sitting on the end of my bed. Still the words keep coming. That last fight. Words I've been trailing over since the maybe not-so accident. I've been holding them up against every return here alone; reached out to touch them in the middle of the night, when I've pawed the other side of the bed and come up once more empty-handed. Words swallowed whole every morning with my medication, setting stomach and spine back to a rock-hard indifference. Words that have kept me sane, I suppose, when one by one every other friend and contact and hidden place disappeared. They are mine, they are not – where do the words end and the voice begin? Is there a difference?

'Bethany ... where in the hell did you hear that?'

Not only the content - how'd she acquire such a perfect imitation of my voice? Right down to half-baked glottal stops and occasional sucking of teeth?

She tells me what I've sort of known from the moment she started to speak.

'It's not you. Never has been.'

So I've been playing back in my head, over and over, a skilful imitation. Explaining the events leading up to the accident with a studio-recorded educated guess. One more trompe l'oeil - trompe l'oreille, more like.

I get up from the chair so swollen with rage that the weight of it sends me tumbling to the carpet. I lie there staring into the weave pattern in the tiles, those many shades of grey, blurring and bleeding. Two firm hands land on my shoulders as she peels me from the floor, wraps me up and just *holds* me, every hair on my skin writhing and buckling at the contact before settling into the warmth. And I cry. That's alright; it's been a long time. Relief, seeing nothing but the red and black of my closed lids pressed to her collarbone, hearing nothing but the cracked vase of my chest opening up. My head rattles with words following *should be* – angry, upset, relieved; then instructions, too, lie down and absorb, take action, do something, *fix this*. I've been needing to see him for as long as we've been apart, but never until now has it been such a matter of *sanity*.

I owe him an apology, and so much more.

I owe *them* ... actions I haven't names or visuals for yet.

She'll do for now. Practice.

Everything goes black. The rest is conjecture.

My left hand thumps the floor, my right her neck, digging deep. She's kind enough to let me think I'm hurting her a little, before she throws me off. I'm right back in there, fists screaming for contact, feet twitching for something solid to shore up against. She takes it, she does; I can't do much damage. Too long removed from up-close contact with another body, I've forgotten what happens when *this* hits *this* and *that* smacks *that*, the noises they make. Which collisions make for recoil, scare up howls. I'm pounding at her stomach, even as I'm registering her drawn-tight panels of flesh, unable to feel a thing. She lets me hit her until I'm worn out, face-down on the carpet again, clots of fluff and errant dust sticking to the dampness on my face.

I sit up, spent. I still have questions. My throat weak from the outburst, every word takes every mote of energy I have to force into the seamy air. Bethany did a far better imitation of my anger than I can manage on my own. She sits cross-legged against the bed-frame, fingers twitching about the front of her mouth in cigarette reflex. Not knowing what else to do, I hand her my pack, too tired to fight anything anymore.

'Bethany. What the fuck is going on?'

Every time she adds something, sketches in another element of the frame, my skin crawls a little further away. Down the stairs and out the door and as far as it can, trying to outrun the speed of sound. I listen. I've no other choice. My own voice can't be relied on anymore, at least not until I've learned how to use it as Caleb always told me it should. To make a noise when *yes* and *no* aren't working anymore. A scream into the faces of those who would tell me where I should be going, and who I should *be* when I get there. I take it one sliver at a time, throwing each new image up on the walls of my mind, looking for hinges, for holes.

So here it is.

There once were premises for people to come and spend time with each other. To work, play, drink, push paper, laugh, dance, eat artisan sandwiches, leave pitiful tips. To argue good-naturedly or otherwise, express opinions without fear of reprisal. Said premises now gutted, dipped in plaster, and hewn into tiny rooms and narrow corridors. High-tech chokes the larger of the caverns. Time-saving devices once used for entertainments and household convenience now remodelled, rewired and turned toward control, containment, management of word and deed and thought and even instinct. The new inhabitants have no first names or personality quirks; no hairstyles or accents, nothing but digits and characters distinguish these stalkers of corridors. All is rank, file, job description. That, and dealings with Interns, those whose unwillingness to bend to edicts necessitated their capture, containment, rehabilitation. People who'd perhaps once drank in a bar or worked in an office in the self-same property now relegated to their very own twelve-foot cube of seeping concrete.

'People like you, Lucy. People like Caleb. Smoothed over and forgotten, until they'd learned how to behave.'

Bethany's quite the multi-tasking talent. People-reading, alley-prowling, bartending, kickboxing and smart-mouthing, and *mimicry* – an asset to the Management. She'd been put to work in a Facility department concerned with fabricating Stories, fictions gifted to such Interns as had potential for release. Studios , scripts, performers acting out Scenarios for those persons deemed in need of an alternate past. And I'd been one of them. She'd stolen my voice, braided it from falsehoods spilling from type-tapping keys of writers I'd never met.

'That's why I had to tell. I know who you are now, Lucy.'

I'm no longer so sure of that, myself.

She's sorry. Wasn't at the time – she'd yet to ask enough questions, yet to test the limits of her conscience – but later on, when she'd encountered an Intern whose mind had refused to be broken and fixed to current specifications. Caleb, my Caleb, had made quite the impression even when simmering in a flood of suppressants. They poured drugs down his throat, re-plumbed his veins, as they'd done for me. I took it, he didn't. He whistled as they beat him. He jumped up from the cot every morning with a grin on his face, a Christmas-cracker joke for the first guard to arrive at his cell.

Caleb insisted there was nothing to tell, that they'd slapped cuffs on a mere vandal and riot-merchant. That they could kick as much stuffing from him as they liked, but they'd only disappointed. Wasting time, effort, manpower, chemistry when there was no information save the obvious – that you couldn't rewire a half-century's worth of dissenting voices in the space of a decade. That he and the rest would need a hell of a beating before they'd be sufficiently discouraged from protesting against the Big Words. Corporations, governments, capitalists, fascists, dictators and the like – words that had been thrown so lightly around glass-strewn tables in university unions that much of the meaning had been lost, until now. Bethany, patrolling the corridors, had looked on through the porthole in the door at the real-life incarnation of her recording-studio counterpart. She'd felt a tug, she said. Somewhere in her torso's refrigerator compartments. A clanking, a battering, a sense that the man on the other side of the door knew something that she didn't about the way of things, both in the Facility and Outside.

'I can relate.' I say. Remembering, without wanting to, the way his eyes and voice and tilt of lip could captivate, enthral.

Bethany – then still Agent, then still Number – had engineered things so as to have a word with Intern Number Nineteen on her own.

She'd told the Manager that she'd been keen to test her reflexes, her upper body strength, against a man of Caleb's weight and height and powers of manipulation. I should get a minor kick out of this, since *I* know from experience that Caleb's a terrier, all yapping mouth and flapping palms, a self-confessed advocate of flight over fight. But I can't unbind my gut from sick creepers of envy as I picture the scene. Bethany, much older, yes, not quite so pretty as she must once have been, but Caleb *was* a captive audience. Who knew what went on in such circumstances? Bethany sees the look on my face. Maybe heard pieces of me crumpling inside, a waste-paper protest.

'Cool it, Lucy. I know what you're thinking, and I don't blame you, but relax. Nothing happened.'

'Uh-huh. *Something* must have, if you're arranging one-to-ones, no?'

'Purely professional interest. At least at first. Which never became more than tenuous friendship. Besides, how do you think I know so much about you? He wouldn't stop talking, telling stories. And always wanting to know where and how you were. Whether you were missing him, or managing without him.'

I guess I'd already been implanted with the fight we'd never had. All I knew torn up by the roots and rearranged. But she's still talking. A broken connection still soothes, even as it murmurs into silence.

'He fought it off. All of it. Every mechanism, implants, tricks and trompes of l'oeil and l'oreille. He knew bullshit when he saw it, heard it, smelt it. He's the …toughest, most resistant guy I've ever seen hauled into the Facility, and you know I'm not talking just muscle, here. By the time the Interns reach the cells,' she says, taking a sudden avid interest in her fingernails and shoelaces, 'They're usually knocked so far sideways that anything on offer from the Management is an improvement. Offers, I mean. Negotiations. Alternatives. Caleb took nothing.'

This hurts almost as much as belief in the fakeries lodged in the tape. I was so fucking eager to choke down their stories as they rolled from the speakers. To wake up convinced that although things were not exactly *splendid*, a signature and set of keys would bring existence right back up to speed.

I dreamed up my own return to consciousness.

They said I would remember it all in time, and if I didn't, it would perhaps be for the best. And I bought it. Asked the wrong questions, the answers to which had been scratched out already, on drawing boards in concrete bunkers a few corridors away. They dragged me from near-death and plunged me into something worse. Made my dream their coma, my coma their dream. When I woke, I *helped* them box it all away. And I left him there. So convinced that I were taking back my *life*.

'You haven't been living,' said Bethany. She's right. I've been existing. A flat, blank disc pushed about a gaming board, neither giving nor receiving any trouble any more.

'Stop. Enough. Where is he right now? And does he know … that I've let him down?'

Bethany shrugs, peels further enamel from her eyes, reaches for another cigarette whilst still smoking the last. Finally she looks up, so slowly I can hear a creak of vertebrae.

'I'd only been able to tell him what I knew.'

'And what did he have to say about what you *did* to me?'

'Nearly killed me. Surprisingly strong, when he's angry.'

'Good. You deserved it.'

After what what she'd done. Stolen my voice and used it to knock him clean out of what I knew. She didn't argue, just looked down once more into the toes of her boots.

'I'm doing what I can, now. Here with you. Cluing you in.'

'Bullshit.'

I'm still thinking in zoetrope, kaleidoscope, scatter-shot pixels of faces long gone. Fair enough, she's helping me out, waking me up, scaring me shitless. What else, though?

'You can't have just *left* him there. *Agent.*'

'I'd no other choice. If Caleb had nearly killed me, that was nothing on what the Manager thought an *appropriate response* to my behaviour. Giving of and taking information without sharing. They could have, should have had me killed.'

Turns out that would be going against the Reconstruction principles driving the Management's system. The proposed outcome was that of a healthier, calmer, more efficient and reliable society, and exterminations were not part of the programme. Those closest to the Manager are all too aware of historical experiments gone drastically wrong, knew that the first droplet of blood would stir up a hunger for more. This must remain a *humanitarian* effort. Resources and personnel will continue to be concentrates on rehabilitating offenders without having to resort to drastic measures. This includes traitors, however passionately the Manager himself wished it could be otherwise.

Bethany was set up with a new job, a new identity, a new home. She would never be permitted access to any Facilities, Interns or

Information again. She would be monitored, she would be called in for reassessments. She was given a treatment. She was given a tape.

I need a minute to absorb this. Caleb would call it poetic justice. But something's missing.

'So ... how d'you manage to *retain the information* you've just given me?'

She laughs again, a tarry rumble from the very core.

'Oh, Lucy. I'm afraid to say there are certain ... *predilections* the Management have yet to knock out of we Agents. Sensational fixes of the chemical persuasion might not be so much of a threat anymore, but as for the usual suspects ...'

'Uh-huh?'

'They'll never lose hold. Money. Power ... and sex.'

Intriguing. Turns out Bethany was a popular figure in the Stories department. I can believe it, too; that *presence* of hers is more than just a bartender's cheek. Certain of the agents in the Arts block of the Facility still believed enough in aesthetics, in the *form* of a thing over the *function*, to remain open to suggestions. To favours.

'To put it politely, certain of these *favours* were enough to persuade the agent in charge of Audio to be gentle with my re-wire. To hold back. To let portions of remain intact. I watched through the glass and winked as he removed one of the tapes, took a blade from his toolkit and slit it lengthways down the middle. Not so much that the Manager would notice any difference, but just enough to make the transmission incomplete.'

'Transmission incomplete? What does that mean, exactly? Half the mind reworked, the other half still clinging to the past?'

God, I hope so. I need to know that there was nothing I could have done for myself, no way I could have resisted the recording. Whether or not this was the case, Bethany was only too happy to oblige. Said she wandered around in a daze for weeks, scraping at the last of the lies clinging to her mind like a cobweb-choked chandelier.

'I wasn't sure who I *was*, never mind what had happened, where I'd been. Next thing I know I'm tending bar in a casino. It all came back so slowly, I wasn't sure whether or not I was losing my mind.'

We both take a moment of silence, for this. I know well the horror of those endless sunrises stared down without sleep. Faces leering from the walls with every re-shuffling of smog-deck outside. Hours spent wandering patches of ground in which I'm still free to do so. Picking up the phone and realising I no longer have anyone to call. Treating my job like an exercise in spatial awareness, the floor thumping my feet instead of the other way around. Hearing people talking, talking, talking and saying absolutely nothing. Being aware of Caleb's absence in purely factual terms, an empty bed, a fading photograph, yet unable to figure out where the hurt was supposed to hit. Thinking very seriously and clinically about killing myself, stopped short by the effort of rounding up the energy and means. Numbed, dumbed, drilled, bored out of my mind, that existential nihilism that hadn't been a popular philosophy or lifestyle choice since the early P-M Nineties. So terribly indulgent, dreadfully unproductive. I didn't even have energy to turn any of it into art, the way Caleb would have done, asked me to do. I just took it. I just *was*. A heartbeat, a pair of lungs, brain patterns traceable if not particularly exciting.

Back on track.

'So how did you do it?'

I want to know how she managed where I haven't, couldn't. How she dug herself out of what had been done, stepped back into her own history. She swallowed thickly, did something brutal to her empty cigarette packet, and fixed me in the eye once more.

'It was you. Walking into the casino.'

'Oh.'

'I didn't know who you were at first, of course, but little pieces of information … swinging back and forth … some began to stick.'

Gestures and inflections, words and tics scurried under the top layer of her memory. She would catch herself humming the backbeat of a sentence I'd spoken to her that day, when we'd both wound up outside on the bench exchanging ever-more personal pleasantries.

She tries to explain once more how sorry she is for taking my past. She said she'd love to promise a future, as always seems called for in epiphanic conversations such as these. She said she was still clawing back much of what she'd lost herself.

'When you walked in again today … I couldn't keep it to myself any longer. Things might look much the same,' she says, 'But one thing she remembers for sure is how easily transitions come about. The idea is to make them look as *organic* and *pre-ordained* as possible, true, but that doesn't mean things aren't getting drastic.'

The upshot is this. If I can forgive, we can do something to stop it. Make things right.

'Lucy. I really could have an ally in you, and you in me. But that's only if you're ready and willing to face down the truth.'

I flick a hand about the room, the site of so many revelations. We're off to a sticky beginning, true, but it's this or straight back to the *nothing*.

'You've already started. I'm still here, still standing. Haven't killed you, attempt notwithstanding. So long as nothing but the truth leaves that talented mouth of yours, I'm game.'

We shake hands. So twee, such a hit of nostalgia, it honestly nearly brings a tear to my awakening eye.

You've been slumped. Sinking. Clutching only to the hope that the more you're able to forget, the better off you'll be. When you do allow a mote to float to the surface, recall tends toward the negative, the prosaic, or worse, the cerebral.

You can't blame the medication.

You can't blame the cracks in your skull.

You can't blame solitude or routine. You're not working hard enough.

Bethany's trying to return what's lost: ownership of your thoughts. This won't work till you're willing to take a closer look. And face it, you're not exactly reeling with distractions, crack-backed around a calendar heaving with better things to do. If you see Caleb again, you'll want to start over, skip the digging-down through all the rot. You won't want him to know just how much effort you've put into forgetting. Think. Pick a nice one, there are more to choose from than you'd have yourself believe.

Here's something to make you smile. One of the first projects you'd got up to in the tower blocks. He'd amassed a team of volunteers; guys with whom he'd shared flats or classes; worked alongside in one of his many bar jobs; or just got talking to when stoned outside a gig. Back then, you both had so many friends. He wouldn't tell you what he had in mind. He wasn't sure yet, himself, but you knew whatever happened would be spectacular.

You shambled about barefoot in your underwear, raking the wardrobe for something that said covert ops, midnight prowlers, secret mission. Still playing a kid's game. He lay on the bed, just watching, talking, drowning in coils of marijuana smoke. Laughed as you wrapped your hand in sticky tape to brush lint from a pair of black jeans.

'Just go naked, Lucy. You can distract the robots whilst the rest of us slip in through the prison laundry.'

'Uh-uh, don't you go objectifying,' you said, a joke between the two of you – political correctness having taken on whole new levels in your Identities seminars on campus. His phone rang as you wrestled on the bed. Freddy. Jake. Colin. One by one they pulled out. He was furious, but he understood – matching the walk to the talk meant climbing higher stakes than ever before.

He took your hands and said, in his best pre-Millennial film star accent, 'Hey kid, looks like it's just you and me.'

The look on your face caught him by surprise. You didn't know just how frightened you were till you saw yourself reflected in his gaze. Dropping your hands, he said, 'Look. This was a stupid idea. Just you wait here. I'll take care of it myself.'

You knew you couldn't turn down the chance to see what he did. You set your jaw.

'Caleb. I'll never know what to be afraid of if I don't get to see for myself. And … and I trust you. To take care of me.'

He didn't say a thing, just kissed your closed lids and led you over to the window. To show you what you were both seeking to protect.

It had been snowing. The last proper winter. No stars in the sky, but no clouds, either. The chill peeled the smog from the city like a milk-skin. A bal three-quarter moon looked on, a great glass eye strung between the distant tower blocks. It turned the snow bright blue, bounced sheets of glare from the flawless spread to the window pane. It was his turn to speak, but you had to say something.

'Maybe this is one of those little things that are supposed to make us glad. Little things to fight for. Like you said.'

He didn't laugh. This was enough.

He led you once more to the wardrobe. Things were getting serious: his spliff forgotten in the ashtray. Soundless, he lifted a black shirt and jacket of his own and dressed you up. Lip caught at mouth-corner, an artist, a patient father. Your eyes locked together, the fraction of a second when you disappeared behind the fabric felt like too much of a strain, too much like a goodbye. You two, the two of you, felt like you were spilling the light of church flames. Every motion a statement footprint over historic dust. Something filled the room for which you didn't have a name.

And even when you were both clothed and ready to go, shutting drawers and pulling blinds and checking locks three, four times over, neither of you tore it down with your characteristic sarcasm. You let it lie. You cherished. Maybe even then you knew there would come a time when such things would be precious, a globe of memory, fully-formed, petrol rainbows swirling the surface.

Then the fun began. He still didn't know what he was doing – he just brought his usual bag of party tricks. The target was a security firm on the other side of the city. They'd been laying folks off to make room for Management experts keen to supervise the manufacture of devices. Device – a word that came up far too often, applied to so many objects that their reputation buried their true purpose. Consumers and technicians were so awed by the numbers, prices, capacities, and qualities that nobody paid much attention to what they could be used for. The target was developing a seventh generation of undetectable, indestructible surveillance equipment. The Management had purchased developments in the hopes of installing them in every home in the city. Complete visibility. No midnight REM or picked nose or pawed-at creature in the depths of sleep would go unrecorded. Dispensing with each and every original employee meant no independent civilian would know enough to disable the equipment. No civilian would ever think to check every last inch of their home for such invasion of privacy. You didn't ask Caleb how he knew this – he had a way with people. They told him things. He had a gift for betraying no reaction at the time to any slice of scandal – he merely nodded, murmured, poured the storyteller another drink and stored away the information for future use.

You did have to ask what was so horrifying about the manoeuvre. You should have known better than to speak without thinking it through.

'I'm not keen on being watched in the bathroom, sure, but if we're not getting up to anything … isn't it something we could all just get used to? I mean, drug dealers and terrorists and paedophiles and murderers get up to their bad shit in their own living rooms. Maybe a little privacy's a small sacrifice for improving the odds of catching them.'

He didn't say a thing at first. He pulled the car over to the side of the road. You sat watching neon mimic sundown. His jaw clicked as he chewed over a response. Finally, 'But that's just how it starts. Has already started. We've been watched, recorded, monitored for years, now. And are we any better off? Wasn't so bad in the Nineties, like – you'd only really notice if you were doing something out of the ordinary, like taking a flight or being fingerprinted in a police station. But since the Millennium, it's just gone crazy. Everything, I mean. I'm not sure what happened first – whether people started pushing the limits of just how fucking insane their criminal – no, fundamentally inhumane acts could get, or whether overreaction on the part of the authorities pushed their limits even higher. It's an interesting premise, don't you think? That maybe some psychotics like a challenge…that maybe they wouldn't have gone to so much bother if the Management hadn't kept trying to make it more difficult.'

You shook your head, lit a spare spliff kept behind the shade on the passenger side.

'You're digressing again. Sum it up, Caleb, for the love of God. I get it, in principle, yeah, but just what so you think you're trying to prevent? They'll have back-ups, they won't …'

He took the joint right from your hands and smiled.

'You've still so much to learn.'

He went on. You listened, trying not to cry. He said your naiveté would be cute only up to a point – a point at which you'd have to decide whether you'd the courage to stand up for yourself. The right to be who and what you were. To exist. To move across the surface of the planet without interference, neither hurting nor being hurt. To remain fascinated by depths of thought and limits of experience. To never, ever believe in one hard-copy, indisputable answer, in one unbending truth. 'Keep it simple –there always have been, and always will be, plenty psychopaths and criminals and deadbeats on hand to keep the Management busy, however many measures they put in place. These just prompt great leaps of imagination, an irony I'm sure they won't appreciate. Look … how old were you when you started smoking?'

'Fourteen, fifteen. I'm not sure.'

'So what was the appeal, at first?'

You felt like a child reading a simple sentence from a chalkboard.

'Because I knew I was doing something I shouldn't.'

'Bingo.'

Caleb winked and handed back the spliff.

'Lucy, you'll start to get it once you've stopped over-analysing. Once you get it into your head that a stripping of permissions and privileges won't happen all at once. The teeniest niggle of something being not quite right ... time to look around and take note of what's happening.'

You made promises. Said you'd keep yourself informed, on the alert, that you'd fear complacency and laziness. Learn to use your voice as a weapon, whether spoken or written, gestured or detailed. He pointed to the rattling spectrum of spray-paints in the backseat of the car. Said they'd never change the world taken purely as they were, a clutch of chemicals and plastics – but that the act itself of doing something other than what was prescribed, permitted, held a shy power of its own. Even better if there were some artistry involved.

'Your idea, Lucy. That day with the fridge ... you got me thinking about ... meaningless destruction. We're not doing that anymore. There should be a context.'

If half the battle was the catching of the eye, the sight had a far better chance of fixing itself to a consciousness if there were a quirk, flair, something undeniably other. The city wasted further every day – a fire or a bomb, a toppling or sabotage, would blend right in. No-one would care.

'Get your beret on, Lucy. How do you think we should spruce the place up?'

'I've a fair few ideas. I'm going to need a screwdriver, a pair of pliers, probably a chisel.'

Caleb flipped out a kit as dextrous as his grin.

Later That Evening

He's stumbling about the kitchen, all excess length of limb, bashing elbows off the counter-tops, tripping over the ratted tendrils of his jeans. You slump on the couch until he's established that there's nothing in the fridge. You're sore all over, a pleasant ache you don't feel often enough these days. You don't know enough to judge whether tonight's been a success, but adrenaline after-burn rocketing through your system assures you that at something has happened.

He enters the lounge cradling a half-bottle of rusty wine you're sure you hadn't spotted on your last raid. You laugh – he's up to it, too.

'Wow, look what you found. Wonder how I missed that.'

Fingers scuttle the mess of hair on his forehead, eyes skewed around stubborn trickles. He sniffles, coughs, skull-bound sounds buying time between where joking ends and interrogation begins.

'You know what it's like ... you hide something, forget all about it, and wonder ...'

'... Whether you're going out of your mind, when you find it again?'

He laughs, takes a seat on the couch beside you instead of the arm of the other settee; his living-room soapbox. A good sign. Skin to skin. He unearths a couple of liquor-embalmed coffee mugs from the battlefield of a coffee table. The vacuum tumble of liquid into porcelain fills your head with a fresh rush of blood. You've both needed this. Compounding crime with misdemeanour makes it taste all the better. You clink rims, drink deep, lean back. Shoulder to shoulder.

'So ... what should we drink to?' he asks.

'I don't know. You're the expert – did you get it done? Everything you wanted?'

'I'll never have done everything I wanted,' he says, 'There's too much still to figure out, and they're just going to make it harder. Maybe we should just drink to trying. To not giving up, not yet.'

'I'll go with that.'

Silence. He really must be exhausted. Two sharp gulps, and he slams the mug to the table, smearing his lips with the back of his hand. He casts his arm over the back of the couch, toward which the follicles on your shoulders begin to strain. You wait. His call.

'You done with yours, yet?' he asks, pursing his lips.

'No. Nursing.'

'Hmmm. You'd think I'd learn.'

His mouth downturned at the corners, he cradles his chin in his hands, staring at the wreckage of the coffee table. His arm gone from the top of the sofa. He's disappointed, less about the liquor than about the restrictions placed by bodies other than he.

You wanted it to be a surprise, but now he's in a slump, you're unlikely to pin down that Kodak moment you've been waiting for.

'You alright?'

'Aye. Just wired. That way when you're ... physically fucked, your body says go to sleep, and you know your head's not about to give you even a tiny wee bit of peace?'

'Yeah. Same here.'

'Which is why I hate not being able to ... properly unwind. Probably not the healthiest of means of getting a kip, but come on—' he lifts the empty wine bottle, taps the halfway mark. 'Even fucking ... school teachers put away more than this, back in the day. My mother was a one-bottle woman, even on weeknights, and she never missed a day's work in her life.'

You'd best get it out now, before he talks himself into a rant. Before you end up on whichever portions of his bad side aren't reserved for the Management.

'In that case ...' you say, 'Had one of those mental blips myself, few days ago. Forgot I had this. Here ...'

101

You dig around under the couch, removing a paper bag. The back of your neck tingles under his gaze as you unveil a litre of wine, a quart of rum, a plastic baggie of decidedly inorganic skunk.

'You are a ... what do they call it?'

'Dark horse?'

'Among other things. Where'd you get all of that?'

'Murray owes me. Tried to scam the lot of us with a set of fixed scales. I didn't yap about it in front of his other customers, so ... I'm milking it.'

He keeps his peace until you've topped up the mugs.

'I thought I told you ... asked you ... not to go to Murray, anymore, Lucy.'

'Why not? Murray's an old friend of mine,' you say. 'And of yours, too. He's not one of them, Caleb. He's just trying to get by, like the rest of us.'

'It's not Murray I'm worried about.'

He leaves it at that. This on the back of several discussions over which he'd expressed concern as to how much you looked to him to see how to act, what to think. Over which you kept it to yourself that you still have no idea what you're doing.

'Okay then, let's hear it,' you say. A thin blade of a challenge slices your tone's mellow haze. 'What's up with Murray's set-up? That's his liquor you're drinking.'

'But you said it was ... never mind.' Caleb's posture deflates, a wistful gaze trailing over the skunk. 'My point was. Was something. But I'm not going to tell you what to do. I'd just rather you didn't ,if you get me. Murray's a decent guy, if you've got something he wants. That crowd of his, though ... I've heard things. About his crew, about what they do when they think they're being taken for a ride. I've seen a few casualties.'

'That's perfectly reasonable, Caleb. He's got to keep himself safe. Can't get a reputation for being a soft touch.'

'What about you, though, Lucy? What happens when you piss him off?'

'I don't. I won't. But if I did, I'd make sure I'm out of his way, long before he figures it out.'

Caleb cracks up, shattering the tension, rattling cups on the table. He plucks the mug from your hands and takes you by the shoulders, turning you around. You sometimes forget just how wide and fluid his gaze can be, when you don't have to fight past a cream of smoke. When you can see past khaki circles rimming the lids like the rings on a tree. Green and gold you can't find anywhere in nature, anymore.

'God, you're a strange one,' he murmurs. 'Never know when you're going to show me what you've got. Never know when you're going to decide you're ... not going quietly.'

Though soaring inside, you're hiding it well. There hasn't been time or space in the Management's manifesto for a revolution of etiquette between women and men – it still pays to be coy, cool, collected. A healthy fear of rejection makes every victory a bonus.

'I just ... I've been going to Murray for a long time, Caleb. I know how he thinks, what he does, what I can get away with. Got to hold on to something. Those ... ah ... little things that make it all worthwhile.'

You share a grin, aware you're speaking in code, yet comfortable enough by now to know there's no shame in falling back on aphorisms, those framed prints of conversation.

'Little things. Big things. It's funny, when you think about it ... the little ones are only little until they're taken off you.'

'Which is why you've got to hold on.'

'Which is why you've got to hold.'

He pulls you close, touches his lips to yours. Gently, now, desperation spent on the evening's activities. He tastes of wine and smoke, rust and brambles, a buzz of re-growth sanding your chin. A kiss with its own dramatic arc: rising toward a peak of intensity, hands on waist and neck and back. Being drunk as a verb, not an adjective. Bright heat, scattered breath, thudding of noses, cheekbones, chin. Then a slow drawing back; a grazing of fingers from the tops of your thighs to your knees, his other hand tilting your chin up.

'I'm ... wow ...' *he says, rubbing a finger across his brow, chuckling.* 'Sorry ... where were we?'

'You were kissing me.'

'Aye, but ...God, I'm no good at this ...'

Part of you enjoys seeing him knocked off his stride. Maybe you have powers of your own. He slackens his grip, points to the baggie.

'I thought we could ... maybe ... if you didn't mind ...' *he says, raising a brow.*

'Fire in. You'd better roll, I'm no good when I've had a drink.'

'You top us up, then,' *he says, setting up the makings of a spliff.* 'See? Teamwork.'

You like to watch his fingers working over the papers and buds; a scientist's precision, an artist's tongue thrust into cheek. It's in everything he does. Tonight's work especially, whether or not the Management will appreciate this when they discover the damage. Once you've both had a hit, you can feel yourself opening up. Your head lolling back on the sofa cushions, you trail a hand across the seat to brush his leg.

'Hmmm?'

'Caleb ...?'

'Yeah?'

'You know you said where were we? Then I'm no good at this ...? What did you mean?'

He blushes, a rare sight you're sure to fold and keep to look at later.

'Nothing.'

'We were talking about little things. Holding on to them. And then ...'

'... and then I was kissing you, I know.'

'Why did you stop?'

Caleb places the spliff in the ashtray, presses the heels of his hands to his temples.

'I knew where it was going,' he murmurs.

'That's kind of how it works,' you say, forcing a chuckle. 'Unless I've been doing it wrong.'

He takes your hand and presses it between both of his, squeezing so hard your fingers begin to numb. He gulps, skin stretching taut across the drawer-handles of his collarbone.

'See. That's the thing. I want to fuck you, Lucy, of course I do. I want to be near you, with you, in you. When we're outside, doing what we do, or even just sitting here, like this, it's ... I don't know if I could ever get as close to you as I want to be.'

Your chest begins to quake, hot beads of hurt rolling from the tip of each rib into your stomach. That doesn't sound good. You don't know what you've done.

'But ... but I'm here, Caleb. As close as you want me to be. I want to be near you, too ... I ... I don't know what you want me to do.'

He shuffles over to wrap arms about your shoulders. Four limbs make a cage around two heads, faces drawn close in the dark, each word now given its own flavour, temperature, density. He speaks so softly you have to hold your breath to catch his every drift.

'Lucy. You know that stuff we get up to? All the trouble we've got into, all the bother we've only just managed to escape? What we're doing now, sitting smoking and drinking and talking ideas?'

'Yeah. Everything we do that we're not really supposed to.'

'That's kind of the point. It's confusing.'

'What do you mean, Caleb? You're always talking about how important it all is, how we can't give up, how we're ... to be honest, I don't know, half the time, what we're trying to do.'

'Do you want to know a secret? In fact, it's not a secret. There's no-one to tell except the Management.'

'Go on, then.'

'I don't know, either. What I'm doing. I just ... I have to do something. I can't just lie down and let all that shit just happen.'

104

You don't say a thing. You've known all along. Protests and anarchies without labels or directions weren't exactly without purpose. That's what you do, after all — the fight had a weight, shape, depth, texture even in the absence of a named enemy. That's what open-ended concepts like system and society were for — a neat wrap around an amorphous dissatisfaction, around an instinct unequipped with an instruction manual. You're still waiting to hear what this all has to do with whether or not you fuck.

'Lucy? You still listening?'

'Uh-huh. Thanks. For telling me your secret. I'm just not sure …'

'I'm getting to that. See … that's where it gets confusing. All the protesting … takes shape mostly around all the things we're not supposed to be doing. That's where the satisfaction lies, otherwise what's the point? And I … I'm worried. I don't want to make love to you just because I know they'd disapprove.'

'Then don't. Do it because you love me, Caleb.'

And he does.

'You gonnae lie there all day, or what?'

A rough damp on my forehead. Pressure increases, behind which I can now sense the ache of a bruise. I sit up and brush off the flannel. Bethany swings up onto the end of the bed, facing me with her legs crossed. I shake my head, scouring temples and sockets with the heels of my hands. Bethany doesn't look much better than I feel; the last of her makeup scattered and ground like a chalked pavement drawing after a rainstorm. Wearing one of my interchangeable assemblies of black jeans, black shirt, black socks. Grudging streaks of dawn fall from the window down one side of her face. She's scratched and bruised about the cheeks and chin, a shallow crack splitting her lower lip.

'Sorry … I'm not a morning person,' I say.

'Not much of an evening person, either,' she replies, dry as cheap vodka, pointing at her forehead, then mine.

'Uh … I didn't …'

'Quite the hook you've got on you, there. Could have made use of *you.*'

'I'm … I'm sorry.'

I want to say *I don't know what came over me,* but we both know that's a lie. Like any recipient of an awful truth, the first reaction is to beat the messenger.

'No worries. Rather enjoyed myself, actually … been a while since I've been in a scrap.'

'Huh?'

'You know … a go-to. A have-at-you. Doesn't half wake you up.'

This shouldn't be beyond me. Caleb used to say much the same thing, albeit about certain other non-contact acts outside the realm of etiquette. Bethany grabs me by the wrists, drags me across the bed for a closer look.

'I want you to remember this. What you did to me. This is what you're capable of, Lucy. If you're angry enough. Had bite at the truth. If you want to keep going. You don't have to run away. Stand and fight.'

'It wasn't *me,* Bethany, it was … those pictures, that voice, it really … *threw* me. I couldn't–'

'–have done it any other way. I deserved this – but not as much as the Management. They're the ones put us where we are. Were.

None of this should have happened. It doesn't have to *keep* happening. To Caleb, I mean.'

A period of quiet reflection. I'm being set up for a pledge, a promise to keep pushing. I've been here before, but there were fringe benefits involved. I had a light to walk toward when it was Caleb pulling me on.

'Did you … ah, sleep well?' I still ask idiot question. Learned responses remain useful for plugging cracks in awkward silences. She raises an eyebrow, lips pursed, awaiting a cigarette. I'm not particularly fussed about being taken seriously.

'Eh … aye. You've a quality floor, there.'

'Oh … ah … do you want some coffee? Tea? Breakfast! I don't know what I have, I mean, there's probably cereal and toast and stuff but no milk and probably no butter, or I could go out and get something from the machines, or–'

'Christ, you really are a charm-school graduate,' says Bethany. 'Calm down. I'm not your house guest, Lucy. We haven't just enjoyed an evening of brandy and bridge, for fuck's sake.'

'I just–'

'–you're just talking for the sake of the sound of your own voice. So's you can't hear a word of what we were discussing last night. Some things never change.'

She unfolds her limbs and rises, slowly, sharp hits of breath hissing through her teeth, squeezing the damp flannel like a barbell. The slightest shift of my own body affirms we've each done quite a number on the other. My knuckles are black grapes of bruised swelling, knees and elbows creaking complaint. Bethany swipes at her eyes, clears her throat, tilts backward over hands jammed into the small of her back like one of those joggers I used to see, warming up for a sprint at the edge of the park. Odd, having had someone else sleeping nearby. Intimacy of sorts, if she has, in fact, been tending my battered face all through the night.

'Bethany?'

'Yeah?'

'I *am* sorry. I mean it. I shouldn't have hit you.'

'Hit? Singular? Come off it. You gave me a kicking, Lucy. I'm … haha … really rather *proud* of you.'

'God … if it's any consolation, I'm pretty sore, myself.'

'Yeah … uh, I was patient with you, Lucy, but you were about to inflict some serious damage, on yourself, mostly. Had to take you out. Don't worry, it's just a surface ache. Just enough to calm you down.'

107

And she'd put me to bed. Cooled the bruising. It didn't seem right that such administrations should seem so *alien*.

'Well,' she says, voice strident, calling up the day, 'It's over with. New day. Business to attend to.'

Stories to be told.

2nd December 2023

The Intern sits in the dead centre of the room. His crossed legs are neat as an ampersand, shoulders and hips equality signs slung either side of his spine. He appears to be coping with bed having been removed from the room, maintaining a steady smile even at the approach of rubber footsteps. In light of recent conversations, The Manager has decided to hand over Nineteen's case to his inferiors. So far, his own efforts have proved damaging to the health of both parties, and thus producing very little by way of chartable results.

Agent X44 strides down the corridor clutching a clipboard. She exchanges terse pleasantries with other Agents on Interview Detail, all the while tightening her shoulder blades in case of an appearance from the Manager. X44 wears full fatigues today: a sharp black canvas jumpsuit whose many zips and buttons rattle with every booted tread, creating an authoritative timpani favoured by certain experts in Intimidation.

'Agent,' she says, nodding to a woman strapped into a taut linen suit.

'Agent,' the woman replies. Her ferocious expression comes courtesy of the painful chignon into which her icy hair is scraped, upper lips drawn up from her front teeth in a feline sneer.

'Progress?' asks X44.

'Some. Intern Forty-Six is certainly comfortable with naming names, Agent, but not quite so ready to associate *himself* with any of the insurgents   mentioned.'

'It's often the way. Has the Manager made an offer?'

'Small holding on the edge of the conurbation. All mod cons ... including full surveillance kit.' The blonde Agent struggles to smirk. X44 nods, forces a grin.

'Let me guess. Forty-Six did not react well to this piece of information?'

'The usual complaint, Agent. Civil liberties, and such.'

'It never ends.'

'They'll never learn.'

'So what's he in for, anyway?' asks X44. She is always keen to switch conversations to the specifics of a case or incident, as opposed to any overhanging ideology.

'Another one of the Film mob. Caught showing portions of banned films, as part of a ... haha ... an *underground film festival*. Agents in Sector Fifteen saw the projector lights against the curtains in one of the old apartment buildings. Walked right in to find about thirty of them squashed into the lounge, watching a woman ... *doing things* to herself.'

'Really?' asks X44. Picturing the scene, it takes some effort to wrap her tones in disapproval. 'Anything any of us would have seen ...from before, I mean? You never know ...what might come up. From the bad old days.'

The blonde Agent snorts.

'I doubt it. Some Dane called ... Von Trier. Pre-Millennium film students have a weakness for his work. Challenging, apparently. That old appetite for controversy. The Intern had more paper material concerned with the riots and criticisms than he had concerning the film itself. I don't think we have much to worry about. It's all hype ... and that's easily dealt with.'

'Remove the materials, the causal factor ...'

'... and thereafter it's merely a matter of persuasion,' the blonde interjects, allowing a sneer full use of her mouth. 'So ...who do you have this afternoon?'

'Number Nineteen. Provided the Manager hasn't changed his mind.'

'Not a chance,' says the blonde, dropping to a whisper. 'He's over-ground today, tomorrow and hopefully the rest of the week. Nineteen's sending him ...a bit ...*you know*. Last time I saw him, he was stomping up the corridor, kicking every single door along the way. Said he'd had it with *words*. That *we* could take care of it. Report back, and keep the output *brief.*'

Both Agents indulge a hint of a snicker, eyes panning the corridor. X44 checks her clipboard again.

'Well, best get started.'

'Good luck with that,' says the blonde. 'Every time someone leaves that room, they're either in a rage, in tears or unable to say a word for hours.'

'I'll handle him. They're only words. Ideas. All that's needed is a touch of *discipline.*'

'Ha. Nineteen doesn't seem to be responding to that, either. The Management left covered in blood, last time – not his own. And the Intern just kept laughing. It was ...' the blonde presses fingertips to her temples, unpicking a word from the Facility's fluorescent gauze. '... odd. Creepy.'

'All the more reason to get in there. Can't have that kind of talk about the Facility, Agent … he's just an Intern. And he's in our custody. Nothing else should matter.'

'Hmm. True. Well, as I say, good luck. You might want to take a chair in with you. The Manager had all the amenities removed.'

'Will do. Good luck yourself, with your … film buff.'

The blonde Agent raises a hand to her face, makes a circle with thumb and forefinger and peers through, muscles around her eye sockets struggling to produce a wink.

'This close, Agent.'

'We always are.'

The Agents exchange nods and handshakes. The blonde squares her shoulders and steps into the room. X44 clanks further down the corridor, lifting an orange plastic chair left outside by a night guard. Peering over her shoulder, checking for witnesses, she slots it into another, entering the Intern's room with both swinging from her index finger.

Unlike the others, the Intern does not flinch at her entrance. He swivels his head slowly toward her, nodding with all the comportment of a headmaster admitting an errant pupil. X44 closes the door and leans briefly against the hinges, listening out.

'Hello, Agent,' says the Intern. 'And to what do I owe the pleasure?'

Bethany can't hold it in any longer. She snorts with laughter, sliding slowly down the door frame.

'Intern Number Nineteen, you aren't half making things difficult for yourself,' she says, waving at the sandworms of blood still streaking the floor. Caleb shrugs, pats the concrete by his knee.

'Won't you sit down, Agent? Or can we skip the double-speak?'

'Just you and me, today, Caleb. Turns out the Manager has more important matters to attend to than Interview detail.'

Bethany draws the metal screen across the porthole in the door. She's well aware of the cameras pointed directly into the centre of the room, but a quick look in the Screening Room in the Manager's absence had proved hand-held gaming consoles to be far more compelling than perusal of the feed.

'I brought you a chair.' There's a slight catch in her voice. This is the first she's seen him since his last Interview with the Manager. Sick heat floods her chest at the sight of his scattered colours, eyes and jaw-line flaring petroleum purple. He's dropped further weight: knees and elbows tenting the fabric of his fatigues, cheekbones and clavicle

111

two pairs of drawer handles, shaved skull a contour map of hollows and planes. Dried blood still crusts the rims of his nostrils, the cracks between nose and mouth. A dip in the flesh of his cheek indicates the recent removal of several bottom teeth.

'Cheers, but … gotta say, I'm loving the *floor* thing they've got going in here. Very Zen. Hones the thought processes. And all great rebel leaders enjoyed a bit of the old Spartan hospitality, right?'

'Just get up off the floor and take a seat, Caleb.'

Bethany faces the wall as Caleb rustles up from the floor and into a chair. Neither wants her watching as he struggles to his feet. Sputters of breath in his abraded throat and the creak of joints stiff from sitting on the floor are quite enough.

'So,' he drawls, once seated, 'Another Interview, eh? Smashing. Somebody must like the look of me.'

'You're not doing yourself any favours, you know. Winding him up like that.'

'I just told him what I knew, Bethany. What the hell else was I supposed to do? Feed him a line? Fabricate a cause? He'd go out looking, find out I was lying, and come back and give me a worse kicking than this one.'

'I … I know, Caleb, it's just …well, hasn't he at least tried to make you a deal?'

'Yeah. Home, bath, bed, book in exchange for information I *don't have*. And in return I get a nice, clean slate. Zapow. Cheerio. I'm not going there. No way.'

Bethany sighs, tosses the clipboard to the floor, folds her arms. Caleb winks and enacts a rude burlesque of her movements.

'Caleb … you're going to have to tell them *something*. I was listening in. I know he mentioned your … that girl.'

'Lucy. Her name is Lucy. And yeah … he told me … told me she'd been in here, too. That they let her go. Since she didn't really have anything to do with … you know. A *hapless accessory*.'

'And doesn't that change anything? Don't you want to get yourself back out there, with your girl? Don't you want things to go back to the way they were?'

Caleb shakes his head, starts up from the seat. He paces, rolling the glue from his shoulders and hips, hands fluttering from one ache to the next over arms, hands, skull, jaw, lips.

'But … it wouldn't *mean* a thing anymore. Neither of us would be who we really were, would we?'

'But you wouldn't *know* that, Caleb. It'd be a fresh start.'

'I just … I can't explain it, Bethany. It wouldn't be *living*. Just existing. And it's already gone way too far. Going back sounds like a prize, true – but that comes at the expense of so many things we don't properly value until they're gone.'

'Such as?'

'Asking questions. Original thought. Knowledge. Inspiration. Reading or seeing or hearing about things that go on in the world over the city limits. Don't you have any idea how *important* that is?'

Caleb's hands fly about his head, bones creaking with every stirring of air. Bethany grabs him by the wrists and leads him back to his seat, trying not to wince at the pitiful girth of his forearms. He's falling apart. He's going to have to start co-operating if he's going to survive.

'In … in theory, yeah. I'm not that much older than you. I did the college thing. The sit-ins. The rallies. Societies – art, books, music, films, debate. Signed any petitions shoved in my face. Even used to date a guy who wrote for a Student Socialist newspaper, haha … jeez, that boy could *talk*. But don't you see? That's all it *was*, all talk, talk, talk, nothing happening but the country continuing to fall apart. Don't you see how much … *easier* it'd be if we all just … went along with it?'

'God, Bethany. I'd have expected better of you. You're right about the college politics stuff, aye – most of us were at it, playing at being so fucking *liberal*, so *informed*. But it's the filter-down effect, Agent. Same principle the Management are so fond of. It works both ways. If one person, just one, shouts loud enough … they can make a difference.'

Bethany stares at her hands knotted taut in her lap. He knows that she doesn't believe in what she's trying to sell, but alternatives to compliance dry up further by the day.

'Caleb … I don't know what to tell you. I'm not in a position to give you advice either way – any offers you've had aren't mine to make. All I *can* tell you is where you *could* go, what would … happen if you choose not to take the Manager up on his … arrangement.'

'So tell me, then, Agent. What's to happen to me?'

'Time's running out, Caleb. If you've nothing to give them, if you're not willing to take the clean slate … they can wipe it by force, if they have to. And I'm not talking a gentle fade, here, a happy-ending story – I'm talking complete and utter deletion of everything you've got up there. Then it won't be a case of *who* you really were – it'll be a fucking miracle if there's anything left at all. I've seen it. It's … I don't want to see it happening to you.'

Caleb, silent, shifts back and forth in the chair, eyes swinging between the door and the patches of floor still bearing the remnants of his last altercation.

'What do you want me to say?'

'Whatever you want, Caleb. You know this isn't an interview.'

Caleb eyes the clipboard on the floor.

'Off the record?'

'I've barely been keeping one in the first place.'

Something unnamed passes between Agent and Intern. This admission cements an arrangement that has so far been tentative, noncommittal. Caleb's mouth twitches into a sly smile. It pleases him to note that even the Agents are partial to snippets of discourse, opinion, subjective impressions of a sterilised environment.

'How old were you, Bethany, that September afternoon?'

'Huh?'

'The only September stamped into our collective consciousness. Twin towers. Aeroplanes. Mass destruction. People leaping from buildings hundreds of floors high. Fire and rubble. Chaos. Terror. Every single television screen showing a silver streak in a bright blue sky.'

'Nine eleven? God, that was ... I'd have been about fourteen, fifteen.'

'What do you remember?'

'Hmmm ... wow ... I must have ... oh, I know. I was at school. Standard Grade Chemistry.'

'What happened?'

'The head ... came into the classroom. Spoke to the teacher in charge. I remember he ... turned white. Hands were shaking. He said *something dreadful has happened, class. We're calling your parents to come and take you home.* Then he turned on the TV, and we watched, and ... wondered.'

'And what were you *wondering?*'

Bethany swallows hard, picks at dry skin around her fingernails.

'Why we should ... care. I mean, it was hellish, truly horrible, but ... it was on *TV*. It wasn't real, it wasn't relevant. We didn't see what New York had to do with us ...sounds awful, I know, but ...'

'Not awful, Bethany. You were just ahead of time, is all.'

'What do you mean?'

Caleb lifts a forefinger to indicate a pause. He slinks from the chair to the floor, inching over on his backside to lean against the wall, cross-legged.

114

'What are you doing?'

'Getting comfortable. You should always be on the floor, for stories.'

Bethany shakes her head. She's still getting used to his oddities. Statements bound to gestures bordering on the theatrical.

'Go on, then. What did you mean, ahead of time?'

'September the eleventh. Arguably the most significant event of the twenty-first century, according to my high school history teachers. From a Western perspective, anyway. It certainly had the most coverage in the media, not to mention pretty much every academic and artistic discipline since. I've seen the archive footage. Influential figures the world over making statements, offering sympathies. Everyone had an opinion. I'd have been about four years old. I remember wondering myself what all the fuss was about. My parents were crying in each other's arms. Scared the shit out of me. My dad ... he was one of the last of the Seventies socialists, the anti-Thatcher noisemakers. Union member, carrier of placards. He hated America and everything it stood for, and yet ... he's always said ...that the events in New York either marked the end of an era, or the beginning of one.'

'The age of terror. I remember.'

' It was, wasn't it? Even up to the point at which I was old enough to understand why my folks were cancelling our holidays to Spain. Bombs in every rucksack, terrorists in every corner shop. But ... it simmered down, didn't it? Soon as the dust had settled ... it didn't take long for the Age of Boredom to take over, guide us all gently past the things we didn't want to hear about. Troops in Afghanistan massacring the innocent, big deal. Mass graves. Torture. Detention camps. Nobody wanted to know. Soon as Blair and Bush fucked up over that little nuclear weapon Chinese Whisper, folks just ... preferred to pretend it was all just a fucking ... *soap opera,* tuned into only when the unfolding events had any direct bearing on Joe Average. Just a wee blurb when a British or American soldier bought it over there. Same thing with seven-seven. Bombing in a London subway carriage. Oh, how perfectly dreadful – and it was, don't get me wrong – but once the country had buried the dead, it just became another excuse, another reason to be pleased that we'd soldiers bombing the fuck out of the Faceless Enemy. Kill the Towel-heads. Nuke the Darkies. Retreat from reality, let the folks in power tell us what to think, what to believe, how to feel, where to direct our rage. We got bored, sat around waiting for something to happen. We laughed in the dark, Bethany, and didn't even know it. Suicide Bomber became a costume to get up in for

Halloween. I remember, couple years ago, Lucy was digging through old copies of some woman's glossy magazine for some sociology paper or other – and guess what? Fucking ... interview and makeover session for the Lady Survivors of Seven Seven. A fucking *photo opportunity*. A chance to *win a Seven Seven goody bag* of products chosen by the Lovely Ladies of the London Bombings ... didn't know where to look, so we all collectively looked *nowhere–*'

'Caleb! Jesus, calm down! You're ranting.'

Caleb *is* holding forth somewhat. Unable to sit still: leaning against the wall; then up on his knees tugging at sleeves; crawling forward, slumping back over his heels; slapping his entomological thighs. His cheeks the lilac of a flush in the absence of blood, scalp visibly twitching in time with the grinding of teeth.

'I thought you wanted me to talk.'

'I do,' says Bethany, dropping from the chair to the floor, scuttling over to kneel alongside Caleb, crossed knees forming a Northern star. 'I just ... I was *there*, Caleb. I remember. And yeah, the Zeros wasn't Western civilisations' finest decade, but ...it's over, yeah? No World War Three. Nobody blew up the planet, countries recovered, international relations are ... polite, if not friendly. It's got nothing to do with the way we live today, okay? We're *safe* now. We know better.'

Caleb begins to laugh again. It's frightening, that so much force of breath can issue from that shrivelled chest, pounding off the concrete floor, swelling the dimensions of the room.

'Caleb! Put a fucking lid on it!'

Howling dims to a trickle; audible damage to respiratory system now a patter of rain on tin.

'You've just,' he stutters, 'Put the fucking ... *stamp* on it, Bethany. We're *safe*, now, eh?'

'Yes!'

'And at what price, eh? Total ... *submission?*'

'Look, Caleb, I know things aren't ideal. But just because you can't go about doing whatever you want, whenever you like, doesn't mean things haven't moved on for the better, eh? Don't have to worry about being killed every time we leave the house, about wars and bombs and–'

'–Bethany. Bethany, Bethany. We're not scared of the world because we can't *see* it anymore. We've drawn ourselves in. The city's all neat and tight, quiet and peaceful. All random factors under control or slung in *here*. And yeah, there are benefits. Crime levels dropped to barely anything at all, people being so very fucking *nice* to each other all the time, everything we could ever want or need right there on our doorsteps and fingertips. Nobody wants to *know* anything anymore, *learn* anything, ask any *questions*. Do you know what they're teaching for Film Studies, these days?'

'Films, presumably.'

'Sarcasm, Bethany. Neither big nor clever. And no, they're not teaching *films* any more. Too risky, too many probable degrees of offence. They're teaching Screen Performance – but not of the greats, the legends. No: they're looking at footage of the – and it pains me to say so – *stars* of those Management Network reality *talent* shows. A bunch of fucking *idiots* with no more talent than troupe of fucking *performing chimps* – no, scratch that, my money's on the chimps any day – and the whole city just *claps* and *cheers* and spends their hard-earned cash *voting* to keep these *troglodytes* on-screen for as long as possible, only for the eventual winners to run out of ideas and wind up hosting *off-shoots* of the same goddamned *freakshows–*'

'Caleb! What's your point?' snaps Bethany, all too aware of the ascending volume, the room rattling like a faulty trolley with Caleb's every mouthful.

'I'm getting to it. That's what they're studying, is what I'm saying. How to piece together a *performance* to rival these *clowns*. A degree in how to waste time, how to lie, how to destroy the very concept of *talent* ...'

'That's nothing new, Caleb. Been around since the Nineties, at least. And who are you to decide what's worthy of study?'

'That's not the point, Bethany. That'd be fine if it weren't all a nice, safe distraction from what's really *important*. We don't go *anywhere* on our own. We can't. Depth of thought arises, progress is made, from reaction to an opposite, a need for change. And that doesn't happen when we're all slumped looking at ourselves looking at ourselves looking at ourselves. You get me? What's the last bit of news you remember from elsewhere?'

'I don't know. What does it matter?'

'It matters because it marks the limits of our ignorance, Bethany. It's a backward spiral. A drawing-in. Nine eleven was a big one. Massive. And a whole ocean away, too. Then we'd Afghanistan. Still pretty far away, good for us, yeah, but it *dwindled*. We didn't want to look too hard, didn't want to have to ask tough questions of ourselves.'

'Nobody ever does, Caleb!' says Bethany, jumping to her feet, pressing her head to the door. 'There's no room for it! It's hard enough carrying yourself through the day in your *own* world, never mind having

117

to ask yourself what the worldwide Big Stuff should mean to you! And yeah, maybe we don't try as hard as we should, but–'

'–okay. Europe, then. Remember Josef Fritzl? Locked his daughter in the basement for *years*, raped her as often as he had hot dinners, had children by her, brought them up underground? Threw her miscarriages in the incinerator? Don't you remember the media circus round *that* one?'

'Christ, yeah, that was horrible.'

'Horrible doesn't begin to cover it, Bethany. Do you remember what they called him? A human monster. That was it. Back when we'd a conception, however vague, of what either of those words might mean. And it tailed off ...'

'... I'm getting the picture, Caleb–'

'–it tailed off and became a fucking ... *urban legend*, a *marketing angle*, or something. Singers were writing songs about - haha - *obsession and control*, dedicating their whiny little ditties to the *families*, whose fucking *names* no-one could even *remember* once the papers lost interest. Burlesque titty-shakers were making up *routines* based on the story. They even optioned a film, until they smacked up against legal troubles. Anonymity, protection. At least they got *that* part right. But ... the whole hellish thing became a fable, something to tell your kids to make them do what they were told. Mr F just another Big Bad Wolf. We put the story on the shelf and left it there, too lazy to gather facts, to know anything more about it than the sensationalist ratings-boosters.'

'People remember what they remember, Caleb. Only what there's *room* for. You don't to see a horror movie, for example, and think too long and hard about the history and psychology of the *victims*, do you? There's no context, no frame of reference, nothing *requiring* you to pin their experience to your own, or vice versa. The Big Bad Wolf sticks around in your head much longer than Red Riding Hood or the Three Little Piggies. You take the element of threat and hold onto *that*, because it's the only part that could potentially *affect* your *own* life. I'm not saying it's right, or fair, or *proper*, but ... your surviving an encounter with the Wolf depends much more on what you know of *him* than it does on what you know of the Piggies. You see what I mean?'

'Fuck, Bethany. Is that how far we've come? All these people buried under statistics, swallowed up in the *sensation*? The murderer becoming the *spokesperson*?'

'We can't. Account. For every single person. In an atrocity. We just ... can't, Caleb.'

'Okay. Fair enough. What about those one-victim crimes? Can't be much of a strain, remembering a single name, eh?'

'What about them?'

'I'm just proving a point. That you can't just pin it on lack of head-space.'

'Okay, then, let's hear it.'

'A beach in Arbroath. Not too far from here. Spring, 2008. Ring any bells?

It does. Bethany smoothes a blank over her expression. She knows she won't have the answers he's looking for.

'There was a murder. Fucking horrific it was, too – couple of little girls found the body. You remember it now?'

'Yeah. It was–'

'–all over the papers, the telly. But back then, dead bodies turned up in Glasgow every day of the week. Why'd this one get so much attention?'

'I don't know.'

'Yes you do, Bethany,' says Caleb, pitch climbing again, knees and elbows trembling, skin around his eyes and mouth stretched pale as cellophane. 'Tell me why the public were so keen on this particular corpse.'

'She was ... in bits. The victim. The children ... found her head in a plastic bag. The rest of her ... a bit at a time.'

'There we go. *Sensation*, Bethany. That's why the papers were all over it.'

'That's not true, Caleb! They couldn't *identify* her – they had to keep the public informed, in case anyone had any information.'

Caleb closes his eyes, tilts his head back, exhaling with care through his traumatized nostrils. 'Information. They didn't know who she was. True. Ask yourself, though, Bethany – after all that, after all the stories and squirmy gossip in bars and trains and offices ...all that work to identify the woman *cut to fucking pieces* ... who remembers her name? What she did? Who she was? Anyone? Do you?'

'No,' says Bethany, quietly, sitting backward on one of the chairs, wrapping her head in her arms. 'No. I don't remember anything about her.'

'Jolanta Bledaite. That's who she was. And you know something? I'm no better than the rest of the gossip hounds. Aye, I made a point of finding out ... the information was there, all I had to do was *look*. But I don't think I'd have bothered, have remembered, if she hadn't first appeared as a severed head in a plastic bag. I just don't see why it has to be one or the other – a monster or a scandal – for people to exist in more than ... soundbites, I guess.'

'Are you reaching a point, here? Yes, we're rotten, the whole lot of us. But there's nothing to be done. It's the way things are.'

'I'm just trying to show you the backward spiral. How soon we forget, how easily, the further we get from the turn of the Millennium. The world getting smaller and smaller, even as we had the technological potential to see wider, further. America and Afghanistan, we finished with after we ran out of news. Didn't care much after the troops pulled out. Europe, a few dirty little horror stories to keep us amused until we'd managed to turn all the players into caricatures. A *human head* on the beach down the *road,* kept us busy until ... woop, done, mystery solved, go about your business. A woman murdered in Queen's Park – I could see my house from the park gates, for Christ's sake – and instead of drawing attention to the victim, to the crime, even, the Management saw another ready-made excuse for tightening the controls. Bad shit in Glasgow, sound the alarm, raise the drawbridge. Because *that's* what we needed. A blotting-out, a drawing-in. Pour concrete over any nasty business. Slam the cell doors on *everyone.'*

'I remember that one, too – you couldn't move on that road for weeks.'

'The Management had to be seen to be doing something – and fair enough, they caught the guy that did it, they put him away, but ... they went too far. They didn't ask questions. They gave orders. They locked us all up *with* him, and made us thank them for the privilege.'

'Well ... you can sort of see their–'

'–no, I fucking can't! I'm not a sociologist or a politician, fair enough, but there's no way locking down the whole goddamned *city* was the right approach! It's ... Jesus, it's throwing toys from the pram! It's giving up! It's basically saying *we're all fucked, look the other way!* And after that ... rewire attention spans. No more violent crime in *this* city, certainly not when public consciousness is focused – rather neatly – on *money, market collapses, real-estate, credit crunch.* All that bullshit, all those rich fucks expecting us to weep over their squeezed wallets. That's all I saw, by the way – I was poor in the first place, so none of that shit made much of a difference. But what a crock! It was all anyone ever talked about! Money troubles diverting attention from the city tightening, closing off ... *cash.* Pieces of paper and metal, numbers on a spreadsheet. That was enough to keep us occupied, Bethany. That was all we seemed to want from our right to *know.'*

120

Bethany is silent for a time, staring through concrete back into the past.

'We're not all like you, you know. Sometimes ... sometimes it's too much effort to remember to *breathe*, never mind trying to figure out what we are or aren't being told. I wish I could say I was ... more curious. I wish a lot of things.'

Caleb opens his eyes. Diode-shock in electric green becomes the whole of his expression; headlights swallowing a vehicle on an unlit road.

'You asked yourself what you're doing in here, Bethany? Listening to my soap-boxing? You could be doing anything you want. Giving me a kicking. You're dressed for it, anyway. I'm giving you nothing you can use. I'm telling you nothing you couldn't find out for yourself. I'm not giving you a lesson, not relating the news. So why are you still listening?'

Bethany can't tell him he fascinates. Feeds a secret hunger running under her days in the Facility. For straight words stripped of codes. Voices with inflections. Expressions matching speech. Such an admission will put both in more danger than they're already courting with each minute passing unchecked on the clipboard.

'Maybe I'm tricking you,' she says. 'Maybe I'm waiting for you to slip up, give me something I can use in a report. Maybe I'm playing the good cop.'

'Maybe you *are* curious,' grins Caleb. 'It's not a full-time occupation. Sometimes it's enough just to have your attention caught by more than an order, something other than having to check you're not up to anything you shouldn't be.'

Bethany begins to pace about the room, footsteps pounding her into her role as the empowered half of the discourse. She's beginning to panic. Whatever she gains from these dialogues, Caleb loses in terms of time, favours, chances at getting out of here. She's going to have to throw up a few more barriers between them.

'Maybe a lot of things, Caleb. Doesn't change the fact that you're still in here, and it's still my job to see if you've any information worth passing along. Sure, we're beyond that, but ...what are you going to do?'

'Already told you. Wait it out. See what happens. Talk to you, if you're still listening.'

'How long *can* you wait?'

'I could ask you the same thing.'

Footsteps scatter the corridor outside. Bethany flinches, makes for the door. Technically, this is only an Interview with a notoriously

121

impenetrable Intern. Still, should the Manager come looking for updates, she's not sure she can hold back from shouting out in Caleb's words.

'Shhhh … hold on …'

Caleb chuckles.

'Hey, hey … no problem here, is there? We're just discussing the news. Recent world history. Unless there's another prohibition I haven't heard about yet.'

'Shut up, Caleb,' hisses Bethany, face flattened to a rubber mask against the door hinge. 'Unless *you* want to tell my *superiors* everything you've just told me.'

'I think I'll pass,' says Caleb, dropping to stage whisper. 'I doubt they'd have the requisite frames of reference for such a discussion. You just can't get decent conversation these days, can you?'

The footsteps trundle further down the hall. Bethany checks her watch – coming up for staff changeover. The Housekeepers would be down before long with rations. Two steel mugs: drinking water, sticky freeze-dried mash with acrylic spoon.

'Nineteen. We're going to have to round this up,' says Bethany, flexing her rote.

'Sure thing, Agent. You get anything useful from that?' Caleb winks.

'Not the damndest thing.' Bethany grins.

'I aim to please.'

Caleb gets to his feet, shaking vertebrae back into place. As he stretches toward the ceiling, Bethany winces once more at the sight of his mug-handle hips, the lower rim of his ribs like the opening of a birdcage.

'Caleb. Your rations are their way. Make sure you take every last bite, eh? You need it.'

'Rations? Not for a few days, now, Agent. Punishment. For soiling the Manager's suit. I'll get over it – can't bitch about being spared the gruel.'

Bethany strides toward the skin-taut Intern. She pokes a fingertip into his breastbone, cups his waist in her hands. A sick tightening in her own stomach. Caleb grins, puzzled. Nothing sexual in the touch, but he's not about to let a touch of skin to skin go past unremarked. He can sense Bethany slipping back, detaching herself from the conversation. Anything to pin it in the memory, the slightest of quips, was more than worth the breath.

'See anything you like?'

122

Bethany prods him again, mouth tight with a clinician's concentration.

'Shut up, Caleb. Have you seen yourself?'

'Do you *see* any full-length mirrors? Must have lost my dressing-room privileges along with the four-poster and the twelve-course meals.'

Bethany shakes her head, folds her arms. Ice chips glint in his eyes. Senses gathered up, honed, concentrated to offset a raging hunger.

'Caleb ... Caleb ... I don't know what to ... I'm going to get this sorted. They can't let you starve.'

'They probably can, Bethany, but I imagine that'd defeat the purpose, somewhat. Corpses aren't party to much by way of information. Besides, it takes much longer than you might think. I've read about it. Takes weeks, months, sometimes.'

'I won't let that happen.'

'Very sweet of you, Bethany. Mothering instincts?'

'No. Aesthetics.'

A word he hasn't heard in years, outside of prohibitions, diktats. He backs away slowly, tracking an arc across the floor, raising and curving his arms around an invisible globe. He rolls his head, as though leaning into a hot shower stream. Smiling without a trace of irony.

'You know,' he drawls, 'There's something to be said for this place. Hadn't noticed until I stopped feeling hungry. Till I stopped needing sleep. It's ... insane, but I feel I'm thinking more clearly than I ever have in my life. It's like ... the Management take away everything you have. Fine. It's harsh, but you deal. You get used to it. Then they take away everything you need. And you're ... almost *glad*. It's like anything else. The more you have, the harder it is to be *satisfied*. The more they take, the more you realize you don't need much of anything at all. You're purer. Cleaner. You belong to yourself, and not to all that stuff you used to let rule your life.'

She can hear, now, the change in his voice, blurring round the edges as adrenaline reserves shuffle from their peak. Falling deeper down into himself, the better to make it through. Too late for further argument, though. A rations cart creaks to a halt outside of the door.

'Right. They're here. I have to go, Caleb, before they start wondering what I've got from you.'

'It's been real, Beh ... Agent. Call in for tea anytime.'

She slips from the room with barely a nod for the Housekeepers. Her head is pressed too tight with words and ideas to manage machinations of speech. Caleb. A genius or a madman, teetering on the prong of that timeless dichotomy. She's not sure how much he really believes in all he unfolds. Whether he's truly convinced that suffering for truth will make what's happening to him worthwhile.

Overground

15th March 2024

Two days, and Bethany's made herself quite the feature in my flat. She takes the blank refrigerator drawer and spreads the edges, makes of it a catwalk, a jungle gym, a proscenium arch. Muscle twitches and rasping breaths of her squats and press-ups seem to swell the room to twice its size. She paces between the bed and the table at which I sit, taking in only a fraction of what she's saying. She's making plans, telling stories. Every so often she remembers I'm here, asks me what I think about such-and-such an idea. I'm running out of synonyms for all my favourite affirmatives.

Whilst she's out running laps, I indulge in the arts of pottering. Opening cupboards and drawers. Arranging tin cans in order of food group, brand name, colour. Examining my two sets of cutlery, plates, bowls and coffee cups for stains, rings,scratches and chips. Half-wishing I'd enough rubbish to justify a trip to the shelter outside.

Medication leaving my system, I wonder how I'd ever kept myself occupied. No interesting developments in the ceiling cracks, no growths worth excising from between bathroom tiles. Me and my skin and my heartbeat and breath. Me and four walls until I get or am given a better idea.

Bethany falls in the door grinning with exertion.

'My, my, Lucy. Don't you look cheerful.'

I say nothing, already feeling like an old coat left out in the rain.

'Lucy, wake up, for Christ's sake.'

I shrug and look down into a mug of black tea, resting on a long-completed book of word puzzles. Wishing she'd shut up.

'This can't go on, you know. You've all the information, now – what are you going to do with it? And don't bother with any more of that shrugging business.'

I'd have to agree that my non-sequiturs are in short supply.

'So …. what, then?'

'It's time for a field trip. I don't know how you do it, sit about in this little box all day and night. It'd drive me nuts.'

I don't tell her how long it's been since I stopped waiting for something to happen.

I let her kit me up for an operation.

'Get into the spirit of the thing,' she says, when I don't look too enthused. 'I know you have it in you. Heard all about your little missions from before.'

I don't want to read too much into the repetition. The black jumper pulled over neck and arms, another pair of hands buckling me into my jeans. Might as well play along.

'So where are we going?'

'I have to show you a place ... no-one else knows about. I wasn't sure whether or not to take you along – can't have you blowing it wide open. You'll have to be discreet. Can you handle that?'

'Knock off the spy movie shit and you're on.'

Fuck it, I'm only there by default, half the time anyway. Any more unobtrusive, I'll disappear. No matter: we're off.

Outside, it's raining a little, just enough to remind my bare skin how it feels. Bethany leads us in the direction of the main street, marching too damn fast again. I've just broke into rhythm when she suddenly veers in to the right, through the gates marking the entrance to the park. Again. I'm not ready for all that staggered nature, not today.

'Bethany, I don't think I want to–'

'–Shut up,' she says, 'Just follow me.'

Staring at my feet again, eyes already swollen with crippled khaki. There's no-one around except an old man in a greasy trench-coat, circling a shattered nymph like he's contemplating a tricky Sudoku. Bethany links her arm through mine, bullying me into a jaunty stroll. Feet scuffling over beige stone chips, skirting the larger cracks in the slabs, I'm soon stood once more in front of the old glass house. Bethany peers over her shoulder, checking for witnesses.

'Think we're alright. Come on. And whatever you do, keep it cool. We're just taking a walk.'

We've circled the inside perimeter of the glass house five times, six, and still she refuses to give it away.

'Bethany. For Christ's sakes, there's nothing here.'

'Just keep it shut, Lucy. We've got to put in a decent bit of sightseeing, just till they stop watching.'

'We've been ... oh, for fuck's sake.'

At least we're boring them senseless. Only so many times I can stare at the same stunted flowers, cracked panes, gutter filth flowing down the centre of the slabs and still feign interest. Like any decent actress, Bethany lives the role, the tourist pointing out the plaques below the statues.

'See that? *Gifted to the great City of Glasgow.*' She sniggers, indicating a cluster of brass oblongs on a bench of splintering oak. *'In memory of Moira Dunne, who so loved this dear green place. For Alfred Maley, who tended this garden for generations to come. Julie Johnson. Kevin Canning. Mark Finch.* All these people used to come here in search of a … I don't know. Solace, solitude, peace. Green stuff. Something different. And just … just *look* at the place.'

'Yeah … I used to come here a lot, too. When I was stressed, when I couldn't come to a decision about something. I'd just walk around for a bit, take the air, people-watch. Shame it's such a shambles, now.'

'It's not a shame,' says Bethany, sucking her teeth, 'It's a fucking scandal. Letting something beautiful go to waste, so's we'll all just …forget there's the option. Don't want us having too many good reasons to go outside.'

I don't point out that nobody had been waiting for the gardens to fall to ruin before getting merrily accustomed to staying inside. I know my history. I've studied sociological patterns as dictated by disseminations of mass media, non-direct consumption, invisible marketing strategies. Green stuff shouldn't need an advertising campaign – it's just *there*, people should just *know* – but without sex, money, glamour or health benefits plotted on a chart or graph, nature slipped off the edge of our cultural consciousness. You don't need a walk in the park when you can jack in to virtual reality safaris. All the exotic blooms and endangered flora you desire can be shipped direct to your front door.

'Uh-huh. Are we done with the tour yet? This place …it kind of …I have to be in a certain frame of mind to be alright with being here.'

'When you're feeling sorry for yourself, aye?' Bethany frowns, a ghost of a sneer playing about her lips.

'No! Just … when I need to think! Okay? And I have to be alone for that.'

She lets it go. I can't explain what it means to have the emotional contours of a landscape reworked on the back of a revelation. I'm up close and personal with the same panes and plants and cracked concrete across which I've walked trying not to think about Caleb.

'Right …' she says, finally. 'I think we're good to go.'

She fights her way past the tangled grasses and braided branches in the central plaza. Once a sculpted attraction, shrubberies overhung with cherry blossoms and willows, blocks of agate and a dainty waterfall, it's now just horticulture's contribution to the circles in hell, a messy plot of scurvy vegetable matter competing for air, light, ground. I follow her into the mass, fighting back whipping branches and nettle shoots, catching my jeans and shirt on every loose thorn, the undergrowth a spray of razor wire.

'Hold it,' she says, once we're pretty much in the centre. 'Christ, look at this. It's only been a month, and it's already choked again.' She paces a three-foot square, flattening the growth, pawing like an animal preparing to lie down. She ferrets in her pocket, withdraws a blade and begins slicing at the carpet of plant matter.

'There!' she says, indicating a small square drain cover.

'You're shitting me. That's your secret place?'

'Wait till you've seen it,' she smirks, opening the trapdoor. A short step-ladder leads down into a narrow passageway, laid with terracotta tiles of the sort they used to use in public swimming baths.

'What *is* this?'

'It's been here for years,' she says. 'Series of tunnels running under the park, so's the caretakers could keep the place irrigated, regulate the temperature for the exotic plants. It didn't occur to the Management to check – I guess it's the last thing you'd look for when the point is to let something just *die*.'

'So you've got yourself a bunker ...'

Caleb would have loved that.

'You coming?'

She drops down without using the ladder. Of course.

'Nice,' I say.

'Come on, then! Jump down!'

'I don't think I'm made of your particular brand of rubber. And this isn't the moment to find out.'

I keep my face pressed close to the ladder. I don't like this at all. Every whisper of feet and hands across the rungs bounds and rebounds across the tiles, handfuls of coins through a vending machine. Every shadow grows a compound doppelganger as motion-sensor fluorescents flicker to life. I've spent more time contemplating confined spaces over the past few days than I have space in my skull to process. When I drop to the floor, it's like a bomb going off from my insides to my edges, every muscle spasm a rumbling bolt, every snap of tendon a slamming of doors.

'Well?' asks Bethany, still grinning.

'Could use a Jacuzzi ...'

'Shut it. We've work to do. Follow me.'

128

Pipes line the corridors, shaking their rust flakes like a terrible skin disease. Others plunge ceiling-ward, presumably feeding sprinklers and irrigation canals. The odd comedy thermometer juts out from the wall, all needles pointing to zero. All this time I've been wandering the park as though it were the essence of the solitary and elemental. And all this time I've been walking over the bones of a different kind of organism, empty corridors echoing with long-abandoned attempts at controlling the spread of the rot.

Every fifteen feet or so, the walls dip back into recessed steel doors. Bethany pays no attention, but there's a thump in my gut every time we approach another. Expecting someone to come crashing into the passageway with a basket of needles, I halt and jump, jump and halt like an engine refusing to catch.

'Lucy! What the hell are you doing?'

I didn't think she'd noticed.

'Sorry. Just ... well, you know. Reminds me of ...'

'Fuck's sake, you've picked a fine time to start being open to associations!'

'I'm *sorry*! You don't *know*, Bethany – you've always been on the *other side* ...'

'Aye, aye, whatever. Rub it in. Wouldn't want you thinking about anyone other than yourself for a minute, would we?'

Okay. It's not that I've *forgotten* what she's been through, that she's been messed with herself, it's just ... she's so *enamelled*, it's difficult to reconcile her with the same sense of helplessness.

'I'm sorry,' I say, for the third time in as many minutes. 'I'm not ... used to this. Shit keeps coming back, like ... flooding up and floating away before I can figure out what I'm seeing ... it's making me edgy ...'

She sighs, a stuttered hiss that fills the corridor with feedback.

'It's fine. I don't much like it down here either.'

She takes my arm again. Maybe needing it as much as I do. We're picking up speed, now, Bethany's lips pursing at each recess we pass. She's counting down to what she's been looking for. Finally we break into a junction, a four-way crossroads leading God knows where. I can't figure out whether the park's far larger than I imagined, or if the corridors seem endless simply because there's so little to look at. We take the left, proceed another hundred yards or so, before Bethany pulls us up short in front of the second door to the left.

'This is us.'

'Uh ... cool.'

'Give me a minute.'

She dips again into the lining of her jacket.

'You ready?' she asks, flipping her head back, jerking upright.

'Ready for what?'

'To see ... to see ... to really *see.*'

She opens the door. We step inside. She locks the door.

There are too many echoes on too many levels.

I will die happy, perhaps, if I never again have to sit on another of these plastic institutional chairs, steel pipes protesting every time I shift my weight. I'd really rather stand, but Bethany tells me I'm better off preparing for the worst.

Underground and windowless, no outside light throws bubbled reflections against the television screen.

'What's that?' I ask, pointing to the box underneath the set.

'It's a VCR.'

'A what, now?' Those are the stuff of legend.

'Oh come on, don't tell me you've never met a die-hard fan of solid media.'

Video tape. I remember. My grandmother used to ask me every birthday or Christmas if there were any *video films* I might like. I've never seen a player for real – it's so *clumsy*. Reassuring, though. When she slips in the tape, the sounds are those of real mechanical processes at work. I rest my hand on the top of the box and grin, a child, to feel the casing humming underneath my fingers. It will not fold itself up or self-destruct or fit into a pocket. It will leave a mark, make a splash, a dreadful racket should it be decanted into a river, thrown out onto the road.

'Here we go. Hang on, Lucy.'

Civilians like me are not supposed to see the recordings. Neither is it my privilege or purpose to pass judgement on aesthetics or artistry – all that attention to composition , mise-en-scene, editing, effects, lens, focus, fidelity of colour and sound and all such errata should mean nothing anymore. Should have had it beaten or bored out, dampened and tamped to a sizzle of something fluttering in the corner of the eye.

I'm watching him move around the room. Not focused on what I *can* see so much as what the cameras have failed to pick up. His face is a poem with many metric feet, each with its own message and inflection, and here they are all run together, blurred together, a mess of soggy pixels and ill-defined parameters. His figure is a moving sculpture through which every jolt of energy flows in a beat, a writhe, skin underlay resolving and dissolving, there and gone, potential and expended. On tape, just a stretch of dripped wax wrapped in Facility fatigues.

Bethany keeps her hands on my shoulder throughout. Again, I'm not going anywhere in the face of what I'm here to see.

'Look at him. Really look at him, Lucy.'

'Uh-huh.' I don't have words for what I'm looking at.

Memory proves surprisingly fluent, compared to this paltry interpretation of same. The tape captures him leaning against the door jamb, listening out for footsteps. Only I can see the twinge in the jaw, the pulling of strings about the eye. Only I know what he's doing with his hands. From here, a wringing hysteric. *I* know he's testing the strength in each finger. I can perceive shattered angles in the set of his back. Gone is the lofty surveyor of territory of midnight screenings at apartment windows. Instead, a motionless cower, tension awaiting a blow. I'm shocked by his baldness. Not so much for aesthetic purposes; more that it means he's nothing to hide behind when they come looking. The vagueness of his scalp frustrates. Up close, I'd be able to chart the ridges and contours of his skull, something I have touched, but never seen. A violation. They've got there first, peeled a layer under which it's never occurred to me to check.

The door flies open. The blow sends his pale streak wheeling across the floor. He lands on a narrow bed which takes up most of the room. In walks a column of beige oblong panels, the head also cropped to the quick. Bethany has to catch me as I topple from the chair, breath seething in my throat like a spiked cigarette. The Manager.

I should have been prepared. Bethany has spared me few details. But it's still a shock to see someone I'd regarded as protector walk into my Caleb's room with shoulders taut with murder. I'm waiting for the Manager to hand over a bag of civilian gear, a clipboard to sign.

Instead he leans over the bed, Caleb scrabbling to sit up, his feet past the Manager's legs and onto the floor. A brief verbal exchange, of which I can't intuit a word. Under more amenable circumstances, it would please me to recognize that secret-keeper's trick of Caleb's. On screen, his mouth a disk-drive slit, whilst for real he'd be talking round corners. Sleight of lips. He used to do it for me, sometimes, playing around. Doing those pre-Millennium movie stars whose cigarette angles said more than their words ever could.

The Manager comes ever closer without a visible shuffle of feet, gliding on castors or strung from the ceiling. He looms without throwing a shadow. Calm down. Just bleak overhead lighting, that's all, that's all.

Caleb's six feet in height don't show up on the tape. He's pushed down, curled up. The Manager presses Caleb's legs to the bed, shin to shin, and grabs Caleb's skull in both hands. Caleb's face disappears for a moment as the Manager bends over, leans in, as though for a kiss. Were I there in the flesh, I'd be able to see tendons flexing in waxen hands, a rare flush of colour on the Manager's lips.

I shrink back in my own chair, my body wheeling, my eyes refusing to follow suit.

I strangle my vowels. There are no lessons here.

'Why do I have to see this, Bethany?'

She steps into my three-quarter gaze. So as not to interfere with my view of the screen.

'There's a difference, Lucy, between hearing something and *feeling* it, knowing it. You've lost things before, even after the accident. This way it's more likely to stick around.'

It's already pasted to the back of my eyelids, will follow into sleep like embroidery on a curtain.

'It's just a shame there's still such a remove – that the *smell* of it, the *taste* of metal filings, the barest tang of the sweat in the room … you don't ever lose *that*.'

I'm already tasting my own blood as the tension makes mincemeat of the inside of my mouth. Bethany steps away. Then action.

The Manager's elbows fly up to the sides, reasserting his grip on Caleb's head, a weary driver stretching arms up from a steering wheel. All moves too fast for the screen resolution to keep up. Caleb is weightless: one twist of the Manager's shoulders and he's throw across the tiny room, impacting the wall on the other side of the bed. His shoulder blades hit before his head, for which I'm obscenely grateful, but the contortions of limb as he crumples to the floor are too manic, too random, to process in terms of probable pain.

Caleb lies still for a long moment. Wicked irony that my heart does not, as it's supposed to, cease to beat.

Finally he unfurls himself from his bodily twist and reaches for the edge of the bed. The Manager glides back, disappearing from the frame. I've a full-length view of Caleb slowly getting to his feet. I can tell from the jut of his hips, the folded arms, the casual spikes of knee and elbow, that he's trying to appear unfazed. I am now glad I can't see the shimmer and shake of his fingers, thigh muscles and lips. I am too aware of how far I've come from him, so far that I haven't even got the right to be proud.

The Manager hasn't finished yet. He enters the frame once more, slowly, still on that strange heavenly glide. Caleb shifts his weight from one leg to the other, turning his head to the wall. I can't quite make out what he's doing with his fingers – either beckoning or unfurling a sly middle finger – but either way he's done with being polite.

The Manager likes straight answers. I remember. Likes things done correctly, by the book. Likes everything in its right place, taking up no more than the necessary space, and a disrespectful digit has no place in his ideal panorama.

This time he needs only one hand. This time Caleb doesn't make it quite all the way across the room. The first blow had landed on the left cheekbone, the second on the jaw. Bethany has her hand on top of my head, now, keeping my eyes tilted up to the screen. I'm half-expecting her to lean into my ear and whisper *This is the best part,* two kids in the back row at an adult movie.

Caleb takes a little longer to recover. The Manager stands off to one side, watching, arms stiff and taut by his side. Caleb struggles to stand. One leg then another fall out from under him like a baby-stepping foal. Eventually he settles for the knees, hands otherwise occupied. One holds his lower jaw to the upper. The other catches mouthfuls of blood and shards of teeth large enough to show up on the tape.

The Manager moves in for another bout of looming. The screen becomes the opening and closing of an Oriental fan in grey and scarlet. Caleb wheels his arm out to one side, unleashing a handful, an armful, of blood and spit and broken teeth. A crimson Rorschach hits the Manager square in the chest. So much of it that the poor grain of the video aids the impression he's just been shot. He rears back, forward, back, gathering momentum. Hands once more strapped around his jaw, Caleb digs his elbows into his chest, his hips and shoulders popping a beat toward each other, snapping back, like a plastic ruler waved before a blackboard. Literally buckled with mirth. I can't help it. I follow him, as in everything else.

Bethany hits a button, freezing the frame to bars of shattered static. But not before I see the Manager charging across the frame toward the source of the blood bomb on his chest.

'What are you doing? I want to see more. I want to know.'

'You're not seeing another damn thing until you stop that laughing.'

My chest hurts. She shakes her head, knots fingers across the nape of her neck, and kneels on the concrete by my chair.

'You're scaring me.'

I say nothing.

' Look at me. Lucy, fucking *look* at me.'

I can't take my eyes off the screen, tilting my head this way and that as though the bars of the static cage have dimensions around which I can look.

'Put it back on.'

'It's just more of the same.'

This rather excites me. More Caleb, more movement, my gap-filling sketches growing ever more detailed.

'Please.'

'No, Lucy. You don't want to see it.'

Bit late to be passing judgements, making assumptions. If it's a matter of taste, I've a six-month window of limit-testing to make up for. I've been dead. I've seen nothing. She can't show me what I've been missing and just cut off the supply. All such trips down memory lane should be nicely rounded, balanced, savoured.

'I'm sorry for putting you through that, Lucy, I just thought you should know.'

I'm waiting for the lesson to scroll across the screen, black and white, capital letters. I'm supposed to twin what I have just seen with what has already happened to me – and with what I know still to be going on. I'm supposed to get up out of the chair and stomp around the room. Tear the place up. Kick a hole in the screen.

I know I'm sure as hell not supposed to be laughing. Maybe I should just pass out again. I seem to have rather a flair for bowing out of consciousness when situations flag up no easier options.

Maybe I should hit her again. I rather enjoyed the last round.

Bethany finally shakes her head and makes for the door. The tumbling of tongues and bolts sounds all too familiar. I'm slowing down. Laughter trickles into that stomach pit in which I keep all that I'm not yet ready to face. She switches off the television and turns the screen to the wall, for reasons I imagine have no real basis in logic. Kneeling down before me once more, she takes me by the wrists and pulls me to my feet. I slacken the outrage in my arms and follow on. There are comforts to be had in playing the invalid. She won't expect too much of me, not yet. She'll push back the talking-over, the making of plans, the querying of impressions, until I appear to have jumped back into myself.

'Whatever you do, Lucy, keep hold of this. I know it's not pleasant, but you can't get to forgetting what we're up against. You can't keep ignoring what's been done to you. What they're doing to Caleb. Do you hear me?'

I nod. I wait. I follow back up into the half-light, already shunting impressions aside to make space for fresh ones. Like, I don't know how I'd ever missed this place. Like, I thought hidden places had all run dry. Like, I can't remember ever having been so tired. Like, I'd be quite happy to go back to my flat, bury myself in the blankets and sleep until whatever is coming is over.

Bethany has to drag me along. I've forgotten what to do with my feet. She seems pleased that I've quit laughing, but not at the expense of my conscious involvement. She tightens her grip.

'Remember this.'

Murder in her voice. Must be half-tempted to give me another kicking. An array of blood-and-sweat smells to hammer this as far into my head as it will go. Not to worry. I can't get rid of it. The active participation element of recall makes it impossible to forget. Like back in the early days of me and Caleb. I'd been unsure where we he going with all of his protests, and whether I was going *with* him. I'd delete and re-enter his telephone number every time we fought and made up, each time determined to have it over with. I did it so often I'd wound up retaining the digits anyway – I could get rid of the LCD entry, but not the act of punching the combination itself. Terribly frustrating, how much I can retain when I really don't want to.

'Time to go back to your place,' Bethany's voice cuts through my reverie.

So. I'll get a sit-down, a cigarette, a blood-sugar boost, some sleep. Then it'll be time to get down to the business of how we react to this *knowing*.

Overground

Infighting. That push and pull between your desire for an easy life, and his belief that there's more for you than that. That flat. The Tube. The perfecting of routines. Speaking only when spoken to.

You tell yourself there's still a kick inside. That thinking about letting your impulses seethe up into action is as good as actually doing something. This delusion will come to be as comfortable as the histories they'll sell you. Reality's just so messy, sometimes.

Try to remember what he was about. You think only in touches, gestures, colours, sounds. Try to remember words. The ones you didn't like, those barriers between you. They're important. Take a leap.

You are walking with him over the railroad bridge. The first hint that something might be going wrong. The last serious conversation over which there was a point of departure – the realisation you were nowhere near as serious about this as he had to be.

Beautiful night for it. Derailing the trains had been a recent development; the points of contact between the wheels and the track were yet to rust. A great silver equality sign unrolling pure and liquid from your feet to the horizon. Under the bridge and far off to the right, the city hissed and brooded, fresh fires throwing up sheets of smoke and powdered glass. Developments lopped apart from the city centre to the outskirts, the braiding, breeding, light-choked motorways enveloping what remained in an infinity of figure eights. Sky overhead tried throwing draperies of mauve and violet over the sprawl of liquid orange; both parties met in the middle, hissed, blackened, prickled the stars to amethyst shards by virtue of the juxtaposition. The tops of the steel and glass towers shimmer that way objects sometimes do when trapped in air currents of extreme heat; faces over birthday cakes blazing with candles. It's not the temperature – it's forever too mild – it's just the a a mass of spare electricity, ions popping like balloons, giving the tower bases the wobble of champagne glasses in the hands of drunken debutantes.

He'd suggested a walk in the interests of a little old-fashioned thinking time. You knew better; those flares to the north-west came blurting from the factory, closed this afternoon. He'd had too many hands on that: trying to win over the owners, and in failing that, trying to stir up the multitudes. Which meant he was under suspicion on both sides.

Which meant he was in for it.

He won't name names. A pattern he'll repeat. You suspect he'd done it himself: he got that way, sometimes, so bored and tired of circular arguments going nowhere. He'd reckoned it time for something to talk about. You don't mind: from afar, at least, the riots are pretty. People taking to the streets again, brave enough, for just one night, get up from their couches, step out from behind those heavy curtains. It gave you hope somewhere inside you don't yet know how to hold on to.

'Jesus. Look at the sky,' he says. 'Fucking ... opaque. That's a sixty-denier firmament. And we're all just stood here underneath like ... like ...'

'Like what? Since when are we meant to do anything else but look and stand underneath? That's kind of the point, unless you've got a massive Brillo pad or something.'

'You don't have to do that. You can't, not forever. Sooner or later you're going to have to make up your mind. Have an opinion about something.'

He stopped, grabbed you by the shoulders. You're unsure as to whether he'd lean in for a kiss or throw you off the bridge.

'So much for quiet, thinking time,' you say, no humour in your voice.

'I think too much. You don't think enough. Can't you hear that? People taking to the streets ...'

He looks so tired, eyes sliding back in his head like a cat's. Time does strange things to people, these days.

'Isn't that what you wanted?' you ask. 'People to start...protesting, or whatever?'

He shook his head. 'It's not enough. They don't know what they're doing.'

'Aren't they a union, or something? That kind of implies organisation.'

'You don't understand. We're looking too hard at the periphery. The details. We're forgetting what we're up against. Every time it seems like we're winning, they...fuck, they turn it around, come up with something else we'll end up going along with all over again.'

'Explain. Please.'

'Right ... okay. Example. The flat situation, right? We ruined the first place because we were pissed off about being kicked out. Right?'

'Yeah, so?'

'So something should have happened. We should have been punished or blacklisted or something. Instead, woops, magic, we're offered a new place, with the powers that be flapping their gums about having listened to our complaints ...'

'And that's a bad thing? Hello, new place!'

'Yeah, but now ... we're owing. For something we could have done without. Flat thing's just an example, Lucy, but a good one – people get into living-situation trouble all the time, or at least they used to. It's awkward, aye, a pain in the arse, but you always manage something, right? Without being told where or when or how, without being practically carried over the fucking threshold by your landlord. It stinks. I don't know of what yet, but it stinks.'

'Better than being homeless. Unless you want me to call in a few favours? One of Murray's lot?'

137

His shoulders tauten, a low growl rising in his throat. You shouldn't have mentioned Murray. You know how it infuriates him to be reminded of his reliance on anyone, never mind your dealer.

'Cheers. Thanks for that. Thanks a fucking bunch.'

'Calm down. What's your problem?'

'You think you'd do better calling favours in with those reprobates than having me sort it out? Is that it? If not the Management, a raft of fucking cokeheads and their heavies?'

'Chrissakes, Caleb, I was only talking hypothetically. Trying to make the point that we've got it alright, with the Management – lesser of two evils, if you like.'

'I'd take care of it, Lucy. If I had to. I'd have gotten us a place.'

He wanders to the edge, leans against a concrete support, slides down to sit with his back to the cityscape. Head in hands, elbows on knees, a body-cage, on the defensive. You hold your own for moment, making much of shuffling shoulder-blades and vertebrae, before moving over to join him, clearing your throat until he looks up.

'Hey. I don't ... want to be in with them any more than you do, Caleb. I don't want to be in with anyone but you. I'm just ... you never get tired? Like ... like watching the city burn, and, seeing nothing coming of it? We're still not free, not the way you want us to be. We'd have to go a lot further – and I'm talking distance, here – for that. Maybe you're going to have to learn to compromise. And if that makes us weak, then ... at least we won't have to be so frightened all the time.'

He frowns, gets to his feet in a slick whip of limb, grabs you by the shoulders.

'Are you frightened?' he asks.

'Aren't you?'

'No. What are you so afraid of?'

'It's happening, Caleb. In spite of all this fun we're having, all the little pranks we're playing. Friends of ours ... colleagues ... neighbours ... all just disappearing, or worse. You seem to forget that part, when you're all kitted up for another night of frolics. You're hitting out at abstracts, missing the real casualties. Things are happening, things I can't explain, and I'm scared. And if you're not, you should be.'

'You think I've forgotten? Why the hell d'you think I keep going? I knew those people too, Lucy. I'm missing folks I care about. And yeah, I'm scared – but not as much as I am of what would happen if I didn't keep trying.'

'And what's that, exactly?'

'I join them. The unquestioning. Mannequins. I have to keep going.'

'And what happens when the Management catch up with you? With us? We're fucked either way, no? At least if we ... play along, we'll be safe.'

He pushes you away, not as gently as you've come to expect. He spits with laughter, shoulder-blades tautening around him like wings.

'Go with what you know, is that it?'

'Yeah. Not particularly sexy, sure, but safe. Aren't you listening?'

'Yeah. I'm listening. I can't believe you, Lucy. You'd be satisfied with that?'

'I don't know.'

'If you were, you're not—'

'—what? I'm not the girl you thought I was? Is that it? Make up your mind, Caleb. You're either with me or you're not. My ideals may not be as sophisticated as yours, but that shouldn't matter. We should be enough. Or is that a cliché, too?'

You're about to start crying. It seems very important to keep it in — this is enough of a melodrama as it is, without the lather of a woman in hysterics. He can hear the hitch in your voice, though —there's still a catalogue of emotional response behind all that soap-boxing. You're sliding round the concrete pillar, out of sight. He follows. You can feel the fizz of his skin, drawing the hairs up from your own. He takes your hand, tentative, not sure yet what to do with it. He pulls you into the crook of his ribs, spreads a spider of fingers across your scalp. You wish he weren't still holding so much kit under his jacket, tool-belts and notebooks and laminates grumbling in the space between you.

'All that talk about what we know ...about being safe ... Lucy. I know it's important. I know how easy it'd be to just give up. You're right, I probably would get used to it. But see ... it's like ...'

You turn your head, tilting back to look at him. The blaze from the city gilds his brow and top lip, tearing the contours from his smile, blackening the sockets of his eyes. You're not going to cry anymore. You're too tired, running low on responses.

'... it's like what?'

'It's like ... there's two routes. Two ways this can go. See, if I do quit it, start doing what I'm told, settle, co-operate ... I know what will happen. Good or bad, get used to it or not, nothing will happen. A known quantity. Whereas ... if I keep going ... sure, it's far from safe. It could get ugly. But at least there's a chance, a random factor, a possibility that things might change. There's got to be somebody, calling up the Management, keeping at it ...'

'But why does it have to be you? What about all those guys who said they'd be there alongside? Where are they? Why do you have to do this on your own?'

'Those guys didn't have it. Didn't care enough. They talk big, Lucy, but the second there's a better offer, they're finished. Lush apartments, cushy jobs, arrangements— can't really blame them for keeping things simple, but that's not for

139

me. Not for you, either, if you really ask yourself … what you want from the way you live.'

You're still waiting for it to crash over, the blood-heat and sweat-reek of the protest to sink into your bones, gear you up, drum-beat your desires. You're going to have to do better than borrowed enthusiasm. So much for honesty – you can't tell him you're still waiting for your heart to catch up with your hands. But not yet. Wind this up. Quitter, peacemaker, headache-protester – this conversation is not going in any direction of yours, had you a compass point tilting in the first place.

'Okay. Okay,' you say, dipping out from under his arms. This is an eye-contact moment. 'I'm shutting up, now.'

'Don't be like that. I'm not going to push it. I'm just telling you where I'm going. However much I want you there with me, it's still your choice to make.'

'I want to. Be there. Just … I'll pick it up as I go along. I will.'

He swivels from the flames. A gaze without depth; stones dropped into the pools would fall forever.

'I love you, Lucy. Whatever else we have to say, or do, or be, I need you to remember that.'

You're supposed to say I love you, too. Your reaction time blurred by hearing it after a quarrel; sugar-clot in powdered glass. It's nice. Tilt your head back, now, kiss him. Hold onto that. Spinning tightly in your own neon cocoon, at least for now.

'It's getting cold,' he says, drawing back for breath.

'Yeah. Let's go.'

No argument as to where or what or why. You'll follow him for now, and that's enough.

PART FOUR

HISTORICITY

18th March 2024

Bethany's been gone since yesterday lunchtime. I have had way too much time to myself. Time to think. Time to work on *not* thinking. So much has happened in such a small space of time, clocks mock, turn their faces from me. Calendars shrug their pages to the floor.

It hits me when I have to fill in forms. Or have them filled in for me by an echo on the other end of a telephone line. Help someone or something plug data into some greater collective. I suppose I'm much like anyone else in this respect – so much of who we are relegated to filing cabinets in the back of the mind until such times as we are called upon to remember. Abstract – for the loggers and speakers as much as the readers and spoken-to. Paper space, a play of pixels and electrons, a slice of an ethereal pie. A sense of it disappearing as soon as it's entered. I resent having to speak of any of it at all: that fence-post jab into the heart, until the next distraction pours fresh concrete over recall.

She's doing a survey. They're clever about it – don't give you room for manoeuvre. It's not like I'm doing anything important – sitting on my bed trying to read around the torn and blackened sections of a book – but the ring of the telephone always scares me, makes me think I'm up to something I shouldn't be. The book splashes to the floor; I bounce up from the mattress, roll toward the telephone table and simply stare it out. The answering machine knows I'm here and won't pick up. The ringing gets progressively louder, a compound screech of metal on metal on metal, rattling up the wall, peeling the windows from their frames. I have to answer. The handset throbs so angry in the cradle I'm scared it'll flay the skin from my palm. I knock it to the floor with the toe of an empty shoe and yell, '*HELLO SORRY I'LL BE RIGHT WITH YOU!*'

Then making scuffling noises like I've just dropped the phone and it's no big deal and I'm not afraid of a plastic brick, a jet engine in wipe-clean acetylene. I'm still flinching when I pick it up and press it to my ear, a half-heard cluster of call-centre voices, employees all trained to match the blurry inflections of a dial tone.

'Miss Lucy Chalmers?' says the telephone, a woman, always a woman tactic. A female voice is supposed to calm you down.

'Yes? Yes …' I'm never quite sure myself, I don't hear my own name very often anymore.

'You're speaking to Department Head A.M Langford. I'm conducting a survey on behalf of Morgan, Steppes, Rithe and Clew. May I ask you a few questions?'

I know what this means. I scan the empty room, clear surfaces, paperback dashed to the carpet tiles and say, 'I'm very sorry, but this isn't a good time. I can't speak to you right now, I'm afraid.'

'I'm sorry to hear that. Why not?'

'I uh … I uh … I have an appointment to attend, I have to get ready.'

'No, no, our records indicate that you have no prior arrangements at this point in time, Miss Chalmers.'

'Can't you call back?'

'No, Miss Chalmers. We have reason to believe it unlikely that you would make yourself available to speak with us, should we arrange a time and date. Now, this will only take up a few minutes of your time.'

'Yes, but—'

'Miss Chalmers, it really is in your best interests to speak to us *now*. Otherwise we'll have to send a staff member along for a door-to-door visit, and we'll have to charge you for the privilege.'

And that's just too much. However desperate I often get for company, something to break the vacuum of my breath built up in the flat, there's no way I'm facing down another clipboard. 'Okay. Okay. I think I can … rearrange.'

'Splendid! Now, we'll just start with the basics …'

I clap the handset to my ear and scrape the book up from the floor, before sprawling once more on the bed to stare up at the ceiling. I'm barely aware of the noises I make in response to her questions – name, age, education, occupation, blood type, medical history – none of it seems to belong to me. I'm going through the motions with the book, turning pages at what seem the right intervals. I'm trying not to hum a tune to mark the beat her questions, my answers, the blear of touch-tone buttons marking the end of level of the questionnaire. It no longer bothers me that I don't have a clue who they are or what they do – those un-pretty names strung over a desk, heading up branded stationery, somewhere in some office on the outskirts of the city.

'Miss Chalmers? Are you still there?'

'Huh?'

There's clearly a fine line between being accommodating and being absent.

'Miss Chalmers, please pay attention.'

'Sorry. I'm listening.'

'Now, to get a fully comprehensive note of your history and circumstances, we need to know about your family. Siblings?'

'None. Only child.'

'Parents' ages and occupations?'

I have to cover my mouth and pinch my nostrils to keep from laughing.

'Miss *Chalmers*. Are you *listening*?'

'Yes. And ... *not applicable*, is what I guess you should put. I have no idea.'

'Of your parents' ages?'

'Oh ... I don't know. D.O.B pre-Millennium seventy-four, seventy-six, mother and father, respectively.'

'Aren't they still ... with us?'

There's a vague hint of tact and tender feeling in the question. It's too much.

'I don't know. I haven't seen them for years. I can't answer any of your questions on the subject, *Miss Langdon.*'

'Langford.'

'Langford. Sorry. Such common names.'

'Please don't change the subject, Miss Chalmers. Where are your parents?'

'I don't *know*. I'm twenty-three years old, living independently of them, as you can see from your records. I don't see why it should matter.'

The telephone sulks in my hand as the voice on the other end sucks its teeth.

'I get the impression, Miss Chalmers, that you may need a little time to think this through. We have plenty of information to work from for now, but we must resume this discussion at a later date, perhaps when you have relevant notes or documentation to hand.'

I don't tell her there's nothing to think about. I don't tell her it's all over, and has been for longer than I care to remember.

'Hmmm.'

'Either myself or one of my colleagues will call back over the next few days. I don't suppose there's any one time or date that's more convenient than another?'

I see her looking at my details on screen. Unemployed, lives alone, no reason for leaving the flat save the odd repeat prescription collection or check-up at the Follow-Up Clinics. Wondering, perhaps, why I'm so often logged as having passed the main street checkpoints or Tube guard boxes at random points of the afternoon and evening.

'No. I can't guarantee when I'll be in, though.'

'That's perfectly alright. We shall leave a message, a number for you to call. I must remind you, though, that if you fail to do so we *will* have to dispatch a representative.'

'Fine. Cool. Whatever.'

'Goodbye, Miss Chalmers. Thank you for your patience. Your time is very important to us.'

One of us cuts the other off before I can ask *Then who the fuck are you?*

I don't act out the way I imagine I'm supposed to. I don't perform a rage, a frustration, an upset. I don't throw the handset across the room, or open drawers and cupboard doors just to slam them shut. I don't crank up the loud music (I don't have any, anymore). I don't draw the curtains closed and cry into my pillow. It's not the same with no-one watching, no-one to soothe, no-one to scream at the messes I'd made. Tantrums and tears aren't in-built ventilation systems. They're meant to be seen, heard, remembered. It's all I can do not to turn on the TV, anything to plug the gaps in the silence. I should go for a walk, get myself some air, but the woman has made it perfectly clear that I'm to expect a call, for which I suppose I'd best get my thoughts in order.

Parents are supposed to teach us how to conduct ourselves in the society into which they've decided to bring us. They're meant to be a generation ahead in terms of learning how to cope with any *changes*, as time and space and progress continue to teeter through their slow, hypnotic dance. I don't know who screwed up which end of the bargain, but ...we were all left, are still left, floundering in our mistakes.

It's difficult to think in terms of fact, gradation, statistic. It's difficult to see the downward spiral when you're standing in the middle, watching what seemed no more troubling than a tacit agreement, a general consensus. Times like this I'm kind of grateful for the numbness, the silence, the blank stare of the walls bouncing back only my own take on the subject. They'll study it in years to come, reference it in sitcoms, bring out a line of joke kitchen aprons and coffee coasters, immortalize forever the tragic upshot of the Tens and Twenties, Third Time Unlucky.

I think my parents and upbringing were as average as they come, at least until I hit my mid-teens and started to pay more attention. My mother was a dental receptionist, my father made deliveries for a catalogue company. We lived in a two-bedroom terraced house in one of the nicer satellite towns on the edge of the conurbation. I went to school and did my homework. They went to work and got home by six, in time for us to all sit around the table for a home-cooked dinner. We watched non-threatening television broadcasts until no later than nine o'clock in the evening. I got five pieces of fruit or vegetables and a glass of half-fat milk every day. Neither of my parents exceeded the recommended daily units of alcohol. They seemed to get on alright – I don't remember either fighting or icy silences, and, at least twice a month, they got me a babysitter and took themselves to dinner or a film. We were left untouched by religion, violence, addiction, terminal or mental illness. I wouldn't say we were *happy*, but neither were we pulled too harshly toward any other extreme. It pains me, sometimes, to think how *pedestrian* we were. There are supposed to be plot-worthy extenuating circumstances behind the disintegration of a family unit.

Then the restrictions became harsher, sharper, grew many more fingers and eyes. I can forgive, I can understand, the means by which the grown-ups just let everything *happen*. There are twenty-four hours to get through each day, seven of these in a week, thus immersing each new diktat in such a slurry of the everyday that it's impossible to devote much consideration to each thump of a portcullis. We don't have space in our heads to elevate every thought, idea, impulse, opinion to universal dimensions. We just want to *get by*, in which case we're all pretty happy to do as we're told.

Everything was illegal, or so heavily advised against that the sheer efforts involved in carrying anything out squeezed any pleasure taken to a shrivel, a pulp. No more drinking or smoking except in the confines of one's own home, and even then there were limits on quantities permitted in any one household at a time. No going out after dark, seeing more than three friends at once. No more theatre or cinema, sports or live music. Public houses became pit-stops. Driving restricted to within the city limits, and in any case severely discouraged. Both father and mother were retrained in order to carry out more efficient versions of their jobs from home, online, on the phone, from a chair. And nobody complained. Folks – mine, anyway – seemed quite satisfied with this new order. Stress, sickness and crime levels dropped to a low hum – movement and human interaction being prerequisites for the germination of each.

But people are people – removal of the spurs of instinct and impulse leaves these inbuilt proclivities struggling toward new and increasingly uncomfortable stimulants. By making everything illegal, everything unacceptable, the Management hadn't accounted for the lengths to which folks would go to push *legal* activities to the limits. Household melodramas and kitchen sink subplots became the order of the day, and I don't mean *fighting*, either. The Management had way too many eyes and ears out for flaring tempers. No. Folks pushed themselves and each other the only way they knew how – subtleties, manipulations and exponential levels of boredom and repetition.

Some folks picked up tips and tricks from the newspapers, magazines and lifestyle shows, and simply dedicated their every moment to standardizing their environments, minds and bodies. My father, sat at the computer, directed toward the homes of other citizens more domestic exercise equipment than had been bought and sold over the entirety of the twentieth century. Everyone jumped on the treadmill or the exercise bike at five p.m., tuned into the workout broadcasts and ran on into *nothing* until nine o'clock or exhausted collapse, whichever came first. My father worked out. He'd spent his late teens in the Navy, and thought it time to reinvest in the arts of stamina and strength. Whenever I picture him, he's multi-tasking. Sweating, closed-faced, staring into a screen strapped to the cross-trainer, muttering the odd affirmative or negative in response to any questions without ever once turning from the abstract movement of goods to addresses.

Whilst they still could, folks who retained a glimmer of creativity turned to cookery and interiors. Thus could whole evenings be spent turning wooden fruit crates into aged-effect media shelving units, stencilling half-drop sunflowers across their living room walls or pushing the culinary boundaries of their microwaves and food processors. My mother's one goal in life for a number of years was to shave an extra five seconds from her three-minute soufflé.

Not that my parents didn't share the odd moment of respite. When energy reserves and craft supplies dried up for the evening, all citizens turned to the back page of the newspaper to tackle crosswords and Sudoku puzzles, on four carefully audited levels of difficulty. My father would tear the page down the middle, hand one half to my

146

mother, and the evening would pass in silence broken only by the damp hissing of breath around pen lids.

And the city simmered down, all was under control, and I got up and went to school and did my homework. And I didn't read the paper, and I didn't worry about war or guns or rape or violence, and in my naivety I looked forward to going to university, where I was sure I'd finally find the stimulation I didn't know I was doing without.

Which all sounds perfectly reasonable, pleasantly benign, but it wasn't enough. Folks who'd have sold their souls for a little peace and quiet and time to themselves began to miss the sound of other voices, particularly craving tones bathed in dissent. Folks grew too accustomed to the touch of their own skin, where once had been other textures, other temperatures. On top of which, all this lifestyle improvement, concentration-honing and body sculpting didn't seem quite so much fun when nobody but immediate family and the odd – increasingly rare – visitor got to see, hear, experience the new and improved version.

Thus, domestic crises and debates began to flare up out of nowhere, founded on problems and lies and slights and habits invented pretty much for their own sake. Marriage was still an ideal lifestyle choice – if facilitated by numerous administrative bodies and matchmaking software – but so too were the processes following on from those unions that didn't work out. People soon didn't mind being set up with spouses they'd never met – the ceremony itself broke up the passage of the year, and the prospect of divorce and all attendant processes guaranteed distractions and entertainments for at least a month or two. Each of these rites still had to take place in public, in a court of law, and this provided plenty of people with excuses to leave the house, perhaps buy a new pair of shoes. By the time I was sixteen, I'd already been approached by five or six men of all ages and disciplines, men I'd never met, never wanted to meet, who wanted to marry me just for the privilege of divorcing me later. I was too naive to think anything of it – the farce was merely something to be folded up with every other adolescent rite of passage.

Affairs, too, became the stuff of routine. From information taken in surveys, from data passed over desks in doctor's surgeries, the Management recognized the need for the populace to inject some interest into their routines. They kindly set up the Extra-Marital Liaison Committee, vetting and matching prospective partners in need of stimulation outside of the confines of marriage, uniting them in so-called Scandal Templates. It seemed to keep people happy for at least a year, maybe two, but only now, hearing stories from colleagues and

147

acquaintances, does it become clear why so many people started *losing* it.

See, affairs had been the stuff of fictions, fantasies, of dreams both good and bad. They were smoke and mirrors, phone calls and clandestine meeting-places – the EMLC just didn't cut it in comparison. Affairs thrived, amid all the heat and haze and murmuring lips silenced with a kiss, on *secrecy*. Permitting – *prescribing* – extra-marital liaisons did away with any satisfaction to be found in the arms of another. The Third Twenties heralded the first and only decade in which those caught either side of a Scandal Template were as likely to protest exhaustion or migraine as they were when in bed with their actual spouses. But, since it provided a decent spot of aerobic exercise for the body, a smudge of stimulation for the mind, and most importantly an excuse to leave the house, it was The Done Thing. By the time the Management realized just how variable the degrees of acceptance could be, the damage had been done.

The papers and broadcasts devoted no attention to these miscalculations. Fights, tantrums, breakdowns, murders and suicides were blamed on random factors requiring further control mechanisms, and had nothing, they claimed, to do with the Liaisons. Everybody was doing it. It was the done thing. If certain citizens could not control their tempers, could not obey the rules, they had only themselves and their partners to blame.

My mother did not fare well. She had old-fashioned ideas passed down from earth-salt parents and grandparents, from watching them cling together through hell and high indifference. By the time I noticed what was happening to her, it was too late. I'd already left home for university. I'd fallen so ravenously on my lessons, those new flavours of experience at many levels of remove, that I'd very little time set aside to catch up with my folks. All I remember is the uncanny silence, each time I *did* manage a visit. My father would be out, visiting one of the many women he'd been set up with, thanks to the Committee. My mother would be curled up on the couch, bent over a puzzle or cross-stitch, her interest in cooking having fallen by the wayside in the absence of anyone to feed. She stopped talking. She stopped moving from her chair, except to get the paper from the mailbox. Stopped going to bed at night, for fear of the cold sheets on the side once occupied by my father. She stopped eating. Slept only if and when her body left her no other choice. Wouldn't answer the door or the phone. Would respond only to my father's name. All she did, all she thought about, were the puzzles on the back page of the newspaper. She'd be at it all day, all night, the only activity she could remember having shared with her husband.

My father saw none of this. He had different bed to sleep in every night of the week, a whole funhouse of different mirrors in which to examine his rebooted physique. Every attempt to get in touch came to nothing. Then his stuff started disappearing – every time I went to check on my mother, there'd be another space in the wardrobe, another empty drawer, another gap in the shelving where his books and records had once been. His exercise bike and treadmill left squashed dents in the living room carpet. Eventually an email reached my student inbox. A brief greeting. A well-wishing. An almost-apology. And a forwarding address, should I ever wish to write to him in his villa in the Maldives. He'd stripped every last penny out of the joint account he shared with my mother, paid the exorbitant emigration fee to the Management's Relocation Committee, and taken one, perhaps more, of his mistresses abroad to more pleasant climes.

Trying to explain this to my mother didn't work at all. She's closed down, a pair of rusty pennies where her eyes had been, corrective stitches for a smile. I called the doctor, the same man who'd given me lollipops in return for being a brave girl through routine injections as a child. He didn't sound too pleased at all, marital strife wasn't his area of expertise. He transferred my case straight back over to the Liaison Committee, who would, he assured me, be only too happy to help.

They sent round a cluster of Medics, who poked and prodded my mother, waved hands in front of her face and received no response. They scowled when she cried at having her puzzles and pen removed from her lap. They gave her two bottles of pills – the first a stimulant, to shake her up from the chair, from the pen, from eyes rolling back in her skull like a babydoll's; the second a tranquilizer, to balance her mood once she'd got to her feet and, presumably, strong enough to face the upshot of my father's departure.

She seemed alright. For a while. Up and about, at least between the lounge and the front door, the bathroom and kitchen. Murmuring vague affirmatives in response to polite enquiries. She'd even sit in a different chair, with the right kind of encouragement. But always she slumped back under, the slightest of movements and vowel sounds plumbing her dry of energy, settling her back into a seat, any seat, for a wait. They upped her medication, again, again, the stuff proving just enough to flick her eyelids apart. They told me this was normal, not to worry, no indication of her condition being life-threatening or progressive. At least not in any classical sense. It took me a while to hone in on the difference.

Oh god, I can't make sense of everything that happened. I don't want to. The telephone telling me to face a past that's not the past, a past that's a dwindling circle, a future-stripped closing of doors, eyes, lips, minds. Maybe I should write it all down, have it all out in black and white, a formula, a checklist, a menu, a prescription. But I'm too scared even to make a start. I've forgotten what it feels like to hold a writing instrument in my hand, what to do with it, which hand to put it into in the first place – I know making the right decision as regards either side is important, somehow, I'm just not sure why. I'd be cribbing out the letters like a child squeezing handfuls of plasticine, dribbling tears, unable to replicate reality with mere fingertip scrabblings. And the TV and telephone would see, would know I don't trust them to tell me what to do anymore.

Some dark, secret part of me wishes she'd just done herself in. Had the faculties to procure the means, the opportunity. God knows, she must have had the will, or the vacuum in place of a will toward the betterment of her situation. She'd had it with *this* world. It had had it with her. Shuffling off the mortal coil – what they call real death, corking of breath, stilling of blood – might as well account for an absence from one's own consciousness. It amounted to the same thing. They used the same phrase – *we've lost her. We're very sorry.* And they didn't mean misplaced. They didn't mean she was wandering unmapped tundra, having taken a wrong turn. They meant the *lost* from which you can never be found.

I remember the day I knew for sure. Up till then, there'd been a back-and-forth monitoring regime struck up between myself and the Medics. We passed my mother's relay baton of an empty head along an hour-divided timetable, muttering vague reports of what couldn't really be deemed *progress* – movement, attempts at speech, bathroom and kitchen motility skills – but kept me from fearing the worst. They upped her medication. Again. Again. I watched and waited for something to happen. I held fast to the glimmer I was sure was still there. I believed in the mere fact of her eyes still showing in colour. It didn't occur to me how tentative a grip held the orbs into the skull, mere nerves pinning them in like picture hooks. One step forward, a teeter, a tumble right over and into the other side.

I got there late. The Medics had already left. She sat in her regular chair. A sheaf of paper on the coffee table at her feet – *NO CHANGE*. Her toes in white marble, inches from her diagnosis. The television a black eye; answering machine offering no comment. Fool that I was, I took this for a good sign. So I went through all the steps, a greeting riding a toothache of false cheer, a clatter round the kitchen making cups of sticky tea. Wittering on about nothing at all, mere words to fill the silence. Trying not to think too hard about how much I missed her advice, her comforts, even her sardonic running commentary. Blowing across the surface of the mug, cooling the tea, pressing the cup to her lips. Her hands locked in her lap, motionless, throughout, no longer attuned to a potential spillage or scalding. I said everything I should have – *come on Mum, drink up, there's a good girl, on you go*. I didn't cheat, and turn on the TV. I let us both sink into what was once known as a comfortable silence – name given to that patch of discourse between two people, once close, anxious to deny that they have run out of things to say to each other – and watched her from the corner of my eye, trying to pick up a hair's breadth of motion. Her chest barely rising, assurance of breath a matter of listening hard at close range, not too difficult in the damp, thick silence of the lounge. Time had swallowed her up, and had set its sights on *me*. I could feel myself being slowly peeled by the air itself, every molecule and mote of dust running through its own life cycle of rot.

Then she moved. I saw it, I know I did. Her fingers twitching, the tip of a right ring finger circling slowly over the knuckle of the left, where once had been a ring, a gold band drawn around a place in a world unmarked by these dank depths of unwavering loneliness. *Mum,* I said, *are you okay?* Wanting to say *are you in there,* knowing this wasn't the time for ill-thought-out stabs at humour. No response. I must have watched for hours, this one small motion of a fingertip, my eyeballs drying up with the intensity of the stare, the edges of the objects in my line of sight growing fur coats as they slipped in and out of focus. Finally she stopped, the moving finger slipping back into its niche in the webbing of her hands, a snail into its shell, a night creature scuttling back under before dawn. Waited, watched. Watched, waited. Nerves jerked toward the telephone, desperate to break the pattern, get her *seen to* before we missed an opportunity to draw her back out. I kept myself very, very still, the weight of my skull rattling an ache down the length of my neck. When she turned to look at me, I couldn't quite believe what I was seeing. Seemed at first like a broken spring, an errant electric impulse in the mechanics of a glass-booth seaside fortune-teller puppet. Head whipped round independent of her torso, her hands and forearms still inert as twice-baked china. Those eyes I'd been relying on still those blue enamelled pennies. Wait, watch. My throat swelling up with all those million things I'd wanted to say before, and held back, knowing they'd hit up against nothing. Then she spoke. She said *Lucy.*

151

I'd almost forgotten the sound of my name in her mouth. She said *Lucy. I'm done.*

And that was it. No *I love you.* No *be strong.* No *I'm proud of you. I'll miss you. I'm off to a better place.* None of that shit that the movies would have us believe lie trapped in the hinges of the tongues of the dying and dead. I froze. I stuttered. I couldn't help it, I'd been embalmed in this inert gelatine for too long. My dear mother had ceased to be an organism capable of accepting or producing effect, till now.

Before I could form a coherent question, her head snapped back round again. Her body reassuming its geometries of parallels and right angles. Her eyes taking up their steady metronome blink. I should have placed my hands over hers, caught a grip of her arm, crouched down at her feet. Clasped her head, patted her cheeks, blew gently over her cobwebbed skin. Instead, I got up, backed slowly away, reaching for the telephone. Telling myself that this could be a *breakthrough.*

I was afraid to touch her, *touch* my own mother. Tiptoeing away as thought she were a piece of delicate machinery on the blink, like one false move would trip a switch. Calling the fucking *repair* men. The Medics showed up in seconds, willing and eager to take the breakage off my hands. I couldn't stop talking, ranting, raving, desperate for them to acknowledge that mote of speech as progress. They politely avoided pointing out the resumption of business as usual, my mother once more an ice sculpture, even as I danced around, waving my hands, mimicking her head-turn, my grin splitting my face with an ache akin to raw dentistry.

They ran through all the right routines – shining a light into her eyes, rapping her knees with a rubber hammer, folding and unfolding her limbs to check resistance.

They made all the right gestures and noises: gentle murmurings, nasal affirmatives, furrows of brow, scratches of pen-nib on clipboard.

They took me into the kitchen. Had to crease me into a chair. Manic and flailing as my mother was kiln-baked. *We're sorry. These things happen. We're afraid we've lost her. We'll take care of her from here. You did everything you could.*

They told me they'd been holding off. That they'd known for a while that things were moving backward. Didn't want to act too soon, just in case, just on the off-chance I could have reached her. I knew I hadn't tried hard enough. I'd let her slip into herself, pleading ignorance of what I thought she wanted. Mothers are mothers, daughters are daughters, and I hadn't been ready to accept responsibilities arcing over a reversal of roles.

I stopped shaking, quit flailing, behaved myself and asked what happened next. I know there's a process, a point at which hysterics need give way to decorum. Just because my mother hadn't yet ceased to exist, didn't mean there weren't arrangements to be made. They'd the decency to look abashed, when I outlined the whereabouts of my father, a different kind of victim of the Liaison Committee. To give me a moment of privacy, head locked in hands over the kitchen table, as I tore my mind apart for any other living relative. None were available. They gave me a bound plastic wallet of worksheets and glossy flyers. A care plan in a very special ward of a very special hospital. I didn't find out until later just how many catatonics frayed the edges of the city, preferring a merry slide off the edge of consciousness to the new-sprung, efficient alternative.

I signed her over. I had to. I honestly had to. I'd no other choice, I wouldn't have had the slightest idea how to take care of her. I'd no imagination, anymore. No energy. The solution was far too neat and clean and shorn of loose threads to pass up. They'd even take care of the house – with my consent, they'd strip the place down, sell it on, profits passed onto a charity of my choice. I staggered, dazed, through the whole thing, all words and sights and senses blurred to everything but a need to have it over with. With my mother stuck somewhere between legitimate presence and utter absence, I'd had no real shot at *closure,* that number-one must-have vaunted by advocates of popular psychology. No chance at a celebration of recovery, no period of mourning with at least an end in sight. The strongest emotion recalled from that period, stronger even than sadness or futility, was *resentment.* I wanted my mother to make up what was left of her mind – in or out, here or gone. With the Liaison Committee's Medics on hand to help, I could hand it over. I could make it all go away.

And I did. I did.

Whenever Caleb asked me about my parents, I was always more than characteristically vague and indecisive. I didn't want him to know just how thoughtless I could be. I didn't half surprise myself with the shape and depth of my own imagination, when called upon to come up with alibis and excuses for the afternoons on which I paid my mother a visit.

But it was a nice enough place. I have to believe that. I *do* believe that. They came to pick me up and take me along, the first couple of times. Told me it was all part of the service, that their clients deserved the very best of care and attention in times of need. It never occurred to me that this was just another neat fold in the contract, another smiling photograph in the brochure. Keep the daughter sweet, since the only other body with viable complaint wasn't exactly in the position to do so.

The wards were so quiet I could hear my own heartbeat, the squeak of single toes moving inside their rubber shoes. Decked out in so many of those old-fashioned fabrics and prints I'd only seen in TV reruns from the eighties, read about in books. I didn't even know what *paisley* and *chintz* really looked like until I set foot in that place. It smelled like age, in spite of the patients being anything from sixteen to eighty-odd – that damp reek of rising damp and cling-film steamed with boiled vegetables. It smelled like giving up. They'd take me to her room, where she'd been kitted out with everything a convalescent could ever need – sugary drinks, plastic carafes, stacks of magazines and digested fiction, a TV in the corner permanently tuned to daytime talk-shows and soap operas, and, of course, her beloved crossword puzzles, everything piling up on the windowsill untouched. Sometimes she'd be in the bed, sometimes in the chair. I was never around to see them move her – I don't think I could have taken it, the sight of my mother in her cartoon-dog print pyjamas being moulded and reworked into position like a Claymation figurine. The Medics always insisted she was doing just fine, a model patient, in remarkable shape for her age, all things considered. I didn't see fit to mention that a life spent indoors, out of reach of all negative influences of weather, environment and other people didn't half keep her out of harm's way. At a cost. She ate and passed waste through a tube, despite being conscious and otherwise capable – she'd simply slipped so far down inside herself that attending to such processes made little difference either way.

At first, I tried to speak to her, tried to interact, excite an interest on what was on television or in the newspapers. I told her what I'd been up to, where I was staying, about work and study and a boy I'd fallen in love with. Eventually, resentment did me in. A captive audience sounds marvellous in principle, but there's nothing worse than feeling like you're screaming into the wind, particularly when things between me and Caleb grew more serious. I hated her for abandoning me, for failing to offer comfort and advice. There was nothing *wrong* with her, as far as I could see, nothing physically keeping her from getting up off the chair or the bed and going back to the business of *living*. I hadn't known, yet, the narcotic tang of sleep, dews of indifference beading the senses. So I stopped going. Not intentionally – these things never are – but simply allowed a slow melt

154

of missed appointments and more important commitments to pour over my duties to my own mother. And whenever I felt guilty about it, whenever I *thought* about it, I ran over what the Medics had repeatedly told me – that there was nothing I could do, that she was in safe hands, that they'd call me immediately if there were any changes.

I kept holding out the hope that I'd hear from my father. I was so sure he'd be waiting for some pall of smoke to clear, to get himself settled, then remember he had a daughter on the other side of the ocean. Double standards, again – never occurred to me that he'd forget as easily as I had. I haven't a clue what he's up to, whether he's still with his new woman or even in the same hemisphere as his old family. I tell myself I don't care, but of course I do. I just don't care enough to be the one doing the seeking-out.

So yeah. When, not if, this woman calls back, I can say in all honesty that I *do* still have parents. If she wants to know the who, where, what and when of the situation, she'd best settle herself down for a hell of a long story. And as always, I don't want to pick up the phone. And as always, I'll do it anyway, since I'll never know who might be watching.

Time to get my furies into shape. She's been in and out and back again in various states of repair all damn week, always too tired to tell me what's gone on. The novelty's worn off.

'Tell me what you're up to, Bethany.'

'I will. I'm still scouting.'

'Looking for what?'

Silence.

'Bethany. I don't know how long you think I'm going to put up with you swinging in and out of *my* flat without so much as a–'

'–Right! I know! I just ... we've got to be ready.'

'Ready for *what*?'

'Whatever it is we're going to do. To get your Caleb back, and ...stuff. I haven't worked it all out yet. That's why we've got to get you on a few practice runs.'

That sounds more like it. First, another coffee from the tar-packed dregs of the percolator. A trickle, a grimace to fill the silence whilst we gather our respective thoughts. She's been pushing hieroglyph-scrawled papers across my table for hours, now, muttering to herself. I might have been out of the game for a while, but I know a vendetta when I hear one. She's got a score to settle: for the treatment, the beating, the humiliating parachute drop into her sham life. Doesn't mean she can keep it all to herself.

I'm starting to feel it. Perhaps I always have. It's starting to come together. Useless energy and slow-burning fragmentary thought. Days spent stalking the landscape for something I didn't know I'd lost. Insomniac dream-scapes making nonsense sprawls of half-remembered dialogue and fact, racing around my skull like so much hangover eye-trash. All leading me here. I just needed a crisis point, a moment of decision. For all those scattered pieces to gather round a core, a nexus, the colour and shape of what I've always known I've had to do. Take it back. Take it all back.

'What did you have in mind?'

I'm peering into the mug as though the answer's written in soap-bubble residue swirling across the meniscus. One can dream. Bethany hums, tapping the end of a pencil against her front teeth. I don't like the look of what's laid out between us – too many numbers, symbols, diagrams, acronyms. Looks like I'm in for an education.

'All that stuff about *knowledge*,' she laughs, 'That's the kicker, Lucy. Here's me telling you everything I know and think *you* should ... and the bastards keep on moving stuff around, changing tactics.

Loosening up a little *here*,' she clenches her right hand, holds up to shoulder level, '… so's we don't notice them tightening it right the way up *here*.' She does the same with the left, glares at her fist, as though clutching an insect, a bullet.

'What you're saying is … you *don't know*,' I mumble into the cup, trying not to look too pleased with myself. She's not amused.

'Don't give me that. Who's shown you stuff you'd never know was there? Told things you'd never have bothered to find out for yourself? Who's sat here *right now* trying to sort this shit? I might not know *exactly* what, yet, but at least I'm doing *something*! You used to be like that too! You used to–'

'–you didn't know me, Bethany. Before. You have no idea. As far as *knowledge* is concerned, you and me, then and now, whatever – you might as well still be fixing my drinks and tapping my smokes. Why do you think I keep telling you I *don't know*? Because I *don't*, okay? Everything's changing, there's all this–'

'–just say the word, Lucy! If you can't take it, I'm gone. Cheerio, goodbye, thank you for your time. You think you're *so* hard-done-by, *oooh, oooh, don't tell me, I don't want to know, I don't want to see* … but you're forgetting how fucking lucky you are. Those people out there …' she chokes off, sweeping a hand in the direction of the window, '… they won't know why they can't sleep at night. Won't know why whole days seem to just … disappear. And if they've lost someone …they won't have any idea where they've got to. Imagine that, Bethany. Thinking your kid or your parents or your partner or flatmate just can't be *bothered* with you anymore. Not being sure whether they're gone for good, or whether they'll walk through the front door any minute …'

Imagine. I can do that. Sleepwalking through your own existence. Never you can put your finger on, just a constant ache, a dread, that something's very wrong, even though it all looks just the same. Oh well. Bethany's still talking. Best pay attention.

'… Aye, for *you*, it's all change, all over again. I didn't like it, either. But that's got to be better than where we were before, no? You've *got* to hold onto that, Lucy. Otherwise you're not the girl–'

'–Ha. Not the girl you thought I was? Could be? Now … where have I heard *that* before? Caleb tell you to say that? Cos he was *wrong*, right! I'm *doing* this!'

'No. I thought it up all by myself. You should try it sometime.'

I throw back the chair, jump to my feet, sweeping mugs and percolator off the table and into the sink. Childish urge to cry at the sight of all that shattered glass and china swilling in the inky murk. My stuff, not my stuff. My home, not my home. I stand at the kitchen door, watching Bethany. She hasn't budged an inch, not even at the crash. Her head pressed into her hands, elbows drilling holes in the table.

'Bethany ...' I try to say, my words dribbling limp from the corners of my mouth. 'Bethany ... can we ... not do this?'

Her head jerks back. Her expression tells me nothing; jaw wired taut, mouth a dash, desultory punctuation, eyes slid deep under a violet haze. So we match. Looking pretty tired these days. Our eyes have had enough, rolling themselves up in shadows for want of anything to look at.

'Do what?'

'Fight. I have – I had – the same argument with Caleb more often than I want to remember.'

'So I've heard.'

'I'm in. I won't flake out, I won't ... *dither*. Just tell me what I have to do.'

She nods, gets to her feet, shoulders hunched over hands shoved in her pockets. She peers up from under a fizz of root-lashed blonde, hair a palm-torn nest.

'It's not about doing what I *tell* you, Lucy. I just know a little more than you do, about all of this. I want you to *work* with me. Neither of us can do this ... whatever it is ... on our own. But for now, you'd have to trust me to know what to start.'

'I trust you.'

I'm not sure I do, but it's easier this way.

'Good. I'd better get moving.'

She's upright again, shaking tension from the lengths of her limbs. She pulls dark gear from my chest of drawers, holding fabrics up to the window to check light absorption. I take a shower, water far too hot for my own good, trying to diffuse some of that prickling in my skull into the spread of my skin.

I don't know why I'm listening to her when I spent too long failing to hear Caleb. Maybe it's a strain of latent feminism. A slow drip-drip of pressure. Boredom, I don't know. Maybe, just maybe, it's the closing of a gap between what I'm ready to learn, and what I'd no hope of understanding.

Caleb went out of his way to keep me from feeling stupid, true, but there was no getting rid of a sense of dragging behind, my own knowledge just a cross-knot in the great all-encompassing badminton net of his own. My expertise was so firmly anchored in the long-outlawed Arts, I could offer only the odd flourish atop his multifaceted political and ideological frames of reference. The odd factoid gleaned from the weekly political digests couldn't stand up to his sprawling internal encyclopaedia. I followed his lead, not for want of brain power, but because I couldn't believe enough in what I *did* know. I couldn't *get* to it any more.

Now, I have a vested interest. If Bethany makes an effort to keep us on a level, that's more than I'd a shot at before. Knowledge, I want it, more, now, again. Got to make up for lost time. The nausea I'd felt, seeing those tapes, hearing the truth of where he and I had been, is slowly being drawn up and out to make room for something else. Something harder. Darker. A hot sharp thrum. A growl rising in the throat. I like it. It means things will be getting done, even if I still feel like I'm being left behind. Little pieces at a time. Energy unexpended on the outside is energy saved computing what's going on. Somebody has to stay and mind the phone and television, I suppose.

Bethany's ready to go, blonde fuzz slicked back in elastics, feet in tightly-buttoned boots already drumming on the floor. I join her once more at the table. The papers again. This time I'll be more accommodating, if it's all I'm getting tonight.

'See … this is the tunnel I took you through, running under the gardens,' she says, unrolling a map of the city's Western quadrant. The tunnel, picked out in red lines, darts back and forth between smallish dark grey rectangles. These are linked to a central oblong, slightly larger, by pale blue lines, some of these crossing the red lines of the tunnel. 'And these are … well, what do you think?'

'I don't know … there's nothing in the park except the glass house and the toilet blocks. Unless those are …'

'Underground. Yep. That's the thing … Glasgow's far smaller than you'd think. We're up close and personal with the Management, even when we think we're in the clear.'

'Those are Management properties?'

'Yeah. Wouldn't have believed it if I hadn't the bruises to prove it.'

All this time, Bethany had been making free and full use of the tunnels under the gardens, unaware that the Management had installed smallish cell-size surveillance foxholes right in between the loops. Their own linking tunnels went deeper than the original, through which I'd walked with Bethany, yet tilting up slightly as they met the cells at either end. She'd taken a couple of wrong turns when investigating the expansion potential of the tunnel, wound up digging right through into one of the dens right where her tunnel and the Management's met at a weak spot.

159

'I'd have laughed if it weren't *me*,' she says. 'Come bursting through the walls in a rain of dirt and plaster dust. Practically landed in the Agent's lap. If I hadn't had a decent kit on me, things would have gotten pretty ugly.'

'That the day you showed up covered in bruises?'

'Yeah.'

'How many of them were there?'

'Three – one to watch, one to listen, one to keep central Management up-to-date.'

'And they hit you?'

'What else were they supposed to do? Intruder falling into their hidden lair? Come on, Lucy – not exactly the point at which you can demand your rights to a question-and-answer session. I just had to get out of there. Did some damage myself, by the way – I haven't forgotten what I'm doing when I've got to go hand-to-hand.'

'Why didn't you just tell me then?'

'Had to work a few things out myself, Lucy. I wasn't sure what ...they were doing, yet.'

Her voice drops into a slight quaver. She's lying – or shaping the truth. She didn't want to talk about it because she'd been in pain. She'd made an error of judgement and had the injuries to prove it. She's not as informed as she thinks she was, her instincts not always infallible. Don't have to ask why she'd kept it from me – if I know anything, I know about having your judgement called cruelly into question.

'Any ideas?'

'More of the same, I think. Spreading out. Digging in. I didn't get much of a look at the set-up, not in detail, but I saw enough. Usual surveillance set-up – computers, monitors, recording devices. Something that looked like a - don't laugh – a *periscope*.'

'Uh ... huh ...?'

She takes a red pencil from behind her ear, and, chuckling, begins to mark dots across the surface of the park, roughly correlating to the grey cells.

'I took a wander, and ... above ground, these cells match up to all sorts of junk you don't bother noticing. Lamp-posts, waste-bins, statues, old post-boxes. You'll remember what I told you, about their not bothering with the park?'

'Yeah.'

'I was wrong. They're all over it.'

'Shit.'

'Which means … they're onto us. They know about the tunnel.'

'Why haven't they—'

'—done anything about it, yet? I don't know. To be honest, I don't think it's worth their time. It's just what you saw – old AV equipment, videos, empty rooms, store-rooms full of junk. They're waiting for us to make some sort of move. And I don't like that at all.'

Bethany leans back in the chair, cradling her head, jaw working to suppress a yawn. She scours her eyes with the heels of her hands, then smacks her palms on the table.

'You know what this means, don't you?'

'You can't – we can't – go down there anymore.'

'More than that. I've busted *them*, they've busted *me* – which means they're closer than we think. Which means they're not invulnerable. I *literally* broke through the walls, Lucy – that's got to mean something. They're running out of spaces to take over. I mean, come on. *Lamp-posts? Waste-bins?* Like one of those Second Nineties spy comedies. Not to mention the set-up on the inside – whatever they had by way of gear, they still didn't see me coming.'

'How'd you get away?'

Bethany grimaces, fingers a bruise on her jaw-line. Making a crutch of her fingers, she stretches her arms, shoulders, back, licking tension from her lips.

'I told you there was damage on both sides. I still know what to do with my hands and feet. And I recovered from the surprise a little quicker than *they* did. For all they know, I'd had it planned for ages.'

'You didn't—'

'—I don't think so. They'll be pretty sore for a couple of weeks, maybe seeing a few of those stars we've been missing, but …needs must. I don't kill people, Lucy. I've never had to, and never want to be in that position. I'm not – ha ha – I'm not *wired* that way. Just so you know.'

I'm supposed to be glad to hear this. I've always been the pacifist in these partnerships, freaking out at the sight of blood, worming my way slowly back from any hint of violent confrontation. Something seething at the back of my throat, though, begs to differ. It's not that I'm craving a kill, it's just …I think I'd be a lot more open to the idea, if it came to it. The same sensation I'd had watching the Management laying into Caleb. Acid thrum along limbs. Creaking of tendons in fingers. A need, a will, to direct such energy into an

161

antagonist. I guess that means I'm ready. To do what Bethany – Caleb – need me to do. Still, can't be shaking her impressions too much. There's always mileage in appearing to be far less dangerous than you are.

'Cool. Well, I'm … uh, glad you're okay. You have to tell me, though, next time. If we're in this together, I'm going to need to know.'

'You won't have to. You'll be coming with me, soon as I've tied up a few loose ends.'

She uncurls her hands, still bunched into fists, and proffers her right across the table. It's been years since I've shaken a hand, since the first impulse upon encountering another being is to reach into your pocket for ID. It's interesting. Particularly since she's still putting me off.

'So … you any clearer about where we're going? When you've … *tied things up?*'

Bethany grins, the first proper expression of glee I've seen for ages.

'Well … all that snuggling going on under the park's given me an idea. I honestly can't believe I didn't think of it before, I'm so stupid … it's kid stuff, for Christ's sake! Okay – you ever play hide and seek when you were a little girl?'

'Of course.'

'Anyone ever show you, tell you how to win?'

'I didn't realize it was that complicated. You hide, they seek, or vice versa.'

'Kid's games are amazing for throwing up little tricks of psychology, manipulation, tactics. All bluffing and double-bluffing. Logically, you're most likely to win by hiding in the last place they'd think to look. Which is?'

'The most obvious place, of course. Which they don't bother checking–'

'–because they know you know it's the first place they'd look. So they don't. So you win.'

Skull plates creak, back and forth, forth and back. I'm starting to notice a pattern, here. Bethany forever drawing out these explanations, teasing, drawing out the cut to the chase. Just like Caleb, so keen to show me just how clever he could be.

'Which means we're looking for them in the most obvious place.'

'Right up close and personal. Where we'd never think to look, cos *we* think *they* would never ever think to hide there.'

'The casino?'

'The casino.'

I resent her indulgent little smile. I don't have to be spoon-fed all the damn time. Still too much I'm not clear on, though. Too many loose ends. If the Management aren't onto all and everything we've got going on – which isn't much, at least not yet – they'll at least be onto *something*.

'So … who's looking for who?' I ask.

Bethany's jaw tightens. She clenches her fists again before scuttling her fingers through the papers.

'I have to believe we're the seekers. At least until we know better.'

'How do you know?'

'I don't. Psychology again, though, Lucy. We've no apparent message or statement. No plan or team of followers. We're just playing soldiers. We'd have to work a damn sight harder to get their attention, to constitute a threat.'

'So … why in the hell are you wanting us to go out and *make* trouble? Isn't that kind of … asking for it?'

'Yep. Two things. First, it'll get us used to working together. You've done this sort of thing with Caleb, aye, but you'll still be rusty. Second – it's not causing a *diversion*, exactly, but it'll … it'll have them thinking we're far less subtle than we actually are. When they're expecting fires and noise and mess and shit, we'll be working on how to be *invisible*. Smoke and mirrors, hiding in plain sight – the oldest tricks in the book.'

'Then what?'

'Then we get in under the skin. We get what we're after. And they'll be so busy watching the sky, listening out for breaking glass, they won't see or hear us coming.'

There are so many flaws in this plan, I wouldn't know where to begin. But it comes down to the same damn thing. Go with it, follow Bethany's lead, or wind up back where I started. Me and four more walls.

'I've got to go, Lucy. I won't be long.'

'I won't wait up.'

'Come on, Lucy! Last thing we need is both of us banged up!'

'Okay. Fine. But *when* will you take me with you?'

'When I know for sure you're keeping nothing to – or from – yourself.'

Eight Hours Later

I do and don't register a homecoming. Can't trust in the wee hours' graphite sketches, eyelash blurred, fragmented. Half-sleep breaks boundaries. Lets in things I've no room for by day; and a backlog of stuff too crazed even for dreams. Pressure and heat on the other side of the mattress. Gusts of breath, murmurs, then silence. All's well. Pre-dawn: off the clock by any reasonable standards. Moments of quiet reflection. Soft chalks and jigsaw puzzles.

I'm the edge of *something,* all the time, some sign I've yet to pick up on, some pattern I'm failing to notice. Something that's there already, it's implied, if I'd only pull in tight and just *look closer.* Something. Not the missions, not the Management, not the movement of bodies or traffic, not the slow-shoe shuffle of my feet. This is different. Noisier. Messier.

Always been something of a stickler for the measured and the calm when it came to the inside of my own head. Drove Caleb crazy; said it killed my creativity. Preferred to take his lead in most anything, thereby passing over responsibility should anything go wrong. Spent more time *thinking* than doing – I'd get the guilt, sure, but got to remember the traditions of culture, education and politics from which I'd sprung.

My parents' generation had been the first to shelve their impulses. Slack-jawed citizens watched slack-jawed governments pick about the wreckage of a country, speaking in axioms, never truths. Puppet hands too feeble and formless to impact on anything they touched. Even the loudest voices trickled to a whine: polemics once written in blood pegged out from behind shielding laptop screens. Every utterance footnoted, referenced, witnessed and double-signed to avoid offending anyone who might be *reading,* still. Protests –my grandparents' weekend mornings – became hollow voices pressed back behind wire fences, microphones in faces, capturing nothing but the words of those who'd no idea what they were talking about. People got more heated over who won some shitty reality television viewer-interactive experience than they did over the latest government fuck-up or scandal.

We dived into the televisual apparatus.

We went online.

We went back to bed.

We disappeared.

Hence my reserve. I can't remember the last time I got properly excited. Or wanting anything except attainment of a level, for some semblance of safety. And there's something wrong, there, I know. I used to do things. I used to *paint,* for fuck's sake. I've been too

164

afraid to pick up a brush for ages, terrified I'll produce nothing but a series of near-perfect circles, variations on the colour *beige*.

See, there it is again. I can't hear myself think over all of this *noise*, all of this stuff from a past so irrelevant I can barely believe I was *there*. Clawing at the back of my skull. Trailing threads or spilled bodily cells in its wake. Like jerking upright in the midnight dark from the murk of a bad dream, trying to orient yourself. Things leering from the shadows, faces swirled into the carpet pile, grabbing hands ruffling the wood grain in the wall panels. Something known and yet not, something out of place and dangerous in the daytime sub-realities. Memories belonging to someone else.

That voice, familiar, mine, could be another imitation. My voice, the one I use today, could be an imitation of an imitation, Bethany's tones picked up from me and re-translated all over again. Collapsing circles, object thrumming out their own facsimiles, squares formed cracking at the limits of what they're trying to contain.

I'm not just hearing things, I'm seeing, feeling things I haven't an entry in my mental catalogue with which to compare them. They told me after discharge I might be a little blurry, but this is almost a year later, and *blurry* is not the word. It's like anything else in the realms of experience – the very heights of perception in the moment itself. So bright I can almost taste colour, see my skin thrilling with touch, yet the second I try to hone in for a closer look, it dissolves like a cloud of laughing pigeons. A child's voice inside wants to ask Bethany to hold my hand whilst I dive in, pull me back before I drown. But come on. Seriously. She's the professional whatever-she-is, the tough-gnarled sceptic, the essentialist. Certainly not my shrink or neurosurgeon.

Worse than laughing at my half-formed descriptions, I get the feeling she'd encourage it. Have me face down these hallucinations as one more sideline in our investigations. Higher stakes means she'll have no problem getting dug right in. I can hear her now: *go on, take a look! Something we've missed! Something we can use!* I've taken to finding a familiar corner whenever things get too heavy. I hate the waking-up – strange positions, chunks of time misplaced, sense of falling through the back of my own skull –more than the sinking itself.

This is not practical. This is not at all comfortable. This may be the point.

She stirs. Shifts his mask from the twin bracket cupping my spine. Damn her. Damn us both. Inside, he may be sharper, clearer, more *present* than when we were heat, bone, skin. I may be sketching details in of wants, preferences, quirks that seem to suit the scenery.

Association games. Every figure in your head a Method actor, so very close to *being* you almost forget the *seeming* end of the deal. Sometimes a block of wood is just a block of wood; however strongly you *emote* at it, it's not about to turn into a baby or a cat.

Bethany rises whilst I clutch onto my inside edge of the mattress, a frozen prawn clinging to the side of the refrigerator. Very, very still, hold on to the compacted illusion. Two bodies caught in space, one still, one mobile, each still tingling from the heat of the other – cling onto these bare facts and the specifics don't matter. I can sketch in the hands I'd have to hold, the lips I'd have to kiss, the nakedness under a set of clothes, not Bethany's, not mine.

'Lucy ...' she whispers, feeling it out. I'm still asleep. She grows braver, slips back into a self freed from the want of another's warmth.

'Lucy!' she says, Agent-sharp, morning-bleached. 'Lucy, wake up!'

She approaches, kicking the blankets about the side of the bed, making it look like she'd slept there all along. She prods me in the small of the back.

'Lucy! We've got work to do.'

I run through the motions of waking.

'Morning,' I murmur. 'What time is it?'

'Getting on for ten.'

This pleases me. She's been so caught up in comfort that she's slept long past her usual dawn automatism. I turn over slowly, squinting against the grey light. Knowing full well I've been indulging in mere sense-memory doesn't hold back a rush of disappointment, as Bethany, not Caleb, coheres fully-formed.

'Hmmm. So ... work? What?'

I can't keep track of where we are, of what she's prepared to let me in on. Still wavering as to whether I can keep up. Just when I think we're on a level, she'll dash off to do something on her own. Still drinking my coffee. Still wearing my socks.

'Get up and dressed. Kettle's boiling.'

Scattershot syllables, the backs of her hands swiped over her eyes. A rough night, perhaps, but I didn't feel a thing. Bethany doesn't have bad dreams; she doesn't have the time.

I do as I'm told whilst she's in the shower. She stalks, dripping, back into the lounge, wrapped in a bath-towel. Scanning the floor; she'd meant to take her gear into the bathroom with her. She cowers when half-clad, the *we're-all-girls-here* ethos clearly having been missing from her childhood. I suspect issues. She's got the towel in her fist, jammed into her neck, a waterfall of cotton draping her from chin to knees. She bends to lift her jeans. Deep blue bruises rise from her vertebrae, a streak of smudged thumbprints, a messy line of Morse code. Catching me looking, she jerks up with a scowl, backing slowly to the wall behind.

'What you looking at?'

'What happened to your back? It's a mess.'

'Took a tumble. Landed hard. No big deal.'

'You sure? That looks dead sore.'

'Nothing a hot shower and a coffee can't fix … if I can just find my fucking *clothes* …'

'Here,' I say, holding out a pile of fabric she'd neatly folded at the foot of the bed. She's in thought-action separation mode; carrying out motions, routines her mind fails to register. She snatches, darts back to the bathroom, from which issues gushes of water, porcelain clanks. I dress with equal inattention to detail, before fixing us both a coffee. A drift of grains on the counter is less a mess than a canvas for drawing fingertip patterns.

Then we're sat at the table, Bethany spreading out yet more of those maps, charts, graphs, lists, some so riddled with ink that neither she nor I can make out what's supposed to be underneath. She makes cathedrals of her fingers, rests her chin on the spire and squints at me through the steam rising from our mugs. It's a stare-out – one of us awaiting instructions, the other questions, neither quite sure anymore where to begin.

'So …' she says, finally, a lawyer, a shrink.

'So?' I reply, not taking the bait.

'So … are you ready?'

'Ready for what?'

'You tell me.'

'Is this some sort of joke, Bethany? Am I supposed to know something, here?'

She smacks her hands off the documents and grabs on tight, papers crumpling in her hands like a nightmare duvet. Her head follows suit, ridges between knuckles moulding her eyebrows. I can't tell whether she's laughing or crying; when it comes right down to it, one wet snuffle, chuckle, engine stutter's much the same as the other. Maybe I should touch her – arm on shoulder, hand on hand – but something in her posture intimates a threat of scalding. Best wait it out – Caleb got like this sometimes, so frustrated and paranoid he'd respond only to church silence or the scent of burning grass.

'Ahem. This is …this isn't good news,' says Bethany, words bounding round the echo chamber of her hands against the table.

'It never is,' I say, feeling stupid, useless. 'What's the problem?'

She snaps her head up, eyes so freshly pink and peeled they look ripe to burst from her sockets. She's neither smiling nor growling, mouth corners wrenched back, her lips a straight and perfect line. She picks up a pen and batters the tip against the papers on the table, shaking her head. Her other hand works its way up and down the small of her back, a spasm jolting the muscles of her arms with every angry button pressed.

'I thought I was onto something,' she says. 'I thought I'd found a way in.'

'You said *casino*. You said they're still *there*, they just keep changing places. You said all we had to do was … speed things up. Catch them before they outran us again.'

'You're missing the point, Lucy. The Management don't *run*.'

'But you said—'

'I was wrong. They're not about to keep moving for the likes of *us*. That's …what I found out, last night. Which means all this shit is *useless*!'

She growls, knocks the papers from the table to the floor.

'I went back for a look around, Lucy.'

'Uh-huh?'

'They weren't supposed to be there. They'd been *breached*, they should have packed up and moved on.'

'And they hadn't?'

'They hadn't. That's the problem – they don't *care* if we know where they are. They can't be *caught at* anything. They can't be *caught* at all. They just *are* where they are, and us knowing or otherwise doesn't bother them at all.'

She fucked up. Miscalculated. Can't do this on her own, any more than I can.

This shouldn't please me as much as does.

I've got to get my kicks where I can.

Underground

Agents scatter down the length of the corridor as word spreads of the Manager's return from the field. D16 and F5, ostensibly watching the feed from individual rooms, leap from their swing chairs and shove their Prohibited Diversions out of sight. Electronic card and dice games, plastic cups of Instant Muffin Mix, pocket-sized puzzle books, vintage trading cards – the repercussions would be dire, should the Manager ever discover these infractions. They couldn't help it: they'd do anything to offset the trundling boredom of being kept in the fluorescent underground all day, despite the Manager's insistence there was always work for idle hands. D16 has to smile at the sight of good old GH64's contribution – a half-pint hip flask, the sign of a man too set in his ways to drop them into any Random Amnesty.

'Go on, get out,' hisses F5.

'I'm *going*, young man,' grumbles GH64. 'Jesus, you'd think the sun shone out his arse, the way you're all running about like a bunch of wee lab rats.'

'You know the drill,' says D16, drily, raising a brow in tacit anarchy. 'Not worth the trouble, mate, although I've got to admire your nerve.'

'I do my job, and do it well. I've class enough to keep it out of sight. He's got a problem with it, he can stick his job.'

All three agents share a smirk, wishing they braved more than mere talk.

GH64 is one of the few Agents whose skills had developed in a similar line of work Outside. Some agency or other named the MI5, now defunct, having failed to move with the times and the Management's lack of compromise. GH64 had apparently been recruited as a bridger of gaps, a man already versed in discipline and secrecy: pseudo-affectionately deemed a *member of the Old Guard*, insincerity puckering the Manager's lips every time he spoke the name. Only a handful of the Agents knew the truth: that GH64's life on the outside had been stripped away to so much *nothing* that the old man had accepted the role in the Manager's favoured frame of mind – that of having no other choice. The old man was flawless, faultless in Interviews, Intimidations, Transfers and Transmissions, still spiritually invested in notions of rewards for hard work; that sheer effort and pure grit will return him to his family, home and the oft-rumoured Quiet Life. Drinking on the job seemed to make this easier to believe.

'Take care of yourself, GH64,' says D16, unable to latch onto something more profound.

'Aye. You too, son. Look sharp – that'll be your man on his way down the hall.'

GH64 flits from the office, disappears between shadow-seams in the opposite direction. The Manager's boots, buttons and belt-buckles clatter and rebound around hollow concrete, a slammed door on the backbeat of his tread. D16 and F5 place clipboards on their knees and peer intently at the banks of CCTV monitors. Agents in the Surveillance Office rarely have to worry much about rogue elements down here – this was the wing of the Facility dedicated to cases long-term and hopeless. Those who'd already learned the hard way the futility of resistance. This does not prevent the Manager from slamming the door against the opposite wall. Both Agents jump to their feet.

'Good afternoon, Sir!' they shout.

'Hmmm.'

The greeting dismissed, the Manager peers at the consoles, grasping his chin to control a quaver in his jaw. A plump earthworm of a scar runs from the left temple to the corner of the mouth. The lids of his right eye tremble in the midst of a violet haze of bruising. The knuckles of both hands are chapped and grazed, the sleeve of his uniform puffy around the right elbow, indicating a padding of bandages and supports. Both Agents know better than to ask. The Manager will not tolerate such over-familiarity.

'Right. Any developments?' asks the Manager, finally. After a cursory check up on the rest of the occupants, his attention remains fixed on Intern Number Nineteen, still sitting straight-backed in his otherwise empty room.

'Nothing to report, Sir,' says D16. 'Usual Interviews, of course –typed, uploaded and filed for your inspection, Sir'

'Nothing from Nineteen?'

'No, Sir.'

'Hmmm. Well, can't expect miracles …' The Manager paces the floor in front of the monitors. His bark dwindles to a mutter as he continues, apparently talking mostly to himself. D16 and F5 lock gazes over the Manager's shoulder, raising eyebrows. '… we're running out of time and patience with this one. Can't go on. Using up resources, taking up space, still refusing to part with any information … in-*tolerable.*'

Suddenly he stops, punches the wall, jerks around to face D16.

'Where's the Agent in charge of the Interview?'

D16 clears his throat, deciding against engaging in verbal responses. He hands the Manager a file taken from a box set into the banks of monitors. The Manager's throat builds up a rumble as he peruses the data.

'Right. Nothing. Not a bloody thing. Right. Change of tactics, today. Is the Communal Laboratory still prepped for use?'

'Not quite, Sir – but we can have it done quick-time, should you–'

'–get to it. A unit for every Intern.'

F5 clears his throat, his line of sight darting between ceiling corners.

'Sir, permission to–'

'What? What is it, F5?'

'It's just – Sir, the Communal Lab hasn't been used since the Facility opened. The electrics, the wiring …it's …we really ought to make a few checks–'

'Don't bother. Either of you. We've all wasted far too much time and effort on these … *ingrates,*' hisses the Manager. 'Efficiency in this Facility is at an all-time low. I will *not* compromise our reputation for the sake of those who have made it perfectly clear that they will not be co-operating. Understood?'

'Understood, Sir,' says F5, staring down at his hands.

'One hour. I'll be back in one hour. I want every Intern set into a unit. I want *results*. One of them has to know *something*.'

'Yes, Sir,' the Agents burr. The Manager tweaks the cuffs of his jacket, straightens his shoulders and turns toward the door.

'I'll be in the Management Lounge. Have a tray and a shower kit sent along.'

'Yes, Sir.'

The Manager drum-rolls his way back down the corridor. F5 and D16 deflate with relief.

'Jesus … he looked rough,' says F5.

'You know how he gets. Over-ground. Feels like he's been conned if he comes back without having had a scrap.'

'Still … must be getting pretty crazy up there.'

'Bullshit,' says D16. 'It's all for show. All talk. You've seen the reports from the others, F5. Folks up there are too bored – or scared – to get up to no good. Nowhere for 'em to go, either – except the casinos. And we've seen the feed from *there* – nobody's looking further than the length of their card-arm, not opening their mouths except to place their bets.'

'Aye, but – did you see his face? His hands?'

171

'I told you. Every time. If he can't find a fight, he'll pick one. Can't really blame him … we're *all* fucking bored.' D16 taps the table-top under which lurks their time-killing contraband.

'Hmmm … I suppose so. Know what I'd be doing if I were up there, though … wee bit of action, aye, but not the kind of hands-on combat the Manager seems to go for.' F5 licks his top lip. The taut muscles of his about-face granted permission to arc into a wink.

'Psshaw. You can dream, pal.'

'Whatever passes the time.'

Both Agents slump into a brief silence, before fumbling into action. D16 rifles through a stack of files, whilst F5 spreads a canvas wrap of tools across the desk.

'I don't know what I'm doing with half this stuff,' he says.

'Don't worry about it. Nobody does,' says D16. 'Think it's enough just to get that lot into their seats, for the show. The Manager will want to take it from there. About the only thing he seems to *like* doing, down here.'

'Right. Shall we?'

One more glance at the monitors. The same stiff, static figures watching time drip down the walls.

'Let's go.'

The Agents nod, gather up tools and files, and depart for the Lab.

A lot of things started happening very quickly.

I might have trouble processing the passage of actual time, but I haven't missed how much has been wasted. No wonder I drift off. Letting my line of sight clot with whorls of dry ice, all sounds simmering to a blurry mumble. At least things have been *moving* in there. Bethany gets annoyed.

'Hello! You still in there?' she says as we step from the Tube down onto the street. Pitch-black glass, bleached pipe, silence: it always makes me sleepy, having always meant, in other circumstances, that I was heading home to bed. Shutting down my faculties, the better to cope with the empty echo chamber of my flat. Not tonight. Got to pay attention.

'Yeah. Sorry, just …'

'Floating, I know. Sharpen up, Lucy.'

We pass the guard box without too much trouble. It's been a heavy night, according to fragments of conversation eavesdropped by the cabin. Instances of sudden catatonia enveloping several users of the Tube. Got themselves lost, stood stock-still at the top of the arc, necessitating search and retrieval operations. The guards would really rather have done without. Bethany catches a chuckle in her hand as we listen, sidles over to whisper into my ear.

'First time they've had to *move* into their supposed *territory* in who knows how long … surprised they could even remember where to go …'

'Shhh, they'll hear you! Let's just … get it over with. We're … where are we going, exactly?'

It's an end of town I'm not familiar with. Another spoke on the wheel of casinos ringing the city lies up ahead, the same orange cream spilling over the horizon, yet the angles and levels of streets and blocks aren't ringing any bells. It's strange. Underlying terrain can still screw with attempts to make the boundaries alike at every point on the circumference: a few foothills push the buildings up on their foundations like knees and elbows under a blanket. The landscape at once alien and known, the features and layout almost exactly the same whilst known to be *other*, a drinking straw severed at water-level.

'Going for a walk, is all,' she says, grinning. 'Haven't been South for a good while … easy pickings, when it's quiet …'

We're not going to the casino. Not yet. Instead Bethany takes my arm and we go striding down the middle of the street, forward and upright as though headed straight for the quiet of home, as promised. On the left, block after block of three-storey tenement buildings, still in half-decent condition, clearly lived-in. Patterned drapes still visible in several of the windows. Half-hearted pots of plastic sunflowers adorn the odd doorstep.

On the right: wasteland. The buildings had been burnt out from behind, the walls facing onto the streets still by and large intact. These soot-clad house-fronts teeter like unearthed Grecian masks; a best-angle tourist's photograph of ancient ruins. Searchlights reeling across the acres of debris beyond shine through the bones of the windows as they pass; the wrecked plates winking at us. I must have been back there before, looking for places to hide, looking for *something*. Pointless looking for souvenirs with nothing but smoking pile after tumbling column to mark your way.

Out of the guard's line of sight, it's down a side-street, picking our way over broken bricks and chunks of flame-scorched plaster.

'They've not got round to flattening these, yet,' she says. 'Running out of funds, Lucy … those Facilities don't run themselves, you know. On top of which … even if they did get a few blocks thrown up, they're running out of people to fill them.'

'So, what, they'll just leave it like this?'

'Aye. Doesn't make much difference – see? That's the city line right there, just a block or two away. A few extra acres of wreckage isn't going to make much difference when there's nowhere to *go*, is it?'

'Do you know the layout?' I ask, fumbling for something that sounds worthy of a plan. Bethany shrugs, removes a laminate from her pocket. Shining a spaghetti-thin torch over the diagram, she indicates blue lines arranged in boxes over a greyish blob.

'That's the South Side' she says, pointing to the blob. 'And those are what we're standing on. Can't do much damage here, anymore, but we *can* cause a bit of trouble. What do you say?'

'Sure. What we going for?'

'I know you and Caleb were into your arty wee messages and statements and all, Lucy, but we don't really have time to plot out anything as grand as that. Thought we'd go for some mindless destruction – we're better off having them thinking *we're* not thinking, if you get me.'

Caleb wouldn't be impressed, but just *going* for it holds a certain appeal. Artful arrangements on previous missions were satisfying, sure, but there was always this sense of restraint. Something holding us back from making full use of our hands and feet.

'Besides,' Bethany continues, 'We're not going to hurt anyone or anything … we'll just be finishing what others started, no?'

'True. Let's go.'

Bethany turns to look me straight in the eye.

'That sounds like an affirmative. No hedging or hemming … you're picking it up.'

'I'm here *now*, Bethany. I want to get this done.'

'Come on over here, then, and I'll get you kitted up.'

From a steel locker half-buried in a tenement's cracked foundations, Bethany unveils all manner of contraband we wouldn't have got past the guards. Petroleum, flares, flints, fireworks, rock hammers and hacksaws, rainbow canisters of spray-paint. Looks familiar.

'How long you been keeping this stuff here?' I ask.

'I haven't. Got a tip-off from a friend. Says he'd left it here quite by accident, after an..uh, unfortunate change in circumstances.'

She winks.

'Caleb!'

'Quite the pack-rat, far as I can make out. He's probably left shit lying all over the bloody city ….must have had big plans for the place. Shame, really – from what he told me, you two made quite the team. He'd the tech head, you'd the flair.'

'We did work well together. When we could agree on why we were doing what we were doing.'

'Well, you know *now*, don't you?'

'Yeah. So …kit me up.'

24th March 2024

In the Management Lounge, the Manager seethes back and forth across the plush carpet, tugging at cuffs with torn fingernails. The gentle ripples of jewelled velvet wallpaper and the scent of dark leather and teak are usually a warm welcome to repose. Today they repel, repress, an all-too-keen reminder of unexpended energy still locked in every tendon, grinding every joint. He does not like to be disappointed. On paper, on file, the calm of the outside could only be a good thing, a clear indication of results from rigorous enforcement of controls.

His reality spoke in a markedly different tone. If the calm continued, if inertia spread, he was looking at a desk-bound existence. A career path marked not in actions, but in *words*. His scalp tightens around an incipient migraine at the very thought.

A klaxon blares. The Manager opens the door to a new recruit, a young Agent too frightened and awkward to know where to look. He bears a tray of streamlined steel dining equipment, each item tinkling in his trembling grip, a wicker basket of bathing products slung into the crook of his arm. The Manager sneers, turns his back on the boy and stands facing the back corner of the room, fingers webbed across the back of his neck.

'Sir? Your tray? Your shower kit?'

'Put it on the table. Come back in three fifteens.'

'Yes, Sir.'

Footsteps whisper across the carpet. Metal murmurs against the teak tabletop. The Manager turns only after the click of the outgoing lock. He sits before his meal, glowering into the high-polished steel plate covers. The Manager, as befit his position, afforded himself certain privileges. One constitutes a diet made up of Raw Materials: gourmet meals pieced together from the few remaining resources of fresh meats, dairy products and vegetable matter. Sunday Roast. Again. He must have a word with the catering staff about their apparent indulgence in nostalgia.

He chokes back a mouthful of bile before pushing the first forkful past his lips. These days, the taste simply bores him. Cognitive energies were sapped, he thought, by the process of registering taste and texture; cells expended here that couldn't be used elsewhere. Time and energy required to fork, saw, chew, swallow was time and energy wasted. Others complained bitterly about foods freeze-dried, stirred to mix, H2O activated: failing to recognize the beauty of the arrangement, the efficiency.

Still, status mattered. He will force down raw fare for the sake of regulation, elevation, a marking of difference. He swallows without tasting, places the utensils back onto the tray and pushes it through the slot in the door. He lifts the wicker basket and makes for the bathroom.

This is his favourite room in the Facility. It bridges perfectly the gap between Management perks and Spartan ideals. Square miles of sleek tile, an angular bathtub and sink in butter-smooth enamel. Toilet bowl a dented seat tucked into the corner of the room, cistern and pipes buried under the floor. All in flawless dental white. The few visible fittings wrought in stain-proof chrome, light fixture an upended toadstool in glass so smooth it disappears into its own bluish halo.

Two facing walls of mirrored glass double the purity to infinite dimensions. The Manager strips without bothering to unfasten buttons. He drops the clothing down into a chasm set under a sliding tile in the floor, from which they will be picked up and taken to the incinerator. A fresh uniform hangs on the back of the door.

As he showers, the Manager examines himself with a clinician's eye. Grecian planes and contours answered back to many years' hard work, but the time for self-congratulatory appraisal had long past. Too much brain power.

His interest lies in tracking the development of scars and bruises, the better to assess the fight still left in those still able to be prodded into a beating. He grins as he washes, relishing the clamour of every ache and sting. It hadn't been the most productive of over-ground trips, he had to concede, but all was not lost. There were still injuries to tend, and to impart.

Finishing up in the shower, he steps onto the tile, dropping each damp towel down toward the collection point. He steps into his uniform as into fresh skin, shrugging shoulders and elongating spine, flexing calves and biceps. He steps back into the lounge as one leaving an airplane on the first day of a long-awaited holiday. He was very much looking forward to refreshing an old Intimidation tactic. The Facility hadn't made use of the Communal Laboratory for far too long, too busy wasting time, he has decided, on words and statements and questions and answers and all their associated lies. It was time to get back to basics. Hands-on. Practicalities. And as for issues of safety and accident prevention: every great historical movement that had ever been, that ever would be, required sacrifices along the way.

Overground

It's a trip. It's a pleasure. Action my insides have been primed for, waiting for me to quit wavering and get moving. I'm using Caleb's stuff, perhaps even finishing off tasks he'd started. A shock to realise I'm actually having fun. I'm doing this because I want to, need to, would have done so even without his encouragement. Shame that these epiphanies do seem to come too late.

We trip between searchlight beams, over remains of low walls, scratching ourselves raw in the frazzled corpses of hedges. Our feet crunch through drifts of rubble, necks and shoulders taut against surveillance.

We knock things over. We tear things up. Bethany lets me get a little crazy with the spray paints. No time or space to run the full gamut of my creative impulses.

'Just think … if we get what we're after, if we get out and away alive, you can spend all damn day painting whatever you fancy. Whole handfuls of the stuff, Lucy …'

Fire comes last. Shaken canisters of fuel scatter rainbow arcs of fluid across collapsed beams and hollowed trees, a series of concentric circles running from the core to the edges of the wasteland. Then matches, flares and fireworks. I'm going first. About time.

'Escape route?' I ask before striking. She shrugs.

'Light up. Then we run till we can't see anything anymore. They won't catch us anyway, there'll be … too much to look at.'

She's right. The first circle starts slowly, blue flames drowsing like a morning stretch. Gathering pace, blue soaks into yellow, then white, spreading faster as each drop of fuel feeds the next. Soon the foundations are ablaze, an orange vivid and rich enough to outstrip the sky's paler cousin. Smoke gathers in a plume over our heads, gathering weight and depth, sandy fragments abrading our throats. We stagger backward, hands thrown out for balance. Bethany nods approval, tearing wrappers from fireworks with her teeth. She splits the pack and hands me half.

'High and far as you possibly can. I don't fancy a Roman Candle up the arse.'

We reel back and let go.

All the power I've ever held in my arms has been leading up to this.

The noise is insane, all the broken teeth of the world crunching in a giant maw. Green, blue, gold, silver, red, violet, crimson, amber shafts and whorls light up the sky, tiny punctuation marks peppering each flare's descent. A grinding of wheels rumbles underneath the pyrotechnics. Red lights atop enforcement vehicles seethe across the spaces between light-shows. The Management have arrived. Surprised to find I'm not that bothered. Glance shifting over blazing fields, the seething crucible of flames *we've* created, there doesn't seem to be a single thing that we can't do. Maybe if Caleb had given me some fire to play with in the first place, I'd have got with the programme far quicker.

'Come on!' gasps Bethany, grabbing my arm, clawing smoke from her eyes. I can't see too well myself. Fixed only on the azure whirl, make sure I'm running the other way.

We're teetering down another raft of side-streets on the well-kempt half of the street, Bethany switching direction at every corner, doubling back, reeling around in circles. The fireworks are long over. I'm rather sorry to have missed them. Still the blaze pours smoke into the sky, striping the orange smog to a tiger's pelt. I'm not sure whether the pounding I hear is my heart or a fleet of steel boots in pursuit. We run forever, time stalled behind the smoke's impassable veil. Finally Bethany stops, then drags us both down a short flight of steps into the doorway of a basement flat. Slipping a wire from her jacket, she pops the lock in half a breath and drags us both inside. A smell of laundry damp and no longer fresh, of dust-slicks, of once-oiled lawnmowers now cultivating only rust. Carnival shapes leer from shadows, bending planes of milky light seeping in from slatted vents. I follow Bethany down basement steps I can't see, severed from my own feet, a child outrunning the darkness in the leap from the light switch to the safety of the duvet. Bethany puts her arm through mine, shoving us both back against the wall, fetid moisture in the concrete spread over my spine and shoulders.

'Bethany ...?'

'Shhh!'

For a moment, I'm sure she's crying. Her torso trembles, a rumbling whine building up in her skull, sniffling and panting and clutching her stomach. I prod her in the ribcage, wave my hand about the basement, losing the edges of my silhouette.

'Bethany?' I try again. The words seem to stick to my lips. 'You okay?'

'Yeah,' she breathes, 'Just ...hold it,' her words up-turned to fit a smile I can't see.

'Where are we?'

'Doesn't matter. The layout's the same for every single one.'

She's struggling to speak without screaming with laughter.

'Let's go, then! We can't stick round here!'

'Take your time, Lucy. It's cool. That, my friend, was an unmitigated success. They'll be kept busy with that for the rest of the night.'

A disgruntled mumble I can't quite control indicates how little I'd like to be down here any longer than I have to. Bethany tightens the controls around her mirth. A rustle of hair marks a shaking of head. She tugs my wrist and leads us both across the floor, both free arms reaching out to anticipate obstacles, both sets of feet kicked out and round in clownish arcs. We're up a second set of stairs before long, pressed up against another door. Bethany deals with the lock in a beat, leading into another stairwell. We stand in on another concrete landing in dust-frazzled amber light, familiar despite never having been here before. From a window leading out onto the street, we can see Management Disaster Vehicles rolling up to the waste ground, spilling drifts of Agents in fatigues and plastic suits out onto the pavement. There's no real urgency in their movements. Once they're assembled in lines around the burning debris, they just stand there *looking*. Some perceptively nodding with what could almost be approval.

'See that?' whispers Bethany. 'See how eager they are to catch the perpetrators? They're all too busy … watching the pretty fire.'

'But they'll—'

'—Oh, don't worry, they'll be all over the clues, all the recordings from the Tube to the street before long, making a lot of noise about clamping down on mindless destruction. They'll have composite photographs of the criminals in their favourite newspapers by the end of the week. Not us, though. We're not any use.'

'What do you mean?' I ask, pressing closer to the window. Some of the fireworks we'd thrown hadn't ignited right away – as the fires bear down on unlit fuses, the odd sheet of coloured sparks splits the sky from the midst of the field. As they do so, the Management Agents' heads all tilt in synch, following the paths of the flares up, round and back down again, a set of vintage marionettes coin-dropped in synch.

'You never taken a good look at those criminal photofits?' she asks, joshing my shoulder with her own. 'Not exactly taking in a wide spectrum of every subset of society, are they?'

'I've never noticed,' I mutter. I'm not telling Bethany about my issues with the paper.

'It's all the same guy, or handful of guys,' she says. 'Males of average height and weight, of indeterminate age, no discernable hair or eye colour. Generally 'male' and 'Caucasian,' although they will chuck in the odd woman or racial minority if they feel the positive discrimination thing's going too far toward one side or another.'

'But ... why?'

'Fear, Lucy. Assigning identifiable features to a criminal *rationalizes* the thing, don't you see? People will be looking out for a marked and notable handful of traits. Feel quite safe going about their business, not seeing anyone who looks like the mad, bad, dangerous person they saw in the news. But if the criminal on the cover looks like your average Joe, it could be anyone, anyone at all, folks you pass on the street or see in the shop or living in a flat in your building. Can't point fingers at a composite, can you? Which means everyone has the potential to be the rogue element.'

'But that's ... fucking ... Jesus, they can't get away with that! Those photos are meant to keep people safe! What if someone really does get hurt?'

'Then the whole thing starts up again. It's rotten, aye, it's scary business, but it's no more or less trustworthy than anything else we see in the paper, is it? Besides, good for us, at this moment in time, no?'

'Hmmm. I guess so.'

'Look, don't get too strung out about it. We've got enough to be dealing with. We'll save the manipulations of the press for another day, eh?'

'Right. Fine.'

'Come on, then. Let's get of here. Might catch a few fireworks on the way, eh?'

And we're gone. Utter silence from the upstairs flats is astounding, it seems incredible that people could just sleep right on through. We circle the building several times before picking a route down the blind side of the sector still standing, coming out at the edge of a block smudged from view by the still-gathering smoke. Soon we're crawling through crisp briars and cracked pathways, circling the Tube checkpoints to come up somewhere under the supporting brackets. Bethany stops, spent, leaning forward to clutch her knees.

'Jesus,' she gasps, 'What a trip!'

She lets it go, laughing so hard and thick and deep I'm expecting her to just drop to the ground, let it take her. It's infectious. Soon we're both sprawled on the slabs, fingers shuffling handfuls of dirt and smoothed pebbles of broken glass, tilting head back to peer up at the underside of the Tube. Neither of us flinching at the drumming of feet passing overhead, neither of us caring about much of anything, I guess. But we can't stay here.

'Bethany ...' I start, reaching over to pull her upright. Her face is a riot of smoke and dirt, skinny trickles of blood on her cheeks from flying shards of glass and rock. I doubt I look much of a school teacher, myself. We can't be seen like this, we may as well present wrists to arresting Agents. 'Bethany ...where to, now? We've got to get showered, changed. No way we can get back in the Tube.'

'We don't have to,' she says. 'We're on foot, tonight. Don't worry, I know where I'm going.'

'–but–'

'–what? You think just because they've given us nice, clean, safe walkways to get from A to B and back again, that there are no other options? We're Scottish, Lucy, hiking's in our blood.'

She snickers, indicates the thorny furze ahead, so thick and high at times it brushes the underside of the tunnel. Shattered slabs pick ancient pathways into the vegetation, vanishing and reappearing at random intervals. She gets to her feet, plunges right on in, beckons. I shrug and follow suit. Painful and treacherous as it is at first, there's something tremendously satisfying about the plunge and grind of bodies through less than accommodating space, a feeling of mastery over what once must have been *the elements*.

The night swallows hours, our breath and sweat and smoky stench disappearing up into the haze. We're back at my place an hour before reluctant dawn, shearing down side-streets, through sealed-off alleyways, over fences and barriers, dropping down always into carefully chosen shadow-thickets. It's an effort to keep from stopping short for a look at my hands and arms, to check and make sure it's really me who's responsible for their actions tonight.

It's me. I am doing something. I am taking it back.

Back at mine, Bethany opens her mouth to speak. She tilts her head up to the ceiling, mouths the air for a good half-minute before sniggering, dropping to her knees and splaying out on the carpet. Rolling over onto her back, she points to me and then the bed, closing her eyes. Rest, then, until tomorrow. I drop a blanket over the scattered limbs on my floor, and crawl up onto the mattress. Bethany is too tired even to snore.

This pattern marks the tumbling of the next few days into a blurry mire. Caleb had indeed left small holdings of tools and decorations in nests all over the city. We don't go quite so far with the fires from now on – we can only risk the dead giveaway of smoke-soaked clothing a few times over before we're asking for it.

182

And she's right. A look at the newspaper for the first time in months throws back faces of no particular note, faces as telling as figures in road-signs, blank illustrations in a first-aid manual. We're getting away with it. Yet I'm ludicrously insulted at the lack of recognition. *We* did it, not Joe Average, and yet the Management still insist on apportioning blame to the Great Anonymous. Bethany notes my ire, however hard I try to hide it.

'You're an idiot,' she says, 'Enjoy it, while it lasts. We're not in this for fame, Lucy, we're working toward cracking open that Facility. If we pull it off …if things keep going our way …we can take credit for all this and much more.'

We take down a couple of derelict buildings, flinching at each thunder of bricks to the ground. We tear out the electric in a few of the offices, and arrive clean and pressed in the morning to witness the confusion. We tip over barrels of burning banned materials, sending half-intact images and legible pages drifting through the streets, perhaps into the hands of the stimulant-hungry. We break out the spray paints as Bethany had promised, although frustration at not being able to produce effects of the kind I'd have got from oils or acrylics keeps me from going too nuts with the stuff. We slash up random communications cables leading from Management blocks to what Bethany posits as central controls. After much lip-nibbling on Bethany's part, we flood the tunnels under the gardens in the hopes of doing some damage to the nearby Management cells. Seen from above, the shards of sparks flowing up from the shorted electrics are a sight to behold, picture-book fairies and goblins scampering across the lawns.

All this and more over the space of a couple of days – you'd have thought they'd have clued in to what we were up to, growing far less subtle with every manoeuvre. Yet every night we return to mine to sink into sleep troubled not by what we'd been doing, but by what we would soon have to do.

D16 and F5 walk the line of Interns gathered in the corridor. Male and female, young and old, fresh and broken: all wear their bodies like waterlogged sandbags slumped the lengths of their spines, hands palming the corridor walls. Only Intern Number Nineteen stands erect at the back of the crocodile, head and shoulders streamline. He keeps eyes fixed on the front of the line, a phantom smile smudging his battered lips. F5 nudges his colleague.

'What's with Nineteen? He looks like a kid on Christmas morning.'

'You never know. Excited about being let out of his room, probably. None of them have any idea where they're going,' says D16. He makes a production out of adjusting the grips on his crowd-control device.

'Neither do we,' says F5. 'Unless you know something I don't ...I've never done a ... what was it? A Fact-Finding Exercise?'

'Aye. Doesn't really have a proper name, yet – there's just this whole bunch of kit in the labs that never gets used ...nasty stuff, mate ...'

F5 elbows D16 in the ribs as a further quartet of Agents enter the corridor. These are from the Technical and Electronics Departments, strapped into fire-retardant aprons and heavy tool belts. All exchange cursory nods and murmured greetings. The new arrivals take point along the length of the line. The last turns to D16.

'Set-up?'

'Uh ... yes. The Manager said you'd know what to do.'

'Yes,' says the Technician. He raises a brow, narrows his eyes. Fresh implications are carefully injected into his tone of voice. 'Any special instructions?'

D16 understands, but refuses to co-operate. This was the Manager's vendetta, not his own.

'No.'

The Technician shakes his head. He knew he couldn't ever rely Arts Agents for a straight answer. He places a jocular hand on D16's shoulder, tightening his grip by degrees.

'Which ... one ... is Nineteen?' he growls, each syllable swelling the limits of his vowel chamber. D16 shrugs, jerks his elbow.

'That one there. At the back. Looking awfully pleased with himself.'

'Thank you, Agent,' says the Technician, and, turning to his fellows, 'Right, men, let's get moving. Down the corridor and to the left. Communal Laboratory 7G.'

The Tech and Electrics Agents begin herding the Interns down the hallway. Some do require a little encouragement, but F5 can't help but pity those who are willing and mobile. Their expressions call up remnants of what it meant to feel insulted, to conceptualise indignity, as they shuffled ahead of sharp blows to the kidneys. Nineteen's strides lengthen, his shoulders open, as he charges before the Agent at the rear, his face a mask of swallowed fury. D16 nudges the Technician he'd spoken to.

'Agent?'

'Agent.'

'What's the deal with Nineteen? *Special instructions?*

The Technician dissolves into a rare grin.

'Oh … nothing *too* special, Agent. We've just to make sure he gets a front-row seat. Now, if you'll excuse me …'

The line trickles down the corridor. Unable to move forward any faster than fellow Interns in front, D16 and F5 can see Nineteen pin-balling across the corridor to avoid the Technicians' jabs. Both Agents need make efforts to hide the slow gleam of pleasure at even this slight defiance. The double doors at the end of the corridor collide closed with a boom, resounding between the concrete walls before sucking the slow shuffle of feet back into silence.

'What do you know, then?' asks F5. 'You said you've seen reports.'

D16 shakes his head, scans the corridor.

'I don't know enough about it,' he says.

'You know *something,'* says F5, dropping into a whisper. 'Don't worry, he's in the Management Lounge. You can tell me.'

D16 grabs F5 by the elbow and manoeuvres him into an empty room. The Agents look one another straight in the eye, a rare occurrence when the Manager is around.

'It's a combination of a whole bunch of different stuff from before. Psychometric testing, analytical exercises, intimidation, control, and …ha ha …*kids party games.* Something called Implicit Association tests, something to stimulate the memory. Show the Interns a bunch of slides. Take the first thing they think of and lead on from there. Except you don't get a prize for the right answer. You get a …something bad happens if you don't see – or say – the right thing. You've seen the units. Nasty shit.'

'And this is supposed to be more effective than the Interviews? If *beating* it out of them isn't working, what makes the Manager think this will make a difference?'

D16 attempts a snigger around an expression taut with horror.

'It's the word thing. You heard the Manager. He's had it with all that *talk* – words aren't giving him the results he's after. All these Interviews ... threats, deals, offers, promises, more threats ... not getting anywhere. We have *zero* information gathered that's of any fucking use – half the time, they're talking a load of shit just to keep from getting another beating. Makes sense, though. The language versus image thing. You remember how it was going, up there. Nobody had the time or the concentration span for *words*, mate – it was all pictures, movement, action, sensation ...and *pain*, the only language *everybody* seemed to understand.'

'God ... but ... does the Manager seriously reckon he'll get something? People don't ... make much sense, when they're in pain. Like you said, they'll say anything.'

'The slides are supposed to help them along. Track reactions, note similar responses to different images. Then plug in the polygraph if there's anything worth following up.'

'And has it worked before? I mean, why hasn't it been used till now?'

D16 slumps to a seat on the edge of the bed, elbows resting on knees, chin cradled in hands. His eyes are backward telescopes, black holes in time, unable to make sense of forced perspective.

'I don't know, mate. I don't think it does. Work, I mean. It's all interpretation, in the end. And I don't know why he's dragging it out. If you want to know the God's honest ... I think he's losing it. You saw what he did to X44 – to Bethany. I think he's ... I don't know, *afraid* ... if that's something he's *able* to be. If Bethany can ... let him down, a trained *Agent*, this whole thing isn't as solid as it should be. Which means he's losing control. Losing grip, on all of this. Which means he'll do pretty much anything to get it back.'

F5 leans against the back of the door, tracking possibilities across the blank pane of the ceiling. He's not so sure. The Manager had seemed to rather enjoy the conflict and resolution, the action plans, the redress, from the X44 situation and many more besides.

'So what does this all mean? What's he looking for? From any of the Interns?'

'I honestly don't think he even *knows* anymore.'

Here are a few reasons why you are in a lot of trouble. Think back. The last great spectacle. The last thing you and Caleb did together. Assuming you don't count your arrest, of course.

Pay attention.

You're running alongside parallel concrete ha-has pinning the rear concourse of the security firm to the building. The tarmac underfoot is latex-soft and soundless. The Management have missed a trick in their preference for surfaces without texture: stone chips would have given you away. It pleases you how easily their blanks and flats can be used against them.

Flashlights are unnecessary. Much of the light source comes courtesy of platinum-effect paint demarcating parking spaces. Halogen overheads rebound, transforming the lot into a silent discotheque. Painted farewells on the tarmac under the entrance barrier: THANK YOU FOR YOUR VISIT PLEASE DRIVE SAFELY under a cartoon moon-man with a smiling face. You don't find this as amusing as you would by day.

You stand before your own sunken reflections in double doors of reinforced glass. Caleb holds his hand up for a time-out, listening. Nothing. He sniggers, throws an arm up into the sky. Behind the glare, the pale rind of the sickening moon. He's done a good job.

'I think you've done it,' you whisper, 'There's no-one in the guard booth.'

Caleb nods and pats his pockets, before sliding a slender metal strip from the lining of his jacket. The minor fire just beyond the cellophane forecourt at the front of the building would keep all eyes and hands occupied for a good twenty minutes, perhaps more. Caleb has already run down for you the psychology of the security guard. So much time spent watching nothing happen meant that the slightest of distractions would be sucked dry, any anomalies peeled like a lover, stretching limits of the moment of return to the watch. Caleb's five steel barrels in pentagram formation stuffed with junk and set alight were all the more disturbing for having no fixed purpose or target.

'Right. Let's get to it, then, shall we?'

Your clumsy hands and unchecked feet flutter, boneless, at the end of your limbs. Noticing, Caleb pulls you close, a hair-muffled murmur into your ear.

'Don't worry about doing anything, yet. Let me take care of getting us inside, and then you're on, Lucy.'

He presses his lips to the top of your head, a desperate crunch of lip between skull and teeth, unspent energy clattering forth from his core to his edges. You love seeing him like this, all that miserable inertia sheared from his frame at the prospect of ideas in motion.

'Just tell me what to do,' you whisper.

187

Just be here,' he says, eyes starting out from socket-skin increasingly fragile, strained. 'Fuck, Lucy, you're here with me. You're here. We're doing something!'

He claps a hand over his mouth, shaking, rib cage bound around a rich stream of belly-laughter. You slide a palm across his back, nudging him toward what you have come to do. He takes a deep breath, stripping his throat of a build-up of thrice-swallowed smoke.

The metal splinter is not a lock-pick. The Management have long dispensed with locks of moving parts: prone to technical problems requiring hands-on servicing from locksmiths, carpenters and glaziers. Coded entrances needed no more than occasional tweaks, tightening knowledge of the systems around a select few. The Management hadn't accounted for the likes of Caleb. He'd spent hours bent over programming dictionaries and electrical diagrams, adding another spoke to the wheel of his otherwise useless skill set. You stand in the shadowy corner of the entryway whilst he examines a button-studded box set into the wall alongside. Framing the box with one hand, tickling with the steel strip with the other, he sets about the wires at the back as though back-stitching over an embroidery frame. The box bleeps, murmurs, bleeps, and settles back into silence several times, each slamming your back to the wall, skin freeze-thawing with tension. He steps back. The box hangs on a mess of wire like a desiccated spider.

'Nearly there,' he says, beckoning. 'Come take a look.'

You have no idea what you're looking at.

'What I've done is … look … if I pull this out … and this … and replace that … with this … the system's tricked into thinking it's just rolled off the factory belt. Brand new, no code yet. So we can put in our own. Cool, eh?'

You nod, wishing he'd get a move on before the fires at the front cease to captivate.

'Any ideas?'

'Hurry up, Caleb. That's pretty cool, go you! – but we can't hang about.'

He's hurt. You're supposed to come up with something cool, funny, dark, intellectual. You're supposed to christen his baby anarchy. And you're too taut and frightened to come up with a single thing.

'Nothing?'

'Just pick something, Caleb. Let's do this.'

He shakes his head and stabs at the box with the metal strip. You're too busy scanning every inch of the car park behind you to make out his chosen code word. It won't register until a long time from now how little attention you'd paid to things that mattered.

'There. Done,' he says, nudging the door. It gives without a whisper, slides across a carpet greased with elegant motifs. 'Come on.'

You step inside. He stands halfway across the entrance, leaning out to tuck the trailing wires back behind the box. You're now locked into a manic garden of shifting shadows, outside light sliding across polished surfaces, the interior of the building a depthless shimmer of the ocean at night. You both stand prone, immersed.

'Best part is,' he whispers, 'The Management won't know it, either. They'll have to rip the whole thing out and start again, if they're going to get into the building at all.'

You don't ask how you're getting out. He never has an exit strategy. The act was the thing, the finale to be improvised as you careened on into it.

'Where are we going?'

He removes a floor-plan laminate from his inside pocket, squinting through anaemic halogen. He shrugs.

'Doesn't matter much. Only the heads are party to the whole works. We fuck with one set of plans and models, we fuck with the lot. I say we go right to the top floor. Nice wee bit of symbolism, eh? Brains of the operation?'

You nod, awaiting a cue. You know there's more to it than a gutting of files. The rooftop offices would house the Management's commanders in chief. He's after the leather swing seats, the crystal decanters, the elevated blindness to the wreckage of the city.

'Come on, then. Need to take the stairs.'

Hinges sprinkle powdered rust across the carpet as you step into a haze of fetid air, a sharp reek of overheated radiator paint, banisters slightly sticky with dried sweat. Nobody's been in here for weeks: no need, what with the gilded cage of the elevators. Every other flight, boxy panes crack open a view onto endless monochrome vistas, the murky heavens indistinct from the concrete below as an eternal reflection of the sky on the sea. You and Caleb lock gazes at the top of each flight, palms on knees, leaning over to catch your ragged breath.

'Got to … quit the smoking …' he wheezes. You nod. That's not it. You're both more than capable of frantic bursts of energy when darting about outlying bridges, remaining parklands, strips of motorway ringing the city. It's the air in here. The accumulated breath of too many people with no reason to move from their seats, cars, office cubicles. It's worsethan the pollution – at least the latter could be identified, could be tackled if the authorities so choose. A population choking on its own breath.

He stops about half-way up for a look out to the front.

'Let's see what they're up to.'

The steel-drum star burns on. Slowing down, dull coals swallowing flames in on themselves. A few silhouettes stand in the midst, turning slowly on the spot. An Environmental Casualty truck is parked by the drums with lights and sirens turned off, two Agents leaning against the hood, arms folded.

'What are they doing?' you whisper. 'They could have had that out with a couple of buckets.'

189

They're waiting to see if it'll go any further. Doesn't look good on paper, if they have to go back and report a couple of dustbin fires. Either that, or it's been a while since they've ... seen something so pretty ...'

'And it wouldn't have occurred to them that there's action inside?'

'Nah. Too fucking smug, the lot of them. No random factors allowed in this crystal palace. See – the fire, right? That's a primal thing, a thug thing. Implies that whoever's responsible is just an idiot with a match and some petrol. Something more sophisticated going on? No way. Too frightening, Lucy. They're comfier assuming we've had all our lateral thinking bored right out of us. Which makes this place easy pickings, no?'

'True. We should hurry, though. You never know.'

'You're still afraid. Aren't you, Lucy?'

'A bit. Maybe. I don't know.'

'Don't be. Save it until we're being chased.'

He's kidding. He's not afraid. He doesn't mind, much, that you are. He takes your hand, grips tightly. He doesn't have to say out loud that he'll take care of you. Matching your steps and breath to his, you can close your eyes for the rest of the climb. The worst kind of silence surrounds: enforced vacuum, sucked dry of human sounds, your heartbeat so loud it could be shaking the glass in the window frames. And he still flows upstairs as easily as melting wax.

'This looks like the place,' he says, finally, drawing to a halt. 'You ready?'

It's an effort to open your eyes.

'It's okay,' he says. 'We'll be in and back out again in fifteen minutes, max.'

It's quite the statement set of doors, at odds with the utilitarian ethos hammered into homes and public buildings. Carved oak reeking of pine-scented polish, its rich ruby hue evident even in the dismal light. Wrought iron handles arc upward like a pair of begging hands. Another of those buttoned boxes set into the panels. Caleb snorts, disgusted.

'Money-grabbing fuckheads,' he says. 'Imagine knocking this door, here ...they'd make you wait, just so you could see what you were dealing with. Waiting, knowing you were in for it. Bastards. I'm going to enjoy this.'

His fingertips flutter across the panel, punching in his brand-new code. These doors do not give so easily, requiring a shoulder-shove, the better to impart a sense of privilege at having been admitted. You can smell the richness as soon as you cross the threshold. The privileges afforded the upper echelons, those with the responsibility to handle it. Leather, polish, heavy wood, phantom clouds of expensive aftershave, floating motes of imported coffee served thick as tar in pewter cups. You can barely feel your feet, sunk into carpets piled ankle-high. The passage lit only by a skylight stretched across the whole of the ceiling, up-lights on the roof donating a few slender rays of star-pale luminescence, glinting off the panel edges in three

190

matching oak doors, two on either side, one facing. Caleb opens each of the side doors, shaking his head.

'Just telephones on tables,' he says of the first, and, trying the second, '. . . and computer shit in boxes. We want that one. Come on.'

He darts back, takes you by the wrist and tugs you gently up the corridor toward the facing door. He presses his head to the edge, listening out once more for any movement.

'This'll be us,' he says. 'You ready?'

'Yeah.'

The first thing you register is the window. Almost a full wall looking out onto the upper limits of the city – so high up, now, the neon-blooming haze blocks the view of anything less than fifteen floors high. You've never seen the star-choking orange clouds from above: at this elevation, they bounce light upward into the office. Not only that – the sky up here is perceptibly clearer, the clotted atmosphere spread out like a carpet below the sill.

'God, look at that,' he mutters, 'Get all of the light, without having to look at what's happening below. I thought it went all the way up. The smog.'

This should be a cause for celebration, you suppose. Instead you're just so very, very tired. Whether or not the damage to the sky wasn't as bad as you'd thought, the reclaimed miles of firmament were not yours to see, to have. You never would be in the position to pay for this chunk of starlight.

'Let's get to it, then.'

It's a pastiche of every luxury bolthole ever featured in books, films, plays, artworks on the subject of power by accumulation, of investment over restraint, of effulgence over taste. It's as though the place were assembled by slotting together a brace of luxury state-funeral coffins. Carved oak panelling. Drifts of silk wallpaper swimming with paisley fishes. Chairs of deepest garnet leather. A desk in the same heavyweight oak stretching almost the full breadth of the room. Micro-computing systems dotting the surface like china figurines. A tang of pollen in the air of the room would indicate that they're real, that dense sprawl of orchids under an enormous cut-glass bell-jar on a side table. You feel ill. All this luxury for those who preach artlessness and austerity, for those who prescribe a stripping-away of all and any slivers of difference, of aspiration, of growth and fecundity, of beauty and splendour for its own sake.

'Sheesh. Where do we start?' he asks.

'Let's just take it all apart,' you say. You are thinking of your mother, crack-backed around a word puzzle. Of your father, whose own self-improvements drew him from his own family. The sweep of your mother's horizons contracting to the breadth of a home, a room, a chair, the palm of her hand. All in the interests of keeping up appearances. Of plumbing all reserves into the doing of the Done Thing – a set of standards clearly at grave odds with the riches wallowed in by those closest

191

to the core of the Management organism. *Trying and failing. Failing and wanting. Wanting and sacrificing more than could be ticked off on an inventory.*

Maybe, at the heart of it, you want to take it apart just to see how it works, to catch a glimpse of rusting springs, fill your hands with spent cogs and foam rubber. You don't have time, you don't have sufficient thought-blanks, for Caleb's messages and statements.

'Huh?'

'Just take. It all. Apart.'

He didn't think you had it in you. You're supposed to be the aesthete of the operation, your constitution wired against mindless destruction. He's always taken care to keep tongue jammed firmly into cheek, to maintain a sense of humour, to pique curiosity. To be childlike about it without being infantile — a kid's tactile experimentation, attraction to colourful and shiny object, the resulting demolition appearing to have occurred almost by accident. Wiring right on into it goes against everything you've so far managed.

'Lucy. We can't just—'

'Burn the fucking place down,' *you say, the pitch of your voice creaking up to brush the carved glass sculptures set in niches around the ceiling.* 'I don't care. Burn it, wreck it, take a fucking axe to the furniture, paint the walls with acid. It's too much. It isn't fair.'

'Lucy. Cool it. We're going to do what we always do. Mess with the place, not mess it up. We want to fuck with their heads, and that's not going to happen if we just take it apart. We need to leave a message.'

'Here's a message,' *you say, striking out at the bell-jar, knocking the orchids to the floor. The fleshy stench of forced tropics fills the room, your eyes watering with what might well be tears. Caleb stands back, open-mouthed, as you grind shards of glass into the floor. Your breath catches in your throat, rough snarls mingling with floral syrup. You want to kill the flowers, now, the flowers that aren't yours, anymore. He lets you stamp yourself to exhaustion, before fixing hands about your forearms, locking you up against his chest to whisper in your ear.*

'Shhhh ... shhh, it's okay,' *he murmurs.* 'You've got to calm down, Lucy. We can't get carried away, we've ... we've got to make a point.'

'Oh, Caleb, you don't get it. This isn't working, none of it. Look! Just fucking look at this place! Think about what's outside. The city's rotting, falling to pieces, we haven't seen the sky for years and people we care about are disappearing, dying, going fucking nuts! Here's a perfectly ordinary office building. And POW, the Management move in, and it's a scene from a Humphrey Bogart movie! They're taking everything from us, and building fucking castles in the air! What the fuck, Caleb! What the fuck!'

You're usually more eloquent than this. Sometimes you're so strapped for words, only a string of expletives will do.

'You knew this already, Lucy. This is extreme, I admit ... didn't think they'd be so quick off the mark, vamping this place up, but ... look, you've got to cool it. This is why we do what we do, yeah? We fight, we show them what we think of their power, their privileges. But we've got to be clever about it. Any fuckhead on the street can wreck a joint. We've got to be ... delicate. Show them we can get inside, go places we aren't meant to go, get our hands on stuff we're not supposed to touch. Besides, destruction's their game. We're more sophisticated than that. We've got to be, if there's to be anything left in the end.'

You are crying, now. You understand, yes, but sometimes you just want to pull things to pieces, stream your desires along taut lengths of thigh and forearm, think with your feet and hands, or not at all. You hurt in colours, textures, weights and shapes more varied and complicated than you'd ever care to explain, to investigate. You don't make space or time for such thoughts very often, so otherwise occupied with the business of continuing to breathe. You lurch from him toward the desk, battering your fists on the oak, making enough noise to attract the attention of the guards out front. Caleb tries to take you by the wrists, your spines a pair of brackets set the wrong way around as he strives to wrap himself around you, bind you, protect you from yourself.

'Lucy! Lucy!' he hisses into your ear, 'Lucy, please, you're hurting yourself!'

One day you will remember this: he thought more of your hands than the attention they could be attracting. One day you will recall this as the first time you've felt anything at all for these missions of dissent. The first time you'd a buzz of fight in your girlish fists. The first time you've ever felt yourself wearing out, true exhaustion overriding studied boredom.

'Lucy ... please!' he murmurs, still refraining from raising his voice. 'Please. For me. I can't do this alone.'

You hear the cliché loud and clear. Those truths, made abhorrent by dint of familiarity, hiding under the tongue like an after-dinner mint. Sometimes you've got to admit to the comfort of a failure of imagination. You're not a sucker unless you're being lied to, and the leather creak in his throat would suggest otherwise. Slowly you rise and turn, a child's defiant uncurling.

'There ...' he murmurs, pupils scattering about your face, watching it recompose. 'Hey ... c'mere ...' He pulls you close. Your ribs squeal complaint. You'll be feeling your tantrum for days.

'Right ... okay ... you still in there?'

'Yeah. Yeah. I ... yeah.' You don't have the energy for an apology, particularly when you're not sure you'll be sincere. He pulls you out of the collapsed circles of broken glass, a gentleman drawing a wallflower up for a dance.

'Okay. I ... maybe we should just get out of here,' he murmurs. 'Save it for another day.'

'No, Caleb. Forget the orchids … just … we'll just do whatever we came here to do.'

'Are you sure? I mean, I don't even know yet, and we've been up here for a while already.'

You both scan the walls for the crimson zoetrope of a Management fleet. You listen out metronome footfalls. You're not ready to leave until he's done whatever he came to do. You're not carrying around an extra weight of guilt at having robbed him of the chance.

'Let's do something … cute,' you say, raising an eyebrow, forcing a smile. 'Random factors. Have them scratching their heads.'

'Oh … here I was, thinking you meant …' He sees your eyebrow, raises you a wink. You've gone through the almost obligatory phase of fucking on desks, carpets, filing cabinets, laboratory benches and car bonnets in each of those places you weren't supposed to be. Fun, yes, but took the shine off your time alone. It was hard enough trying to slough the taint of surveillance from your skins once you'd closed you flat door on the city. By tacit and mutual agreement, you'd both decided the Management shouldn't have the right to your steam prints and claw marks on their wipe-clean surfaces. You've always enjoyed the irony – almost a century of thorny male-female negotiations, things were looking up, a balance was imminent, and yet it had taken such an extreme shift in societal constructs to enforce the specialness of sex.

'Nah … wouldn't want to get up to any of that in here,' you say. Don't like that dirty feeling, you know? This place is crawling … we might catch something.'

Then you're both chuckling and everything seems like it might be okay. Caleb scuttles around the perimeter of the room, peering from the window.

'I think they're still messing about down there,' he says, 'Can't see or hear a thing.'

Neither of you want to talk about the smog-clot buoying up the upper floors. Too raw, still.

'So. What's the angle, then?' you ask.

'Ech … weird and wonderful modern art?' he drawls.

'Sounds like a plan.'

Caleb starts with the wall panels.

'These aren't built-in,' he says. 'They're just stuck on. Wasters … this stuff would have cost a fortune, and they've cheaped out on putting it up properly.'

He reaches into the lining of his pocket and hands you a slender steel tool, smooth on one side, rough on the other, much like a giant nail file. He has a long, fine hook, the end of which he slips in behind each wall panel.

'Dig it around, like … file it off,' he says. 'They used to do this back in the Second Twenties, you know …workers would go around stripping roofs for sheet metal, selling it on. Theft, aye, but when you think of all the effort that must have

194

been, on top of eighteen-hour days ... just to put a bread-crust in their kids' mouths ... some things never fucking change ...'

You let him rant on for a minute or two before eyeing the window, the door. Time presses.

'Sorry. Let's just do this, eh?' You move like clockwork dancers, each action demanding its answer, empty hands seeking to be filled, stilled flesh craving the burr of the file, the splintering of wood. The transference of energy from thought and speech to deed.

'Okay. So what now?' you ask.

'Hmmm ... want to get rid of that shit ...' he gestures to the technology on the desk, 'But we'll leave that to the end. Some basic defenestration, eh?' He shifts the silicone boxes to the corner of the room. Already, the place is a theatre set between productions: drifts of sawdust peppering the carpets, gormless trails of electrics, detached panels and bared plaster reinforcing an air of the half-made, the abandoned.

'Paper files?'

'In a bit. Let's get the desk, first.'

You remove the drawers. Caleb removes his tool belt and spreads it on the desk. He hands you a claw hammer, takes up the hacksaw.

'We'll take it apart,' he says, 'We'll just be delicate about it, eh?'

It's tremendous fun, a children's game of blocks. Like the walls, it's a construct of grandeur, heavy-weight pieces pulled from their feeble joints with no more than a wrench of the arm. You're soon stood by neat piles of wood with your arms folded, feeling rather pleased with yourself.

'What now? What do we do with this stuff?'

'Mmmph. I dunno. Quick swap?'

You've done this before. Switching car doors for bonnet lids. Turning signal boxes upside down. Stringing lights from lamp-posts with hot-pink elastic bands. Peeling warning posters from windows, doors and guard boxes and replacing them with prints of forbidden artworks, mimeographed album covers, T-shirt slogans. Wrapping barbed-wire spokes with paper flowers. Pointed pointlessness: the message lay in the polite smile of the insult, the buckling of routine, the slipping of random factors between sheets of glass and concrete. All carried on under the black eyes of the cameras. Proving to the Management that systems were fallible, that a warped sense of humour has a power of its own.

'Here,' he hands you a hammer, a cluster of nails. 'Make whatever you like. Can you manage? It's not as heavy as it looks.'

'Yeah. Cool.'

'Watch yourself on ... that, there,' he says, tilting his chin toward the broken bell jar.

'Will do. What are you doing?'

'Messing around with the files. An old trick, but a good one.'

195

You set about the wall panels as Caleb fumbles in the desk drawers, removing a pair of paper shears, a pot of glue. He empties the contents of a filing cabinet, crouches down in the paper wasteland and begins cutting the sheets to pieces.

You have a project. You're able to lose yourself for a while, in the movement of panels, thumping of nails, the warm burr of effort settling into your bones. You get carried away. You can't help yourself. Still silence outside, on the stairs, no shifting of light kicking heartbeats out of joint.

You step back when you're finished shifting, pounding, sawing.

You've made a Wendy house. A fairy lodge out of a vast, polished assertion of dominance.

'Look!' you say.

Caleb drops papers to the floor.

'That's awesome,' he says, 'How did you—'

'I don't know,' you say. 'It just sort of ... came to me.'

The sloping roof comes roughly to hip-height, the door just about large enough to admit a small child. You're especially proud of the windows, sawn into tipped archways; of the roof built for picnics, for pointing out starsInside, motes of sawdust dance up ghosts of dwarfs and talking dogs. The back of your necks pricks with a flush; you've taken it a bit far, perhaps. Failed to mark the boundaries between statement and rank sentiment.

'What made you ... a house? I was thinking ... I don't know ...'

'Been on my mind, I guess. That's a message, don't you think? Show them what we still take to be ... important, I guess?'

'Hmmm ... wouldn't give them too much credit for picking up on stuff like that. They see a house, they think office space. Almost wish we could take it away with us, eh?'

'Ech. That'd just be robbery, though,' you say, giving him a pointed look. 'Besides ... I wouldn't want to have it around. Nice to look at, aye, but a bit cack-handed in terms of that ... symbology we're going for. Might as well be one of those cosy wee Nativity scenes.'

'I like it. Maybe it's best they don't understand ...one less thing they'll have to use against us.'

You don't mention the battery cages in which you and Caleb have lived for years, now. You don't mention the supermarket shelving slat of your mother's in the Catatonics Wing of the reality-bypassed. The sight of your own gingerbread house, once the Estate Sale Agents in the Management's employ had come by to strip the skin from your childhood. Change the subject.

'Huh. Yeah. You're right. It's not like we're giving them anything. Except a headache, and an afternoon trying to put the place back to the way it was.'

'And you enjoyed that, didn't you?'

196

You did. A child again, building sandcastles in full cognisance of their eventual removal by the tide. Using your hands, your eyes, your spatial awareness and critical faculties, none of which you feel the lack of until you've had need of them.

'Mmm-hmm. God, I used to be so into it. Arts and crafts.'

'Next time, you're getting full creative control. How about it?'

'Cool,' you say, wishing he weren't already plotting another round. The odds are slowly stacking against him, you know. He can only get away with so much for so long. Yet still you'll be standing by his side in your borrowed fatigues, as always and always and always again. 'What are you doing with those files? Anything in there?'

'Hmm. Not really — well, probably. It's all in that code-that's-not-a-code. Management speak. Fifteen million technical terms to dress up a simple concept or routine. I reckon if we mess it up and ditch the computer, we'll have at least put a dent in their info bank.'

'What's with the scissors and glue?'

He grins, winks, shrugs. 'More kid stuff. Kind of.'

'Cut and paste?'

'Yeah. You remember that shelf of books I had in the last place? The ones I didn't get back?'

You remember. It had been an ugly afternoon. Caleb dervish-wheeled from box to box of your belongings, tearing the rooms apart, hollering down the telephone at the Management's removal men. They hadn't been valuable, those books — crack-spined and dog-eared, tea-stained and grass-scorched from multiple readings — but Caleb knew he'd never be able to lay hands on other copies. Such books, explained the worksheets in plastic wallets dropped into your mail slot, did not sit well with the Management. They did not fit a system built on order, manners and good behaviour. They were full, Caleb had explained with a sneer, of ideas. Bad words, scandals, revolutions: recipes for chaos, should the reader be sufficiently divorced from reality to attempt recreations. Caleb had given you a potted history of a branch of literature once concerned with the telling of truths, the pushing of parameters, immersed in a healthy disregard for authority. You'd followed him out into the street, chased him along to the concrete quadrangle set alongside one of the Management's strongholds. There, in the same steel drums he'd lit out front this evening, burned a seemingly endless supply of contraband. The fires had been going for months, weeks, as the Management rounded up every record, book, artwork, film or artefact at odds with a calmer, safer, cleaner future. Caleb had cried as the embers crawled over the names of his literary heroes. He knew he'd never again read their words, drink their wisdoms, lean into the creamy smoke of a world with potential to be other than it was. Even now, you'll catch him murmuring to himself in another voice, trying to track back over the pages once propped before his eyes.

'Yeah. I remember. Ideas?'

Just a thought. Burroughs. One of my favourites. He published whole books of cut-and-paste. Taking a text, slicing it up, rearranging whole pages, words, sentences. Half the pleasure in reading was trying to crack the code. You need imagination for that. And these Management fucks don't have a sliver of that. Like to see them trying to figure out any of this.'

He throws a hand over the snowfall of paper scraps.

'We make them a collage,' he says. 'Want to help?'

'Sure. Hold on.'

You check the door, the window, the depth of night still clinging to the firmament.

'What do you think—'

'I don't much care, Lucy. I reckon they're all still sat out front, waiting for something to happen. Either that, or they're still trying to figure out the codes on the door. We haven't left a trace, you know. They probably figure they've forgotten it. They're too stupid, too arrogant, to think anyone's smart enough to get past the door without a battering ram.'

You shrug, start to help him move the desk pieces. Caleb hammering, you holding, you've the desk nailed to the wall in less than five minutes. It looks pretty cool already, the skewed angles and mismatched dimensions giving the room an air of a funhouse mirror gallery. He hands you a glue stick and staple-gun, gesturing to the shreds at his feet.

'Go for it. Anything you like. You don't even have to read a thing; just make sure no two pieces from the same sheet go up side-by-side.'

You both work quickly, in silence. At first, you try to pick up a little information from the scraps in your hands — there may be something important there, a warning, a whiff of plot, maybe even a sliver of hope — but Caleb's right. It's all in code. You can feel your eyes tilting back in your head at the sight. Technical terms, extrapolated naming devices, rewrites of synonyms accepted as politically correct, numbers and acronyms standing in for what could be anything, objects, places, people, continents, planets, philosophical constructs. You pause over a sheet still left intact. A bar chart, a gathering of statistics, an incomprehensible cluster of jargon. At the top, a heading — INTERNAL REPORT CONCERNING PURCHASE AND DIVISION OF DIETETICS-APPROVED DAIRY PRODUCTS. It's a milk chart. whose turn to buy, who's owed what from a petty cash supply. Your stomach buckles with mirth. They were not impervious to the same piddling concerns besetting the civilians they controlled. Caleb is having much the same reaction — he snorts, disgusted, every time his eyes move over yet another meaningless edict. Soon you're both pasting without looking, smearing words and glue across every available inch of the wood. When you run out of space, you continue up the walls, smothering the paisley fish. Out of space, you and Caleb lock eyes, stare down at your handfuls of scraps. You're not touching the house. It wouldn't be right, to sully your work with their banal abuses

198

of language. The remaining scraps you each place into a brass wastepaper basket. Caleb pours glue over the top, clotting it to nonsense.

'Right ...' he says, dropping into a crouch, smearing sticky hands on the plush carpets. 'What do you think?'

'A beautiful mess, I guess,' you say. 'Isn't that what we wanted?'

'Done and done. Making something from nothing.'

He's right – aside from the shattered bell-jar, the sweet-rot corpses of the orchids, there's nothing in the room suggesting destruction for its own sake. It's merely a matter of a switching of places, a changing of forms – neat lines of type in place of the wallpaper; desk deconstructed and laid up against the walls; a dollhouse from yards of heavy panelling. Creativity supplanting rote, skewed angles in place of orderly oblongs. Foul baroque excesses slung aside to make way for what you're tempted to call art. You can almost understand the Management's blanket ban on such things. Too many loose ends, blurred edges, too many multifarious interpretations for a system locked in binary. Risky business, might just inspire original thought.

'What now?' you ask. Danger that's dogged you from the very first step now seems to belong to another day, another place, as abstract as the words cut from the pages. You can't stay here, though. Morning is coming, daylight's enthusiasm notwithstanding.

'Huh?' He's lost in thought, still smiling at your dollhouse.

'How are we getting out of here?'

Another of his freakish grins, blue-tinted now as the dawn begins to trudge toward the skylight.

'I don't know about you, but I can't face being stuck in that staircase again. How's about we take the scenic route?'

'Window?'

'Fire escape. We can take all that computer shit with us, and this way we can watch it hit the ground.'

'Cool. Let's move.'

You're quick enough gathering up boxes and wires, but you're not quick enough. Breeze whipping through the window at your back keeps you from hearing footsteps on the stairs. You're each taking one last look at the job, sketching dollhouse architecture and wallpaper patterns deep into memory, to be examined and gloried over later, back home. Caleb has his free arm locked around yours, a pair of parachutists buddying up before jumping.

The door hits the wall hard enough to crack the plaster. In the entrance stands a red-faced man, glossy as a hydrant, barrelling ahead of a tall, thin man in a suit the colour and texture of a rot-damp mushroom. You shriek, and jerk toward the window, craning your neck to catch sight of the first run of the fire escape. Caleb's arm tightens on yours, keeping you in place.

'Don't! We're not ready yet!' he yells.

199

'What in the HELL is the meaning of this?!' bellows the fat red man in the security uniform. This is not the time for quips or feints or negotiations. They're marching slowly toward you, the open window still a window, after all, not an exit or entryway by any Management regulations.

'We were just leaving,' says Caleb, any humour in his voice choked to a rasp. You don't know where to look. The two men glide across the floor, then suddenly stop. They're taking a long, hard look at your dollhouse.

'What on earth ...' says the thin man, strain making sharp arrows of his arms.

Their art appreciation lasts a mere few seconds as Caleb leans on the window pane, trying to take a measure of the fire escape. The red man snarls, heaves himself around the dollhouse, running toward you with outstretched arms like a vengeful housewife. Divided attention between the fat man and Caleb's fidgeting with the window pane doesn't keep you from noting the tall man's reaction. He doesn't look angry at all: instead, an indulgent smile plays about his lips, his arms folded as he walks slowly around the room, peering at your creations as one would in a gallery. His interest in you is transitory, incidental, his partner clearly trusted to take care of any grunt work.

'Curious ...' you hear him murmur, 'Thought we'd gotten rid of all that ...'

Caleb grabs the leather swing chair and shoves it into the path of the red man, the whirling star of wheels at the base starting up from the floor, at an angle most unfortunate for a pursuer short in the legs. The man does not go over right away, but falls into the upturned bucket of the chair, howling and cupping his hands over his crotch.

'Get out!' shouts Caleb, 'Come on!'

Revolving panes of light and shade make it impossible to see where your feet are landing. You close your eyes and trust Caleb's guidance, his hands on your arms manoeuvring you into place on the platform below. Only then do you open your eyes. He's still up there. You hear pieces of furniture crashing to the floor, Caleb's shadow a flurry of limbs and oblongs as he throws into the path of the red man anything he can put hands on. You laugh, you can't help it. The, something strange. The tall, pale man appears at the other end of the wide window. He barely moves, head facing outward in spite of the commotion at the other end of the sill. He sees you, stood down here on the fire escape, and nods very slowly, grasping his chin in his hand. You don't have long to ponder this oddity: Caleb finally rolls over the sill and drops down to the platform, grasping your shoulders to catch his breath, cords and wires from the electronics wrapped around his forearm. The red man leans over, swiping for Caleb's head, howling something barely intelligible. Caleb can't move yet, can't breathe, and you're not strong enough to carry him. Your eyes catch another glimpse of the pale man, still stood in the window, this time turned toward his companion, saying something, barely moving his lips. The red man spits a final *curse and pulls back from the window and into the room. Caleb grips your shoulders tighter, hauling himself upright.*

'Come on,' he rasps, 'Let's get out of here.'

You tug at the wires still binding his wrists, trying to free him.

'No!' he shouts, wriggling to loosen them up, yet refusing to let go. Once you're on the next story, he's breathing more easily, standing upright, gazing at the steps you've just descended, free of pursuers. He laughs, shaking with glee. He always gets like this after an exercise, celebrating long before you're both in the clear. He's looking outward and down, seeing only the way you're headed.

'Fuck yes!' he whoops, dropping your arms to raise his own in triumph. You're exhilarated too, you can't help it, but as you round the angle onto the next set of steps, your eyes are drawn back to the scene of the crime you've just departed. The jagged pane still seethes with that careful mood lighting, warm glow from oak and leather simmering like the death throes of a fire. The red man is gone. The pale man still watches, hands folded behind his back, the trace of a smile still coasting his lips.

You have to make your way through the blanket of smog. It's not like you'd imagined – you've been hill-walking before, a lifetime ago, and you remember the cold-shower froth of damp cloud infiltrating clothes and hair and skin eyes, a potentially unpleasant sensation rendered glorious by virtue of the freshness of altitude and open space. This is nothing of the sort. This is a dry heat, a walk between walls of a painted radiator, hot specks of toxic dust lodging in your throat, pushing past your drawn-tight eyelids, forming a layer of fluorescent eye-trash far outstripping those midnight tadpoles. In the thick of it, you can't see a thing, trusting to your feet and Caleb's breath to lead the way.

'You alright there, Lucy?'

'Yeah. How can you see?'

'I can't. Just … ha ha … better down than up, eh? Least we know where we're not wanted.'

You're making it into the clear a few steps further down. You can see your feet, at least. You still feel you'll never quite be clean again, your skin crackling with dust as though you'd been wrapped in cellophane.

'Time for the finale.'

'Huh?'

Caleb grabs your wrist with his free hand, shoves you down the steps ahead of him, and gives the wires an almighty tug. Then it's a race to emerge fully from the fog, two steps at a time, thundering blind, praying your knees and ankles will hold out. An irony strikes – that it seems the faster you try to move, the more your movements seep into cinematic slow motion.

You're both on the next level by the time you hear the crash, sheltered from the rain of shattered glass by the landing overhead. Caleb whoops as the boxes of metal and silicone soar past you both to smash on the ground, both of you upping speed on your downward descent as though trying to match the speed of gravity, whipping cords trailing behind the equipment like the cosmic dust of shooting stars you've never seen. Caleb draws you over the balcony just in time for the impact: plastic casing cracking like an egg, shards of glass flying from the point of collision for what seems an incredible distance, silver streaks of silicone and wire all heaving from the casing like a pit of glossy snakes. You're too far up to hear the noise. The city skyline blushes in the spaces between buildings, gearing up for another unspectacular dawn. Already the motorway loops heave with cars, a plague of giant beetles enamelled in one of five regulation shades of taupe – already heaving, or still backed up from yesterday, it's impossible to tell. The casino lights provide the only startling hits of colour – lurid green bank notes, pink cocktail cherries, bell-bottomed guitarists strutting between shapes in bright blue tubing – and from a distance, it could be any other city, seen from motorway overpass leading from any airport in any country in the world. You know better. Neon boxed around an empty frame. And that's where you're both headed, back down into grey banks of concrete, blurring the lines between shadows and solids.

'Caleb. We've got to move. They'll be down the elevator and out the front door, by now.'

'We'll see,' he says, a smirk playing about his lips.

The rest of the descent is something of an anticlimax, speed in itself being the only impetus. When you hit the ground, your first impulse is to run. You stagger three metres and stop, your thigh muscles giving out after the strain of the descent. Caleb laughs, circling the wreckage of the computer systems, stretching out his calves.

'Take your time, Lucy. We're going nowhere in a hurry after that.'

You don't understand. He's lost his mind. He wants you both caught.

'Caleb! We've got to get out of here!'

He grins, saunters up on oiled hips, rolling the sensation back into his legs. He takes your arm and leads you from the back alley, right back around to the front of the building. You struggle, pull at his wrists, your head reeling back and forth on your neck as you try to find a hidden exit.

'Are you crazy?'

'Come on, Lucy, Trust me. You'll want to see this, it's a riot.'

Back over the ha-has, over the cellophane lawn, and you're facing onto the double doors of the entryway. Behind the glass, the red-faced man smacks fists against the door frames, against the wall, against the inside buttoned buzzer box corresponding to the one outside. This latter hangs half-dead from the wall, wires dribbling sparks to the ground. The man sees you both and notches up his rage, now hurling himself against the glass like a wasp in a bottle.

'What the ...' you mutter, eyeing the entry systems.

'You saw. Tap in a few wee odds and ends, and ...poof, you're not only in charge of the codes, you're in charge of what happens if anyone tries to fuck with them ...'

'But they got in!'

'Aye, but they had to wreck the thing first. Self-destruct, oldest trick in the book. Bugger up the works, all locks slam shut automatically, can't be opened even from the inside. It's how they used to trap bank robbers. Lock them in with their own swag.'

You laugh. This time you mean it. However many times you tell yourself you've had enough, that, whatever his charms, Caleb's extra-curricular activities were becoming just too much for you, he manages to surprise you. That's no cheap trick, no daft little prank – he's gotten you both out of the building in safety, without being pursued, and he's done so with no more than a few lines of code. Later, you'll remember this, the next time he's buried in a book. The glass in the door rattles, trembles, each time the little red man smacks off the surface.

'Isn't he going to …?' you ask.

'Nah. Reinforced safety glass. Fire and bullet-proof. Just a shame for them they didn't bother glazing the upper floors with the same stuff, eh?'

He takes your hand and tugs you gently toward the door, to look the red man in the eye. He nudges the outside security system with his finger, and shrugs as it topples to smash on the ground.

'Shame … if only they'd the patience …'

He locks his arm through yours as you face down the door. The red man's eyes are rolling in his head, whitening from strain at the rims of his sockets, pale circles set in his ruddy face like a skier's sunburn. His jaw flaps, mouth jabbering words you can't make out.

'Soundproof, mate,' says Caleb in jest, making a burlesque of every syllable. 'You'll have to speak up!'

You both chuckle. The red man can't get any wilder.

'Look at that, Lucy …' Caleb murmurs. 'I want you to look at what we're up against …'

He draws you up closer, closer, whispering into your ear.

'I know you're not always with me on this … not quite getting what I mean, half the time. Tonight, though, you were … you were amazing, Lucy. And I know you were scared – I'm scared too, sometimes, but it's moments like this that we've got to remember. What we can do. And what they can't. I mean, look at that. That's the sum of their power … at least at this moment in time. A pig in a cage, watching us walk away. We can do this. I'm not saying we can beat them, not right away, but … if we make enough of an inroads, if we scare them enough, we can really show them. Show them they can't take control of every little thing. That they're not impervious. That we can make something with their nothing.'

You're caught up in this speech, you admit. It sounds pretty cool. And you do appear to be getting away with it. You won't wonder until later what had become of the tall, pale man. It won't occur to you till later that you've both been

203

seen, in flesh and on camera. That you've made them pretty angry, and they're willing to wait to get you when it's you two caught with your guard down.

Underground

Interns form a trembling line against the wall outside the Laboratory. Instructions are to take them inside no more than two at a time. Things could get out of hand, if those still waiting were to see what's inside.

The Lab is accessed via two sets of steel double doors. Two Agents control of the line whilst two others lead an Intern each into the passage between the doors. Here, Interns are cuffed and blindfolded before being inside. Only once each are strapped into the Units are the blindfolds removed. One row at a time, starting from the front, thus preventing Interns panicking at the sight of their fellows. They have enough to deal with, getting used to their shackles and gags.

Caleb is on his best behaviour. Crowd-Control Devices did not have to be detonated to do some damage, and he's already boasting fresh bruises. He's having a hard time keeping his sudden good mood in check. Wherever else is going on, he's out of his room for the first time in months. Leg muscles flood with a freshness at being able to walk further than the length of himself without having to turn on the spot. Even the air, dank as it was, didn't have quite the same reek as the ceaseless build-up of a body's own breath.

He accepts his blindfold without protest. Senses drawn in, the staggered breath of the other Interns is a wall of white noise. Moulded into a hard plastic seat, he feels straps binding his wrists and ankles, buckling him into his infant's high chair. Hands lock around his scalp, jerking his head back. Another grabs him by the chin. Fingers in dusty latex probe his lips apart, thrusting a hard, cold metal disc into his mouth. The hands clamp together the upper and lower halves of his skull, sealing the object into place between teeth and cheek. A telephone-thickness of wire attached to the device keeps him from closing his mouth. It's worse than the chair, the blindfold, the hairs-breadth shuffles of the other Interns. It's a mouthful of every blood-letting injury he's ever had, every half-chewed word he hadn't permission to speak. It's every struggle for breath in the middle of the night when he jerks awake, unsure of where he is.

'Listen up, Interns,' comes a voice clipped and slick, half-wrapped in plastic. 'We're going to remove your blindfolds in just a moment. Do not panic, no not shout, do not try to move. You won't be able to, in any case, but this exercise will be far easier on all of you if you co-operate.'

Agents spread out amid the rows. It seems to take forever, each gasp from the rows behind Caleb drawing his scalp tighter. The Agent charged with removing Caleb's blindfold takes especial pleasure in stringing the act out to screaming limits. Fingertips dig into the sensitive skin behind each ear. Shoving his head back and forth on his neck like a bowler weighting a ball. Peeling the blindfold by slow degrees before permitting a full view of the room.

Caleb sees the floor before anything else, the Agent's forearms still bearing down on the back of his neck. Initial impressions are of high school classrooms, of mandatory assemblies in sunless auditoriums. Floorboards waxed, polished and trod to shellac shards many times over. Dust floating up to lodge in the nostrils until permission is granted to sneeze. Then his own feet, naked and tight-sprung with veins protruding baby-blue and pink from flesh as cool and pale as waterlogged soap, wrapped in wide plastic ties. The same ties he'd once used to hold together an ancient fuse box in a flat he'd occupied in another universe. These same ties fix his wrists to the arms of the unit. Between his spread knees, just under his mouth, a kidney-shaped steel pan. He is certain this is not to catch the foreign body crouched in the secret places in his mouth. Further wires spread from his chest, back, arms and forehead, streaming into a control-studded box on the chair's left arm.

'Let him up. We're about to begin.'

Pressure leaves the back of Caleb's neck. He struggles to sit back; heavy fittings jammed into his shoulder blades keep him from doing so. Another strap runs across his chest and under either arm, leaving barely an inch of give for the rising of his chest. He and the others are bound in such a way as to prevent their spines meeting the back of the seat: heads must either be craned up or left to slump on the chest, necessitating an awkward Rodin's Thinker's posture throughout, save for that wonderer's luxury of a hand upon which to lean.

Caleb can see the others only in flashes between eye-trash in his peripheral vision. He is in the centre of the front row; for optimum view of the wide projection screen. Two Agents stand at either side, while a third paces before the screen, tapping a Device against his thighs. The slamming of a heavy steel door accounts for the position of the fourth. The Intern has seen none of these Agents before. Their figures and features are beyond note, save an surplus matte in their skin's uniform pallor, indicative of long stretches in poorly-lit rooms. Save a brutal fixation in their gazes, adding depth to ridges around the eyes. Men invested in this business of sight. Men craving detail, ripe to detect the slightest of anomalies in confused scrawls of wire and vein.

206

Energies diverted into such scrutiny, Caleb knew, left little in reserve for the emotional, psychological, the human.

'You Interns!' begins the middle Agent, mouth writhing at the taste of the word. 'Pay attention!'

Caleb hears but cannot see the struggles of the others as they shift in their seats. Lifting and dropping his head, Caleb decides he prefers the former contortion, if only for a touch of defiance. But footsteps up and down the rows behind, then dull thuds against flesh and bone, suggests he'd best look up instead. An Agent hits him anyway, just to make sure he knows what's coming, should his concentration waver. Caleb's teeth jar against the object in his mouth. He's oddly grateful for the wash of blood across his tongue; anything to rival the taste of oiled metal.

'Right! Are you watching?'

The Agents seem to be expecting a response. All heads roll in approximation of a nod; muffled tongues meet palates in blurry affirmatives.

'We're going to have a bit of fun,' says the central Agent. 'We're all rather tired of the Interviews – you're giving us nothing, and we don't appreciate time-wasters. So we've a picture show instead. You like pictures, don't you? Yes. You're to watch the screen. And since we've put in so much effort, we'd love to hear your thoughts.'

The room swells with a collective damp smack, as each Intern gulps back a coppery mouthful of saliva. The Agent grins, increases the tempo of the beating of the Device against his leg. The Agent on the left takes a turn, swivelling about the front of the room. A stage director taking measure of attendance.

'We are, in fact, so keen to know what you think that we've taken the trouble to wire you to the chair. This will measure your reactions – temperature, heart rate, brain patterns and so forth. You'll also note that we've placed a small device into your mouth. This will require your concentration. Right now, it's stopping you from speaking, but won't keep you from getting our attention. If and when – and I think you *will* – you see a picture that reminds you of something you want to *share* with us, you bite down hard on the device. This lets us know we've to have a word with you, and that you're *willing* to co-operate. You'll have plenty of time with each slide to make up your mind … chew it over, if you will …'

All four Agents snigger. The middle Agent picks up the trail.

'… so there's really no excuse. We're tracking you responses anyway, so there's no real point in lying. If you *do* feel like pushing us, though … that device in your mouth will take care of that, also. There are several thousand volts of electricity running along that wire. A high current. And as those of you who paid attention in Physics will know … the human body can manufacture only so much of its own resistance. So. Use it wisely. Indicate when you want to tell us something. If you don't, well … the device will do it for you. And *that* will definitely interfere with your enjoyment of the show.'

All four Agents assemble before the projector. The first speaker steps forward, arms spread in the air. A maestro.

'Any questions?'

Another black reel of laughter.

'No? Excellent. We'll get right to it, then.'

Two Agents attend to the screen, a third to the projector in front. The Agents make much of keeping their Devices on display, thus indicating that their repertoire of punishment does not begin and end with the electrodes.

Caleb has been in the Facility for months, now, perhaps longer. It's impossible to keep track without Bethany's updates.

Not until now has he been truly afraid.

Solitude, Intimidation, Tactical Applications of violence and starvation; the slow removal of all upon which he could fix his eyes and mind – that could be dealt with. Unpleasant, yes, often horrific, but there have always been apertures though which to dive inside himself. Always the merest millimetres of resistance, just enough to keep them from taking away everything he is. He could shut down, slip off and think of Lucy, keep her image fixed between bulls-eye and vanishing point. Remember, even when he could barely breath or speak or move, that there were still reasons to refuse all offers of a clean slate, crafted falsehoods. He had clung to all of this, cloaked in these microscopic anarchies, and remained, he hoped, truthful and true.

And now they have him. Everything accounted for. No room for sly gestures or anglings of brows, shoulders, mouth corners. No option to close eyes and wait for the latest interrogation to end. No drifting, his full concentration required to control the implant in his mouth. Neither he nor the others even have the benefit of a preamble, should they wish to break their silence – a binary chattering of teeth on metal all that stands between Agents and as-yet formless information. He can't risk a split into two channels of thought – that which kept against that which he could give; that which was happening to his body against how he'd been and hoped to be once more; that which he had lost against fixation on finding. Persons of fists, not faces, against his and Lucy's locked lips, eyes, minds, breath.

Yes, now they had him. He would now see what they could do. That there won't always be places inside him they can't reach. With the right equipment.

An Agent flips a switch, plunging the room into dust-brittle twilight. Another cranks up the projector. The screen sputters like streetlights through snowfall, a pure white point gathering in the centre.

'Are you ready?' All Interns repeat their strained affirmatives.

'Remember … this can go either way … pay attention …'

Images begin to fill the screen, one by one, slowly resolving to maximum clarity before peeling off once more in a fade.

'What's this?' the Agent on left asks his colleague at the projector. 'I thought it'd be–'

'This is just to start them off. A few pretty ones to get them warmed up. We jack up the intensity once they're nice and *relaxed* …'

Caleb hadn't known what to expect. He's oddly pleased to realise there's still room for irony, however cack-handed, in the Management's Fact-Finding programme. The slides begin with scenes that could have been culled from a souvenir shop in pre-Millennium Blackpool. Fibreglass ice-cream cones. Sunset over a milky sea stippled with seagulls and boats. A flower-sprigged china teapot set before a stand of luxury confectionery. The crowd shot has potential for disturbance. A mass jostling across the foreground was an all too familiar sight in less amenable circumstances – but smiles, handfuls of flags and paper windmills soften the scene.

Caleb is engaged in the bizarre exercise of trying to assess the beating of his own heart. There must be holes to pick. The very fact of being strapped into the unit, of being under pressure from the start, must impact somehow on the devices, compromising data arguably produced by the images themselves. Trying to control the heart was like trying to control thought –the harder he works to breathe steadily, to keep calm, the closer he edges toward panic.

The Agent at the projector turns to his colleague.

'See? No alerts, yet, but wait – we're going to have some Glasgow slides, now. See if that doesn't get them all a bit dreamy.'

Caleb has spent so long unpicking the wreckage of his city that he has almost forgotten what it had looked like before. As he city unfolds for him once more, in horizon-skimming panoramas and microscopic close-ups, there is a real twinge somewhere at the back of his ribcage at the sight of all that is no longer there. Sepia simmering, balmy ideals, existing now only in spoken words and written records.

Byre's Road, lit up with Christmas lights. Bright blue orchids against the etched glass of the Botanic Gardens glasshouse. A brass knocker on a tenement door. Banners flying from university turrets. A book face-down on the seat of a train carriage. A man strumming a beaten guitar on the steps of the train station. Airplanes shearing the night-time high-beams, a sky too clear and clean for even the photograph to capture. Chocolate sprinkles on a cappuccino saucer. The art gallery glowing in autumn reds and golds. A lost glove hooked over the railing of a fence. A clock tower in the old church near the inner city university. A hand flailing for a taxi. A pair of feet in dancing shoes ticking over wooden floorboards. Red velvet curtains peeling back over a darkened stage.

Caleb can hear sucking sounds as the others fumble with their implants. Two Agents fan out into the rows to check readings on the monitors. No stories yet. Nothing but childhood fables and teenage romances. The Agent at the front waves to his colleague at the projector, raising an eyebrow. The other returns the glance with a nod, a grin, an upturned thumb. Shutter speed cranks up as postcard scenes are interspersed with far more stimulating sights. Whilst retaining a certain degree of control, Caleb mentally twists a critical lip. Zero points for subtlety. No artistry, no craftsmanship, nothing save chartable blows to the memory.

A glass of beer dripping condensation down onto a marble tabletop. Fans of long-banned team sports gathered outside a public house in a clash of primary colours. A loaded syringe perched on the lip of an ashtray. The initial bloom of the fire at the airport, a swollen nova of molten orange spreading from terminal to terminal. An obese man fucking an emaciated prostitute in the back of a taxi. The same woman leaning from the other door of the vehicle to vomit onto the road. Books burning in tin drums on Royal Exchange Square, long-dead fairy lights trailing buckled vines down the walls of the buildings on either side. A red-eyed close-up of a young man drinking deeply of a joint. The same man framed in household wreckage. Shattered cars blocking the underside of the Kingston Bridge. Looters picking the ruins for valuables even as paramedics seek survivors.

Caleb's stomach tightens as he remembers Lucy's words, spoken through a cloud of marijuana smoke and steeped in blackest irony: *All our fault, we did it to ourselves.* Several of the others begin to murmur, mutter, blubber wetly. The Agent at the projector locks eyes with his colleague at the front, a question on his brow. The latter shakes his head, motions to a third. They make their way into the rows,

210

peering closely at the screens of Interns who appear most agitated. The Agent at the front steps before the screen, spreads his arms wide.

'Now, you Interns,' he says, 'We're noticing a few of you look like you might have a few comments to make about the show. You have to *indicate* whether or not you want to speak – remember your mouthpieces. We're not mind-readers. And we won't be pleased, should you have a reaction without letting us *know* first, eh? Bite down, that's all you have to do – otherwise …'

Caleb can hear the Agent speaking to the Intern right behind him. The Intern's breath is a mess of wet plops and snorts as he struggles to speak, nostrils thundering as he gasps for air. Under the wind and rain of respiration, Caleb can just hear the tempo of the monitors rolling up, up, up, touching the edge of an alarm before backing away.

'Come on, then, Thirty-Nine. Can't help you out unless you show us you want to say something. All you have to do is *bite down*. You can do that, can't you? You have to prove you're willing to co-operate, otherwise we're off on entirely the wrong foot, aren't we?'

No response bar a wet plop, a high whine gathering in the nostrils.

'Hmmm. Well, I'm afraid I've others to attend to. You know what to do. Might want to think about it, Thirty-Nine. Your output doesn't look so good … you're sailing close to a …well, you'll soon know all about it …'

Again, and again, and again. No Agents come anywhere near Caleb. He's not sure what's going on, whether his body has somehow sensed the importance of maintaining his heart, breath, temperature out of reach of the Agent's attention.

More images fill the screen. The streets outside pubs at closing time. A man with the broken neck of a beer bottle jammed into his eye socket. A baby in a pink hat seen through a clot of smoke, the child's mother sucking deeply on a filter as she leans into the carriage. Close-ups of the stretch marks fanning out over the thighs of an obese woman in lace underwear. A quivering dog defecating over the pavement. A skinny stripper tumbling from a splintered stage.

Several klaxons in the rows behind. Caleb hears scuffling, heavy breathing, the snapping of plastic ties as the Agents answer the alerts. Whether the Interns have anything of sense to say remains to be seen.

More images. A city rotting from the core to the edges. Crumbling, burning, tumbling. Rains of ash and acids, floods of gasoline and blood. Broken glass and bones. Faces desperate and blind, howling and spitting. Caleb wishes they'd get to the point. He's seen it all before, up close, and his memory is not so easily rewired as some.

Fizzing pops and cracks as several Interns meet with the wrong end of the device. Caleb isn't sure whether or not to be grateful that he can't see to the rows behind him, see what happens when Interns fail to follow simple instructions. The room fills with the autumn stench of burning hair.

'I see some of you still insist on making this difficult,' says an Agent. 'And after we've put so much effort into putting on a show. You're really going to have to do better than that – for your own good, you understand.'

Caleb squeezes his eyes shut, giving up. A different kind of boredom, sure, but the same four walls if stared at long enough. A blow to the delicate strap of muscle between shoulder blades brings an end to his brief rest period.

'Nineteen. Pay attention,' says the Agent, out loud, before leaning down to whisper into Caleb's ear.

'You're a lucky man indeed,' he says, a voice choked with the dust of abandoned subway tunnels. 'Not only have you been given a front-row seat ... you're also getting a few slides of ... specialist interest.'

He grabs Caleb by the loose skin on the back of the neck. Tilts his head up to the screen.

It's everything he's never wanted to see.

You're starting to feel it. Good. This is progress.

But you've no idea what you're dealing with. Not yet.

It's one thing looking into the smudged grey planes of a video screen. Seeing yourself naked and blemished from a safe, controlled distance. Or Bethany returning from another lost adventure, her nose running down her face. Or hearing the truths you've worked so hard to keep from yourself. Interfaces. All distance, intermediaries, second-hand. Unreal.

It's quite another meeting the flesh and blood of ghosts sheeting the surface of Bethany's eyes. Coming palm to palm with hands who'd last touched you to draw blood.

What are you going to do? Are you ready for that, yet? Drastic decisions? Crisis point? Ironic, really. All that time you were clamouring for an easy life. A blow to the head, a few trained actors on the brain, and you'd got what you wanted. Now you're throwing it all away for the sake of circumstances you can't even begin to comprehend.

Bethany won't take care of you. Yes, she's been indulgent of your slackened instincts. Coached you well, broken you in, given you time and space to absorb and reflect. But she's got just as much riding on this as you do, and she's been fully conscious for far longer. Stoking up her poisons, fanning the flames of her vendettas, fists clenched, tongue bitten raw whilst you've been strolling round the gardens, watching the walls, smoking badly rolled cigarettes and thinking you were so damned deep for being so easily satiated. She's been in training all the while, leading herself up to this. Perhaps you aren't a cause or sponsor so much as an initial itch, a trembling spark dying out in the hand, leaving nothing but a phantom sniff of cordite. You are not as important to the making of the event as your ties to Caleb on the inside might have led you to think. Ties? What ties? You've only just started to listen again.

Here's another approach. Have you yet thought about taking it back for yourself? Yes, Caleb's in a bad way. Suffering for his beliefs. But know this: he asked for it, at least on some level. Think about it. He'd be quite the celebrity if he ever got out of the Facility. They'd love him in America. Have him on all the hippest talk shows. Screen those cheekbones onto fridge magnets and T-shirts. Have him quote motes of wisdom for car bumper stickers and samplings for rap records. If he ever gets out of there, there's a fair chance he'll be quite insufferable.

Another thing: where was he when they took you? Okay, so it wasn't exactly a fair fight, for either of you, but should he have let it get that far in the first place? Not to suggest for a moment that you're a weak and precious child, but he'd egged you on for the sake of his beliefs. He was the target from the start, even as they were beating you raw in the next room. Why else do you think they let you go? Good behaviour? Not quite. That you got off lightly doesn't change the fact that you shouldn't have been there in the first place. If you loved him enough to want to jump on board with the motions, if not emotions, of his beliefs, he should have loved you enough to slacken off a bit. No? Okay, just a thought.

Maybe you're right, maybe you loved him specifically because he was so passionate about what he was trying to do. And yes, if you'd both compromised, you'd be rotting in a slack mire of false consciousness. You would, though, like a little recognition on the matter. Store it up for the fights you'll have when you get him out of here. You like fighting, by the way. You've missed it; all this talking to yourself has weakened the musculature of your rhetoric, your flair for debate. One more item on the plus-side.

But back to what you're facing once you're in there. You have scores to settle. Greater minds would have cracked with what they put you through. In your old flat, on the floor, the bed, against walls, thrown and kicked and jabbed full of tiny needle-holes. That you can't remember is a mere technicality. It happened — all impressions are still in here, waiting. That prickling at the underside of your skin. That rustle of old newspaper against the inside of your skull. That free-falling through half-sleep, teeth snapping in terror, waking with your mouth full of blood. That numbness in your feet and hands, trying to remember where they've been. It's all in here. You're just waiting for the furies to course up. Maybe save it for your bleached and glossed Samaritan. Channel it all into rearranging the square planes of his face.

For now, you have to concentrate on what you're doing with your body. Reawaken your reaction times, hone your instincts, move fast and light and traceless down the pathways Bethany will mark for you. That's fine for the graft portion of the exercise. Just don't move too far away from what's inside. Nothing you have learned since Bethany sat down beside you outstrips what you know already. You just have to keep looking.

214

PART FIVE

TRANSPARENCY

Underground

24th March 2024

And now they have him, and they have him, and they have him.

Lucy fills the screen. An old shot, Caleb notes, from way back when. She'd let her hair grow long, plait tiny fish herringbone braids along the top. She looks happy. Properly happy. No evidence of chemicals, sedatives or intense concentration on the business of not looking directly into anything. Caleb scrabbles at the chair arm, barely feeling the plastic ties bite into his wrists.

An Agent takes a sidelong glance at Caleb as the current shot fades into the next. He is pleased to see evidence of affect. Something to carry him through the tedium of subsequent reports. Caleb does not try to speak, his tongue a dead slab weighted under the implant. The Agent knows there's nothing useful by way of information in this simple close-up of a girl in need of a hairbrush: just a starter, an establishing shot. The running order was so orchestrated as to spin the exercise out for as long as possible, and the Agents had nothing but time as far as Nineteen was concerned.

The show mellows for a handful of slides. Prosaic shots of the harbour, the skyline, the museums and libraries blurred violet at night. Caleb waits, checks his breath. A voice burrows into his ear.

'You know to do, Nineteen. Just…bite down. Before it bites you.'

Caleb stiffens lips as far as he can around the restraints. He can tell by the slackening of breath in the room, the diminished volume of rustling bodies, that there aren't many left now. Soon it will be him

215

and the Agents. The screen and the threat. He shoves his tongue to the other side of his mouth. Whatever happens, he doesn't want it to stop. He wants to see Lucy.

Another shot. His own flat. Lucy sprawls on the couch, wrapped in a ratty harlequin throw acquired years ago from a junk shop. She's feigning sleep, the fakery belied by the close-lipped grin, the hand pressed to her stomach to hold in a laugh. The aftermath of a party; Lucy shy, embarrassed at having given over to sleep. Caleb murmurs, swallows hard. An Agent picks a semi-circle in front of him, hands on waist, elbows creaking at his side like a bird pondering flight. Caleb has never wanted so much to beat a smirk from his otherwise immoveable face. He can feel his chest tightening, warming up a pounding. Deep breath, deep breath, this is nothing. Okay.

The next one's simply scenic. It's no less painful. Winter twilight over the Botanic Garden, a long time ago. The sky still a fluid azure, speckled with the promise of stars like kitten claws through silk. The flat he shared with Lucy just seen in the bottom right corner. The window against which they'd pressed night on night, peering for remnants, even as the sky cultivated its murk. It had been near done for, the last time he'd seen it; he was loath to imagine just what now hung overhead. Caleb closes his eyes for a second, the better to concentrate on his heartbeat. It appears to have calmed somewhat – however much energy he'd plunged into the business of anger at such things before, his frame of reference has by now inalterably shifted. Having seen nothing but planes of grey and white; variable only by degrees of dry rot, damp and hollow faces peering through barred portholes, thoughts of the sky now just made him feel sad. The Agent picking an arc surges up to the unit, beats on the arm of the chair, a single blow to Caleb's head. Not too hard. They need him conscious.

'Nineteen! Pay attention!'

Caleb's eyes fly open. They're picking up speed, now, the slides, losing patience with the wait. No doubt hoping the surge in tempo will provoke reactions necessary to kick off a shock. Enthusiastic at first, the Agents seem to be growing bored. Most of the Interns being gone took the fun right out of watching, waiting. The Agents had been swapping small-change bets, a pool based on which of the Interns would crack first. Now they were down to Nineteen, alone. Slides that meant no more to the Agents than pre-Millennium holiday-snaps. Still, the Manager's orders. Patience, patience.

A shot of a street Caleb doesn't recognise, at first, without the bustling crowds, seething colours and leafy overhang of old. Lucy walks along cracked concrete from the vanishing point toward the unseen camera. She keeps her hands shoved into the pockets of a shapeless coat, head down, shoulders sheltering her rib cage. The shops and businesses, pubs and markets that had once bracketed the pavement are now shuttered; plastered with red and black warning signs. The only hits of colour in a plain of grey and beige. No other figures save a man in a trench coat crouched down in front of a once-regular pub. Byers Road: closed for business.

Caleb's gut kicks up a clamour. She looks tired. Smaller, too, drowning in that coat. Her skin, her eyes, neither giving nor receiving any light, so swamped is she in the scene's colourless seep of pale fluff. Caleb's concept of time and its passage now so shattered he can't be sure when the photograph was taken. A year, a month, a week, it didn't matter. Lucy did. Lucy fading out into the city, blown in drifts of pallid dust. Far from his sight, his help, his hands.

'See anything you like?' snickers an Agent, striding over to the unit, leaning into Caleb's face. He can smell his breath, damp with rot. 'Quite the catch, your lass …'

Caleb seethes, forearms tensed for a blow, the skin around his bindings flooding crimson with strain. He struggles to speak, speech bubbling around the implant.

'You sure you don't want a word with us? Positive? Oh, well then … let's move on.'

Lucy disappears from the screen. More shots of the city. A skyline. A smogline. Empty buildings with shattered windows disappear into the clouds. Another of the clot of burnt-outs near the old university, Halloween pumpkins, smouldering palings gritting black teeth against the embers. Caleb keeps calm, breathes deep, his body taking his side for a change. He'll be seeing no more of Lucy unless he remains out of reach.

Another of a building so familiar Caleb can almost feel his feet sinking into plush carpet. The last job they'd managed before Caleb had ended up in here. The Management have been making repairs. All broken windows re-paned with chessboards of clear and clouded glass; the functional front entrances brocaded with columns, a Modernist fountain nestling in the cellophane lawn. Caleb smirks around the implant. They're running out of subtleties – he's never denied having had something to do with this particular break-in. He'd smiled for the cameras on his way out. The Agent by the screen notes his disdain, and flips a hand signal toward the projectionist. A fist looping a circle at shoulder level: *crank it up*.

Lucy staring up into a camera pointed down at the entrance to one of the tunnels, arms folded, glaring, as a guard runs his hands down the insides of her trouser leg. Lucy spreading arms and legs, pulling apart her coat lapels, looking into the lens as though pleading intercession. Lucy sat in a doctor's chair, drilling fingertips into her temples. Caleb's breath whirrs in his chest like a desk fan. Three Agents take point around the unit, slowly circling, peering in and tilting back.

'Oh-oh.' A muttering in Caleb's right ear, 'You're not getting upset, are you? A touch too much?'

'Uh-huh,' says another, into his left, 'All that nasty *nostalgia*, Nineteen, it's *messy*, isn't it? You *know* you don't have to watch, you *know* you'll feel better if you let us take you out for a little chat, instead …'

Caleb shakes his head as best he can, blowing his cheek out around the device. Minor bleeps in the seat and handles of the unit skip up in frequency, shadowing his heartbeat like an oven timer.

'Tsk-tsk,' says the first, 'That's a shame … nice-looking girl you've got, there. Thought you'd have rather remembered her that way …'

Another of the cranking hand signals. The projectionist cackles, hissing through his teeth.

'You had your chance,' comes the voice to his left, all mock friendliness discarded, his voice a gutter-crunch of powdered glass. 'Right. Get the latest up there.'

Caleb's imagination has always been in high definition and surround-sound as regards the activities of the Management. He had spoken of it often to Lucy, sketching in probabilities and extremes befitting pre-Millennium horror movies – or newsreel footage, as became more pertinent. But these existed, and remained, in the abstract, on the turn of a change of subject. Never has Caleb imagined having to paint injuries, indignities, cell walls and Intern fatigues onto and around someone he loves. As the slides roll, Caleb wonders, for the first time since his incarceration, whether his current circumstances were truly of the actual. Just for a moment, he falls into hackneyed patterns of self-preservation, desperate to be convinced that *this was not really happening.*

Lucy in a room just like his own. The rooms in which all such things must happen. She lies on a cot under a white sheet. She'd be as pale as the linen if it weren't for a rainbow bloom of bruising running from her temples along her cheeks to her jaw-line, two water-dropped ink blots in place of her eyes. Her lips fade into the pallor, save for a black crack of dried blood splitting the lower in two. Further clots pick out her nostrils, nasal contours otherwise indistinguishable from

218

swelling on the bridge. Her hair, in his memory, a fall of honeyed liqueur, is now ratted from many days without washing. Her hands and forearms strapped into a webbing of tubes and wiring, hooked up to drip feeds and monitors with jagged green liquid-crystal screens. Lucy in a room just like his own. Lucy, an honorary corpse, a first-aid training dummy. Caleb lurches forward, vomits into the bucket between his legs. The Agents begin to laugh. Two of them cheer, clapping their hands.

'There we go! Not so pretty now, is she?'

Caleb slams back into the seat, upper arms clenching, uselessly trying to fold his arms. An Agent taps the screen the point of a Disciplinary Device.

'Interesting piece,' he drawls, a mock gallery guide. 'Here we see the Subject taken unawares … a candid shot, we think, that really brings out her colours. Wouldn't you agree?'

'Oh, indeed,' chimes another, in a ham-actor's drawing-room drawl. 'Posing often does detract from the *honesty* of a piece, yet … here we have the Subject in her natural environment, giving us a real *flavour* of her condition … flawless composition, I must say.'

Caleb's tongue tweaks the underside of the implant. No more. He squeezes his eyes shut, awaiting another blow to the head.

'Snap out of it, Nineteen! Uncultured scum!' comes the voice from behind. 'You're very lucky, you know – you're seeing pieces from a *most* private collection!'

'For a champion of the *Arts*, he doesn't seem very interested. Such a *shame*.'

'True,' says the Agent by the screen. 'Not everybody can afford to be a critic. These days, you've got to take your culture where you can get it!'

All four Agents howl with laughter. Caleb tweaks, presses, tweaks again. Nothing. The monitors in the unit squeak up once more in pitch. Caleb stares once more at the image on screen. Folding it away. He was giving up. He had no right to look at her. Lucy. Held for so long on the other side of the fight he's now about to lose.

He bites down. Nothing happens. Something is wrong. He hums, squeals into the front of his mouth, trying to attract the Agents' attention. Nothing. They're having too much fun, interest in the exercise rejuvenated by their Intern's distress.

Lucy sitting up in bed, staring blank into the corner of the frame. Fingers locked around raised knees: a childish posture at odds with the aging effects of the bruising. Beginning to heal, it would appear. Bloody purples simmered to chilled yellows, but still tender.

Her face somehow half-finished, each streak sculptor's desultory poke. Caleb's chest aches. He can't make out the colour of her eyes, so sheathed are they in high-denier violet shadow.

Another shot, almost identical, save for the Manager stood to the right of the frame. Shot from the rear, hands clasped behind his back, there is still no mistaking that breadth of shoulder, that scalloped close-clipped skull. Worse: the expression on Lucy's face. She leans forward with a grin, eyebrows drawn up in pleasant surprise.

'Look familiar?' calls an Agent from the front. 'Good pals, so they are. The Manager and your girl. Maybe want to think about being a bit nicer to the man, eh?'

Caleb tries once more to speak, biting down so hard on the device he takes several chunks of his own flesh alongside. Mouth full of blood, he bubbles, chokes, keens into the front of his nose. An Agent snorts.

'What's this, then? Jesus, you Interns are a bunch of animals,' he sneers, tracking the streamers running down Caleb's chin. 'You'll just have to sit in it, won't you? Not our damned job to clean you up.'

'He knows what to do,' says another, at the front. 'He's just being awkward. It's his own bloody fault if he's not going to play the game.'

The projectionist rifles in a box of slides by the machine. He calls to the others.

'Got a few here we took from the traitor,' he says. 'Not on file yet, but worth a look. What do you think?'

'Get them up there,' comes the reply. 'Let's move this up a notch.'

'How's he doing?' asks a third. The Agent at Caleb's side crouches down to read the screens.

'Not too bad, so far,' he replies. 'All those funny cigarettes, I'll bet. Doesn't half slow the old reaction time.'

'These'll sort him out,' says the projectionist, loading the slides.

This wasn't supposed to happen.

A strange species of outrage. Caleb first registers not the *condition* of the body on the table, but the owner of the gaze as dictated by the lens. Lucy, naked, should have been seen only by him. This transitory affront is nudged aside once he's taken in the full flood of damage covering his lover's skin. He was right about the pallor. Lucy's form is defined almost solely in contusions, lacerations, grazes and dents, the few faultless inches fading into the sheet below, drank into the fluorescence above. Further clicks herald a series of skin shots in

220

various angles, sections, front, back, full-body, headless, footless. Just to give Caleb a full and detailed portrait of Lucy as he's never seen her before. Caleb spasms in the chair, green fluid mingling with the blood tumbling from his mouth into the bucket, fingertips scrabbling at the arms of the chair. The mouthpiece severs his shrieks at the root as he tries, still, to bite, speak, cough, spit.

And now they have him, and they have her, too.

Caleb's recollection of the day of his arrest remains uncertain. Blows to his chest and skull reverberating in time with the slamming of doors, the tipping of furniture. No room for Lucy in the mise-en-scene, she wasn't to be a part of the experience – was she? He can't remember where she was …not in the flat, surely? He's been so certain, all this time, that they'd come for him alone. They'd left with him alone. They'd banged him up alone. Any mention made of Lucy's whereabouts or circumstances had, up until now, been components of encouragement, reasons as to why he should accept their offers of release. Even through grief, it doesn't take Caleb long to work it out. Taken backward, from the raw slides of injury, to the shots from a room like his own, to that of Lucy walking alone down the street that had so changed, it's clear there's been a dreadful mistake. They've hurt her, then fixed her. Changed her in the same way they've offered to change *him*. Any relief he might have felt at having her absence explained, her failure to track him accounted for, is blown away by the sight of her poor broken body lying prone under the careless eye of the camera.

The Agents have gone back to laughing amongst themselves, sometimes turning to the screen to point at a breast, a neck, a lip, a crotch, then turning to Caleb with a snigger, a wink.

'Quite the wild thing, your girlfriend,' comes a sneer, 'Seems she likes it *rough.*'

'Och aye,' says another, 'Just a shame she's not more *lively.* Hate it when they just *lie* there.'

Caleb's head, heart, ribcage all quake at the edges, thrilling to burst. He'd no idea he had so much violence inside. Rage raw and ripe enough to tear up the inside of his mouth, draw gashes across his bound wrists and ankles. Lucy. Lucy. Skin. Hair. Teeth. Stomach. Breasts. Legs. Fingers. Flash after flash of bruised flesh. His every nerve searing with need. To see her as she's meant to be seen. To kiss her in better in those secret places no longer quite so secret.

The machines in the unit keep frantic time, bleeps tracking upsurge of internal mechanisms.

'Hey ... might want to be careful.' An Agent notes blood dripping to the floor. 'Take your arm off, there.'

'D'you think he's forgotten?' one asks, mock-curious. 'We *have* told him over and over what he needs to do to get out of that chair ...seems a bit daft to me, going about it *that* way.'

'These Interns, Agent ...' drawls the projectionist, 'They'll never learn.'

'I'm half tempted just to leave him to it. See if a wee bit of time and quiet reflection won't sway him either way.'

'Shall we, then? It's been a long afternoon, and I'm sure we could all use a cup of tea.'

'One last chance, then.'

Three Agents circle Caleb once more, making sure not to block his view of the projector. Still he jerks, tears streaming down his cheeks, a braid of blood and bile running down his chin. It is the ultimate in humiliation, the unit. Quite ingenious. With the straps on the limbs, the chest-tray and mouthpiece, it's only a matter of time before the inevitable potage of bodily fluids renders the occupant a helpless infant. Caleb sees himself reflected in the blank pennies of their eyes, struggling, helpless. He carries on. Around the mouthpiece, he presses his lips together as tightly as he can, gathering a mouthful of pink spittle. As they come closer, heads tilted in bogus concern, he g launches a mouthful of spume. It would have been a good one, too, were it not for the wires interfering with the trajectory. The globule cuts a pitiful arc before plopping into his own lap. The Agents howl once more.

'Will you look at that! What a lack of respect for superiors ... I'm not looking forward to telling the Manager how little progress he's made.'

Another leans down to inspect the screens, murmuring over the kick-up in Caleb's read-outs.

'Well, that's it, then, isn't it? Can't reason with *that.*'

'How *rude.*'

'You'd think they'd learn some manners, away from all those nasty outside influences.'

'That's alright, there's time yet.' The Agent shuffles a hand across Caleb's scalp in a burlesque of parental indulgence, before shifting his grip, digging fingertips deep into either side of his spine. Caleb moans into the front of his mouth. His body has taken quite enough of his attempts to keep control. The monitors whirr, beeps kicking up a frantic riot, even as the Agents turn to leave. The projectionist has kindly left the screen fixed on Lucy's broken nudity.

They're halfway out the door when the reaction occurs, Caleb's form writhing in a sparkling web of wires.

'Oh-oh ... see, the lengths we have to go to for some *honesty?*' drawls the projectionist.

'Should we take him out? Switch it off?'

'Don't bother. Let him baste for a bit, might put a spring in his step.'

'What'll we tell the Manager?'

'The truth – no co-operation, no information. Punishment dispensed as agreed.'

The Agents flip the lights and slam the door.

After a time, the juddering ceases. Caleb's skin fizzes, sick-rot smoke rising from points of contact with the electrodes. Only the rubber guard between implant and tongue has prevented its being snapped off in his teeth. But alive. The units are calibrated to cut the power before Interns reach the point of no return. Extremities numbed and baked bare, he'll be unable to understand much of anything but varying textures of pain.

Crucially, his mental faculties are not beyond repair – the Agents were quite correct, a touch of voltage often rendered Interns rather more voluble than before. Memories of a session in the unit would shimmer with such clarity as to make Interns willing to do anything to keep from returning. However neat, clean and measured the healing process, though, Interns couldn't help but leave a session in the unit irreparably change. Damaged in patches sunk far deeper than skin.

27th March 2024

We can't hold off any longer. We've hit the wastelands, plundered the Caleb's bunkers, wandered off, dragging smoke trails in our wake. I'm seeing things, or possibly just *seeing,* men in mushroom-coloured suits passing my building in the grey dawn. I heard murmurs in clipped voices seeping out from under the doors to flats below. They are onto us. We'd be fools to think otherwise, that's how they work. But Bethany insists they're still trying to figure us out.

'We've not given them anything to worry about, Lucy – wee bit of chaos here and there, is all. We've got to give it time to settle down. Let them think we've run out of steam and equipment. They're not going to bother watching *us* – they'll be watching the sky, following the smell of burning ...'

She's drunk on the idea. Not that I wasn't enjoying myself, but – at some point we'd have to get it together. Remember why we're doing what we're doing.

'We're playing at it, Bethany,' I tell her across the table. I wave a hand over sprawls of crinkled blue-prints and smoke-stained clothing strewn over every surface, every inch of floor-space. 'This is still kid stuff. I thought you had a plan.'

'I told you, I need time,' she says, taking a pull on her coffee cup. I can hear the rim creaking under pressure from her teeth.

'Well?'

'I figure .... we just go for it. I *know* there's got to be a link-up somewhere in the casinos. Too bloody *quiet* and *polite* in there. All this time, here's me thinking the *bouncers* were enough to ... Jesus, what an idiot ...'

'So you've definitely decided that's where we're headed? We need an angle, though.'

'Aye. We're *celebrating,* that's what we're doing. If they're watching us. We've had an exciting week, ay? Need to blow off some steam ...?'

'You'd better have some idea of what we're doing when we get there.'

'I know my way around.'

'Why didn't you look around before, then? When you were tending bar?'

I shouldn't have asked. Bethany glares, makes cages of her fingers on the table-top. Her eyes drop deep into her skull, leaving nothing but violet smears dashed round the sockets. Suddenly she bangs both fists on the surface, shoving back her chair to pace the room, hands pawing at the hair behind her ears.

'Because I was *fucked*, Lucy, okay? You don't think I'm kicking myself, every time I think about what I must have missed, all those months of making fucking *lattes*?'

'Bethany, I–'

'But it wasn't my fault! I've *told* you what happened, I *told* you how long it took to get back into myself, and I *told* you how afraid I was for *months* after I did! They nearly killed me, Lucy – if all I had to do was keep quiet, do my job and not make any fuss, I didn't have to be told twice. I wasn't about to go poking around when I was still *healing* from a *beating*, was I?'

'Sorry. I'm sorry, Bethany, I just … you're so different, now. I forget. What you went through. I didn't mean … I don't know what I meant.'

I should have learned from Caleb not to expect infallibility from those who talked the talk, from those whom I admired. Their mistakes or omissions only *seem* far worse than those of we ordinary human beings, by virtue of the flair with which they otherwise conduct themselves. Bethany takes her hands from her head by jilted degrees.

'Look, it's fine. It was a long time ago. I remember enough of the surface stuff to know what to look for, once we're in there.'

'I really am sorry, Bethany.'

'Just get yourself ready. We're having ourselves a night out on the town.'

We approach in silence. Strange, planting steps on the same slabs I'd trod over just days ago, knowing nothing. It's a trek from the main drag to the outskirts, heavy-treading past miles of wreckage I'd rather not see by daylight. Me and Bethany have entered an unspoken agreement to use the breathing space for as many cigarettes as we can possibly chain-smoke. Her lips are flooded deep red, her gnawing outstripping the rouging effects of lip-sticks or stains. The expression on her face when I tipped out the sum total of my cosmetic items was positively mutinous. Dried mascaras, cracked discs of eye shadow and knuckle-length liners do not, apparently, bespeak of a decent attitude toward self-care. It's becoming ever clearer that Bethany's as subject as the rest of us to a skewing of priorities. Or maybe it's me. It's been a long time since any of that stuff seemed in the least way important.

The casino doors murmur open onto the same acres of sheen I may as well have seen in another life. But I'm a dealer in multiple existence, now. I can handle another trompe l'oeil. We move across the floor like as gracefully as we can – it's been a while, for me, at least. Blurry smiles smooth our faces to marble eggs. We're just a couple of girlfriends out for a good time.

It's interesting to watch Bethany walk so softly. Lazy, almost. A flow of limb and vertebra. Tilted back on her hips, tugged into the building by the pelvic bones, shoulders rolling like a jungle cat's. Approaching the desk, she tips a wink and murmurs, 'Hey! We're okay … just, ah, *act natural,* as they say.'

I clamp a hand to my mouth to keep it in a hysterical giggle. Seems a cruel irony that nervousness – a condition of being in which you want most to disappear, be unobtrusive – carries such symptoms as the kind of histrionics even more likely to draw attention. My gut sits at upper rim of my ribcage, so heavy with dread it must be affecting my balance. I've never been one for the poker-face. Bethany darts an elbow into my waist, yet unable to fully hide the upward curve of her mouth. She's loving it. Practically strutting through the lobby to the beat of some power-rock record, a peachy montage of previous exploits intercut with every step.

'Good evening,' Bethany murmurs, her voice a muted jangling of bells. 'I realize we haven't booked, but … we were looking to come in for a few games, if that's okay?'

The lady behind the desk nods without smiling, without a half-inch of movement in the rest of her frame. She's about my mother's age, I'd guess, silver-streaked hair wound up about her head like grey ice-cream, spectacles on a braided rope resting on her chest.

'Curfew applies. Six o'clock. You'll need to leave your ID here if you want to use the tables.'

'That's just fine,' Bethany drawls, placing a hand on the small of my back. 'Hold on.'

She digs in into her trouser pockets, flipping a laminated card onto the desk. Whilst the receptionist checks it over, Bethany slips something into my hand. We haven't discussed this before. There's a flash of satisfaction when I realize I know exactly what to do.

'And yourself, miss?' asks the lady, darting out her arm. Ruler-straight, no elbow angles. Prostheses and wires. She glances over the card, nods, scans the barcode, and places it with Bethany's into the top drawer of the desk. The computer screen fizzes with blue light. An automated voice chimes in *APPROVED.* Neither the name nor the photograph on the card have anything to do with me, fakes so painfully obvious I'm waiting for an alarm to sound. Only when she's clicking a stack of gambling chips into a cloth bag that I realise she's yet to look either of us in the eye, to move more than the muscles required for a twenty-degree nod. Those spectacles remain untouched. A prop. Her gaze fixed on some formless middle distance whilst she runs through motions from memory, from habit.

'Thank you very much,' says Bethany.

'Thanks,' I add, at her prompting. The woman folds her lips around her teeth and nods again. Picking a metronome beat, half-drop down, up, down, levelling out.

'Enjoy your evening,' she says. We are dismissed.

It's moderately crowded. Folks still wrapped up in their outdoor coats hunch over tables and games machines, feeding chips into slots without taking their eyes from the screens. The odd group of two or three sit stiffly around small tables, placing playing cards with utmost care in piles or rows. No sudden movements, no fanned handfuls, no eye contact: just this endless game of Patience, a terribly terminal definition. Some drink from old-fashioned cocktail glasses, shallow cones on stems. Not touching, afraid to lift the receptacles themselves: instead they nip, birdlike, through short plastic drinking straws. No heads lift from tabletops as we cross the floor, looking for a table far enough from the others to insure against eavesdropping – an unnecessary precaution, since nothing outside of jealously guarded personal space grabs much attention. Two youngish men stand behind the bar, arms folded, half-asleep, overseeing their wax-house customers.

'So, lovey, what do you want to drink?' ask Bethany, cheer loud enough to break over the hiss of air conditioning, the hum of the games machines. 'Tea, coffee?' she drops into a murmur, 'Re-constituted pineapple juice? Orange-flavoured, orange-flavoured, orange-flavoured juice drink? At only fourteen removes from the real thing …?'

'Shhh, Bethany. Let's just get a coffee and a table. Then you're going to have to tell me what to do.'

We've already agreed on sticking around for a couple of games before moving deeper into the building. Best to fix ourselves in time and space for longer than five minutes, for the sake of the cameras. I'm not remotely happy about drawing it out like this, every nerve screaming, peeled raw. We approach the bar and order up. There's a brief scuffle of bored bartenders around the coffee machine, warring desperate over something to do.

'What do we do now?'

We're sipping coffee from our cups with pinkie fingers extended. An unspoken concession to an ad-libbed burlesque.

'Well, see, what you do is, you put your chips in the slot, pull the lever, press the buttons to hold ... you try for three of the same kinds of fruit, all in a nice little row, to win yourself *more* chips, to put in the slot, to press the lever, to–'

'Shut up, Bethany, I'm serious.'

'So am I. We're here for a *good time,* Lucy, you'd better start acting the part.'

Although Bethany trusts the employees to let us mind our own business, I need a little convincing. It's far too easy, walking around like we own the place.

'Bethany, I don't like this,' I mutter, as she circles among the machines with her head tilted to one side, a mock-up of a discerning eye. 'Shouldn't we get a corner, or something? They can *see* us.'

'That's the idea,' she says. 'We've now been witnessed. And now they've seen us, they'll do everything they can to make sure they *don't have to interact.*'

'What do you mean?'

'They won't want to talk to the likes of us. Of them.' Bethany casts a hand over the hard-line old-timers, brittle jaws grinding over consoles and card tables as they stuff the machines full of tokens. 'The staff come here to escape just as much as the customers, Lucy. You know that. All those times we got talking outside ... a wee unreality check, no? We were two different people. Inside, it's all business, never saying or hearing more than we needed to.'

'So what's your point?'

'Ever get talking to a crusty old regular in a bar? In fact, you'll have done it yourself – come over to give some poor guy a pint, and you end up standing there for hours listening to his life story.'

'Yeah. It's ... painful.'

'Tending bar in here, Lucy, it's ... it's a good job, if you just do what you're supposed to do. If you keep your mouth shut. Soon as you're hearing more than you're ready to hear, that's you in trouble. Which is why you're better keeping an about-face. Please and thank you, nothing personal. So long as the bar folks have registered we're *here,* they'll forget all about us unless we're looking for something.'

'Hmmm. Fair enough.'

I'd argue, but I've done it myself. We all have. Eyes fixed on overhead middle-distance. Rarely willing or able to function through interactions demanding more than perfunctory contributions. Too many people, too many problems – self-preservation at the heart of every brush-off, every pavement gaze.

Bethany picks a machine, jabs an elbow into my waist.

'This'll do. Grab a chair.'

We each grab a Second Fifties artefact; much like dentist's chairs, high-backed and wide-armed, teetering on chrome spikes.

'Check it out,' says Bethany, slipping onto the seat, shifting round to face into the machine. She disappears from view, aside from the lower half of her legs dangling below.

'So what ... we sit here and *hide*?'

'Nope. More ... trompe l'oeil. See, every machine is numbered, wired to monitors in the front desk. An LED floor-plan shows whoever's in charge how many machines are in use. Easier than tracking bodies, with all their shifting about back and forth from tables to bathrooms to bars and back again. If the machine's on and running, *that's where we are.*'

I get it. I swallow a laugh.

'How're you going to keep it running, though?'

'Oldest trick in the book,' she snickers, removing a chip from her pocket. Casting an eye over the back of the chair, she takes a toolkit from the lining of her coat.

'Put a chip in, pull the lever,' she says. 'We've time for a couple before the real games begin.'   I do so, half an eye on the arts and crafts going on in her lap. She's got the chip clamped in pair of pliers, squeezing hard, pulling the edged of the disc into a shallow arc.

'Ever lost cash to a faulty vending machine?' she asks.

'Yeah. Too many times to count.'

'It's not the machine. It's your coin. The slightest flaw, and the machine goes haywire. This time, though, it's a total bonus. Jam it in just right, and you override any attempts to default back to the start. Which means it's stuck on a loop. Watch.'

She pulls her chair in even tighter to the machine, all the pretence of intent on the game furrowing her forehead, curling her lip. She hits a random sequence of buttons, pulls the lever with her left hand, holds it in place, slips the warped chip into the slot. Easing up on the lever, she sits back, a smirk tweaking the corners of her mouth.

The machine judders, clatters, the screen flickering with bright green heart-monitor strata. The lever rattles in its anchor like an epileptic limb; the metal plates around the coin slot squeaking their bolts and screws, scrabbling for purchase on an edible coin. Bethany looks on over screen, serene. Startled, I'm checking for curious gazes from the bar. They're all still stood with their arms folded, eyes glazed pink and tired. The machine picks up a gear, internal mechanisms a whirr of washing on a fast-spin cycle; red and amber diodes on top of the screen picking out a patchwork of manic Morse. Making the same noise microwaves do when you're nuking something you shouldn't. Speaking through my teeth, I make my case for action.

'Bethany, do something! It's going to–'

'–relax. Give it a minute.'

The shutter-clack soon drops in frequency. The screen slowly gathers resolution, solid images caught and dropped, caught and held. Whirring trundles to wheeze, to a sigh, to silence. Cherries and pears defend their edges. Bethany flicks the lever, now hanging loose and useless in its cradle. Unbound, the fruit begins to dance its same old reel, whirling and holding, switching and stopping. The game now plays itself. None of the employees have seen a damn thing.

'Very clever,' I say, 'Now what?'

'Now we take a wander. Right. One at a time. You go first, Lucy. Just … slip round the back of the machine. Wait a minute. Then keep going, dead easy, like, along the row. There's a bathroom up at the back, to the left. There'll be an *out of order* sign on the door. Stand there a minute, in case they notice you've moved from here. Act it out. Pissed off, confused. Too slow to remember there's another in the lobby. Natural reaction. Get me?'

'What about you, though? I'm not standing staring at a locked door all night. I don't look *that* stupid.'

'I'll be right behind you. Need to keep an eye on this,' she caresses the machine, 'For a minute or two, just to make sure it won't let us down.'

'Cool. Right. Whatever.'

'On you go, then. Don't look at the bar, or over your shoulder, or up at the cameras. You're just needing a pee, that's all. Daft lass on a night out. You know how it is.'

I'm getting it. There's an uncertain but no less pleasurable irony in being asked to *play* dumb, having truly been so for far too long. I slip from the seat, shift behind the chassis of the game. I pause, gaze picking through the wire guts of the machine, as though looking for a chip I might have dropped. Marking one-twenty seconds in the whirr of the fan, I make my way between the rows spread out behind, a proper country wander, feet picking arcs instead of lines.

It begins to get darker, the carpet thicker with dust. Long-silent game screens throw back no reflection, so frowsy with cobwebs and grime. I've never been this deep into the casino before. How easily curiosity is dulled. With everything a customer could possibly want or need within range of the bar and front desk, there's no point expending energy seeking out anything else. Shapes wrought in dead neon tubing line the walls, guitars and grinning showgirls in cameo-

relief, dulled with age and neglect. Machines track a pattern of eras –
touch-screens to push-buttons; buttons to levers; smooth LCD flat-
screens melting back to make room for bulky sets in thick glass,
promising screen resolution in pixels large as abacus beads. Running
over interfaces, my hands come away gritty and greased. A mock-up of
a history of mechanised leisure. All that's missing are coin-operated
peepshows, mannequin mediums in glass booths, stuffed toys in
telephone boxes menaced by motorized claws. My trouser cuffs drag
clusters of fluff, nose and eyes streaming with itch. I'm making mental
notes as I reach the back row, looking forward to telling Caleb all
about this when I see him. No room in my head for an *if.*

Three doors lead off from a short corridor; ladies on the right,
gents on the left, a code-button locking system on the door at the end
marked, predictably, *Private.* Yellowing sticky-tape peels at the edges of
helpful notices – *Out of Order.* I make a show of trying the door;
scratching my head; tilting my hands to the ceiling in mock frustration.
Waiting for a sign.

'Jeez, what a joke. Should have a word with the housekeeping
staff,' Bethany mutters, so close to my ear I almost smack her with
fright.

'Christ, don't do that!' I hiss.

'Calm down. We're in business – that daft game'll be looping
all bloody night, the number I've done on it. Nobody's seen a thing.'

'You sure about that?'

It's too easy. We've got to have missed something.

'Yep. Told you, it's the way of things, in here. Coffee, drinks,
stock and clean the bar, please and thank you and goodnight. Better for
the nerves, not to pay too much attention.'

I grin a little, wondering what we'd have to do in here to
attract some. Broken glasses, howling, brawling. Like old times. Caleb
would have had a few ideas. But enough. Got to keep a fix on what
we're here for, take it from there when he's with us again. I throw a
hand about the corridor, still burlesquing annoyance at the signs on the
doors.

'So what now? Since I take it we're not down here for a slash.'

Bethany shrugs. Clearly pointless to be asking so many
questions, since, going by our cyclical discussions, she's still making it
up as she goes along.

'Anything marked *Private,* we're interested,' she mutters. 'Got
to be … something … So many fucking *doors* in this place, and I never
bothered …' She trails off, pale spider of her hand over her forehead.

I no longer enjoy moments of weakness in which she admits to my same lack of curiosity. Back then, strung out, confused. Taking things at face value was the only guarantee of safety, of sleeping at night. But we're fixing it now. I have to believe it's not too late.

'Bethany. Come on. You were the one who said *not to look back*.'

She squares her shoulders and glares at the offending portal, humming a little in the back of her throat. A minor internal war with what she knows now, and what she should have known. She clamps a hand around my arm, tendons visibly flexing even under her jacket.

'Right. Fuck it. Now it's time.'

We shuffle along the corridor to lean against the door marked *Private*. She murmurs to herself as she fumbles in the lining of her coat, her free hand intermittently drumming fingernails across her forehead. She's got to calm down, snap to it. This can't be any worse than going it alone. Than giving up. Than not knowing. She hands me a soft moleskin wrap, the contents tinkling between my hands.

'Why don't you have a go, this time?' she says. 'You've seen me do it often enough.'

'What?'

'I'll deal with this thing here,' she gestures to the push-button code box, 'You pick the lock. It's easy.'

'I don't know what I'm doing.'

'You'll manage. Just be gentle. Like anything else – if you want something ... treat it right ... and you'll feel your way.'

She takes a miniature screwdriver to the coded panel, jaw set, all business. Selecting a pick, I face down the keyhole set below the handle. Can't be many eyes on us now, unless we can pass this off on really, really needing to find a bathroom. With the sliver of metal, I jiggle, twist, flick, waiting for an indication of give. Frustrating as hell, nothing's happening. I can't match the three-second job Bethany makes of such things, and a mockery of me, it seems. Screws from the code-box above fall past my head to hit the carpet; a shower of metal dust in my eyes. Bethany drops to a crouch by my side, sneering at the box in her hand.

'Amateurish as hell,' she mutters. 'Doesn't look like they've updated a damn thing in this place for *years*, going by the nick of *this* piece of crap.'

'Bethany, I can't do this. Nothing's happening.'

'Take your time. I told you, *feel it out*.'

She places a hand over my clenched fist, revolving it in a slow circle.

232

'Tickle it. I mean *tickle* it; you're looking for the tiniest little ridges.'

She removes her hand. I set my jaw. I quit straining, start stroking. Her hand on my shoulder, reassurance. One, two, three soft scourings of the mechanism eventually betrays anomalies, a rough grate pitting a smooth arc.

'Got it.'

'Easy, now. Just a *slight* tug.'

The lock shrugs open, tired of playing coy. I stare at the slit in the now-open door, amazed to find I'm still capable of shock and awe at the works of my own hands. Bethany grins.

'Told you, it's easy. The next one's yours, too, if you like – but watch it with my picks. If you lose them, I'll have to kill you.'

We stand, turn back to face the end of the corridor. Still nothing but dust-clotted chrome and dead neon. Bethany's pressed up close enough to hear my throat buckling with nerves.

'Hey. You okay?'

'Shitting it, as they say. I don't know if I'm ready ... to see whatever's down there.'

Neither of us need draw attention to the fact that I've already been. In flesh, on screen, projected, discharged. Whether interface, unconsciousness or amended memory, it's not the same at a remove.

'Can't go back now. Unless you can fix *that*,' she grins, indicating the hole in the door.

'Hmmm. Right. Let's do this.'

We step into darkness thick and gritty as black chalk. Hands held out to either side fix first upon smooth arcs of metal and plastic – more ancient machinery – and the odd stack of cardboard boxes which clink at the touch. Glasses for the bar in which nobody drinks anymore. The taste of hot and dusty fan-blades in my mouth. Skin fizzing a warning of walking-in-darkness, that sense of being seen without seeing. That primitive panic that makes you run from light switch to bed, vaulting invisible monsters crouched behind the valance. Bethany walks a steady beat, arms held out in front, never once grazing an obstacle.

'How do you—' I whisper, clutching the back of her jacket.

'Shhh ...' she hisses. 'Listen.'

From somewhere far back in the room, the passage, the vault, or wherever the hell we are, I can hear a thrill of water through pipes. Porcelain harp notes of dripping on concrete. A low hum of electricity. And behind it, somewhere, a tread of measured heavy-duty footsteps.

The humming is insane, felt rather than heard, a thrum pushing at the insides of the bones like a mouthful of dental appliances. A generator.

'We're so close,' she murmurs, 'I just have to figure out–'

She stops dead, pulls me up behind her, back to chest, my chin on her shoulder. I spread my left arm, then my right, always keeping one hand bunched around the fabric of her jacket. I can't feel anything out there, now; empty space, still no hint of light breaking a chink into the gloom. Standing, perhaps, on invisible cliff edge, that feeling I've carried inside me made real.

'What is it?' I whisper, my insides rattling like a car-trunk of shopping.

'Stay close.'

She takes my hand in hers and holds it out in front, to land on a smooth concrete wall, slimy with damp. The wall buzzes with that same manic electricity.

'Right ... through ... there ...' she murmurs. 'The Management.'

25th March 2024

At the sight of the burn-scabbed Intern, the receiving Medic at the Infirmary can't maintain his customary impassivity.

'Jesus …' he breathes, spreading a sterile handkerchief over his airway. D16 and H5 set the stretcher on a gurney. Two Nurses roll Caleb onto the mattress. All five in attendance take a step back. All clasp their hands to their abdomens.

'Thank you,' says the Medic to the Nurses, opening the door. For a change, curt dismissal is welcome. The Medic smoothes the front of his lab coat, rolls up his sleeves.

'Another from the Laboratory?' he asks.

'Yes,' barks H5, wishing his colleagues weren't quite so committed to stating the obvious.

'This one's in a bad way,' mutters the Medic, circling Caleb without touching him. Walking the floor of an anatomy museum. 'Not like the others. What happened?'

'He got the full dosage,' says D16. 'The, uh, Agents running the exercise left him in the unit without cutting the power. He'd been sat there for a while, still … buzzing.'

'Any information?' asks the Medic. H5 and D16 spread their hands, stunned, waiting for the Medic to attend to his patient.

'No! Does he look like he's up for a chat?' snaps H5.

Distracted, the Medic shakes his head, mentally running through a list of procedures. Lowering his gaze once more to the hospital bed, he spreads a professional smile over his face. Reassurance, capability, authority. That was it.

'Well! Let's get to it, then! But you needn't waste your time hanging about. I'll handle this from here.'

'We're staying,' say the Agents in synch, turning, surprised, to lock glances. D16 takes over, smoothes out the exchange. Neither will admit, not even to each other, how important it has suddenly become that the Intern can and will be repaired.

'Our instructions were to keep an eye on this one,' he says. 'We've to report back immediately, should he regain consciousness.'

'Fair enough.'

'You might want to get started, you know,' says H5. 'He's been *in a bad way* for a couple hours, now.'

'Well …' says the Medic, exhaling. He leans forward to press a stethoscope to an uncharred patch of flesh on the chest in his fingers.

Discounting the flayed wrists, he takes a femoral pulse from Caleb's left leg. 'He's stable, good breath sounds, steady pulse … these are all surface injuries. Control the spread of infection, and he'll be just fine, I think … shouldn't have left him so long, though … these are going to scar …'

He takes a pen-light from his pocket and flicks open the Intern's eyes, one by one.

'Pupils … hmmm … fixed and dilated. He's …not quite *there*, is he?'

'He's been hooked up to a unit, *Doctor*. You've seen this before – you've seen it this afternoon already. You *must* know exactly what's happened to him.'

The Medic peers over his shoulder. Approaching the door, he peers out into the corridor before pulling it closed. He then draws the blinds over the examination room windows.

'I'm going to strip him down, then put in a drip, for now,' he says, 'Standard procedure. Then … I'll have to check for internal burns.'

The Agents watch, silent, as the Medic slides a pair of scissors up the front of the Intern's fatigue shirt and trouser legs, peeling the fabric slowly from the skin. A delicate process, D16 notes: removing the clothing without taking the flesh with it. Muscles around the Medic's jaw and eye sockets tauten with every snip, every revelation of another plane of carnage. Without being asked, the attending Agents each slide on a pair of latex gloves, picking up detached fabric scraps, dropping them into a kidney-shaped dish. The Medic then straps a plastic packet of saline to a metal stand, before swabbing the Intern's arm with disinfectant. The Medic jabs a thick needle on a length of plastic tubing into the sensitive flesh of the Intern's inner elbow. The Agents avert their eyes, loathing themselves for doing so.

'Right,' says the Medic, sighing. 'That should do it for now, until we know more. Thank you for your help, gentlemen.'

'*Now* are you going to tell us what that means? His *not being quite there*?' asks H5. D16 thumps him in the back, shaking his head.

'Shut up! Let the man do his job!'

'We've got to know!' says H5. 'For … for the reports. We've got to know what we're dealing with, here.'

The Medic checks the blinds again, pulls the lapels of his lab coat tighter about his shoulders.

'I don't quite know what to tell you, gentlemen. I haven't seen anything like this before, at least not since the early days of the Management. You're familiar with the rewiring process, I presume?'

236

Both Agents nod, having had more to do with it than either is strictly comfortable with.

'A fresh start. For the greater good. All very, very carefully constructed, no loose ends, every detail lovingly prepared, every unpleasant prior circumstance erased or accounted for.'

'We know! We do it every day!' says H5.

D16 curbs the urge to hit him again. He's becoming rather concerned about his partner. H5 would be in trouble if he didn't watch his mouth. D16 can already sense his partner constructing fantasies of revolt. Such romance was dangerous, was never fully-formed, and all either need do to assess the consequences was take another long look at the inert body on the gurney.

H5 didn't care much, anymore. Every fresh injury made it all the more crucial that he find out everything he can. He's feeling out for weak spots in every interaction, testing others for potential doubts as to their role in the Management's schemes. He half-consciously wonders if the Intern can hear him, taking up a slim sliver of a cause he can't quite understand, yet.

The Medic is not pleased at having been interrupted. He clears his throat, arching a brow.

'Sorry, Doctor,' H5 mutters. 'Please. Carry on.'

'Right. Well. The careful construction of clean-slate realities we do here – that's a rehabilitation exercise. You know that. Give the Interns concerned a fresh start, so that they can safely begin their lives anew on the outside. Correct?'

'I suppose so,' says H5. However he felt about the rewiring process, he had to admit that it was remarkably clean, clear, and injury-free. Interns emerged from the booths with little more than a temporary sense of disorientation, the new memories still bedding down in the brain cells. They all seemed in satisfactory health when they arrived at the clinics for follow-up check-ins, perfectly stable and competent, if a little dulled.

'This ... exercise ... the units, the slides ... for all the monitoring of temperature, pulse and whatnot ... it's decidedly *random*. There is no telling which of the slides will react with which of the Interns, or however *controlled* the Interns themselves can be when faced with the images. You're familiar with certain psychological tactics? Rorschach diagrams, word association, Pavlovian responses?'

'Yes.'

'These all rely on a degree of *interaction* between test subject and professional. Reward or punishment, depending. In this case, however, there is nothing of the former. All there is, is *pain*. All that links the subject to the image is a greater or lesser degree of the stuff. And that …well, that leads to all sorts of psychological chaos. The mind, when faced with circumstances beyond a certain level of tolerance … the mind can only hold so much. It beats a retreat, carries the subject back into him or herself, thinking only of escape. In response to the degree of trauma brought on by the, uh, *exercise,* the Intern has been left with no other recourse but to … absent himself from the proceedings.'

'But … but that doesn't make sense,' says D16. 'The whole point of the exercise was to … ah, encourage the Interns to talk! He's no use to anyone if he's *absent,* as you say!'

The Medic sighs once more, folds his arms, moves the side of the bed. He looks down the length of Caleb's spackled body, already tiring of talk.

'I don't think …' he begins, trails off, changes his mind. He coughs. 'It's not for me to pass judgement on the efficacy of the exercises. I just patch up the Interns when it's over. After that, it's out of my hands. You Agents can find out for yourselves whether they have anything left to say.'

H5 steps forward, lowering his eyes, shrugging off D16's grip on the back of his shirt.

'You know it, too, don't you? You know there's no point to *any* of it except the Manager's keeping control! They can't let them out, you know! Not anymore! He's got to be seen to be doing something, and he's *losing* it, Doctor! He's out of his fucking mind!'

'Shut up!' say the Medic and D16 at once, the latter grabbing his partner from behind, by the throat. D16 hisses into H5's ear, hot breath beading on the skin of the neck. D16 takes the Manager's pen from his pocket, jabs it into the small of H5's back.

'Shut your fucking mouth, you *fool,* you don't know what you're doing! You're the one losing it, *Rick,* so get a grip!'

The Medic reels back into the corner, hiding his face behind a clipboard, humming into the front of his mouth. H5 snaps his jaw shut, holds himself very still, until D16 loosens his grip.

'Sorry …' he murmurs, eventually. 'It's … I just … don't know anymore.'

The Medic places the clipboard onto the Intern's shins, leans in to adjust the tube from the drip. Looking up at H5, he casts a limp hand about the room.

'None of us are, Agent. That's why it doesn't pay to ask questions. We all have a job to do, down here. We just have to do the best that we can.'

'Let's get out of here,' says D16. 'We *do* have work to do. I think the good Doctor can handle things from now on. You'll alert us if the Intern regains consciousness?'

'Of course.'

'Thank you, Doctor.'

H5 says nothing as he follows D16 down the corridor, back to the surveillance room to check up on the monitors. Passing the unscreened windows of the Infirmary, he can see all too clearly the beds full of wreckage of each of the other Interns fresh from the exercise. Some of them are awake, staring glazed at the corners of ceilings. Some are moaning, a terrible sound, thick and rasping with loose phlegm over prickling throats. Some, the lucky ones, remain quite unconscious, their bodies still twitching with static residue. All will be properly taken care of, of course, at least until they are ready to start answering questions.

*   *   *

H5 hadn't been far wrong. Caleb can hear everything, from spoken words to general ambience. They begin as kernels at the core of his skull, tiny fingernail scratches on crystal. Gathering depth, sounds seethe at the boundaries of tissue and bone. The noise is too much for his body to hold.

Pain. Caleb thought he knew all about it. Gotten almost to like it: proof he was still alive and fighting. Up till now, it had come from hands and feet at the ends of a limb. Implying a body. A head. A pair of eyes. A set of teeth. A consciousness. A source. Something to look at. Pain had a context, an initiating event, purposive motions of muscle and heartbeat.

This is different. There's nothing to take hold of. Nothing for it but to keep eyes jammed manhole-tight. Praying for surrounding sounds to stop jolting him back into his body. Time slips further from his grip. Echoes plant echoes. Space drops away.

He recognizes voices. Those two Agents. The ones with the slight apology on their faces, more often than not. The one with the vague remnants of an Islands accent had brought him a pitcher of ice, once, after a beating. He'd sometimes stayed to talk a little, under the pretence of fishing for information. Never taking notes. Just listening. A strange expression on his face, pondering. The other had once helped him back into bed. When he'd still had one. Gruff, yes, but kind when he hadn't had to be. Caleb's oddly glad they'd been the ones to bring him here. To the Infirmary.

239

The Infirmary. Yes, that's where he is. Picking at the edges of white noise, he can isolate instruments chinking into steel bowls, respirators hissing. Intermittent bleeps of his own machinery. The Medic had been quick to attend to the rest of the procedures after the Agents had left. Running through familiar motions helped erase the remnants of the outgoing conversation.

Caleb retraces the conversation carried out over his head. Tugging words past pain proves difficult. Words scatter like feathers, the first half of a sentence falling away whilst he grappled with the tail end.

Something about power and control. Things not being right. Some sense of Agents' disgust at the exercise. Pity in the Medic's voice. Panic in one of the Agent's, syllables shattering, urgency usually absent from their toneless inflections.

Something about the Manager *losing it*. Helpless anger in the voice of the other. *Get a grip*, he'd said. Somewhere above the gauze pinning Caleb down, Agents were having doubts. Infighting. Speaking out of turn. Caleb's in no position to encourage them. All he wants is to sleep. Proper sleep. No spill of red light around edges, no relentless pinpricking of sound. His flesh feels larger and heavier than it should, his whole body a chink in a tooth at the end of a tongue. Every inch shrieking and hissing, demanding more than was reasonable of his sensory receptors.

Behind it all, gaining pace, sharpening up, the marquee of images rolls on. Reverse order. Lucy's bruises seep away, clothed, too, a little at a time. Lucy inches up from her sprawl. Sitting, then standing. Then walking with ease along a sunlit street. Lucy climbs up to the flat they'd once shared, her arm slung through his, her hair catching in his teeth and lashes. Lucy and her morning warmth. Her pineapple shampoo and cinnamon cigarette papers. Lucy out there, maybe waiting, maybe forgetting . Lucy smoothes a blanket over the ache, pulls him gently past the shards and scalds of being conscious. Lucy's soft kiss as he tries to retreat, pushing him back up to the surface.

*   *   *

The Manager takes a turn around his suite. With every footstep planted, the plush carpet sucks at his heels. Chuckling, he looks over his shoulder. A man of simple pleasures, he likes to watch the indentations disappear. He needs as little stimulation as possible at moments such as these: a medicinal gathering of thoughts. Every paced length of wall a glorious reminder of space to be had in comparison to the Interns' miserable cells.

Today has been another odd one. No visible results. Nothing to chart, no observation of likely changes, but still a keen sense of motion. The whole Facility is abuzz: even studied silences unfold in shape and texture. Interns who'd missed out on the Laboratory exercise are huddled in the corners of their rooms, facing the wall, grinding their teeth so vigorously it can be heard even through walls. Agents on Interview and Surveillance detail are sliding along the corridor walls as the Manager approaches, staring at spots over his shoulder when he pauses for a check-in. The Technicians and Electricians who'd carried out the exercise now walk with a deeper clunk to their boots, legs and shoulders spread a little wider, smiles unrestrained. The Manager had had a word with each of them, promising promotions, privileges, increased access to cloistered information. They have also been assured frequent and recurring use of the Laboratory. All in the interests of research, of course. In hope of unpicking fixed quantities from a mess of random factors.

In a shriek of leather, The Manager takes a seat. He reaches under the table for a tray, upon which sits bottle of viscid amber liquid and a crystal flute. From a drawer he takes a small pewter dish. Lumps of real sugar. Most expensive. He drops one of these into the flute, then drizzles it with acacia-honey cordial. As he takes a sip, a slow smile spreads, lips squeaking over teeth tacky with syrup. He really can't understand civilians' tight, fast hold onto cravings for alcoholic liquor. All the Manager needs is a measure of his own worth and influence to feel completely at ease in both self and surroundings. The potency of the cordial resides purely on the tongue, a transitory sensation without sedative effect. A taste with no real flavour, appreciated solely for its exclusivity. Civilians were weak, that was all. Never to savour the ennobling tonic of control. Never to partake of the natural high granted by privileged space and information.

Satiated, he lifts the handset embedded in the seat of the settee, idly counting the pinpricks in the mouthpiece. Anything spoken through these tiny holes would carry out through the Facility, through central control, through the whole of the city, should he wish it so. All demands answered for, all concerns taken care of. All at the touch of a button, the unclipping of a jaw. He flutters a fingertip over the console pad, barely caring to say or hear anything at all. It was just pleasant to remind himself of his prestige.

'Sir, yes, Sir, ah, Agent D16 speaking, Sir!' says the Agent on the other end, making a mess of the regulation greeting. All did so whenever they registered the Manager's Suite's indicator light on the corresponding machine. The Manager considers a reprimand, then decides he'd prefer to do so face to face. His inferiors take lessons to heart far more effectively when facing the full unmediated weight of a voice.

'D16. Any news on Nineteen? Has he decided to join us yet?'

'Sir, no, Sir. He's with the Medics right now in the Infirmary, on a monitors and a drip. Myself and H5 are to be alerted in the instance of any change – of which we shall of course inform you right away, Sir!'

'Hmmm. Fine. That's fine ... but tell me, Agent – how did he look?'

A brief silence on the other end of the phone, save the click of saliva in D16's throat.

'Uh ... well, *scorched,* Sir. Blisters and marks on the skin. Surface wounds, the Doctor tells me. He's stable. He'll be ...alright, once he's had time to recover.'

'I don't care about that, D16! Tell me how he *looks!* Does he seem ... smaller, yet?'

'Smaller, Sir?'

'Smaller, Agent. Does he seem ready, yet? To do what he's told?'

'Uh ...I'm not sure what you mean, Sir. Shall I have the Medics pass you on a report? Some slides, perhaps?'

'I'm perfectly capable, Agent, of making my own way to the Infirmary to take a look myself. I just want your unalloyed opinion. What do you think? Do we have him, yet?'

Another brief silence. D16 clears his throat.

'Most definitely, Sir. He's a terrible mess. He'll be thinking very carefully from now on about what he chooses to share with us. We have left him no choice.'

'Thank you, Agent. And again, contact me immediately in case of any change.'

'Certainly, Sir ... And it's been my pleasure. Of course.'

The Manager hangs up without another word and tilts back in the seat with a luxuriant sigh. This is a rare moment of down-time. He should really be making the most of it. Calling in a meal, taking a bath. Perhaps reading over success stories found in the files of more accommodating Interns. All available. More, anything he desired, should he ask for it.

And yet, he wants nothing more right now than for Nineteen to waken up. He would like a few words.

An alert passes through the Facility, speeding H5 and D16 back to the Infirmary. A very special Intern is awakening from sleep, far sooner than expected.

Caleb still feels wrapped in a nylon face-mask, all between his slit lids abraded with contrails of eye-trash. The trials of consciousness beats back every attempt. Furry flutters of lashes a too-tempting reminder of peace to be found on the other side of giving up.

Rubber fingertips prod at his lids. The Medic shines his light into his eyes. Caleb makes out a silhouette, back-lit by hallway fluorescents.

'Well, what do we have here, then ...?'

A carnival drawl behind layers of cotton and glass. Real Medics don't talk like that, do they? Clichés uncurl from his memory like worms from an apple. Waking to find it's all been a dream. Being asked if he knows the year or the season. Damp flannels. Straitjackets. Dreams bleeding into reality. He knows perfectly well where he is, what's happening, who's responsible. He's just fuzzy on the point of departure. Lucy's image remains the last thing he can remember before dropping like a stone into a world of pain.

Two Medics, H5 and D16 stand over the hospital bed, watching. Caleb's eyelids and fingers twitch toward the light.

'What do you think?' the admitting Doctor asks his second.

'Looks just as you said. Surface wounds, good vitals. Should be fine.'

'What about ... cognition?'

'That's not really our concern,' says the second, turning to D16.

'That's up to your colleagues in Stories, no?'

'He won't be needing a story,' mutters D16. 'The Manager will want everything intact. This wasn't a rewiring, Doctor, as you well know.'

The second Medic shrugs. He checks the level on the saline drip, the monitor output. Redundant activities employed when responsibilities are about to leave their hands.

'Shall we call the Manager ...?' asks D16. 'I mean, is that it? Is he on his way back up?'

The first Doctor peels back the Intern's eyelids, shrugs, opens his palms to the ceiling. It's out of his control.

'I don't see any reason why not. In my professional opinion, I'd recommend giving the Intern a little time to ... recover. He's been through a hell of an ordeal, and I wouldn't be expecting too much sense from him, at least not at first. But it's your call, Agents. I imagine the Manager *did* mean for you to get in touch *right away*, at the first sign of ... wakening.'

*   *   *

There's something odd in the Manager's progression down the corridor. A hurtling jerk augments his customary glide. For the very first time, he resents the fact that all cell doors look exactly the same. Pressing his face up to the grilles as he passes, he flinches back with a snarl at each incorrect guess. A light sheen of sweat beads the back of his neck: a sign of inefficient expenditure of energy for which he knows he would reprimand his underlings.

Although they could easily have led the way to Intern Number Nineteen's room, D16 and H5 follow at a distance of several feet. An explosion is imminent. Neither wishes to be within arms' reach.

Finally the Manager stops at the correct room. Hands pressed flat to the surface of the door, he takes a jagged breath and turns to D16.

'Thank you, Agents. Anything I should take into account?'

'No, Sir.'

'Hmmm ... he's just ... *lying* there. I wouldn't have expected–'

The Manager breaks off, tongue tip rolling about the inside of his cheek. Jerking back from the door, he points at the Agents.

'I don't recall giving permission for a bed to be re-installed! Would either of you care to explain?'

H5 prods D16 in the small of the back, prompting a response.

'Uh ... Sir, Nineteen's just come ... uh, from the Infirmary. He's still in quite a bad way–'

'–he gets *nothing* unless I specifically say so! You!' he points to H5. 'Did you have anything to do with this?'

'Sir, it's – ah – as D16 says, he's come straight from the Infirmary. That's a hospital bed, not a standard cot. Nothing's been *re-installed*, it's just ... come with him. He's not yet fit to support himself, and ...'

H5 launches for and fails to grasp a means of prompting leniency. He mouths dead air, unbelieving. It's too much, even from the Manager. D16 takes over.

244

'Sir, we're very sorry. There's clearly been a few crossed wires. We'll have a word with the Medics – they couldn't have known. Shall we take it back right now, or would you rather we waited until you've had a word with the Intern yourself?'

The Manager's eye sockets are stretched taut, paler even than the whites of his eyes. He shakes his head quickly and turns to press his hands back to the door.

'No. It's too late, now. It doesn't matter. I'll have it removed myself, later on. Just … tell me. How is he? What's he saying?'

'He's not saying much, Sir,' says D16. 'The Medics tell us he'll be disoriented for quite a while yet – which explains their failure to remove him from the bed.'

'This is not acceptable. You told me he was awake.'

'Sir, he's going to be slipping in and out of consciousness for quite a while yet – look …'

D16 taps a paragraph on a sheet pinned to a clipboard. He is still using the Manager's pen, a fact the latter notes for later questioning. He scans the print and shakes his head.

'Explain.'

'Basically, Sir … from what I can make out … all that electricity's creating some unpredictable patterns of brain function. No discernable changes in IQ, language capacity and so forth, as far as we can tell, but … according to the Medics, he's having trouble fixing on the *time*. His realities are jumbled – sometimes he's here in the now, sometimes convinced he's still on the outside, in the past. We've heard him having … *conversations* with somebody in his head, telling of his experiences here in the Facility as though … as though he's no longer here.'

'The girl,' growls the Manager. 'He's talking to the girl. What's he telling her, then?'

D16 curbs a shrug, coughs instead, mumbles.

'Oh, nothing of note, Sir. All terribly incoherent. Nonsense.'

H5, D16 and several of the Medics have been present at the Intern's bedside for these storytelling exercises. All agree it's quite dreadful thing to hear. Painful. Hopeless. Tales of besting the Manager. Clever trickeries. Fights won. Breaking out of the Facility. Returning home. All related with breathless excitement, a smile coasting the sleeping face.

The listeners are also uncomfortable aware of how much things have changed. Caleb's flat long since taken over. All traces of his extra-curricular activities erased. And the girl upon whom he remains fixated has been through the rewiring process. The Intern has nothing to return to, even if any of the elements of his hallucinations remotely probable. There's a tacit agreement between each of the listeners not to elaborate as to the specifics for the Manager's benefit. It didn't seem fair to provide yet more ammunition.

'Well. We'll soon have *that* sorted,' mutters the Manager. 'Telling stories, eh? Not on my watch.'

'We just thought you should know, Sir,' says D16, swallowing a depth of sighs, 'Not to expect too much ... *efficiency* or rationale of speech. The Medics have made it clear that he'll need quite a bit of time.'

'Did they, now? Hmmm ... I'm afraid *time* is something we don't have, Agents. We've wasted quite enough of it on this particular Intern already. Not to mention *energy*, haha. Come back half an hour before shift-change, Agents, and we'll take it from there.'

The Manager angles a thumb over his shoulder, pointing the Agents in the direction of the end of the corridor. H5 blanches.

'Sir, are you sure? You don't need us in attendance?'

'No. Off you go. I'll handle this. It's been a long time coming.'

*   *   *

Even through the lead-weight of the door, through murky cognitive clot-webs, Caleb can sense the Manager coming. It's not the voice. Those modulated syllables barely break through the thudding of Caleb's own heartbeat and breath. It's more a shifting pattern of retreating currents; concrete molecules shrinking back to let him pass. Caleb can feel the heat of the Manager's hands moving across the door; a tang of bleach and sterile sweat leaching through.

Caleb presses shoulder blades and hips down into the mattress, knowing he won't be this comfortable for much longer. H5's been to visit him in the Infirmary, ostensibly checking whether he's ready to be moved. The Agent's tone of voice had grown ever more frantic, pleading with Caleb to start making sense. Escape fantasies and backward glances have thus been shelved in favour of the here and the now.

You have to hold on, he'd said. *You can't let the Manager hear you talking like that. Not doing yourself any favours telling yourself wee stories, eh? Come on, buck up. This isn't over, yet.*

Caleb is no longer in the position to knock back advice. It's not the time to indulge in parallel happenings. He requires all concentration in re-establishing contact with his limbs and senses.

246

The door does not crash against the wall, but drawls slowly open. The Manager takes his time letting go of the handle. He leans back against the closed door, gaze floating over the figure on the hospital gurney. An intake of breath into lungs ocean-deep. A wet smacking of lips, teeth and tongue.

'Intern. Number. Nineteen,' says the Manager, savouring the taste of each catalogue article. 'Quite the mess you've got yourself into, eh?'

Caleb neither speaks nor moves. It seems wise to maintain an illusion of weakness, at least for now. Footsteps shift from a shuffle to a firmness of tread, each sole a hard slap to the concrete. Caleb feels the heat of the Manager's breath on his face.

'I know you're awake, Nineteen. I've just spoken with my colleagues. So – you've been telling stories, have you? Care to share …?'

Still Caleb remains motionless. The Manager drills two thumbs into the flesh underneath Caleb's eyebrows, hauling open the lids to peer into the eyes.

'Morning, sunshine.' The Manager's mouthful of Scrabble-tile teeth is wrenched into a terrible grin. Caleb's eyes swivel in their sockets, desperate to look away. He starts, the Manager removes his thumbs, and Caleb allows himself to be hauled upright to a half-seated position. The Manager yanks at the front of Caleb's hospital gown until his spine is parallel to the wall.

'We can't talk man to man if you won't get to your feet. Care to have a go?'

The Manager steps back, still grinning. Caleb glares, shifts the twin humps of his knees. He still can't feel a thing below mid-thigh. Even his hands are still giving him trouble, despite the rehabilitative mouldings and squeezings applied by the Medics, checking for sensation and strength. Caleb won't be getting to his feet when he's having trouble even holding a drinking straw to his lips.

'Would you look at that …' drawls the Manager. 'Not quite so quick off the mark now, are you? For the best, I should think. Conversing with the likes of you …? Well, let's just say that's far from *my* interpretation of man to man.' He ends with a scattershot of spittle, his grin giving way to a leer. Caleb closes his eyes, choking on his inability to respond with his customary smarts. The Manager swipes a palm across Caleb's jaw.

'Pay attention, Nineteen. You've been down and out long enough, had yourself quite the holiday. Mattress and everything. We've got some catching up to do.'

Caleb gags, fresh blood flowing from oral blisters and cuts. Despite the rubber bracing, the implant had done a fair amount of damage. The top layer of skin and a couple of teeth had been removed by the Medics along with it. The Manager, ever the gentleman, proffers a pressed linen napkin from his front pocket. Caleb's hands flail at the fabric, numbed fingers unable to take hold. The Manager snorts, folds it away, as blood and spittle course down Caleb's chin.

'How rude. Oh well, never mind. We've more interesting things to be getting on with.'

The Manager places a hand on either of Caleb's juddering knees, smiling again.

'You appear to be having some trouble, here ... would you like me to give you a hand?'

The Manager notes with interest the dwindling hues in the Intern. Already pallid of complexion, the colour seems to have been drained from his eyes. No longer fixing the Manager between hectic points of brightest green; the irises are a muddy blur of dishwater, pupils taut, picking up no light. This was good, this was progress. Perhaps now it will be time for long-overdue co-operation. Two fists jammed into Caleb's armpits, the Manager hauls him bodily from the mattress, legs still twisted in the sheets. Setting Caleb's feet on the floor, he removes his hands. Caleb teeters, eyes wide, teeth making further mincemeat of the inside his mouth, before tumbling to the concrete with a groan. The Manager laughs.

'You're going to have to do better than that, Nineteen.'

Caleb, winded, scrabbles at the floor, trying to free his useless legs from the sheets.

'I'm not helping you up,' says the Manager. 'I shouldn't have to do *everything* around here.'

Caleb wheezes, shifts around on the floor. Fumbling at the frame of the gurney, he eventually manoeuvres into an almost-seated position.

'You ... fucking ... you ...'

'Oh, oh, that's not how this goes!' The Manager clouts Caleb once more, in the torso this time. He wants Caleb conscious. The attempt at speech is encouraging, if not the content. 'You've got much more than that to say for yourself, Nineteen! I know all about it! I've read all the reports! Didn't have yourself too much fun in the Laboratory, did you? After we went to all that trouble, tracking down pretty pictures. Everyone's a critic. Still, I'm very keen to hear your thoughts. Anything you'd care to share? Now you've had a nice long rest?'

'I've never ... you didn't ...'

'Oh, we did. Don't you worry about your girlfriend, Nineteen. We took good care of her, afterward. Accidents will happen, you know. She was lucky ...but then, *she* was willing to co-operate. Knew what was good for her.'

'Where is she? What happened?'

Even blurred and mumbled, Caleb's words carry more inflection than any of the Manager's scripted sound-bites. The Manager growls a warning. He shoves the supporting hospital gurney to the other side of the room, leaving Caleb to writhe himself upright.

'You don't ask questions, Nineteen, you answer them. Tell me ... what sprung to mind when you were watching the show?'

No response. Caleb dips his head down into his useless hands. The Manager takes a moment to identify the sound coming from between the fingers. Damp hissing. Heavy breathing.

Caleb is crying.

As a rule, Interns tend to cease all such futile expressions of sentiment after a couple of weeks in the Facility. Every day being, by and large, exactly the same, there's nothing to trigger an outburst. With surroundings a motionless and unresponsive blank, there's nothing to delineate one mood from the other. The Manager is thus taken aback. He's rarely around for the initial interrogations, when Interns still have tears to spill. His tastes for efficacy keep him from taking over until Interviews are less likely to be interrupted by hysterics. He responds the only way he knows. Fetching another blow to Caleb's head, he catches him hard with the blade of his palm just below the right ear. Caleb unleashes a full-throated howl, mouth and throat working up to their sensory capacity. Some of the feeling begins to return to his hands, as they scramble over the hot skin of his skull.

'This is how it's going to go. You are going to sit up and pay attention. You are going to tell me anything and everything inspired by your session in the Laboratory. The more you tell, the easier things will be. I won't have to hit you. If you say nothing at all, you'll be sent back to the Lab for another round of slides. Am I making myself clear?'

Caleb is weakening, has been since he laid eyes on Lucy's battered body. There's something very wrong with the man leaning over him. Caleb knows there's no information he could give worth anywhere near the time or effort the Manager seems willing to expend. That exercise was a case in point. Caleb may have been talking, but nothing he said was of any relevance. Nothing could be used to root out further dissent, particularly when so little of it made temporal sense. Coasting over all of this, there's the palpable relish in each blow the Manager applies. No longer pausing for answers. Lashing out for no reason at all. This is no longer an Interview, if it ever was. This is the Manager's show. Caleb a puppet, a prop, each slap or punch a punctuation mark in the Manager's running commentary.

And there is no fighting with that. The realization takes time to take hold. Streamers of futility braid their way along each of Caleb's veins and nerve endings. He isn't going to win. There is no longer a game being played. The Manager meant what he said about their being unable to talk *man-to-man*. Caleb is something else. No longer human. A soft landing for the Manager's fists. A crash-test dummy inserted into experiments and set-pieces.

'I asked you a question, Nineteen. I said, *am I making myself clear?*'

'Yes.'

'Then let's get started.'

PART SIX

ILLUMINATION

27th March 2024

Time spins out further and wider the closer we get to the Management. Disorienting, but not so heavy and sticky as hours slain before everything kicked off. Just the right kind of dark. Could get used to measuring spaces around myself by echolocation against invisible walls. Less to see frees up headspace.

The silence between us feels awkward in such an intimate space. Two strangers taking an elevator to the same floor. Crammed onto a seat on an old city bus. Sat tight in the waiting rooms at the follow-up Clinic. Shared destination, space, purpose, yet unable to take pleasure in identification of same. Bethany's breath gathers pace, the further we press on. Not panic, but eagerness. I can tell the difference now. It staggers me how much I'd have otherwise missed between the slightest degrees of paying attention to what's going on.

'Shhtt!' she murmurs. Reflex. I haven't said a word. A hot hand on my breastbone pushes me into the wall. The wall. Another potted history tracked back. Plasterboard to concrete runnelled with gobbets of paint. Now bare rock, granular damp. The kind of wall whose cracks and niches I'd once have peered into for interesting patterns, as folks once did with clouds in the sky.

'Listen,' she says.

More damp drip-dripping from the ceiling to the floor. She slows her breathing to a seep from a punctured balloon. Then something else. I wasn't sorry to leave behind the casino games bleeping down the corridor in our wake — too much like a funhouse from a dream you can't escape — but I'm not sure I like that scattered set of rhythms, at all. Beats marked out on snare drums in different rooms in a house. Rhythms circling, crossing over, stopping and starting again, but maintaining a metronome tempo. Footsteps. Beyond the passage in which we're standing, footsteps heading in many different directions. None of the feet in any more of a hurry than any of the others.

I remember this. A brief flash between scattered patches of sleep. Catching strands of the beat and feeling so reassured. Knowing the Manager and his colleagues were on hand. Watching over. Taking care of me.

I don't have time to feel sick.

'We're nearly there,' she says, lips right up against my ear. 'I just have to ... there's got to be a door somewhere. I just ...'

'Here,' I say, handing her the flashlight, 'I think it's time to use it, now.'

'Hmmm.'

Annoyed. My coming up with something she should have remembered has altered the balance of power. I don't believe half of that bullshit about her being able to see in the dark.

This is coming to be far simpler than her stories, gadgets, warnings and technicalities imply. Feints and sleights. Human error. Taking advantage of boredom's tendency to slacken surveillance. Picking and slipping between shadows and cracks. And so we've finally made it. Down here with the Management. Maybe one day they'll put up a plaque.

Fumbling with the flashlight, Bethany sprays a skewed halogen circle along the walls of the corridor. I'm pleased to note a spattering of ancient graffiti. We're not the first to have come this way. Neither, it seems, were the Management. So much for there being nowhere left to go sight unseen. Bethany fixes on a set of intertwined initials in thick-set three-dimensional cursive. It staggers me to note the time and care taken over shading and lighting the letters. The artists have even ensured the loops follow a logical arc, a knot to reach in and untie like a parcel.

'Check that out,' she whispers, 'Art's gone *literally* underground.'

Below the main body of the image, a few words in regular capitals. An ellipsis, then *WAS HERE. AND WE'LL BE BACK. GET IT UP YE.* Brilliant.

Bethany lingers longer than she reasonably should, panning the beam over histories spray-painted and scratched. I'm up for interacting with past, sure, but not here, and not now.

I have to concentrate.

If I look hard enough, I'm bound to come upon something of Caleb's. I'm not ready for any more of his input until I'm looking him straight in the eye. Bethany picks up on the tremor running along my arms. Hissing softly through her front teeth, she places a hand in the small of my back and presses us on. I keep my eyes fixed on a spot overhead in the dark, as far as I can see along the tunnel. The footsteps are picking up in volume, if not speed. Coming from a corridor directly parallel to this one. Bethany agrees. After another few miles out of time, she stops, presses palms to the wall on the right.

'We can't go much further,' she whispers. 'If I'm right, we'll be coming out just beyond the central surveillance rooms. This'll be one of the back passages I told you about. If you get me.'

I do. She'd explained. Levels of privilege assigned to information passed between particular ranks of Agents. Some fresh recruits are still rather *delicate* as regarded the lengths to which the Management will go, and must be kept from seeing the results of certain interrogatory techniques. They might grow frightened. Start talking amongst themselves. Or worse, to persons on the Outside. So these corridors come in handy for transporting Interns or pieces of equipment through the Facility without being seen. This one can just about admit the width of a hospital gurney. An observations which sets off a craving for something *interactive* to look at. I don't want to think about what these walls must have seen.

'Here!' she hisses, planting her elbow in my chest. I stop short, stagger back, eyes flying open to take in a heavy metal door. No handle. No window. Just a skinny little keyhole halfway down: my shout. I drop to my knees and select a pick. Not shaking anymore. My whole body moves with cement-heavy purpose, regular and deliberate as the footsteps beyond. Three scratches at the inside and I've got it, sliders tumbling between sheets of steel. Bethany's hands stiffen on my shoulder. For all her talk about my getting involved, she doesn't seem too pleased that I'm picking this stuff up.

'Wait,' she says. Still doesn't trust me. Skewed priorities, since this is insane. Found the tunnel, found the door, and we've nothing but Bethany's orientation and vague sense memory. She presses an ear to the surface, nodding in time to audible footsteps.

'Follow me,' she says. Like I've a better idea. 'Stay close to the wall.'

Everything has been leading up to this. Months of blank silence. A year's worth of waiting for something I couldn't see, name or touch. A burst of adventure larger and wider than the whole of the year gone before. I'm *doing* something. I'm *moving*, I'm *seeking*, I'm trying to be someone to be proud of. Whatever happens has got to be better than returning to boredom, to fear. All the boxes are ticked: prickling on the back of the neck, hitch in the breath, blood pounding like shoes in a washing machine.

And I'm disappointed.

No light shows, no sound effects, no fireworks or explosions. Just two women of average height, weight and intelligence sneaking onto a premises. A pair of teenagers trailing home after curfew. I drink deep of the dank air in the corridor. I'm pretty sure it's the last chance I'll have to be reflective. I press my chest to Bethany's back, and wait for the magic to happen.

It's dark, still. The same motion-sensor fluorescents they use in the Tube. Lights watching us watching the lights, following on. A giving and taking of cues. It's empty down here as far as we can see. Footsteps ring out from much further away than they'd seemed from the echo gallery of the passageway.

'Where are we, Bethany?'

'We're circling the central block. The back way, past the labs. All the cells are on the other side. If we take the long way round, we can have a look round before we do anything stupid.'

'Won't they see us? On camera?'

'No. Same idea as the side-tunnels. Don't want anyone on surveillance detail seeing something they're not ready for, yet.'

'Hmm. Right. So …?'

'Let's go. Quickly and quietly as you can. Stay close.'

It is done. Finally. Everything is in motion.

The Manager paces the carpet in his suite. His jaws ache from denying himself an incipient smile. Soon it will all be over. He is not yet sure whether or not this pleases him as much as it should. The Intern is out of his hands for the time being, though, which lent itself to a switching of disciplines.

He has grown tired of watching the ex-Agent and her pet Candidate ducking and diving in and out of the tunnels. Wasting Management time with their minor anarchies. Causing no small amount of damage with their breakings and enterings. Once this charade reaches its final stage, though, there will remain only the other, far less stimulating Interns to hold his attention. He may never say as much to assisting Agents, but petty war games with these idiot women proved beyond doubt that there are no limits to his power. He – and the System – have two marvellous assets. One, the freedom to *play*. And two, the authority to draw the game to a halt when he was no longer being amused.

Having won, of course. That went without saying.

Having plugged codes into the lead from surveillance control to his suite, he has blocked signals and alarms for the next couple of hours. Agents on duty have been informed that he has much work to do in his office, and does not wish to be disturbed.

He will *not* be informed that Agents have captured intruders. Such would drain delight right out of pursuit. He won't be denied the pleasure of scuffles between shadows. He's been waiting for this for a very long time. A chance to deploy tactics and techniques picked up in the field. From times before his job became an endless film reel, a paper chase, the tip of a pen rattling Morse on a clipboard. There is very little gratification to be had in baiting Interns once they'd been in for a while. Too weak to beat back a blow. Too dizzy to circle or parry. Too stupid to engage in a parlay.

The women – Agent, Candidate, they *did* have their identity crises – are worthier opponents in the absence of much by way of competition. No challenges down here was a given, true, but even the walkers Overground are growing meek and mild. Indifferent. Pliant. Obedient. Useless. No, the women are the freshest bounty in a long time. Perfect. It's almost a pity the odds can only ever be skewed beyond their favour.

The Manager leans his forehead against the door to the corridor. Among his many other talents: spectrum analysis. Discerning levels of permission and intent from discrete sets of footsteps. All it would take would be a call to the control centre for a live feed, to have it done with. But he is not so far removed from his field days to have forgotten that this blind *waiting* is, more often than not, an opportunity to relax. Reflect. Savour the moment, that the finale be all the more glorious when it arrived.

We gather fluidity the closer we get. Rattling jerks of limb smooth out as we adapt to changes of light and space. Lungs recover from the first hit of hot paint and lemon-scented sterility. Hearts simmer to a drumming of fingernails. We're doing it.

Strobes down here don't flicker before jolting to life, but instead flow gently one by one. Heat rising in a liquid thermometer. We're almost *welcome,* so much so that we're treading down the centre of the passage, no longer pressing vertebrae to concrete. I'm cloaking potential fits of terror in concentration on my footstep. On listening out for others, in these corridors with which I should be familiar.

Bethany must be working to push back her own conflicting set of impressions. She has known this space before, too. Employee like them. Candidate like me. Two strands bleeding together must create

255

some clamour of confused associations. I feel it, too. Her stories made stone. No room for questioning truth when my very own breath bounces from the reality of the walls.

I can see it all as it happened. As it happens still. Takes every mote of energy to keep from following one of two instincts. One: slip back into the dark belly of the tunnel, run away as fast and far as we can without leaving another trace. Two: sink to the ground with my back to the wall. Hide my face in my lap. Wait to be taken back to my cell for a talking-to. A session. Another go-round with the Manager. Armed only with what I now know.

'Well …?' I mutter. We're approaching a branch at the end of the passage. 'Right or left?'

'Left,' says Bethany. 'We want the cells.'

'What's on the right?'

'Departments. Offices. Labs.'

I pause at the junction, looking down into the murk of the right-hand passage. Quiet, now. Hands-on endeavours must be over for the day. Nothing but a half-drop pattern of double doors, shuttered screens, chains and padlocks draped between the handles. Protecting something far more precious than cash and assets. Voices and stories, mock-ups and recording equipment, edits and deletions. Means of entry into another consciousness. I can almost hear the thrum of unfathomable machinery, a metronome tick embedded in minds in need of regulation. Bethany steers me from the Departments, perhaps hearing in her own head the squeak of gurney wheels passing through. However tempting it is explore the engineering of initiating events, that's not why we're here.

Walls and floor grow markedly smoother and cleaner the closer the pair get to the centre of the Facility. Noise picks up, too. Footsteps and murmuring voices so close they almost seem to be all around. Above, behind, underneath. Sneaking up on the sneaks. Bethany's accustomed to sonic distortions. Lucy's relieved to feel a tight grip of fingers round wrists. Offsetting panic.

They pass a few single doors set almost at random into the walls. A quick look around the edges of the window panels reveals nothing but computing and cleaning equipment. Odd-looking machines wrapped in plastic sheeting. Stacks of gurneys propped up lengthways against the walls. So many supplies left idle. There could be a number of reasons. Increase in Interns rehabilitated and released. Fewer Candidates giving the Management cause for arrest. Disposal of Interns that can't be conditioned. Can't be *saved*. Either way, the system is clearly working.

Another wide arc at the end of the corridor leads to a central pillar. This houses surveillance and administration offices. It looks impressive enough. Large plate-glass windows half-shrouded in sheets of corrugated steel. On one side, a murky view of rooms packed with heavy desks, filing cabinets, computer equipment and banks of telephones. On the other, a room whose walls are comprised of flat-screen closed-circuit televisions, casting blue-grey light across the concrete floor outside. Each monitors a different cell, a different stretch of corridor.

Before the screens sits an Agent in a high-backed swing-chair. He has his head buried deep in plump leatherette cushioning, his hands resting gently on the arms. Trusting in the chairs' promises of ergonomics and posture to maintain the illusion that the screens are being paid the slightest attention.

H5 makes such a performance out of professing to loathe night-time surveillance detail that, as expected, he has been assigned exactly that for the foreseeable future. Only D16 knows the truth. H5 savours the motionless silence. Rarely needing to take any kind of action, to make any decisions. On top of which, it keeps him out of the way of the Manager. More and more often, these days, H5 has been fantasizing about telling the Manager exactly what he thinks of his job, the Facility, the treatment of Interns. Disgust rolls up the back of his throat and sits there, pressing back logical sentences. Growing larger and darker every time another piece of human wreckage squeaks past on a gurney, headed for the Infirmary.

But he's seen it happen before. He knows exactly the measures the Manager takes when he suspects Agents are muttering treason. H5 feels his skull cracking apart under the weight of self-loathing, it's true, but nowhere near enough to run headlong into the same fate that had beset his friend Bethany Trenton.

A shift in the fabric of half-sleep. Starting, H5 checks his watch, heart pounding, before his body gathers up its regular rhythm. It's the slowest, gentlest portion of the evening. Night-duty Agents sleep on rotation in the bunk rooms in the next wing. Exhausted Interns finally crashed out, having accepted that they're now unlikely to be jolted awake for an Interview. The Manager pushing paper his suite, having forbidden interruptions. Footsteps mark a length of pace decreasing, as Facility stillness slowed alerts to a crawl. Smacking dry lips together, H5 smears hands across his eyes, then shifts the chair to point a little further from the window and door. It's surmised that if the Manager is not to be disturbed, H5 is unlikely to be caught drowsing. He checks his watch once more. Marking how much time he has left to idle. He does not check the monitors.

Rounding the corner, Bethany pauses before the first set of windows, pressing her back to the wall before peering around the edge of the frame. Nobody in the office. Taking Lucy's arm, she proceeds to the window to the surveillance unit. She notes the slack in forearms draped across the chair. Below the seat, feet quiver gently as the owner takes a wander through a half-lit dream-scape. On a monitor in the top corner of the room, she and Lucy stand in greyscale pixels. The figure in the chair does not budge. Bethany snickers. '*Rick* ...' she murmurs. '*Always asleep at the wheel* ...'

Lucy jerks away from the window, eyes perfect circles of fright. Bethany shakes her head, smiles, pulls Lucy close to whisper in her ear.

'It's okay. He's asleep, or near enough. He's not paying attention.'

'But—'

'Trust me. We were friends. Before. He's ... let's just say he's not about to pass a loyalty test ...'

'Okay. Let's go.'

Bethany starts back, narrows her eyes. That Lucy seems to know where they're both headed should have been a good sign. Memory unfolding from layers of implanted material. Asserting itself. Empowering the beholder. But there's no guarantee these echoes will be limited to directions and floor plans. Every step closer to the cells brought with it reeling, writhing sensory activity requiring every mote of concentration to contain. Measures must be taken. Memories must be used only to their mutual advantage. Kept technical. Precise. Bloodless.

'Wait here,' says Bethany, 'This'll only take a minute.'

Lucy swallows hard, steps back into the recessed doorway of the paper office. Bethany presses down gently on the handle of the door to the feed room. As expected, H5 has neglected to lock it behind him. She slips inside, pauses, listening. A soft whistling issuing from the chair confirms that he's out for the count. Bethany chokes down a foam of guilt for hitting an easy target. It's unsporting. She'd liked H5, back then. She knows he'll be the first to catch hell when the Manager discovers the intrusion. Unwilling to see H5's face in repose, Bethany drops to her knees and scurries over the linoleum. She lies staring up at the underside of a steel box at the far side of the room, riddled with buttons, spewing a mess of wires. Closes her eyes for a quarter minute. Instinct takes care of the rest. She reaches up and yanks hard, shorting the electrics on the feed from the cells down the corridor. Looking up, she's pleased to note few changes in the level of light and motion shown on-screen. A hash of static sprawl shows little marked difference to the grey haze of the feed from the cells. It's no surprise H5 finds it so easy to drop off to sleep. Outside, Lucy keeps watch, her face a pale smear in the half-light of the doorway. All of this strange, yet known, all at once. Threads of a dream picked up after a brief pre-dawn wakening.

I'd be a fool if I'd thought this would be *easy*. That it comes down to simply shelving reworked impressions in the context of fresh lessons from Bethany. I've just been waiting, I suppose, for a loophole. Some intervention or other to keep us from getting this far.

It's all too *real*. Concrete too solid beneath my feet. A frost of my very own breath paints petals on the glass of the door. In some unspeakable cell in the pit of my skull, possibilities whisper in dark patterns. Indulged for a blank spot, a black hole in time.

One more shot at the rewire.

No more Bethany. No more blueprints. No more crawling through tunnels like some pale, blind insect looking for a hole to curl up into and die. No more Caleb, maybe, if they take custom orders. Sculpt the alternative to my demands. I'm running out of energy. Losing conviction that this will all be worth it in the end. The end. Whatever *that* means. Dangerous thinking. Can't let that get in. I have to concentrate. I can do this.

Okay. So what now? That we don't have a *plan* isn't the meat of the problem. Even if we do manage to get Caleb out of here and back up into reality, what then? We're *different*, now, both of us. I've seen more of the truth these past few weeks than he's ever managed to show me before. Even if the Management don't tail off in pursuit, we're going to have to make a few changes. Establish a new framework, not to mention power structure. We can't just pick up where we've left off, not now. But that doesn't mean I'm going to give up. I just have to *concentrate*.

Bethany springs from the surveillance room with her expression unwinding. I let myself jump shotgun on her high. It's infectious. We're doing something. If we let it happen, these rooms and walls become less a bank of bad memories than a system of triggers and nerves over which we can be in control. Bethany links her arms through mine with a vigour approaching *joy*. I match Bethany's rhythms, still trying to absorb her enthusiasm. That brief reverie has me rattled. But hell, I can't expect to know what to expect when I'm finally stood facing Caleb. I've already let him exist as more of a figure of myth than of flesh, blood and bone. Got to remember who's taking control, here. That would be *me*, for a change.

Motion-sensor lights drink us in as we approach, dimming as we move on. Soon the corridor behind is as tar-thick as the corridor ahead. All footsteps are, Bethany surmises, coming from *above*. Guard activity restricted to watching overground entrances. If we're lucky, we'll be able to leave the same way we came in. Nobody any the wiser till morning. If we're lucky.

Cell doors offer no clues, metal grilles locked up tight for the evening. I remember. I'm *sure* I remember just how dark it can be in the cells at night-time. No spill of light from the corridors. No illumination penetrating to the depths of the underground. Just a thick wash of black so deep it has texture and shape. So dark it takes a good hour to regain sight after the first halogen shock of the morning. From under the doors spills a slow hiss of deep breathing, punctuated here and there with a sticky hitch in the back of the throat. Bethany sets her jaw.

'Bethany,' I whisper. 'What do we do about the rest of the Interns?'

We've spoken about this already. But I can't just walk on past and say nothing.

'Lucy ... we're in enough trouble as it is, going after just the one.'

She sounds suitably pained. Guilty. But I know she's right. We're barely heroes enough for Caleb, never mind the others. Besides, we've already battered out the extenuating circumstances. Excuses, in other words. Chances are, the others are too weak and tired to care anymore. No means of manoeuvre out of the Facility without *all* of us being caught and banged up. If there's anything to be done, we'll have to figure it out later. If this little audacity comes off as planned. I nudge Bethany's shoulder, going for a sympathetic pat. Bethany loses control of her nerves, whirling sharply enough to almost knock us both over.

'Jesus! Watch it!' Bethany hisses.

'Sorry. It's just ...'

'What is it?'

'How do we know how to find him? They all look exactly the same.'

'I remember. I know where we're going.'

I feel around in my pockets for the handful of lock-picks. Much as I've appreciated Bethany's leading the way, when it comes to the springing of locks, it has to be me with my hands on the mechanism.

260

The Manager's forehead is beginning to hurt, so firmly is he pressed to the door. Every muscle pushes against the seams of his suit. Waiting for call to be able to follow his blood. He can hear them for real, now. Just a few doors down from the end of the corridor.

Certain Agents had been a little bemused when he'd decided to have his suite installed so close to the Interns' cells, so far from the central control tower. He'd insisted it would be advantageous to have Management presence at both ends of the Facility. Not only in terms of tactics; but being properly *involved* on every level of the Facility's routines and procedures.

Privilege kept him from having to share the pleasures he's been taking in his nightly strolls past the cells. It paid to be close to one's captives in every respect, conscious or otherwise. Listening to their breathing. Their dreamscape ramblings. Occasional night-terrors. The better he *knows* them, the more pleasure could be taken in their division of power and circumstance. And he *knows* them now, certainly. Every flicker of respiration. Every murmur of name or place wrestled in sleep. Every scratching at walls in the dead of night. No other ruler, commander or parent ever knew their charges so well as the Manager.

Closer, now. They must be outside Nineteen's cell. The Manager half-wishes they'd get a move on. Half-hopes they'll drag it out as long as they can. Ideally, he'd have been on hand to watch the first moments of the reunion. A shame it simply wasn't appropriate: his presence would halt the proceedings entirely. Peeling his forehead from the door, he works on loosening muscles in his arms and chest. He knows it's best to let it happen by degrees instead of wasting the whole finale on just one great explosion, returns diminished. Such was the preserve of anarchists, after all. They never did learn of the pleasures to be taken from patience.

I don't know if I'm ready for this. I'm still waiting for an intervention. A shattering of glass. A blast of heat and light from somewhere down the corridor. It shouldn't be this neat and easy. He's right there on the other side of the door. I can hear him breathing, shifting around on the top of the sheets. Like he used to do for hours, those nights following one of his little adventures. Despite what Bethany's been telling me, I can't rely on his having been thinking about me as much as I've been thinking about him. Too much time has passed, since he and Bethany had their *chats*.

Whatever they've been doing to him in here will have thrown up a distance between us. Levels and degrees of experience I can finally match, sure, but the narrative framework remains irreconcilable. But I

261

get to my knees with the lock-picks in hand. No way in hell I can leave him down here. Even if it's just to have been the one to do the saving.

D5 can't sleep in the night-shift lounge. His head is too full of H5's earlier outburst. Constancy prickling at the edges of acceptable discourse. D5 knows he should just have gone back to his Management-protected apartment block for the evening, his presence no longer required. But he's wrestling with the agonies of one half-possessed of a secret liable to get him into trouble. Such a silly thing, he knows. Worrying about nothing. It's just that wants to be near both H5 and the Management, should H5 open his mouth and implicate them both. To defend himself, deny his part in any untoward discussions, if need be. That's all it is.

He hoists himself from the bunk and works knots from his shoulders. It's been an irregularly hands-on shift: much fetching and carrying, pushing and shoving. The Interns themselves may not weigh much, but the gurneys and equipment made up in awkwardness for what they lacked in load. Exertions have been helping with work he's been doing on his patterns of thought. Viewing the events surrounding the exercise in such purely physical, statistical and gestural terms kept back the eruptions rising in his own throat. Depth of thought made his stomach hurt, his scalp rigid with dread. H5 and the Medic should have kept their mouths shut as regarded psychological specifics. Too much loose thought in the heads of the Interns can be too easily spread to Agents in charge. And they were *in charge*, after all. There is a *way* of things.

He swings his legs from the bed and straight into his shoes, perpendicular-precise on the concrete below. Aside from a slight dent in the spine of the mattress, the taut surface of the bed shows little sign of disturbance. Making for the door, he's irritated to note a betrayal of limbs. He's teetering ever so slightly. Lacking sleep. Lacking nourishment. Lacking light. Space between shifts barely counts for much anymore in terms of separating an Agent's quality of life from that of an Intern's. Stress, pressure, exhaustion, the unholy Trinity. That's all it is.

Pausing only to peer into the other night-shift bunk rooms, D16 proceeds down the corridor. All sound asleep, the others. Those lucky enough to have missed the day's entertainments. D16's last word on the Manager was that he'd insisted on an evening undisturbed in his suite. In the odd stolen moment out from under the black eyes of surveillance, he and H5 have often speculated as to what the Manager actually got up to in there. H5 had a feeling he was watching old footage, reading old files. Kicks came few and far between, down here, and H5 reckoned it the kind of interfaced voyeurism the Manager would surely enjoy. D16 himself didn't go quite so far. It's enough, for him, to resent the added extras such privilege afforded. He's never seen further than the slim isosceles of carpet at the front door to the Manager's suite, but that had been enough for a measure of sheen. A whiff of leather and genuine coffee. Un-reconstituted fruit juice and non-medicinal soap. On the plus side, such luxuries implied the Manager had plenty to keep himself occupied. D16 would slacken off, too, he knows. If he'd had a place like that. A place of his own. Retired from eyes.

H5 is, as predicted, asleep on the job. D16 frowns, noting the static fuzz on the CCTV monitors, before placing his left hand on his partner's shoulder. Making sure, first, to hold his right over H5's mouth. The entirety of H5's skin buckles and leaps as he jerks from sleep, mouthing at D16's palm. D16 drops to the floor by the chair, slowly loosening his grip.

'Shhhhh ... it's only me.'

'Jesus, mate, you scared the shit out of me! What are you doing here?'

'I could ask you the same thing, mate. What the hell's this you're watching? Weather reports in Alaska?'

H5 blinks, staggers up out of the chair and squints at the nearest monitor. Lightly smacking a palm against the side of the box, in the time-honoured tradition of the technically inept.

'Shit. I don't know what the hell's going on with *this* ... must have been an error, or something ...'

'Caught at ease again, mate. You're lucky it was me who came by.'

H5 still mutters, rummaging in the plugs and wires behind the screens.

'I don't know how this happened ... It was just fine, a wee while ago ...'

'Wasn't the Manager buggering about with the feeds, or something?' asks D16, vaguely remembering a pale presence flipping switches in central control not too long before he left for the bunk rooms. H5 nods.

'Aye, well, last thing he said to all of us was that he didn't want to be disturbed. *In any way, shape or form,* he says. Told me he'd pulled all feeds and alarms from here to his suite, for the rest of the evening. Must have yanked some other stuff, too, and not realized.'

'Which is your job,' says D16. The grin on his face assures H5 he's still only teasing. H5 slumps back into the chair, fingers kneading his scalp. D16 takes a seat on top of a control panel, showing no signs of leaving, nor of looking for help.

'Fuck, mate, I'm buggered now,' moans H5. 'All the Techs have left for the night. And if the Manager's not to be disturbed – *not under any circumstances,* he says – I don't have a bloody clue what to do about this.'

'Do nothing,' says D16, a strange, slack, smile unfurling. 'Do nothing. You'd just be following orders, after all.'

'But–'

'I'm serious. You've one of two choices. Maybe three. Sit here and wait for the Techs to come in the morning. You don't have much to worry about, and I'm sure the Manager would agree – all the Interns are bedded down for the night, doors are locked, guards on patrol at all the Overground entrances. Everything's all very quiet and peaceful, as it should be, as it always is. Two. Leave your post, take a walk along to the Manager's suite, and tell him you're having some technical trouble. True, aye, but blatant disregard for his request. And you know how he is about manners …'

D16 drawls to a halt. H5 sits up straight in the chair, peering with intent enough to pierce the blue-grey gloom.

'And?'

'What?'

'You said three choices. That's only two.'

D16 swallows thickly.

'Well, for the third, you're going to have to shut up for a bit whilst I tell you something.'

'I don't think I'm going to like it.'

'Neither do I. But I can't keep it to myself, mate. Why'd d'you think I've missed fucking off at the end of my shift? I have to have a word.'

'What's up?'

D16 holds up a hand, requesting a pause. He's still not sure what he's doing. This was madness. Went against everything he knows to be correct, everything about which he's already expended so much energy and breath warning his partner. But he's been working alongside H5 for far too long to be holding back information. Particularly when it concerned the issue that's already provoked so many breaches of propriety.

'You know something, Rick?'

H5 starts once more at the sound of his own name. Twice in the one twenty-four hour period. A full-body shock when held up alongside years of living as a two-digit chunk of a barcode.

264

'Mmmm-hmmm?'

'I thought I came down here because I couldn't sleep. I thought I couldn't sleep because I was worried you couldn't keep your mouth shut. And here I am. Yapping. I guess I needed to talk just as much as you always seem to do.'

'What did you think I'd be saying? *Tony?*'

D16 drops his head and hunches his shoulders. Accusation in the voice of a friend. Funny, it has the same effect down here as it would Overground.

'You know. What you were saying earlier. About stuff not being right. I thought you might wind up saying something to the Manager.'

'And get you into trouble, aye? Is that it? Do you think I'm *stupid*, Tony? Think I don't remember what he did to X44 –to Bethany?'

'I don't think you're stupid, Rick. I think you're right.'

'What?'

'It's happened. I overheard Stories leaving for the day. It's not good. It's not *right.*'

'What's happened?'

'He's taken it, Rick. Intern Number Nineteen. He's taken the rewire.'

'Holy fuck.'

Silence in the surveillance office crawls over skin with etymological legs. Groaning, H5 presses his temples between his palms. Blank static screens on the monitors now seem all too appropriate. Black humour. A bad joke at a funeral. Faith shaken on a few more levels than whether an Agent's duties contribute to a worthwhile cause.

'I thought you should know,' says D16. 'Since …'

'Since we were the ones to hand him over.'

It takes a moment for D16 to register the tones carrying through H5's voice. Self-loathing. Self-pity. Guilt. Emotions that, down here, served absolutely no practical purpose.

'No. Since we're the ones who've been talking to him. We know who he is. What he's giving up. And …I don't know what I'm doing. I just thought you'd rather hear it from me. Didn't want you to find out yourself, without warning.'

'Fucking … *bastard* …' hisses H5. 'He *knew* Nineteen was too fucked after that *exercise* to know his own name, never mind any damn *information!* He couldn't just *leave* him? He hadn't done *enough?*'

Both have watched months pass as the Manager has had his offer of rewiring refuted again and again. Neither are able to take much

265

comfort from the fact that Caleb had had to be tortured and fried beyond all concept of sense to reach a point by which it became an attractive prospect.

'I want to see him,' says D16. 'I have to know how ... how he'll be.'

'But why? You know how it goes, Tony. They're not in there, anymore.'

'Not Nineteen, though. Don't you think there's a chance, just the slightest chance, that it's not taken hold? Nineteen's not like the others, Rick. He's too ... well, *strong* for a rewire. I have to know whether he's really, truly gone.'

H5 is silent. It's a nice idea. A touch of that old Romantic heroism the Manager so rigidly abhors. Whether or not there was anything left, a visit with Nineteen will offer the closure H5 and his partner so desperately need. In the former circumstance, proof that the system was fallible. That there may be ways and means of getting around it. In the latter, proof, should either require it, that their days were not spent crafting and maintaining a worthy and valuable system of government. Reason enough to pick up and leave. Get the hell out of the city before they were no longer able to notice or see just what happened at the other end of so many flipped switches.

'Right. You're right. We should go and take a look. Maybe see if he needs anything. But if the Manager–'

D16 swept a hand across the static-blank screens.

'If the Manager comes looking, you're investigating a disturbance. You're out checking whether there's anything behind *this.*'

'Right. Right.'

H5 gets to his feet, grabbing the tops of the monitors for support. None of his mantras were working anymore – *only an Intern. For their own good. Stability, efficiency, Management.* Whatever had gone on in the Stories department that evening, whatever *had* been going on for months, years, now, was something he could no longer ignore. No longer condone.

'What are we going to say to Nineteen?' he asks his partner. D16 shrugs.

'I don't know. I'm not sure what kind of state he'll be in. But it's only right to go and have a look. Even the Manager would agree that it's the gentlemanly thing to do.'

Locking the door on the fizzing surveillance screens, H5 and D16 proceed down the corridor. The silence staggers, as it always does in the evening. Punctured by nothing but the sound of minds slowly peeling themselves to the quick. The lights drink them in and spit them out.

Movement at the very horizon of visibility. H5 punches D16 in the arm, then drags him back into the dark. Stood very, very still, they can watch the two figures making their way down the corridor without drawing attention themselves.

'Jesus ...' murmurs D16. 'I think that's ...'

'... Bethany,' breathes H5. Tones to match names revered in the highest of pre-Millennial churches.

'What the hell is she doing down here? What are *we* going to do?'

H5 grins.

'You know something? I don't give a flying fuck. And *we're* not going to do a damn thing. At least not yet.'

H5 knows exactly where the ex-Agent is going. The same cell toward which he and D16 were headed. Bethany and Nineteen went way back, he remembers. His face falls when he realizes just what she's going to have to encounter.

'Who's that with her?' he asks D16. 'Have you seen her before?'

D16 frowns, scratches at a memory lodged behind his brow. It could be only her. The girl. The girl who came in with Nineteen. The girl from the photographs. The girl whose name he cried out through both torture and sleep. The girl who might not be *in there*, anymore.

'It's Nineteen's girlfriend,' croaks D16. 'She'll be down here with Bethany, trying to break him out.'

'Jesus ... but ... oh, fuck ...'

The Agents share a moment of silence. Admiration for audacity. Reverence for the taking of action. Sorrow for what they knew to be coming. Finally H5 slinks a little further along the wall, angling for a closer look. He was right: the girl was on her knees at the keyhole; Bethany standing guard, staring up into the tarry murk at the other end of the corridor. The Manager's suite. Still no action forthcoming, but they still had to do *something*.

'Should we ... you know? Back-up?'

D16 shakes his head.

'They've come this far. They have to do this on their own.'

'But what if–'

'Bethany can handle herself. We can't be around for this part. It wouldn't be right.'

H5 nods, sinks back into the blackness. Whilst the Agents do not make a move toward Caleb's cell, neither do they retreat back down the corridor. It had nothing to do with the threat simmering in the suite at the end of the corridor. Whether or not the Manager missed the whole thing, something unspeakable is about to happen.

*   *   *

Caleb stares through the ceiling at the sky as it might have looked many years before. The Agents in Scenarios have done what they could to make it a little easier on the Intern. No recordings. No fabrications. Just deletions. Taking him back, way back. More than a decade's worth of rot skimmed away. And with it, all he'd learned since he threw away his childish books and toys. All he'd come to know about what made being human worthwhile. All he'd seen and known and done with the promise of love on the other side of dawn.

It's a nice place to be. Quiet. Calm. Indifferent. No Management. No *city*. Caleb's frames of reference are tightened to the breadth of a parental home, a school classroom, a back garden. No thrum of protest nipping at the inside of his ribcage. No sense of having anything to protest *against*. Caleb is at ease. Everything is so dark in here. So pin-drop silent. Although his head rather aches, his mouth and ears numb, he is warm and fairly comfortable. He is to understand that he's not feeling too well, and must rest in his room in his bed for a while. This goes some way toward explaining the riot of red stars exploding across the backs of his eyes every time he squeezes too tightly shut. The way his skin feels hot from the core to the surface, yet cool to the touch of his fingertips. The powdery crumble of the inside of his mouth. Sticky clots at the corner of his eyelids and lips. He can smell rubbing alcohol, the same stuff his dad used to swab grazed knees whenever Caleb took a tumble. It was all going to be okay. He just has to relax, like the man said. Get some rest. Then he'll be right as rain.

*   *   *

Lucy's vision refuses to adjust to the sheer pitch of black in the room. Opening wider doesn't help at all. More black rushes in, pressing down. Her eyes are drowning. Bethany's hand on her back proves to be less of a reassurance when she can't see what she's being pushed toward. She can smell disinfectant. This is not a comforting odour.

'What the fuck …?' says Bethany. A swipe of dry palms against concrete walls. Looking for a light switch. She hasn't counted on

Caleb's cell being tailored to such blankness as to shift all controls to the outside wall. For the best, she supposes. Less chance of attracting attention. But still. No shift of light, temperature or space takes place in here without the Manager's say-so. He has relented on the issue of the bed. Caleb was neutralized. Baiting him with such details as furniture removal had as much effect on him as it would on a freshly shelled hatchling.

'Caleb ...?' Lucy begins, skating across the floor, hands grabbing at nothing. The warm presence on the bed in the room does not budge an inch. Lucy can hear respiration growing markedly gentler, shallower. The way kids breathe when they played hide and seek, and the seekers draw closer.

'Careful,' says Bethany. She's not quite sure why. Something about approaching a body in the dark sparked a reel of fears dark and primal in the pit of her torso. Too many bad horror movies as a teenager. Before the Management had done away with such nonsense.

Lucy's knees hit the edge of the bed. Blinking, shaking, she crouches down to the floor. Moves hands over bare mattress. The tips of her middle fingers soon meet the give of flesh wrapped in rough blankets. She jerks back. No response. She remembers she's come equipped. She flips the flashlight from her pocket and agitates the switch, a process impaired by her trembling fingers. Shocked to finally meet the mark, she drops the torch to the floor where it spins and spins, peeling and repainting the pitch.

A flash of green. Eyes open very wide. Set in deep pits of starved sockets.

'Caleb!' Lucy moans. Disregarding the torch, following the impression scorched on her retina by the brief flash of light, she leans over the bed and pulls herself up to kneel on the mattress. Reaches for body, for shape. Finally locking hands around shoulders hard and brittle as glass.

'Caleb ...' a sigh. A name murmured over so many half-sleeps, long after she told herself she was growing accustomed to waking alone. Finally, a warmth on the mattress beside her.

'Caleb? It's me. It's Lucy. We've ... haha ... we've come to take you home.'

Bethany stands pressed to the door frame. She has missed something. Possibilities she hasn't accounted for. All this talk of liberating the guy, and she's an Agent again. Discounting the mind in service of the body. Transport of flesh from one location to another without being seen. Building blocks and binary. Not enough. Against the frame, she smacks the back of her head as hard as she can without making a sound. Her whole body is screaming *ABORT*. This is not what's supposed to happen.

Lucy shifts her hands up the body on the bed, looking for the right spot to press to make him say something. Say her name. A body she's known almost as well as her own, yet drawn so taut and spare and *weightless*. She worries her fingers might just poke through the skin, like indelicate treatment of a paper lantern. Bethany finally reaches into her own pocket and unsheathes another flashlight. Squeezing her eyes shut, that she may not have to see what Lucy is about to, she throws a halogen spotlight over the bed.

Caleb lies wrapped tight in his Facility blanket, hands scissor-folded over his chest, legs perfect parallels with the walls alongside. His charred skullcap of hair pressed deep as is possible into a scrawny Facility pillow. He is a carving, all visible skin riddled with potholes of bruising. Face pitted with shiny scabs from blisters formed and bursting. Twin dents in the curve of his jaw intimate bridges' worth of missing teeth. Were she to place finger and thumb to his cheeks on either side of his mouth, they'd be able to meet in the space between tongue and hard palate.

Still staring. Not at the ceiling. At something he can't ever share. Lucy's throat buckles. It is Caleb, and yet it is not. The eyes in the skull in the figure on the bed should be looking into Lucy's own, promising *everything* she's been missing since he left. Full of whatever it was Caleb *had* that has sent Lucy looking, down here in the dark, for something without which she feels incomplete. Of whatever made Bethany want to help him out, even after everything that had been done to her also. Of whatever had driven the Manager to do what she'd seen him doing to Caleb in pixels and brief shreds of footage. Lucy is not so foolish as to think the eyes are all of what he *is*, but they do provide an aperture. A glance into what might be, should have been forthcoming.

She shifts further down the mattress. Tries again to jerk him upright, arms grappling an ungainly bag of bones. His head lolls on his neck, pupils unchanging. A broken clock spilling the springs from its gut. Lucy snaps, shakes him by the shoulders, her face right up against his own. The instincts that had led her to this point in time had implied such a position would have been a prelude to a kiss. She can't do it. Slack lips dry-dribble down his chin.

'Lucy, please ...' murmurs Bethany, still pressed to the doorway with her eyes closed. The torch beam trembles on the wall. Lucy snaps her head round.

'Something's wrong! He won't talk to me! What have they done to him?'

Without waiting for an answer, she presses her mouth to Caleb's ear.

'Caleb. Caleb, I know you're in there. I've got so much to tell you. Loads of mental stuff, you won't believe it. But you have to snap out of it. We've come to get you out. Take you home. See? That's Bethany over there. Remember her? She told me all about this place. All about what was going on with you. Told me you were always in trouble for running your mouth off … why am I not surprised, eh! Caleb, come on. I know you can hear me …'

'Lucy,' says Bethany, 'I'm not sure he can.'

'Don't be stupid. He's just a bit whacked out. They've given him a doing, and now he's sleeping it off. Come on. You have to help me get him to his feet.'

Lucy can hear tones of her own idiot denial. The bullying cheer of the oncologist. The rally-cry of the faithful, unwilling to face down the terminal truth. As though voicing such gentler patterns of circumstance would make it so. Bald lies, yet she can't stop trying. Shaking. Squeezing. Disregarding the greys she knows not to be Caleb's, she rubs hands on either side of his face. Calling on colours from a bottled genie long since run to dust.

*　　*　　*

The girl looms at Caleb out of a scattershot pattern of darkness and light. A nice face, he thinks. Pretty mouth, wide eyes. Her hair's a bit of a mess, though. Smudges on her cheeks. A rich, thick scent of mud inches up from her clothing. Can't be a nurse. Maybe one of his sister's friends. A cousin he hasn't seen since they've been little kids. Too tired to care. He shouldn't *have* to care. She should leave him alone and come back when he's feeling better.

But she's soft and warm, like the bed. Would be nice if she'd stop yanking at his shoulders. They hurt. He hurts, somewhere. Everywhere.

He can hear her. She's talking to him. He can understand every word as a *word*, sentence as sentence. But nothing with anything to do with him. Doesn't she know he's not well? If he's very quiet, very still, like the man said he must need to, want to be, maybe she'll go away.

*　　*　　*

271

At either end of seams of light in the corridor outside, both sets of onlookers strain heads on stalks, trying to make out what's going on in Nineteen's cell. It's not yet as exciting as it could be. But give it time.

The Manager shifts along the wall, gritty hunks of concrete catching on the fabric of his suit. He's never before slunk around his own premises, as far as he can remember. Curious. He can hear low murmurs and deep hitches of breath. Can make out the reeling beams of poorly-handled manual light sources. The occasional near-scream of the Intern's civilian name. The girl, the stupid girl. He remembers her well. He couldn't not. Professional satisfaction: a tremendously successful rewire off the back of a potential mess of mistakes. Until she'd got talking to the traitor, of course. But that just made things all the more interesting.

He smiles. One hand leaps to the corners of his mouth to find out what it feels like from the fingertip-exterior. A proper smile. It doesn't matter, in the dark. In spite of elation at the prospect of facing down the women, there had been a couple of small dips in his mood since he had retired to his suite. Caught up with the prospect of the whole charade soon being over, he had been having doubts as to whether Nineteen's accepting the rewire was as desirable an outcome as he'd initially thought. There had been no real alternative save another round of shocks in the unit, and the Manager knows there's no way the Intern's body would have stood up to that quite so soon. There was no time to *wait* for him to recover, either, not with the women digging ever deeper into the tunnels. The Manager had been hoping at least for another exciting round of Interviews in the aftermath of the exercise. Nineteen had let him down. Barely a whimper. Not the slightest mote of density of body or mind in the entire frame. Useless.

The rewire hadn't been the plan, at all. The Manager had offered such because he knew it to be, second to the unit, the process Nineteen most feared, rejected, abhorred. If it proved an easy escape route, a path of least resistance for certain lesser Interns, so too did it strike the Manager as somewhat anti-climactic. He still wants light shows. Motion sickness. Sound effects. Choreographed chaos. The rewire seemed to promise nothing but somatic silence.

Until he'd factored in the women. So many associations between persons, between processes. The very walls thrum with psychic disturbance. Three bodies. One cell. One thing in common. It would not be a point of identification. It would be – it *is* – now the very thing cracking them apart. Levels of knowledge strung up alongside the self-same experience sent all measuring devices haywire. Moral compasses. Frames of reference. Nothing can hold them together, not now. He can hear it in the pitch of the girl's voice. Crying out the Intern's name. Stories muttered, incomprehensible, yet there was no missing the panic snaking between whispered syllables. He notes that the Agent – X44, the traitor, the disappointment – is still stood in the entryway. Her spine blocking the spill of light down one side of the door. Unwilling to come any closer to her old friend, or her new one. So many ungainly expressions of rank sentiment rolling between the walls of that one tiny room. It seems almost a shame to break in on the scene. It seems they are already doing one another a fair amount of damage.

*   *   *

D16 and H5 remain locked in painful contortions of stillness. They'd heard the latch click on the door to the Manager's suite. They see the light bloom at the other end of the corridor too soon to turn and run the other way without illuminating their own end of the corridor. They have to wait it out. They watch as the halogen lozenges proceed up the corridor, almost as far as Nineteen's cell. Then suddenly stop. The Manager waits, watches, listens also. The Agents sense tension and disgust radiating from the tight flesh of the other. By unspoken agreement, both hold their positions. They have to wait to see what the Manager will do.

PART SEVEN

CHOICES

'Lucy,' says Bethany, finally opening her eyes. She places the torch on the floor, the puddle of light splashing from the concrete up over the feet of the bed. Peeling herself from the wall, Bethany crosses the floor to stand over the pair bunched on the mattress. Caleb is moulded as far as Lucy can gather him upright. Her arms tendon-wrenched as she struggles to keep his upper body to a near-seated position. His legs stuck straight out under the wrap of the blankets. Arms firmly locked to his sides. A quartet of prostheses. His head kept from dropping back to his chest only by Lucy's grip of his chin. Eyes still beads of clouded glass, repulsing even the glow of the flashlight. Bethany swallows hard. She has no idea of knowing exactly what's happened beforehand. Lucky enough never to have seen the Labs put to use in her time at the Facility. But she knows perfectly well what's happened since.

The dull glaze. The slack limbs. The voluntary shut-down of senses. She's seen it before. She's been there before. Countless impressions batter at the frames of what she knows about the rewire. Inside. Outside. Seen. Unseeing. Being trained as to the steps in the process. Her own voice recorded as Lucy's. Her own voice in someone else's mouth. Escorting rewired Interns back Overground. Being half-carried up to her own new premises. Telling Lucy how it all worked. Clicking back through archives of interfaced memories. Peeling back her own rewire to uncover what lay underneath. Doing the same for Lucy. Doing and done-to. Pressing buttons and walking through footsteps. At no point in any of these colliding impressions has there been space for how Caleb might fit into the process.

This is not supposed to happen. This is not supposed to *be*.

'Lucy. Listen to me.'

Lucy jerks her head from hovering at Caleb's ear. Fixes Bethany between a pair of death stars. Opens her mouth to speak, words meeting air without making a sound.

'Lucy. We have to get out of here. Right now. Caleb's not in there. Not anymore.'

'What the fuck are you talking about?'

'They've done to him what they've done to you. To us. He's taken the rewire. He's gone.'

Lucy shakes her head. Shakes Caleb's shoulders. Her chest and throat hitching with a prelude to tears. Still no response from the mannequin in her arms. No sign that he's just tired. Just playing. Just waiting for her to loosen her guard before slinging arms, hands, lips around her for a kiss. A surprise. Lucy knows she's got to move.

'Then help me out, here, Bethany. If he can't walk, we'll have to carry him.'

'But … Lucy, you don't get it. He's not *in* there.'

'So what? We just leave him? No way, Bethany. It doesn't have to be like this. I can help him. Tell him all about it. Do for what you did for me.'

Bethany sighs, drops to her knees, takes one of Caleb's clammy hands between her own.

'I don't think it's that simple. Look at him, Lucy. There's more than a rewire gone on. Remember. I only got a half-shot. Took time, but I got better. And you were only in here a couple of weeks. That's all you lost. You had Medics to help bring you back up. And you might not have got the *right* story, but it was story enough. You didn't have to go as far back as some to remember who you are.'

'I don't care. I'll work at it.'

'Lucy, would you *look* at him? He's a *wreck*! Where are the Medics? The tubes? The machines? Why do you think they're keeping him locked up in here without so much as a goddamn *light switch*? There is *nothing there*. It's a waste of time.'

Bethany runs a tongue-tip across the last sentence in her mouth. It tasted strange. Not unpleasant. Familiar. She knows she has a point. She does. They've been lucky enough to get all the way down here without being caught. Trying to manoeuvre an inert block of bone and skin from here back Overground wasn't just inefficient, it was suicidal. Being down here doesn't feel as awkward as it had done the first few steps into the tunnel. She knows what she's doing. Getting to work.

'Waste of time? Fuck you, Bethany. If you're not going to help me, I'll do it myself.'

275

Bethany backs away toward the door. Opposing instincts pulling her apart. The right thing to. The sane, sensible, efficient alternative. Mutually exclusive.

Lucy begins to cry. Spare as he is, she knows she can't carry Caleb herself, all the way back up to the casino. Even then, they're not going to pass the lobby unnoticed. A lone woman and her life-size doll. This is not how it's supposed to happen. She hadn't been expecting Caleb to be in the peak of health, true, but she'd been relying at least on some semblance of consciousness. She can't take him with her. Yet she can't leave. She eases her legs up onto the mattress and presses her body to his. Hoping that heat, those familiar contours, might reach in somewhere her words simply can't.

The Manager hears weeping. Shuffling of feet as the traitor resumes her post at the door.

'You've got to snap out of this,' he hears the Agent say to the girl. 'This isn't how it's supposed to go.'

No response from the girl. The Manager tunes into every ebb and flow of breath and damp. Tears and bed sheets. Hitches and sputters. A low moan outstripping all the night-time cries he's heard from other Interns calling out in sleep.

'Lucy!' The traitor still trying to gather some sense. He has to admire her for sticking around as long as she has. Although that left much efficiency to be desired. She's evidently lost her flair for assessing situations. That this one was hopeless should have been perfectly clear. 'Lucy, this isn't going to work. Look, we don't have to do this right now. We can get out of here, have another look at what we might do, and come back better prepared. You know I'm right.'

'Fuck you, Bethany. Fuck you. Get out of here if you want. I'm staying.'

'What? So you can get a nice little cell for yourself, too? Isn't this enough? You're not going to *win*, here, Lucy. You've got to get out of here before we get caught.'

'Fuck you.'

More weeping. Angrier, this time. Growling in the pit of the ribcage. Each breath a painful exercise in control. Caught, though. That was his cue. The Manager moves toward the door just in time to see the crack of light shifting by degrees. The traitor is making a move. She won't be getting very far.

All cell doors in the Facility swing inward. Better for the pinning of Interns into their rooms. Ticking fingertips over the coded box on the outside wall, the Manager unlocks the cell's inner light source, blinding the occupants with a sudden blaze of halogen. Caleb sees none of this but a shift behind the eyelids from black ink to blood roses. Lucy flinches, gasps, cants an arm over her eyes. Bethany shrinks back further from the bed, smacking her spine against the door frame. Neither were ready to see Caleb bathed in the white glow of the cell. Fully deformed. Every burn scar glowing violet, still seeping yellow fluid. The charcoal smear of the scalp's melted hair offsetting the putty pallor of the rest of his skin. Facial dents accentuated by missing teeth and acute starvation make him look like something long dead, dug up, poorly reanimated.

Lucy and Bethany don't have time to look, never mind avert their eyes.

The Manager puts his body's every last mote of energy into his shoulders, legs, arms, throwing the door against the wall. Bethany, caught behind, slams against the concrete in a rasp of beaten breath. The Manager steps inside with all the calm command of one entering an elevator. Letting the door swing shut behind him, he watches with a smile as Bethany worms along the floor, clutching her winded stomach. Lucy says nothing. Jerks upright, pulling Caleb closer. Lips moving around innumerable opening lines – accusations, pleas, challenges, explanations. Whatever has happened between their first meeting and their last, he's still the Manager. Still in charge of her care.

Outside in the hall, D16 and H5 move closer, closer, until they're standing with their backs against the outside wall of the cell, inches from the door frame. They can hear everything, now. It's just a matter of knowing how to act, if and when.

'What do we do?' asks H5.

'We can't do anything till we know what's going on in there.'

Violence, he means. Still clinging onto the hope that it might not have to come to anything at all involving *them*. That, should the Manager throw down a few words and sweep from the cell, H5 and his partner could still feasibly be checking out a *disturbance* in the corridor. Doing their duty.

Inside, the Manager doesn't know where to begin. It's glorious. The traitor on the floor, where she belongs, belly-crawling. The Intern silent. No riposte, no parlay. No smart manoeuvres of brow, of eye and mouth corners. No gestures requiring interpretation. The girl prone on the bed, as she had been the first time they'd met.

Fingers brush the tops of his boot, flutter the cuffs of his trousers. The Manager stamps both feet, flipping Bethany across the floor like a loose flagstone. He laughs. That's as good a place to start as any.

'Agent X44. Decommissioned, and still such a *presence* in the Facility. To what do I owe the pleasure?'

A wheeze, a hitch. Bethany struggles up from the floor, shifts to lean her back to the wall.

'Well? I wish you'd told me you were coming, X44. I would have put on my favourite suit.'

'You … fuh …'

'I didn't hear a *Sir,* there. You may no longer be on my payroll, X44, but manners cost nothing.'

Lucy clutches Caleb tighter. As he moved closer to Bethany, the gap widens between the Manager and the door, the opening edge closer to Lucy's side of the room than to his. Bethany's face beads with pale dew as she struggles still to catch her breath. The Manager's presence in the room has had no discernable effect on Caleb: his breath still even, his heartbeat a sluggish drip of syrup from a spoon. Lucy is on her own. Her only chance at making it out of here is to leap for the door, snatch out into the hallway and run for it as fast as she can. But that would mean leaving Caleb. And however much sense Bethany may have been making about practicalities, liabilities and second chances, Lucy has come too far to entertain the thought. There is nothing out there for her but an endless backtracking over what she would now have lost twice. Forming and reforming alternate endings in which she'd done the right thing.

'Agent X44, I'm speaking to you. I must say, I'm rather astounded by your rudeness. Not only have you failed to inform me that you were coming to call, you've brought an uninvited *guest.* Poor form, Agent. Poor form.'

The Manager shakes his head at Bethany, turns to fix his attention on the pair on the bed. Moving closer, thereby blocking Lucy's exit. She is not as distressed by this as she might otherwise have been. She has already made up her mind that wherever she's going, she's going with Caleb.

'And who might you be?' asks the Manager. Knowing she knows he knows perfectly well just made the answer that much more delicious. It was always interesting to hear how Interns and Candidates so identified themselves outside of their assigned number and status.

'You know who I am,' says Lucy. Her voice comes as a shock. Harder, rounder than her desiccated throat felt capable of. 'We've met before.'

'Have we? You'll forgive my not being able to remember. I see so many of your kind, day on day, week on week … so many faces … so many useless *words* …'

278

Bethany gathers breath enough to speak. Still struggling to push herself up off the floor, she manages to unearth a sentence.

'Lucy! Her name is Lucy!'

'I don't recall asking *you*, X44.'

'And *my* name is Bethany. I'm not your fucking *Agent* anymore.'

'Language! My, my, you really *have* changed since we last met. I don't recall your being anywhere near this … *voluble* when we last had chance to speak.'

The Manager offers Bethany a horrible wink. Both fall back into a picture of the Agent on her way out of the Facility. Many shades of black, blue, purple, green. Dragging a plaster cast behind her. Unable to form a coherent thought, never mind a sentence. The Manager may not have enjoyed having to discipline and decommission a skilled and talented Agent, but he *had* been rather pleased with the overall upshot of the penalty. The Facility had been running smooth as glass ever since, not so much as a whimper of the kind of deviant behaviour that had gotten this one into so much trouble.

'I've had a bit of time to get my thoughts in order,' says Bethany. 'Thoughts you'd so kindly had removed, without my permission.'

'You needed a bit of a clear-out, X44. A terrible amount of disorder in there … what a mess …'

'You had no right!' yells Lucy. She didn't know she had it in her. She tightens her grip on Caleb enough to produce a muted moan. This shifts her attention to the body in her arms, tilting his chin up with her free hand. She snaps back to the Manager. His reply deferred to bubbles of laughter crawling from his barrel of a chest.

'Look what you've done! After what you did to me! Who the fuck do you think you are?'

This latter question comes from so far outside of the Manager's frame of reference that he is taken aback, for a moment. He strolls slowly into the centre of the room, jangling keys in his pocket, lip thrust out in thought. Behind his back, Bethany slowly gets to her feet.

'Who do I think I *am..?* Curious, very curious. You Candidates, you Interns, you're always the same. Always grabbing for *stories*. When, in systems as efficient as mine, things just *are* as they *are*. All is fixed. Stabilised. Efficient. But …in answer to your question … I am the Manager. *Your* Manager. That's all you'll ever have to know. Isn't that a comfort?'

'There is nothing,' says Lucy, every syllable a cyanide capsule, 'That lets you get away with what you're doing to people. I didn't understand, before ... I thought you were ... I don't know. But you're ...you're *wrong*. Things aren't just what they *are*, they are what *you* say they are. And that's just not right. Look. Look at him.' Lucy tilts Caleb's blank face up to the Manager. 'How can you think this is the way things should be?'

'Because I'm the Manager!' he bellows. 'I'm in charge!'

'Who says so?' snaps Lucy. 'Since you're clearly insane ...'

She stops short. She knows baiting the Manager when he's stood between herself and the door was a terrible move, but she has to do *something*. Say something. Buy time for Bethany to get her act together, unleash all the skills possessed of a former Agent. Get them out of there. At least that's the way it *should* happen. The Manager grows bored of talk, though. It was time to move things on to the next stage.

'It's a shame you have such a problem with my running of things,' he says. 'Since there are no alternate options available. My way or the highway, I believe is the expression. Like it or lump it, is another. Enough of this nonsense. The only decisions you'll be able to make are what you'd rather I did with you next.'

'What? What are you talking about?' says Lucy, looking over Caleb's burn-scarred flesh.

'Well, you've come all the way down here for a visit. I can't let you leave without extending offers of hospitality.'

'We're leaving,' says Lucy, very firmly. As though conviction bled into the voice would run concrete rivets into forthcoming developments. 'All of us. We don't want anything to do with you or your Facility or your *hospitality*, you crazy—'

'—my goodness, I never would have expected such cheek from a former guest! After all I did for you, Candidate Number Forty-Two. Gave you a place to sleep, food to eat, fixed you up good as new after your little accident ...sorted you out with a home and a care plan—'

'—no *accident*, no nothing. I know everything, now. I know what you are.'

The Manager clears his throat. Shrugs. Tilts his palms to the ceiling, a cartoon burglar caught in the act.

'Oh well. I suppose that means we can dispense with the niceties. You have two choices. You'll get a cell for the evening, of course, but come the morning shift, it'll be time to let me know what you'd prefer. You either go with one of my talented Agents in Stories, for another shot at a fresh start ... or you remain in the cells indefinitely. It's up to you.'

'I'm taking nothing, and going nowhere with you,' says Lucy.

'I'm afraid you're on my premises,' says the Manager, 'And such petty declarations of intent mean nothing down here. I know all about you and your anarchist, there ...' The Manager sneers at Caleb, still inert. 'All your little adventures. Well. Where have you ended up, after all that? He's going nowhere. He *is* nowhere. Is nothing. And you're on your own. I suggest you give some thought to a fresh Story, Forty-Two. Because you'll not be leaving here without my say-so, if at all.'

'I'm not taking your fucking story.'

'Your decision. I'm afraid we can't offer a cell with a view, but if you're on your best behaviour, I'm sure we can scare up a cot. Maybe even let you have the lights on, during the day. You'll have plenty of time to get used to it, since it'll be the only home you'll ever know from now on. And I know how fond you are of playing houses ... quite the little carpenter ...'

Bethany springs onto the Manager's back, wrapping both arms around his ham of a neck. His face briefly creases as he registers the extra weight. Then a smile at her efforts to liven things up. He lets her hang there, suspended, for a moment or two, before flipping her back to the floor with all the ease of a man swatting a fly. He turns, tutting, shaking his head.

'Ah ... Agent X44, you were always a favourite. So ... *athletic.* Skills I could have put to excellent use in the field, if you hadn't let me down so badly ... but we haven't heard *your* thoughts on the subject of where you're each going from here. What about you? Are you for a time-out ... or a fresh start? A Story ... or a cell?'

Bethany's first attempts at speech emerge crooked from around the folds of another winding.

'What ... she said ... Lucy ... fuck your stories ...'

'Now, now. Let's not make any snap decisions. I realize we all find ourselves in a situation of rather ... heightened emotions. And throwing our lot in with our *compatriots* ... it would seem the Done Thing. But there's no shame in thinking things through a little, first. Real life doesn't move half so fast as you might think. As you'll find out, if you opt out of a Story.'

The Manager leans over Bethany with a smile. He crouches down to the floor beside her, takes her wrists and pulls her up to her feet. Surprisingly gentle.

'There we go, Agent. Bethany. See? Things don't have to get rough every time, do they?'

Lucy mouth gapes around words she can't quite form. She shakes Caleb's hand in hers, willing him to say something, do something. Bethany stands, dazed, for a moment or two before flinching out from under the Manager's grip.

'I don't want a story,' she says, dulled syllables spilled without inflection. A phrase learned by rote. Muttered without quite being understood. The Manager steps before her, blocking her view of the pair on the cot. Lucy swings her feet to the floor with every intention of standing upright, before realising that to do so would have Caleb slumping boneless to the mattress.

'Oh, Bethany. Agent. Bethany. Who are you, really? Can you be one without the other? I'm offering you what I offer *everyone* who walks both ways through my Facility. Another chance, a fresh start. A life. You don't *have* one, up there. Following, hiding. Slipping in and out of other people's business. Do you?'

'Shut up!' shouts Lucy. 'Bethany, don't listen to him!'

The Manager turns to face the bed, still blocking Bethany from Lucy's line of sight. He smiles, spreads his hands.

'Well, what we have here is a case in point! My dear, ask yourself ... and be honest ... weren't you better off before your friend here interfered? You were *safe*, you had a home to go to, a routine, a presence. A healthy mind in a healthy body. A *way of things*. *We* did that for you. We took you out of that anarchic mess you'd let yourself be dragged into by *him,* there. Set you up on your very own. If you had just *let it be*, if you'd stuck to what you knew, you wouldn't be down here, right now, would you? You'd have let go of all of those little *niggles* eventually. Had yourself a nice, neat, clean and purposeful existence ... but you had to go poking around into things that don't concern you–'

'–excuse me?' snaps Lucy, pressing her hands to either side of Caleb's head. 'I think this – *this* – very much concerns me! You've *ruined* him!'

'We did nothing we didn't have to do,' says the Manager. 'If there's no information, we expect co-operation. If there's none of either, well ... we need make examples.'

'But–'

'–And you're consistently failing to get the point, here. Which is that none of this would have mattered to you in the *slightest* if you'd just left well enough alone.'

'If you think it's as easy as–'

'–but it *is*, don't you see? We've been running a successful rehabilitation programme for as long as the Management have been in power. Never the slightest *ripple* of bother following release. Until *you* … well, let's just call it a series of unhappy coincidences. Rogue conversations. A few too many anomalies in the same place at the same time. Which is all fixable. If you think carefully about your options.'

'I don't want your–'

'–quiet, please. Lucy. I know you better than you might think. I know you know when to keep your mouth shut. And this isn't about you, not yet. Right now, I'll be needing a word with your friend, here. So please. Take your time. Relax. We'll be right back.'

Bethany's head flicks back and forth across the room as the Manager opens the door, waves her into the corridor. Her eyes full of switchblades of light gathered from all corners of the room.

'Lucy, I–'

'–Lucy will be just fine. It's been quite a while since she's seen her … since she's had a little *visit*. I'm sure they'll appreciate a touch of privacy, whilst they get on with some catching up.'

Bethany follows the Manager into the corridor. Two shadows further down take the flicker of light as distraction enough to edge a little further away, out of sight, holding pattern in a deeper dredge of gloom. The Manager flickers fingertips over the box on the outside. Locks ring out a neat series of clicks, a rhythm comfortable enough to elicit a sigh. He leans against the door facing Bethany, who stands with her arms firmly folded.

'I meant what I said, you know,' he begins, 'About jumping the gun. It's all very well playing the hero when there's a fixed outcome in sight, a prize, a … well, why don't *you* tell *me* what you're doing down here?'

Her throat clicks as steady as the tongues in the lock.

'Because … because it was the right thing to do.'

'Interesting. Very interesting,' says the Manager, noting the past tense. 'And now? Now you've seen just how *pointless* the whole exercise has been?'

'It's not pointless.'

'So what's the point?'

'I don't know.'

Bethany's shoulders slump over her ribcage, angling toward a firm surface, any surface, against which to lean. The Manager steps away from the door, circles back as Bethany's feet pick an arc, her fingers tangling in the hair at her temples.

'Shall I run it through for you?' he asks. He does not wait for a response.

'You stay down here with you *cause,* and you'll be down here indefinitely. Cells and Agents with whom you will be *familiar,* but never in this particular configuration. And that will be that. No room for manoeuvre, no variables, nothing. And all for that girl and her *boyfriend,* neither of whom have done or will do a damn thing for *you.* The girl's a waste of space, I don't need to tell you that. Jumps on whichever bandwagon's coming her way. As for the Intern ... I can see why one might find him *interesting, stimulating,* what with all those *ways with words* he has ... but he's not so tricky now, is he? Not much left to say for himself. And all he had to do was *co-operate* ... that's all *any* of us have to do, to keep things running smoothly ... Agent?'

Bethany stops circling, stands with her back to the Manager. He's not wrong. Nothing has changed. She has dropped her semblance of a life on the Outside for the sake of the Intern and his girlfriend. She has no idea what she has hoped to achieve. Either way, she has wound up with nothing. A cause. The word implies momentum. Purpose. Consequences. And yet here she stands, again, between the same set of walls, with the same powerlessness.

I should be crying. Howling. Screaming. Renting claw marks in the cement. Caleb's arm has barely enough flesh hold fingernail half-moons, however I tighten my grip. So many things I hadn't counted on. No room in my head. I should have thought it'd have been easier, knowing exactly what you were running after. But however present the fact of the flesh, skin and heat remain dead meat without an animating spark.

Bethany is out there making negotiations. I've known, somewhere at least, that I can't rely on her when there's more than one life at stake. The Manager still charms. I remember it well. I can't say for sure I wouldn't take him up, if I were her. If I didn't have these rivets of blood and bone between my hands.

I know why I am still holding on. Why I won't take a Story, even if another version of myself still wavers. A version caught between the first and the last. I am both stronger and weaker than those who'd have accepted. My shift in perspective is doing me no favours.

It's not principle. That's never been my style. Given a bait appealing enough, hell, I'd bite. Few wouldn't. Me, I can't take down something that spans more than the breadth of the Manager's chest, floods wider, roots deeper than the wires and tunnels we've already breached.

It's not honour. There are no assessment criteria of such old-fashioned concerns anymore. Not down here.

It's not about a *cause*. I have no banner, no acronym. Not a statement. I don't have the right words, never have.

Not consequence. I haven't the arrogance to assume I have influence.

I want nothing from this but what I've come for in the first place.

And I am not leaving without him. So simple. It should hurt more than it does.

I know where she's been. Potent. Respected. And *useful* . It's hard to twin the *used* with the power gleaned from being so. But I've wasted too many empty days to deny there's a pleasure to be taken from having your potential invoked. I know where she wound up: like me, looking over her shoulder, watching her footprints disappear the second they sunk. Choking on routines of self-preservation. Not sure whether she should be seeking meanings in sunrise, whether her head was picking up strands of errant radio streams. Whether she was going crazy. But she's not as lucky as me. She had no real *before* except what had been built all around her down here. No Caleb. Which probably makes this a glorious irony.

I'm already working on how to forgive her. She has her reasons. Everybody does. For giving up. She has nothing to go back to, now. Not even a rotten bar job over which every muscle movement is curtailed before unfurled. No familiar faces leering from the walls. A cavalcade of gargoyles made less horrendous by virtue of familiarity. No home, or whatever she'd managed to make of the same kind of blank compartment at whose walls I'd stared for hours, wondering who the hell I really was. No friends. Her treason had severed at the knees any relationships she'd built up down here, upon which she'd relied for her identity, the frame of her days. Nothing but what she's given me. For which the Manager will make sure she's getting no reward. I'd be sorry, if I didn't have more pressing matters at hand. Curled up with me, whether he knows it or not. Brackets around a rank of manic slash marks. Digital invective.

Caleb shifts in my arms. Or maybe it's me. I can't tell anymore. Numb from muscles knit in one place for so long. Since before I got here, probably. Waiting.

This isn't how it's supposed to go. There's meant to be a proper confrontation, an exchange of blows. So far the only giving and receiving have been between the Manager and Bethany. Agent. Agent X44. I'm a fool if I think that's irrelevant. The same way I'm clinging to Caleb over logic, over safety, over an easy out, so will she, too, be reaching out for what she knows. Nothing more pathetic than a hunting down of glory days. Not when they can be clawed back. Both of us down here looking for something we've lost. The winners and losers are no longer between ourselves and the Manager. It's whoever can hang on tightest to what we have found.

I'm supposed to say something, here. It's only right. I've read things about the subconscious: absorbing sounds and sensations from the outside even when nothing appears to register. I can't hear what they're talking about outside. And it's not like the movies. No ear pressed to the door, to the crack underneath. I don't want to hear either way. The inventory of what she might be giving up for us. Me and Caleb. Or what a person says, what they sound like, when they are betraying you through the thickness of a door.

'Caleb. I'm saying I want you to listen to me. I don't know how much choice you have, but if you can *try*, please do. I want you to know what's at stake, here, if you can't help yourself out of here. I'm not going to leave you. But I can't move you. I need you on your feet. I need your smart mouth more than anything, probably, but … I can make do with one foot, then the other. The Manager's outside. Which means we're not getting out unless something *happens*. And I need you for that. Two against two evens the odds …or makes it less likely we're going to wind up far worse than we started. Caleb … Caleb, please. I know you can hear me. I just need you to be here for as long as it takes to get us both back Overground. We'll take it from there. I'll take care of you, I promise.'

I am talking myself into this as much as talking to him. My tongue thuds in my mouth like a length of spent movie reel, slapping over and over the tears on its idiot sequence. No response. He's not going to snap back just because I will it so. I'm already kidding myself I can see shivers of a smile of recognition. Screwing my eyes up in the hope of seeing light-crystals blossoming in Caleb's. Telling myself there's a purpose to crippling my own vertebrae for the sake of propping his spine into a mimicry of alert; that there's no way he wouldn't know the difference if I just let him slump back to the bed. There's my cause, my statement, I guess. Sheared of frames crafted by anything bigger than this: me, Caleb, a surface to share. The only skin as comfortable as my own.

I can hear give of slivers in the door. Garments catching in the hangnails of its painted surface. A blocking of access. Or a slump of defeat. It's almost a shame he's missing out on it all happening as it unfolds. His scene. The final *something* of which I had to come down here to be convinced.

The oddest sound issues from Bethany's throat. A clicking of ponderous draughts. Mastication. The Manager has quit tripping slow circles around her and stands with his back to the wall. Bethany presses hers to the door. As though the body temperatures through the panel could swing the mercury of the decision either way. As though any of that mattered when faced with what *mere words* could really do. The Manager's fingers twitch at the cuffs of his jacket, trying to keep from checking his watch. He needn't bother: it's panning out far longer than he could have hoped for.

'So what you're saying is … it'll be what I want it to be?'

'Yes. That's correct. I meant what I said, Agent X44. I was very sorry to have had to let you go in the first place. You were always one of my most valued employees. Why do you think I put you on Nineteen in the first place? I knew you'd the skills to get what I wanted from him. Just a shame you clearly had a different target in mind.'

'He talked, Sir. I mean, he *talked.* I couldn't … I got confused.'

The Manager nods, slowly, murmurs affirmatives. Places hands gently on Bethany's shoulders. A father's forgiveness in the wake of a blistering tantrum.

'I understand. You know as well as I do just how much trouble we had with him. But that's over. *He's* over. There's nothing you could do for him, even if you wanted to. And I think you may well be getting tired of running yourself into the ground for the likes of those who can offer you nothing in return.'

'It's been … yes. She doesn't know what she's doing. Lucy. Comes all the way down here for a *boyfriend* who can't even remember her *name,* not even stopping to think of all the ways he might be *different,* always complaining about how she just wants things to be *the way they were,* like that's ever going to happen, what an idiot–'

'–Shhh. It's okay. She'll be dealt with. The Intern, too. Let's worry about *you* for a minute, Agent. Bethany. What do *you* want?'

Bethany presses her hands to her face and laughs. Dank dribbles between tunnel pipes. Snapping her head up, peeling her hands away one finger at a time, she yanks hard at the ends of her hair and jerks a thumb at the door behind.

'I want what she wants. The idiot girl. I want what she's been after all along – for things to be the way they were before.'

'Done.'

'You can't mean that. Not after–'

'Order. Efficiency. Stability. That's what I'm after, Agent X44. Your earlier mistake shook that up: not beyond *repair*, of course, but things weren't quite the way I liked them after you'd left the Facility. With you on board again – resumption of your role, Agency apartment, wages, health plan, uniform, clearance, everything – I'll be running as tight a ship as I ever have. Which goes a little way toward answering your next question.'

Bethany rolls her eyes. Nods.

'Which would be, ah … *what's in it for you?*'

The Manager beams, as far as a grey pearl gleam dribbling the edges of his tombstone teeth could be considered so.

'Exactly! But there, that's what's in it. I get a highly respected and valuable Agent back on the team … and, of course, I'm able to keep an eye on you, too. *I'm* lucky it's just that stupid girl you managed to bring down here. You did some damage, overhead. To tunnels. To Agents. I'd rather have you on my side.'

Bethany nods. Thick-click swallowing so loud even D16 and H5 can hear it.

'How do I know I can trust you to do what you're saying you will?'

'You don't know. You won't. You'll just have to ask yourself if you can pass up this chance in the face of the alternative.'

Bethany already knows she'll take it. Better a shot at something working out than opting for a one-way route to a cell.

'So what now?'

'You come back in there with me for now. A word with the girl. She's been following your example for a while, now – perhaps hearing of your turn in the direction of sense will change her mind about accepting a Story.'

Bethany shakes her head, threading fingers across the back of her neck.

'Uh-uhn. I can't … I don't want to see her. I can't.'

'This isn't the time to start feeling *guilty*, X44. You're not doing anything you should be ashamed of. If anything, you should be *proud*, being strong enough to see past all that *protest* and *cause* with its' associated *glamour* …' Scowling, the Manager pauses, shaking a tick of disgust from his scalp. 'And see that there's no dishonour in taking the rational, sensible, *workable* option. One with a *future*, Agent. You're taking a future. Those two are sacrificing theirs for a past so irrelevant it has ceased to mean anything at all.'

'But …'

'You're coming back in there. If you're still a little fond of the girl, think of this as your chance to help her see sense.'

I'm still muttering into Caleb's ear when the door clicks open. Feet clip domino-neat across the floor. I already know what's coming by the expression on her face. She's taken it.

'Lucy.'

The Manager makes a cathedral of his fingertips, half-standing in front of Bethany. That the door's still open and she's showing no sign of making a run for it underlines what I'm looking at, here. The bitch.

'Lucy,' he says again. I make a production out of finishing up what I'm saying to Caleb – nonsense drawn out for dramatic effect – before tilting my head up to look at him.

'Yes?'

'I hope you've been thinking about my proposition. Because I've had a word with Bethany, here, and she's agreed–'

'–to do the sensible thing, aye? Might have known. Once a traitor–'

'–now, now. You've come a long way together, you and Bethany,' he says. 'She's shown and taught you a great deal. I'd have thought you'd be more inclined to follow her example.'

'No way. If she's back in your lap, fair enough. I'm just as fucked either way.'

The Manager stiffens, moves to the centre of the room with. A starched squeak of thread in his neatly pressed suit. Bethany slips further behind him, still making no move for the door. Eyes pressed Jolly Roger-deep in her head.

'So ... all these options laid out ...a catch-up with your sweetheart ... and still you think you're better off carrying on the way you are. You're a very stupid girl, Lucy.'

Cradling his skull, I lower Caleb back onto the mattress. A jerk in the cords of my insides as he produces the tiniest puff of a sigh. But I need to be on my feet for what's coming. Swinging my legs from the bed to the floor, I find myself still a whole head and a half under the Manager's height. He's smiling, the bastard.

'I might be a *stupid girl*, but at least I know what's important. *She* clearly doesn't have a clue.' Bethany sidles back and forth behind the Manager's back, still hiding. 'Bethany! Look at me! What the fuck do you think you're playing at?'

The Manager steps forward, makes to put his hands on my shoulders. I slip round his bulk to face Bethany head-on. She shrinks back, burying her head in her collar. The Manager doesn't intervene, but stands back with arms folded. Still smiling. A parent overlooking a squabble between children.

'Bethany! Talk to me, for Christ's sake! What's going on?'

I take her by the shoulders and shake. Harder than I should. Her head flops back and forth, lifeless. A broken marionette. Finally, she looks up.

'Lucy, I have to. You've heard it. The way things are. The way they were. I can't go back to *that* if I have a shot at *this*. I'm sorry, I'm so sorry, but …it's too late anyway. He's gone. You've nothing left, not unless you take what's on offer. It's your only shot – and mine – to … to be alright. To get by. To manage.'

To manage. A running theme. Take a Story, neatly pressed. Insert. Switch on. Release into the Overground, all anomalies accounted for. No risk of quirks or idiosyncrasies or original thought. Caleb's been right all along. The Management don't take care of the city for the citizens: they manage the citizens to take care of the city. I will not be a part of that.

'No, *I'm* sorry, Bethany. That you're taking the easy way out. Letting us down. Sounds like you've made up your mind, though. You're not going to help me out of here, are you?'

She shakes her head.

'That's not my job anymore.'

I tighten my grip with my left hand, rear back with my right. I'm inches from meeting her jaw with my palm when his fingers tighten round my wrist.

'Now, now. We won't be having that, Lucy.'

He pulls me away from her and sets me in front. The muscles required to work the mouth into a smile have no knock-on effect on the rest of his face. A finger drawn through damp cement, left to set.

'Sounds like you're having some problems with questions of loyalty, Lucy. Betrayal, and so forth.'

'That doesn't even begin to cover it.'

'What do I need to do to convince you that such outdated nonsense as loyalty and honour are as worthless as the fictions in which they occur? You're behind the times. Catch up.'

'What?'

'Come on, Lucy. You know perfectly well that all manner of beings act only ever in their own interest. And that your only loyalties should be to the Management, the system in which you can *pursue* said self-interest. The only entity against which you *can* commit treason.'

'Bullshit.'

'I'll show you. Where loyalties should lie.'

The Manager steps away from me, spreads his arms across the expanse of the room like a magician. Bethany still cowers in the corner. He beckons her over.

'Now, here we have someone who knows her place. Knows what's best for the Management, for her city. Stops playing around with idiot girls like yourself, and steps back into line. And you feel betrayed by her?'

I don't understand.

'Of course I fucking do! She's back with you and your … fucking system!'

'No loyalty but to the Management, Lucy. Motions of tiny little people and their problems do not matter. Think about what you're facing if you still refuse a Story. Here's your *loyalty*.'

It happens so quickly I can't figure out what I'm seeing till it's already half-over. Limbs locked too neatly into place to be called a *struggle*. It takes longer than I'd have imagined for her to stop struggling. Or maybe it just feels that way, seconds elongating, heartbeats heard underwater. One of the Manager's arms about Bethany's waist, the other wrapping her shoulders, his massive hand making a fist about her neck. She is too surprised to scream. I am too appalled to do anything but *stand* there. I think I cry out. *No. Stop. What are you doing?* Her rigid frame begins a slow dribble to the floor. Complexion shifting from a soft flush to a raw rash, then fading to a damp puce as her body clocks click to a stop. I've never seen a corpse before. And she *is* dead, I know this. I saw something pass from the inner rims of her eyes, something drizzling off the limits of her body like medication from a spoon. It doesn't *look* right, with her still *vertical* like that, held up alongside the Manager's frame. Gathered firewood. Office furniture. He doesn't look about to let her go.

Maybe this is shock. When you're supposed to feel something and instead find yourself stepping back from the scene. Making notes. Reporting back as accurately as you can to another version of yourself. She has been sleeping on my floor, in my bed. She has been linking her arms through mine as we walked concrete, as we walked the remainder of the grass. She's the one who told me what I was looking for, what I'd been missing all along. And I'm stepping back and watching a Management broadcast. Slack-jawed. Blank. Half-blind.

'Here's your beloved *loyalty*,' he says, loosening his grip on her waist, reaching up to tilt her face toward mine. Until we're finally seeing eye to eye. 'You are always on your own. It makes no difference how many of you rally round: in the end, each individual need keep

291

only two sets of interests in mind: his own, and that of the Management.'

He lets her slide to the floor. No longer *she*, just a bag of clothes and skin. A puddle person. Like Davie. Like all the others walling the corridors. Like Caleb. Maybe luckier. An outrage bitter enough to prompt me toward speech.

'You … fucking … you were going to *help* her!'

'It did occur to me to keep her around, of course. She was a spectacular Agent, Lucy: you should have seen her in action. On our side, not yours. She knew all about *precision*. She also understood that, sometimes, even such quality cannot redeem uncertainty. She couldn't keep her considerable talents aligned to the principles and purposes advocated by myself. She was too skilful, too *devious*, for her own good–'

'–so you just – how could you–'

'–I can't be having uncertainties in my Facility! I've already wasted far too much time on this backing and forthing of yours! Story or cell! Cell or story! Or do you want this to be over for you and your *sweetheart* as quickly as it has for your pet Agent?'

He nudges the pool of rags on the floor with the tip of a well-polished shoe. I've figured him out. Or rather, figured out he's not *for* figuring out. His systems of logic, the lines of his argument, are beyond error because they're beyond comprehension. He is talking himself through a set of feasible circumstances in which there can be reasonable causes and consequences for what he's just done. Trapping me and Caleb in a room governed by a rule book read upside down and back to front. For a man who professes a loathing of words, he's certainly fond of them. Of the ways in which they can be manipulated to *manage* his affairs.

'No story. No cell,' I reply. An expression almost breaks over his face. A watercolour sketch of fury. I don't have to step back, out of the reach of his hands. Others are moving over his shoulders, out of his line of sight. I've seen them coming and have given nothing away. Poker face picked up over all those long afternoons in the casino.

Bethany would appreciate that, I think.

The Manager's boom from the cell masks a muttered exchange in the corridor.

'Jesus Christ,' breathes H5. 'He *has* lost his mind.'

'How can he put Bethany back on the team, just like that? *She* might not know, but the rest of us will! She'll find out before long that she hasn't been off on her bloody holidays.'

'I don't think … I don't think he'll go through with it,' says H5, sliding further down the wall toward the cell door. 'He can't. He's planning something else.'

They press ears to the walls for a handful of beats.

'Why isn't she just taking the damn *Story*?' hisses D16. 'I mean, I get she's pissed off, but you'd think she'd listen to an Agent …'

'Shhhh! Something's wrong.'

'They'll be having a cat fight,' mutters D16. 'Girls are like that, eh? All about the *sticking-together*.'

Another dark throatful of silence. The Manager's voice rings out again.   A scuffling of feet. Not a fight: that would need two pairs. A sequence of gasps. Damp spurts of breath inside a crumpled windpipe. H5 moves toward the door, stopped only by D16's tight grip on his upper arm. H5 jerks back, turns to his partner, perfect circles of his eyes communicating his horror, his need to move. D16 shakes his head.

'Wait a minute. We can't–'

It's too late. H5 bolts, even as the Manager continues to speak. He halts in the door as instinct kicks in, just in time. Surveying the scene. The wide plain of the back of the Manager's suit. The Intern on the bed. Bethany on the floor. Limbs tangled in patterns complex enough to keep H5 from seeing her face. Obscene gratitude for same. Mourning comes later. He locks eyes with Lucy as D16 fills the rest of the doorway. Only the need go unnoticed keeps D16 from landing a punch in his partner's gut. But they needn't worry. The Manager is on a roll. Nothing will shift him from a lofty oration.

They watch. They wait. They note the cords rising in the Manager's neck at Lucy's final words. He shakes his head and steps toward her. Taking this as their cue, H5 and D16 move in synch, no longer afraid. Their own infractions are small change compared to far more profound rules broken this evening. They leap for the Manager just as he opens his mouth to reply.

H5 and D16 each grab a shoulder and one beefy forearm. Lucy staggers back as one of the Manager's hands grazes her cheekbone. Though far larger than either of the Agents, the Manager is not match enough for both, although at times each side of the struggle seem on level pegging. The tangle of three sets of limbs picks messy circles across the floor. H5 is thrown off, cracking his spine off a rung of the hospital bed. D16 wriggles around on the Manager's back, trying to keep from his loosened half-grip. The Manager hunches over, head to the floor, free hand clawing at the Agent, trying to tip D16 to the concrete. Reaching around his back, the Manager's blows meet their mark on D16's kidneys and ribcage. D16 smacks a fist against the Manager's temples. Lucy snaps out of it, hauling H5 to his feet, and makes to attack the Manager from the front just as D16 finally loses his grip. A tearing of seams in the Manager's blazer heralds D16's clatter to the concrete. The Manager snaps upright, roaring, arms wheeling, momentarily filling the whole of the room.

Later, examining mental snapshots of the fight, Lucy will be struck by the expression on the Manager's face. Angry, yes, but also *euphoric*. Muscles and tendons finally able to swell to their full capacity. Blows finally raining down unchecked. She's never been in a fight before, never known quite what to do. But no matter. It all rolls off the back of a long-buried gland into the tips of her fingers and toes. She swings as the Manager descends from his animal rear, driving her fist into his chest, once, twice. As she rears back for the third, he looks down at his lapel as though he's dribbled a beverage. He swats her aside with one sweep of his palm, but not before she clatters her shoe-tips against his shins. The Manager howls, stamps his feet, grabs at her shoulder, hectic blotches of pain adding points of interest to his milk skin of a face. She kicks up her legs at his grabbing hands, redressing her balance with both palms on the wall before pushing off and whirling around. H5 leaps, locks arms round the Manager's neck from the front. A burlesque of an embrace, were it not for the scatter of punches into each of their stomachs. Having gathered his breath, D16 leaps up to join in, smacking a fist off the back of the Manager's head before joining his partner in front. Neither Agent can see where their blows are landing. Neither is there much difference of give in skin and bone; chest and stomach packed as dense as forehead and shoulder blade. Lucy circles the pack, throwing a messy punch wherever she can see an opening, before settling on the Manager's ankles in the interests of avoiding her aides. She can't see the Manager's head, his hands, so thickly are all three entwined. Once or twice her blows produce grunts of pain: it is nowhere near as satisfying as it should be. Not with Bethany lying there on the floor, head tilted at an angle threatening to roll right back, direct a dead eye to the mob.

Caleb lies flat on his back throughout. Images processed in changes in the quality of light: limbs scissoring beams with shadows as the brawl moves closer to then farther from the bed. He can hear shuffling. Panting. Pained yelps register briefly in his consciousness before trickling to rest at the back of his skull. The girl, the nice girl with the pretty eyes is no longer there to keep him company, keep him warm. He'd be able to go back to sleep if they weren't making so much noise.

294

D16 flies off once more from the brawl. He staggers back, half-landing on the bed at Caleb's feet, before dribbling off onto the floor, clutching his gut. A bright red blot uncurls on the fabric of his shirt. A short, sharp metal object protrudes from between his fingers.

The manual keys to the Manager's suite.

'RICK!' roars H5, unclasping his arms from the Manager's neck. Winded, the Manager staggers back to lean against the wall, the heave of his chest tugging at his shirt buttons.

'You BASTARD,' shouts H5, examining his partner's wound. He does not look over his shoulder. No fear or care as to whether he's left himself exposed. Lucy stands in the corner, trapped between the bleeding body and the hulk of the Manager. Hers is the face to whom he turns once he's caught his breath. Never has he been had at by a *woman* before. His shins and ankles tinkle alarm bells from the sting of her kicking.

'Lucy ... that wasn't part of the deal,' he says. The wheeze leaves his voice syllable by syllable, gathering tenor and weight. 'I knew you were a very stupid girl, but that ... *that* ... my goodness, you have no idea what you're in for after that.'

'Get away from me!'

He closes in, backing her into the corner.

'Jesus, help me out here!' she yells at H5, his hands pressed to either side of D16's wound. The key was a decorative object, kept more for the purposes of the Manager's titular keyring than anything else. Having yet to be blunted in the turning, it had parted panels of muscle in D16's stomach to the tune of two inches deep. H5 is all too familiar with the sight of blood – nosebleeds, broken teeth, a few more critical injuries on occasions Interviews got a little too intensive – but never seeping from under an Agent's fatigues. Never like this, a role reversal. Always, the upshot came down to simply closing the door. Having the offending sight whisked away to the Infirmary. Utensils deployed as per instructions, with manual precision. This is a brute act with no intention but pain. Fatality. This is the act of a man who no longer stops to tick past the bullet points of a formulated and scrupulous plan. H5 realizes he hasn't the slightest idea what such a bodily crisis called for. These things never happen down here.

'Rick ... Rick, is it?'

'I can't feel a fucking thing, mate,' grins D16, mouth corners drooling a thick carmine froth.

'Jesus, what do I–'

D16 can't form an answer round the admixture of seepage and pain. He jerks his head in the direction of the Manager, moving in on

Lucy with outstretched arms. Lucy stands poised with hands bunched into fists, breathing hard, knowing she stands little chance of outstripping him twice.

'Hang on, right?' hisses H5. 'It can't be as bad as it–'

'Hurry up ...'

The Manager had been expecting an assault from H5, eventually. H5 lands on a back taut as a shelled amphibian's, impenetrable. H5 does not yet attempt to land any blows, just fixes a firm grip around the Manager's neck. Lucy starts breathing again. Her hair, thick with sweat, ropes her face like a trawler's net, fear-bright eyes the only discernable feature. She steps forward to throw a few unpractised punches, and draws back, confused. The Manager stands stock still, face impassive, a wry brow tilted over his shoulder at the dangling Agent.

'Aren't you tiring of this, yet, Agent?' he asks. Lucy swipes at his face, her blow beaten back with loose dart of palm.

'You ... bastard ...' H5 hisses into his ear. 'This'll be finished when you are.'

Lucy moves to swipe. H5 shakes his head.

'No! Back off!'

Lucy's on automatic, though, and takes another shot with her left. The Manager roars with laughter, catches her whole hand in his fist. Snatching a passing fly from the air. They struggle, Lucy yelling, trying to reclaim her hand, the tendons on H5's right arm purple with tension as he strains to keep hold.

'Let me go!' Lucy swipes the fingernails of her right hand across the Manager's face. That he bleeds, and bleeds red, gives her sufficient pause to stop struggling, instead rearing back out of range of a retaliating shot.

'Stay back!' roars H5. The Manager is still laughing too hard to bother attempting to shake H5 off. The sight of the girl, pink and white, limp as a broken flower dangling at the end of his arm, is one worth savouring. So much better, even, than the pliancy following a rewire. So much better, he does not absorb the pain of impact until droplets of blood begin spattering his well-polished shoes.

H5 slackens his grip, spent, and trickles to the floor at the Manager's back. Lucy tugs once more at her hand and breaks free, ducking under the Manager's arm to stand by the bed, ready to defend Caleb should she need to.

The Manager revolves slowly away from the corner, hands framing the injury at the bottom of his breast-plate. It had gone in far deeper than even H5 had expected. Turned out it was true what they said about adrenaline. Sweat beads the Manager's forehead, trickles the length of his nose, dribbles across his upper lip. As shocked as the onlookers at the sight of his own bodily excretions. His hands fixed around the assault weapon, he teeters back and forth on his toe-tips before crashing to the ground. Felled by the none-too-blunt tip of his very own pen, plucked from D16's front pocket.

It's like watching a tree fall. A building. A monument. The sheer mass of the Manager is enough to rattle the concrete. Wouldn't be surprised if he's put a crack in the floor. I leap to the Agent who'd toppled him, helping him to his feet. He clutches onto my hand far longer than necessary; communication between his brain and extremities slowed from the shock of what he's just done.

'Mate ... is that a ... *pen*?'

The Agent peels lips apart very slowly, allowing a hysterical giggle to escape by degrees.

'Mmm-hmm! I didn't ... it was in Rick's pocket, it was the only thing I could ... wait ...'

Stepping in place for a minute, assessing muscular control, he pushes me behind him a little and prods a toe into the Manager's side. He groans, bubbles a little, then heaves back into unconsciousness with a bovine sigh.

'He's out,' says the Agent, 'But he's the Manager. No telling for sure.'

This doesn't keep him from rearing back for a deep-gut kick. Down or not, it seems only fair. The Manager makes no sound save a wet puff of air between lips even stiffer and paler than usual.

'Is that serious?' I ask.

'I doubt it. Fucking sore, in the belly, like, but nothing the Medics can't fix. If they want to.'

'Want to?'

'Things are going to have to change, around here. The Manager never backs down. Never gives up. Never. This means ... this means questions.'

A wheeze from the floor by the bed whips attention from the seeping mass of managerial flesh. The other Agent isn't bleeding as freely as he had after the initial plunge. No fresh rivulets. Stale blood clots black in the fabric of his shirt into a gory papier-mâché.

'What about him?' I ask.

'I don't know,' moans the Agent, pressing hands to his cheeks. 'I've never had to do anything like this before!'

'You said *Medics*. And I know there's an Infirmary down here. Shouldn't we get him along there? Call them? And we ... we have to do something about Bethany.'

Shame stings, then burns on slowly, gathering heat. How quickly I've forgotten. Turning from the Agents, I crouch to the concrete and roll her over. It's not easy. She's absolutely rigid. This does not lend itself to great expectations when I press two fingers to her empurpled neck. Nothing. Cold as a night in the glass-house.

'Miss? ... *Lucy*?' says the Agent. 'It's too late. She's gone.'

I don't realize how long I've been stretching the moment until I see splotches of damp gathering on the front of her shirt. It appears that I'm crying. It's strange. Coming up with an appropriate reaction long after the passage of the appropriate moment. Maybe adrenaline dried them all up at first. Instincts borrowing energy from other sources.

'Okay. Okay. Okay okay okay.' I say, got to keep going. 'Agent ... eh, what do they call you?'

'Rick,' he says, an audible click in his throat at the alien syllable.

'Rick. Hi,' I say. Stupid. Working backwards, meeting properly long after we've shared something as huge as we have. 'Look, we're going to have to get moving.'

Neither he nor I can keep our gazes flickering back to the hulk in the corner. Both of us expecting him to rear up, come barrelling toward us like a grizzly bear wrenched from hibernation. Like in the movies. They always come back.

'Come here. Help me with Tony.'

Rick takes the arms, I take the legs. We swing the Agent up onto the bed next to Caleb. We each release the brakes at either end of the gurney, working in silence, in rhythm, pushing it out into the hall.

'So the plan is,' I find myself saying, 'We get them down to the Infirmary and ... you can get hold of a Medic, right?'

'Yeah. Yeah. I've never had to ... I'll get through.'

The Agent's condition doesn't look to be worsening, at least. Still no obvious blurts of fresh bleeding. Every now and then he tilts his eyes up toward us, a sluggish smile moving across his lips. Rick keeps patting him on the shoulder, saying, 'Don't try to speak. We'll talk later, man. We'll talk later.'

As though they've been pushing back a catch-up for eons.

'What about him?'

'The Manager? Uh ...'

Rick flushes. A schoolboy caught setting up a prank.

'Only one thing for it, eh?'

He pulls the door closed, closing his eye at the click of the latch, and punches a code into the mechanism.

'What if he … you know? Doesn't he know the code?'

Rick chuckles, muddles a mouthful of sardonic spit.

'Not from the inside. The Facility doesn't work like that. Besides, even if he *could* trip it, he's left his manual keys in my friend, here.'

I nod, saying nothing. There's something appalling about leaving Bethany in there with him. Rick picks up on my unease. Turns out they haven't been drummed dry of all human sentiment, all emotional cues in a crisis.

'Look, it's just for a minute. Just till we've made a few phone calls. God, none of them are going to believe what we've … what we've *done* …'

He stops, shudders, fastens fists tighter around his end of the gurney. I'm far too fixated on getting Caleb as far from the Manager as possible to have the patience for an anarchist's doubts. Because that's what he *is,* now, I guess. More in common with Caleb, laid out prone between us, than with the clattering sack of tumbled Scrabble tiles on the other side of that door.

'Worry about that later. Just move. Before he wakes up.'

Because he will. The bad guys always come back for one more shot.

'Right. Right.'

He's a lot like me when it comes to how to function in situations such as these. Prop yourself up on logistics, in plans, motions, checklists, thereby forestalling emotional collapse. I have too much hanging on this to waste time falling apart.

After helping me shift his partner onto another gurney, Rick absents himself to the room adjoining the Infirmary to ring the Medics on call. Perhaps ferret out any first aid supplies he has any idea how to use. I get a few moments alone with Caleb. Long enough, stroking that forehead still damp with nightmares, clutching that hand with no responding grip, to make up my mind as to what happens next. Rick enters the Infirmary cubicle, swiping at his forehead. Still looking very much on the brink of being sick.

'They're on their way down. Look, Lucy … you're not in any trouble as far as I'm concerned, but … maybe it's best they don't see you, not yet. I mean, things *have* changed, but I don't know how ready the rest of them will be.'

'Fine by me. I need to know … where's the thing they used on Caleb?'

'What?'

'You know what I'm talking about. I need your help.'

'The Lab … it's closed up for the night.'

'I doubt that's a detail bound to stop either of us. Not now.'

'What do you—'

'I'm taking a gurney back down to the cell. You'll need to let me in. Follow me on once you've talked to the Medics. Tell them there's a body they'll need to pick up, but only after they've taken care of Caleb and your friend. We'll have to be quick. And bring something … something more reliable than a stick pen. Just in case.'

We lock gazes for a long moment. I don't have to try particularly hard to track back through years of plugging through *this*. The cells. The Management. The fucked-up shit they're expected to do daily down here. The sight of Bethany crumpled on the floor like a vegetable sack. His friend, his partner, seeping blood to red to be real. He wouldn't have done what he did if he didn't want out. All he has to do is help me out, here. First steps lead to seconds lead to paths changing altogether.

'Right. Hurry up. And be quiet.'

Rick then does the oddest thing. He holds out his hand. I'm staring at it as something I've never seen before, some ancient artefact plucked from a museum cabinet. Which, I suppose, is exactly what it is. We shake. Every finger on each side thrumming from the contact.

'See you in a bit,' he murmurs. 'Hurry.'

'Rick …' I have to add, pointing to Caleb. 'I know he's … stable, or whatever you'd call it, but …have them take a look. Make sure they do everything they can. Tell them he's got some information, or something, I don't care, just make sure they don't hurt him.'

'That won't happen. The Medics are the only ones who still try to … look, they won't hurt him, Lucy. I promise.'

'Thank you.'

I can't remember the last time I said that and truly meant it.

I'm not long down the corridor when I hear the brittle mutterings of Medics and on-call Agents flooding in from the direction I'd come in the first place. This place must be a bloody Swiss cheese of entrances, exits and tunnels. Stood motionless by the gurney, darkness remains liquid-thick as far as the eye can see. Pressing my ear to the door like a ghost-hunting kid, I can hear nothing bar the wet slurp of a snore. It's no longer so unsettling, standing in the naked murk. All that practice in the tunnels has me honed to the movement of air

300

molecules, sensitive to those thrumming in nearby walls, to those displaced by the approach of bodies in space. Maybe Bethany wasn't so full of bullshit. Maybe she really could see in the dark.

Muttering at the end of the corridor is swallowed up behind the closing of doors. A single set of footsteps shuffles my way. I know it's Rick because he's the only other body down here who has a need to walk in secrecy.

'Is it done?' I ask.

'They're on it. They're both going to be fine. Now, are you going to tell me what you're wanting with that gurney? Cos we've about ninety seconds before someone comes to … pick Bethany up.'

'Did you bring something?'

He presses something slick and hard into my hand. I know enough to know it's not a gun: I just have to trust it'll do me a favour, should it be necessary.

'Open the door.'

'Don't you–'

'Just open the door.'

There's nowhere else to go. Nothing else to do. I now know what folks mean when they say they're as ready as they'll ever be.

The Manager does not move from his squat in the corner. Not even after we slam the door. Not even after we turn on the bright lights. I can't help laughing: he's just *lying* there. I'm half-expecting a decoy, a wigged watermelon and rags stuffed into arms and legs, if it weren't for the raw snuffle of staggered breath bounding between his mouth and the concrete. It's almost embarrassing.

'Shit,' says Rick. 'I think we've really …'

I shake my head. That's not the way it's supposed to go. They're meant to come back for one last crack. I approach on phantom footsteps, too aware of the pretzel twist of a corpse on the floor. Something has gone missing in me, I guess. Parts of me left behind in tunnels, in empty apartments. My soft spots are needed more urgently on Caleb's hospital bed. Soon. Soon. We'll deal with Bethany. We will. But not till I've had my way.

'You awake, then?' I ask, kicking him in the chest. He emits a piñata squeak and says nothing. Doesn't move. I turn to Rick.

'It's time. I don't know what was in that pen of yours–'

'–his. It was his.'

'Okay … but whatever it was, it's done the trick. Help me shift him onto the gurney.'

We don't move with the ease we'd gathered to ourselves when shifting Tony. Too scared, still, that the hands and feet at the end of hefted limbs with sparkle to life, administer his bastard brand of justice. Yet once he's lying on the gurney, slack as a broken balloon, all the clout dribbles from the tips of his extremities. Mouth hanging open, drooling. Dried sweat plastering to a pudding-batter mess. None of the rumours turned out to be true. After all that he's done, he's still just a man in a suit.

And we've a treat for him.

'You sure about this?' asks Rick, still all kinds of anxious. 'I saw ... you saw what happens in there. Even the Manager—'

'—the Manager will be getting no more than he deserves. Besides, you heard me. I don't believe in Stories. I don't believe in cells. So it's either this, or we give him to the Medics. And that's not an option. Not after all that he's done. Show me the way to the Lab.'

And he does. Excepting the horror of closing the door once again on poor Bethany, every movement I'm making feels just as it should be. Each muscle, tendon, fibre, nerve ending and brain cell stretching up and out to its full potential. Caleb was right. All the talking in the world, whatever the intention, will only ever take you so far. Some truth in those dusty old axioms: that actions speak louder than words. In this case, that a picture's worth a thousand of them. Sometimes you have to drop the rhetoric and look inside. Plug in your instincts. The same thing we'll be doing in a moment for our beloved Manager.

No more than he deserves. A coy rewrite of his favourite slogan.

EPILOGUE

RECONSTRUCTION

So there it is. Here we are. Standing – well, sitting, give it time – at the window again, trawling for traces of sky. Opinions differ as to whether the damage is permanent. Small changes are going down, to counter the damage. Cars slowly crawling off the road as the blocks clear. People are finally getting to their *homes,* and don't seem to be in a hurry to get back behind the wheel. Power plugs pulled on the casinos and Management buildings. None of the neon girding the former, no more violent halogen lowering from countless double-glazed windows, so the orange haze slowly retreats. Maybe someday we'll see what's above. Nothing burns in the Management's amnesty trashcans, nothing burns anymore in the wreckage of cars, nothing burns at city limits or in empty lots where anarchies were once mounted. It could happen. We could clean up. I have to believe in something. Seems foolish to fixate on whether we'll ever get the stars back again, what with so much else going on. I guess it's enough to know they're still up there. Me and Caleb, we've seen them up close, close enough almost to reach out for a handful. And now we're Overground again, we're at only one strata of remove.

So. The fall of the Management. My recall of how it all went down might be my own this time, crystal-clear untainted precision, but it's still a scatter-shot of zoetrope images. Action. Cut. Action. Seems more complicated than it actually was.

We put the Manager in the chair closest to the screen. So much lighter than I thought he'd be, all slack and pliable like that. Then we got started. Neither me nor Rick had any idea how to work the damn thing, but between us we figured it out. Ancient machineries, like the lumpy slicks of plastic in the casino. Turns out technical wizardry's more in common with sideshow magics; all smoke and mirrors once you pull back the curtains.

I remember feeling sort of hot and fizzy when we put the straps on. Like my skin were itching to head for the door. Rick found the slides left in the machine from that afternoon. Handed over the shots of myself without saying a word. Put them in my pocket, to later be destroyed.

There was plenty left to work with. Scenes from the city. Anarchic landscapes crumbling to the ground. Fires and garbage. Whores and drug addicts. And a plenty of folks just *having fun,* kicking legs over the backs of beer garden benches. Foaming glasses in hands, smiles on faces. Back in the day, as they say.

And that was it. All it came down to was the Newtons required to flip switches, push buttons. We plugged in the Manager. We turned on the projector. We left him with the images of all that *was.* Lost. Regained. Could be again. All the rogue ideologies and random factors he'd thought – and *we'd* thought, for a long time – he'd been fighting against. For our own good. It never should have happened. No city's problems ever needed the kind of crackdown he'd been allowed to get away with for so long.

But the details aren't important. Just a flickering of light, the low bleed of smoke from under the door upon our return. He was burnt so black he could have been anyone at all, but there was no mistaking the size of him. Staggered oblongs slumping toward the ground, a padded simulacra of the chair in which he sat. Rick took care of it. A trip to the incinerator to finish the job. Came back wiping bile from his mouth with the back of his hand. The Medics were already on to Bethany. There was nothing they could do but bag her up and see she got a decent send-off.

Once Rick had told the Medics and Agents that the Manager was gone for good, all sprung into a crazy domino-tumble of action. He made it pretty clear there were other Interns in need of attention. Injured or otherwise, they were all moving down toward the dark end of a spectrum of sanity. They needed freed from the cells before they got any worse.

A murmur distracts me from the replay.

'Tired now,' Caleb mutters. 'Need to sleep.'

Enough smog-peeling for now. I jerk the blinds shut and lead Caleb to bed. He's getting better at telling me what he's after. Too hot, too cold, tired, hungry. My new favourite is *bored:* that means it's time for a lesson. A book, a film, a piece of music. Or even just my telling him a Story, something I've never been called on to do before. So many things I could have done for my mother, if I'd just given her – and myself – a chance. But missing the boat on one act of kindness doesn't mean it's too late for another.

I have to be careful. With the Stories. If there's one thing I now know, it's that there are often too many versions of the same series of events. I'm not in the position to be balanced or fair about what happened in the Facility. I don't want to make a running joke or a Big Bad Wolf of the Manager, extremes between which I find myself swinging still. If Caleb's faculties are improving by degrees, there's got to be a good chance his memories will return, too.

And I can't ever know what really happened to him.

The mechanics of the thing I understand, but I'll never get a feed from the inside of his head. Won't ever see what he saw through his eyes. Felt what he felt all the time he was down there. I don't want to tell him my side and later stand accused of feeding him a palliative falsehood, a line. Worse, I don't want to run the risk of him scaring himself back underneath. I am not, and never should be, the sounding board for the construction of the mind of another. I looked too long and hard to others for firm versions of myself. I thought Caleb, the Manager, Bethany, whoever, knew better than I did who I was. Took a sequence of events I'll never wish to repeat to find out that underneath the Stories, there was only me. That's all. It still scares me a little how much I've still to find out. Scary, yes. But at least things now have the chance to get interesting.

So I'll be Caleb's crutch only insofar as he needs me; as far as he'd *want* to need me without bruising his dignity. I can do that. Daily rituals. Well-rounded meals. Watch over waking and sleeping, just to make sure he's on the right side of both. Engage him in fragile onion-shells of conversations. He can only grow stronger the harder we work at this business of being alive. He has to. I have to believe in that, too.

It's not so bad. Peaceful. Soft. His violet-frilled lids drawing back of a morning and instinctively looking for, reaching for me. Gentle ablutions, slow murmurs, playful dips and feints between stimuli.

As to the latter, it's getting more exciting. On cue, as he's been doing almost every day, Rick comes round with batches of material that had somehow escaped being destroyed. Probably a backlog, a queue for the ash-cans, the wider the Manager threw his prohibitions.

'I don't know why he hung onto this stuff for so long,' he says, handing over a particularly scandalous haul. 'Some of it's ... pretty, uh ...'

'Know your enemy, I guess,' I reply, trying to keep a rein on my glee. There *is* some fabulous stuff still there for the taking. I'm looking forward to treating Caleb to some Burroughs. An education for us both.

Information seeps back and forth in uncertain flurries. If you've *contacts,* which I guess I have, now, you're barely better off in the knowledge stakes than anyone else. Whatever's going on down there, we're eventually going to need *some* sort of regulation, which is where the folks who know what they're doing come in. As usual, Rick sticks around for a chat, keep me up to date on how things are progressing out there. *As far as he knows* remains the pre-fix looping the sum all data in an infinity sign. Still pretty shaky down there, folks not quite sure what to do with themselves. Still teetering over whether they can truly trust in the fall of the system into which they'd been gridlocked for so long.

The Nurses and Medics are the folks to look to for a model of behaviour, according to Rick. At the sight of the Infirmary filling up with Interns in greater or lesser states of disrepair, they didn't ask any questions. They just got on with it. Did what they could to fix them up. The first thing to do was to get them to Infirmaries Overground: better equipment and easier access was the reason given, but I suspect it has more to do with the healing properties of light and open space. Many of the Interns are apparently improving at an unbelievable rate: the race toward health requiring no more, it seems, than the chance to do so without battering at concrete. Tech and Admin Agents have been transporting paper and electronic files from Underground, in the interests of finding out where each Intern has come from, whether they have homes to go to once they're fit to leave.

In the interim, they need somewhere to go. There's been a committee assembled of Agents seeking ways to help restore some sort of order. In the absence of the Manager's assigning his usual glut of crazed and pointless missions, they're actually getting things done. They're mostly from Scenarios. Calling upon their backgrounds in the Arts, they're putting heads together, throwing ideas around. Maybe coming up with ways and means of making something of all this destruction. They've all been pitching in when it comes to finding homes for patched-up Interns. In the wake of the Manager's mass rash of arrests, those disappearances we never read about in the newspapers, a lot of the freezer-drawer flats just like mine have been standing empty for months. Agents have been clearing them out, fixing them up. Interns now have places to stay until they've found a more attractive – or even better, familiar – proposition.

306

'A set of keys. An address. But not a home,' I mutter at Rick. He shakes his head.

'Not a home. Just a practicality, just temporary, Lucy. I mean, they can't stay in the Infirmary, right? And it's an improvement on …you know.'

'I know.'

Hell, I'm living in my own freezer drawer, still. It hasn't undergone some sepia-steeped transformation after the fall of the Management. Watery light still lashes the blank walls whose cracks I've still got committed to memory. The cupboards still neatly stacked with identikit utensils and crockery. There's still a marked dearth of anything remotely approaching a personal touch. *I'm* still as studiedly featureless as ever, sticking to black on black on black. Safety measures yet to shift. But there's a feature in here now that I've been missing. A soft warmth under the palm of my hand when I run hands over the mattress at my side. No more blank mornings. I needn't care about the sun's failure to give me a light show in the morning, when I've green candles burning on the pillow by my head. I just hope the others will soon be gathering to themselves the lives they'd lost.

'Are they … you know, in their own heads?' I ask. I have to. You never know. Rick shrugs.

'I don't think that's quite how I'd put it, if you get me. You're never going to be the same after having been down there. But they've never had a rewire, if that's what you're asking. I don't know which I'd prefer, myself.'

'Not a rewire. Not a story, Rick. I've been there. And having seen both sides, I'd rather come away with my memory intact. Even if it were the worst thing that had ever happened to me, I'd want to know. I'd have to. That's something to build on. Still being who you are. Not just a *nothing.* A non-person. A whole lot of blank space. They'll be fine, right?'

'Eventually. What was it they used to say, ages ago? What doesn't kill you–'

'–makes you stronger. Makes sense. Sometimes the old ways don't seem as daft as you'd think. So there's hope?'

'Aye, I'd say so. Most of them are doing pretty well, now you're asking. Desperate to get outside and take a look around. See what the city really looks like. Not having to look over their shoulders or flip out their ID cards …'

'So what's happening with the Tube, then? The guards?'

'Some are still clearing the roads. Shifting the wrecked motors, so's we can get things moving even quicker. I've never seen so many folks so over the moon, just to get *home*. But anyway. There's still guards and Agents down in the Facility, clearing the place out. There's a shitload of stuff to go through before we can seal it all off.'

'Fair play. And the Tube?'

'Most folks are still using it to get from A to B, convenience and all. Forgotten how to get where they're going on street level.'

'But that'll change, right?'

Rick laughs.

'Aye, it's already happening. Couple of clowns are already charging folks a few quid a pop for a tour of the city on foot. Show the ones who're still feart that there's nothing to be scared of.'

'Might get in on that myself,' I wink. 'Me and Bethany, we took a few wee tours ourselves.'

I'm getting used to the taste of her name in my mouth. Rick and I have a tacit agreement that it's alright. It has to be. She doesn't deserve to be censored right out of our vocabulary. We've each spent too long watching what we say, to whom we say it, to waste time and energy swallowing precious words. Unsaid, something ugly happens to them. Words, statements, truths, tales. They twist and fester into lies, or grow dusty and misunderstood through underuse. Bethany was a part of this. To withhold a mention would do as much damage as forgetting the Manager and everything he'd done. We need to talk to keep ourselves alive. Including, but not limited to, stuff we've got to drag from the past into the light. Otherwise – as Caleb would have told me, had I needed reminding – the same thing will happen all over again.

A moment of respectful silence passes. Aside from a few Agents in Scenarios, we're the only ones left to pay tribute to the Manager's last victim. We tried as hard as we could to track down anyone who might have known her before – friends, relatives, lovers – but she'd been telling the sorry truth. She'd have had nothing to go back to, had she passed up a Story. I'm thus quicker to mourn her than to hold her a grudge for what had seemed at the time such a betrayal. Distance smacks home the impression that, roles reversed, I'd have done the same thing. Which means I owe more than ever to Caleb, however slowly he's reaching the surface. If Caleb hadn't been there, laid out on the bed like a blank plot of earth promising spring, I'd have trailed the Manager down that same old corridor for another dose of machinated fiction.

'So how's he doing, anyway?' asks Rick, offering a welcome change of subject.

'A tiny bit better every day,' I reply. 'Not so you'd notice, maybe, but better. Little snippets of conversation, aye, but they tire him out pretty quickly. But it's enough. Enough to keep trying. Enough to be glad we both made it. I've memory enough for both of us, for now.'

Rick nods, checks his watch. I know he's got some visiting detail of his own.

'That's smashing, Lucy. I can tell, you know. A wee bit of recognition in the eyes, like. Looking forward to getting a proper chat when he's up for it.'

'You'll be first to know. But anyway. How's Tony?'

Rick breaks into a glorious grin. A full lip-stretch. I've been seeing them more and more often on my trips down to street level. Makes you wonder what else folks are learning almost from scratch.

'Still milking the fuck out of it,' he laughs. 'A wee dunt in the belly, and you'd think he took a rocket launcher in the gut. Proper war hero, so he is. But I can't fault him for wanting to stretch out the down-time as far as he can ...'

'It's been a long ...however long it's been, since he last had the chance, I'll bet.'

'Hmm. Aye, been a long time for us all.'

Which might well go some way toward explaining how *quiet* it is, out there. We've both been expecting all manner of chaos, now that the Management are no longer around to clamp down on that sort of thing. But so far there's been nothing but calm. Folks unfolding their leaves a little at a time, stretching tendrils by degrees into the outside. Maybe the very fact of just knowing they're not about to be dragged off for infractions is enough to make relaxation a very pleasure in itself. Taking tiny little nips at books and films and pieces of music as though they were all still red hot, apt to burn the fingers. Peeling back the prohibitions by degrees, enjoying each fresh facet all the more for its staggered and delicate unveiling. The city performs her great striptease.

'I'll call in on you tomorrow, then, Lucy?'

'Eh ...aye, aye, sure, but gonnae give us a call, first? We might not be at home.'

Rick butters a smile across his lips.

'We? You taking Caleb with you, this time?'

'Wee field trip. I think he'd progress a little quicker if he saw more than the walls of this room.'

'Aye, fair point. Just be careful, eh? And give *me* a shout if you think you might need a hand.'

'Should be alright, but cheers.'

And he's gone, leaving my head ringing with his final offer. For its own sake, without ulterior motives or an undercurrent of exchange. No latent threat of informing the Management. Just a favour from a friend. We are heading the right way.

Caleb stirs. I spread out alongside him by the bed, the better to catch a whisper from the depths of his dreams. He's lucid when he's out, which doesn't surprise me. Means it's just a matter of tearing the veil, a little at a time.

'We're going out tomorrow,' I murmur. 'Someplace I haven't seen since the Management collapse. I think you'll like it. Maybe you'll remember it. Maybe you'll have a Story for me, this time. The way you used to do.'

Of all the places now freed up to human traffic, there's one place I'm desperate to see flourish. I'm holding out for no miracles, at least not in these early stages, but there's potential for change. If the sky is peeling itself free from its shackles of smog, you never know. Concrete, stone and glass give nothing back. Fires are pretty enough, but never last. But there's still one place we can go and never know what to expect. The garden.

We're going to plumb the cracks between the slabs. We're going down to the place where it all began. See if we can't watch – or make – something grow.

AFTERWORD

I wrote *Abstract/Concrete* between Autumn 2009 and Spring 2010 whilst resuming university studies after a couple years' absence. The summer before term began, I'd been bored enough to begin to take notice of warring factions in the media with regard to what was and was not appropriate behaviour: it seemed like everyone had an opinion on what constituted acceptable levels of permission to drink, smoke, eat, spend or behave however they wanted. For every advertisement or celebrity promotion, there was a health warning's or so-called expert's damnation, and this seemed to be extending into every decision the average person had to make day-to-day. I realised I was living in a society afraid to choose for itself, for fear of some error calculated on some unfathomable scale of correctness, image, arbitrary morality. The terms 'police state' and 'totalitarianism' began to ring in my head; only, it relied less on brutality (at least not at first) than on coercion, on an apathetic populace easily herded into line for the want of a quiet life. It's easier, after all, to do what you're told than to have to expend energy on weighing up costs, benefits and consequences, especially when the dictators are that nice bloke off the telly recommending Sainsbury's; and the bad examples are once-pretty, now cocaine-ravaged soap stars falling out of nightclubs drunk and sans underwear. Another factor in the portrait of Glasgow's urban decay was the financial crisis still raging in Britain. It's an odd situation: we're being advised by one set of 'experts' to cut back, and by another, flashier troupe, to spend, spend, spend on things we don't need and can't afford anyway, leaving the average citizen bitter with want. Our culture of consumption made promises the economy couldn't keep, even as branding, advertising and 'free' credit diverted attention from that fundamental error still inherent in our forward-thinking, democratic

311

society: the rich and powerful continuing to flourish whilst the poor and voiceless are submerged. This model forms the basis of the struggle in *Abstract/Concrete,* but little did I know how much scarier things were to become for our country following last May's election. As a freshman back in 2004, I began an MA in Film & Television Studies with English Literature. Back then, the upshot of gaining this qualification had a multitude of options for employment after graduation: writing, researching, lecturing, teaching, publishing, journalism, working in television or film, curating, librarianship ... I could go on, but the point is, that was seven years ago. When the coalition government came to an agreement which effectively stabbed the whole country (bar the wealthy, powerful, *connected* and obscenely well-protected percentage whose interests would always, it seems, be met), the words that set everyone trembling were 'reforms' and 'cuts'. Something had to give to heal our ailing economy, and that something mirrored the issues explored in *Abstract/Concrete*: the deletion of the Arts from the agenda as unnecessary padding. Organisations were shut down or absorbed into 'portfolio'-driven umbrella companies. Funding was drained from artists of all disciplines seeking to start up something special. Postgraduate studies in Arts subjects were afforded a paltry nip at the collective cherry. Universities were hit hard: not only in terms of investment, but of access – the message broadcast with the introduction of backbreaking fees, with or without the small print, seemed to be that only the privileged had the right to a higher education. And despite protests (to which the police and the media were extraordinarily antagonistic) everything, everywhere, began to look and sound very much the same. And that's what this book is about, among other things – a pitting of art, accumulating knowledge and the awe that comes with it against sameness, colourlessness, boredom, apathy. It's a solid – *concrete* – yell of protest on behalf of every author whose local bookshop sells mostly three-for-two on airport fiction; for the exhausted Arts professors overworked or nudged toward retirement; for musicians, painters, filmmakers too shattered by their day jobs to remember why they *must* create; for those who graduated with me this June and are looking at a lengthy spell in a customer-service Purgatory. Art may not save a life by jumping in with defibrillators, food, shelter or money, but what comes after these basic needs are fulfilled? Those who wrongly belief art means excess are forgetting to ask a very simple question: what are we living *for*?

ACKNOWLEDGEMENTS

I couldn't have written this, or anything else, without the undaunted support of my family. Mum and Dad, living with a daughter of, shall we say, an 'artistic temperament' isn't always easy, and never has your support, encouragement, pride or love budged an inch in my disfavour. Your strength was my strength to draw on whenever I needed it, without question, and I'm so proud of you both for being true to yourselves always and for teaching me the value of same.

For providing both comic relief and a shoulder to cry on, thank you to Mairi Neary. I'm so lucky to have you around, little sis. Alex, thank you for proving me wrong in thinking you'd never grow out of being a sulky teenager. Siblings of mine, your humour, resilience and encouragement (not to mention fashion sense and music taste) gives me cause not to despair for the future just yet.

A novel about strong women has its foundations in a corps of remarkable ladies. Mother and sister, you're the blood-hot heart, but I also want to thank you, Anne, for your energy and (if it hurts, it works) brutal honesty; Cari for sharing your wisdom and strength right from the very beginning, and for bringing so much happiness into our family; and you, Granny Margaret, for being so full of love and kindness I can't think of you as any less than a saint.

Thank you also to Duncan for your cool head, Melanie for your household magicks; Spike for your stories, songs and critical appraisal; and James for your priceless banter (and for not laughing *too* hard when Kent drank Glasgow under the table).

For their encouragement to explore further, think harder, and to always bring imagination into academia, I am indebted to Drs Donald Mackenzie, Robert Maslen, Ian Goode, and Karen Lury, with an extra-special thanks to my adviser Dr Ian Garwood for helping me get my education back on track.

Thank you also Andrew Raymond Drennan for your friendship, critique and for piquing my interest (and honing my debating skills) in subjects I hadn't yet explored; Aniko Szilagyi for shamelessly geeky book chat and cake; Daniel Carr for having faith in me, still, and Gerald Anderson for keeping me entertained when I've been tearing my hair out (and for encouraging me to look to the skies!).

Finally, thank you to all the friends who've stuck by me with this (whether picking me up or *holding* me up); professionals who've given me advice and support; and the hardworking folks keeping the momentum going on Glasgow's spoken-word performance circuit.

We can win the day. This isn't over.

BIOGRAPHY

Kirsty Neary was born in 1986, and grew up in and around Glasgow. Kirsty specialises in illustrating her written work with visual media such as painting, filmmaking and photography. She performs her various works at events across Scotland such as Words Per Minute, Initial Itch, Forge of the Wordsmiths and the Wigtown Book Festival, and lectures on the craft of writing, and the industry itself, at writer's networking events and discussion groups. Her first novel **The Stately Pantheon** was published in 2009, and her short fictions are featured in magazines such as *dotdotdash, From Glasgow to Saturn, qwerty!* and *Spilling Ink Review,* for which she has also won prizes. She recently graduated with a First Class degree in English Literature an Film & Television Studies, writes freelance journalism for Glasgow newspapers, and is looking forward to following up her second novel, **Abstract/Concrete**, with yet more tales inspired and informed by that notorious city. She would get a lot more done if her cat didn't insist on sitting on the keyboard.

www.ingramcontent.com/pod-product-compliance
Lightning Source LLC
Chambersburg PA
CBHW030933260626
47169CB00002B/460